A Similar Devotion

— SUSAN BELL —

Sacristy
Press

Sacristy Press
PO Box 612, Durham, DH1 9HT

www.sacristy.co.uk

Published in 2014 by Sacristy Press, Durham

Copyright © Susan Bell 2013

Sacristy Limited, registered in England & Wales, number 7565667

British Library Cataloguing-in-Publication Data
A catalogue record for the book is available from the British Library

ISBN 978-1-908381-09-5

In memory of my much loved husband John;
always in my thoughts.

ACKNOWLEDGEMENTS

My thanks go to my friend Sal, who was there at the beginning and end of writing this novel and was generous with her valuable comments and her expertise in proof reading; to friends Kate, Liz, Irene and Margaret, whose suggestions made me think again; to Brian Cook in Australia for useful appraisal, and to Noel and Bet Bates in Cairns, Australia, who were researching their Armstrong ancestors in Northumberland; to Helen, Kathryn, Ayisha and their inspirational readers from Cornerstones, who gave me praise and reason to hope and challenged me to reassess and improve my manuscript; to friends Judy and Mary in America; also to my friend Julia Jarman—a writer of children's books—who suggested I get in touch with Cornerstones; to Richard from Sacristy Press, who encouraged me to send my manuscript, to Thomas who read it and approved publication, Gemma who edited the final drafts and for their combined faith to publish my book; and to my late husband, John, and my family for encouragement and being proud that I managed to get into print.

BAMBURGH, NORTHUMBERLAND

1740

I am young again, remembering the pleasures of bare feet on dewy grass, the salty scent of the sea, thundering waves dissolving into lacy foam that fans across the wide sands, the plaintive cries of gulls and the moan of the wind in my ears. My senses drink in the splendour of the land and seascape before me and flood my body with contentment. How I savour the joy of being in this place once more!

To my left across a reflective ribbon of sea, Lindisfarne, the Holy Isle: the isle of St Cuthbert and St Aidan, the island castle perched on a sheer outcrop near the southern tip. Further out to sea, southwards, the rocky Farne Islands, surrounded by fishing boats and weighed down by innumerable birds. To the right, across the swelling and often turbulent waters of the North Sea to the soft golden sand, our castle of Bamburgh, standing tall above all else, clinging proudly to the towering mass of craggy cliff as if it grew there long ago. Closer to me, a scattering of houses, our manor house and the church of St Aidan.

Leaning against this rough stone wall, the coarse grass beyond dipping and rolling toward the sea, I smile in remembrance. So familiar is the unchanged scene that the past is but a moment away; a setting to momentous events of which we were a part.

The grey, granite walls of the church stir memories of the souls that filled its hallowed halls and are now no more—where Thomas and I sat as first family of the parish, above all others in our places in St Aidan's chancel, unexpectedly raised to this lofty position through successive and untimely deaths in the Bamburgh branch of the Forster family. We sat even above

1

our father, stepmother, and the Catholic Radcliffes who shared our services.

All this was ours, mine and Thomas's, for but a short time.

Many have misjudged and blamed Thomas unfairly for what he did in the so-called Rebellion. They were not there, and those present had reason to find a scapegoat. He did what he thought right and should be remembered for his refusal to make cowardly excuses and for his unwavering loyalty to his friends and our King over the water.

I have no regret for what I did. There was anxiety, fear, thrilling highs and dreadful lows, but also excitement never matched since and a love that comforts me still. Life presents its opportunities. I shudder even now at the thought I might have left to others, what only I could have done.

CHAPTER 1

THE BEACH AT BAMBURGH

1715

I sat down, plunged my hand into the soft sand and let the golden grains pour through my fingers. The sea was unusually calm and I watched as the placid waves broke gently into curved ripples, revealing darkened sand as they retreated. I looked to the horizon and wished I was on one of the misty Farne islands, beyond the reach of everyone and everything that demanded so much of me.

My wayward hair, at that hour in the morning not yet confined by ribbon or bonnet, hung loosely about my shoulders. A sudden breeze caught my locks and briefly blotted out the islands from my vision. I tossed my head and felt, rather than saw, the brooding presence of the dark, crumbling castle standing on the cliff that towered above the beach to my left. It was part of the vast wealth and lands that branches of my family had owned and squandered. My more recent ancestors had lived with no apparent thought of preserving the inheritance for future heirs. Thomas and I soon realised that he had inherited debts too great to repay and the only answer was to sell the inheritance we had so joyfully thought was his. Life could have been pleasant and leisurely, ours to determine its course, but now was dependent on the kindness of our uncle, Lord Crewe Prince Bishop of Durham.

I stood up and pulled my shawl about me. I climbed up and down the sand hills until I reached the path that would take me round the land side of the castle.

I had to accept that my time merely managing the household accounts and finding ways of curbing Thomas's spending was over. There was a great deal more to think about than simple matters of money. The moment had come when decisions had to be made and action taken which might have momentous consequences. Thomas's news had both excited and frightened me. I had needed time to mull over the bare bones of what he felt able to tell me, about an enterprise so long in coming and yet suddenly too close not to inspire apprehension as well as excitement.

I had left the manor house just after dawn, as I often did. I walked down to the sea and along the beach past the castle, high on the massive rocky cliff, and climbed up into the sand hills beyond. I ran down the dunes as I had once done as a child with my nurse holding my hand. I sighed. Such carefree days were gone.

I reassured myself that I at least had the satisfaction of knowing that my uncle was happy with my accounts and the decisions I had made to economise. It was hard for Thomas to change the life he had led so long. Hunting, shooting, gambling and drinking with his many friends were his ways of passing his time when not at Parliament in London or about the business of his constituency.

That was the life he considered his right, when the last of our uncles died so tragically in a duel outside an inn in Newcastle. I shuddered, remembering the hanging of John Fenwick on the spot where my uncle died. He was condemned, it was said, because of his unsporting actions, running my uncle through while he was picking up the sword he'd dropped on the cobbles.

◆　　◆　　◆

In 1701, at the age of eighteen, Thomas was informed that he would share the inheritance of the Forster family's Bamburgh branch with our Aunt Dorothy, sister to our late, beloved mother Frances, who had died shortly after my brother John was born. I remembered the moment three years later, when Thomas came fully into his inheritance at twenty-one and asked if I would come and live with him in Bamburgh. Though only eighteen, I accepted joyfully and was happy to leave Adderstone Manor.

I knew I would miss my father and my brother John, but I was thankful that Thomas was willing to take me away from the step-mother we both disliked. For many years I had ridden there from Adderstone and galloped along the sands, or trotted through its streets. I felt it would be a delight to live in Bamburgh, close to the castle I had always admired. We talked of restoring parts of the castle to its former glory. But it was not to be. Only the keep was now habitable and made so by our uncle.

It was agreed that Thomas and I should live in the Bamburgh Forsters' splendid stone-built manor house that still stands next to St Aidan's Church. Aunt Dorothy did, however, caution us to live moderately and keep strict accounts of all our expenditure. Thomas scorned her miserly instructions, and although I was happy to use my arithmetical abilities to help him with the book-keeping, I inquired why such economies were needed. Aunt Dorothy did not explain, so there was no way we could have known the truth. The shock of finding out the true state of the Bamburgh Forsters' legacy made Thomas sullen and angry. Not long after he came of age, creditors petitioned Chancery to order the sale of the estates and a decree was issued. Thomas would not at first accept the unwelcome truth. In the end his only choice was to agree with Aunt Dorothy that her wealthy husband should buy up all the lands, farms, manors and townships that Thomas and she owned in Northumberland and Durham. And, more painful for me, he was to lose the manor of Blanchland and my beloved manor and castle of Bamburgh.

In all, Uncle Crewe paid more than twenty thousand pounds to the Crown to save the family honour. We knew it was all done for the sake of our aunt whom he adored. Over time it became clear that there was barely £1,000 to be shared between Thomas and Aunt Dorothy. Thomas owned lead mines in Northumberland and County Durham from his Adderstone Forster family inheritance, and this quarterly revenue, and a small allowance from our Aunt, was now all we had to live on.

I doggedly stuck to my duties and tried to make Thomas more aware of our income's limitations, but he always pointed out that he would one day inherit the lands and properties of our father's estate in Adderstone. He had a generous and friendly nature and a desire to share with all his friends what he still saw as his comparative good fortune. Although reduced to an income of about six hundred pounds a year, he continued to keep a good stable of horses and took part in hunting, fishing, cock fighting and hawking. Much of it was done to find food for the table, but he always expected to entertain his friends with food and drink when they returned.

It was just as well that, young as I was, I realised that the servants could not be relied upon to rein in such lavish generosity, however experienced they might be. For almost eleven years I gradually made myself responsible for scolding, cajoling and managing Thomas's excesses in a way that kept our easy and affectionate relationship intact.

I learned how to prepare conserves, jellies and wines. I made many of my own clothes and perfumes and saw to it that the servants made roasts, pies, cakes, biscuits and puddings without waste or excessive enthusiasm. I knew that my aunt and uncle relied on my ability to prevent our financial position from worsening.

They had spent most of that year in London or at my uncle's seat at Stene in Northamptonshire, so on receiving a message that they would be in Durham a short while, I hastily prepared myself and my maid, Jenny Lee, to visit them to report on the last twelve months. Aunt Dorothy seemed happy with my accounts. "My Lord Crewe admires the firm way you handle Thomas too," she confided one evening, "He only wishes Thomas had profited from his education as much as you have."

I felt anxious at this criticism of Thomas, but tried to disguise my resentment of my aunt's words. "I believe there were many things to distract him from his studies, Aunt."

Aunt Dorothy looked sternly at me. "Ha! Like drinking and gambling! Even at the tender age of fifteen he was already beyond the pale."

I kept my face expressionless. "I cannot argue with you, Aunt; I was preoccupied with my own studies. But life with our housekeeper was very difficult to bear. He kicked against being constantly scolded by that woman. It was impossible for him to stay at home with her constant tales against us and always making our father's life a misery. Margaret and I escaped into our books; John was absorbed in his own little world of make-believe. Thomas escaped to his friends. Mrs Lawes had such power even before she persuaded father to marry her. She restricted Thomas's income to such an extent that he got into debt."

My aunt snorted, "Aye, and he added to the financial worries, no doubt. He most certainly wasted his time at Cambridge. What a missed opportunity! I know you've always been loyal to your brother, Dorothy, but take care he doesn't ruin your life as he seems to be intent on doing his own. It's he who should have a firm hold of the household management, not you. You should be married with a family of your own."

Controlling my anger at this unwaveringly harsh judgement of Thomas, I continued quietly, "He does help when he is able, but his work as a member of Parliament takes up a great deal of his time."

"Hem . . . when it suits him." Aunt Dorothy's face was set in a look of disapproval. I lowered my eyes and held my tongue. I knew too well my aunt's opinion of my brother and I also knew that nothing good could come of a serious disagreement with her. Thomas and I relied on the continued patronage of the Bishop, and Aunt Dorothy was his most trusted advisor, as well as his wife. Inwardly, I raged at our prodigal ancestors, but knew I must be grateful to the Bishop that he allowed us to live without paying rent for the manor houses in Bamburgh and Blanchland and merely required us to look after his interests.

My aunt, though obviously pleased to see me and full of praise for my management of the estates, was strangely subdued a good deal of the time and later begged me to find a husband, and encourage John to marry to secure the continuation of the family line. She said she'd given up any hopes of Thomas settling down. He was too fond of high living to take on the responsibilities of wife and family.

She confided her long held sorrow that she'd been unable to give her beloved Nathaniel a son. "My only regret is that I turned him down when he first asked me to become his wife. I thought that at only nineteen and him fifty-seven, the gap was too great and I too young to help him in such an important and lofty position. Now I think I could at least have given him children then."

"But my dear Aunt Dorothy, you were near my age when you did marry him. Why should you blame yourself? You were not quite twenty-nine;

he was sixty-seven. Perhaps it was too late for him."

My aunt cast her eyes to the ground. "Even so, it was my fault for waiting." She raised her head and fixed me with her pale, watery eyes. "Have you no young man calling on you?"

I shook my head. "Those that call are seeking Thomas to go hunting or hawking and others that come to socialise often have their wives in tow."

I kept from her my thoughts that I had long since given up hope of finding a husband. Had I not already found a place at my brother's side? I knew he would not be inclined to relinquish my post to a wife who would expect more than he was able to provide. And I knew of no unmarried young man willing to take on a woman like myself who had the position but not the wealth to be a good match.

CHAPTER 2

DURHAM CASTLE

I dismissed my musings on my situation in life as Aunt Dorothy and I slowly descended the wide, dark stairs in Durham Castle. We passed her portrait, painted in her late twenties. It showed her breathtaking beauty; the gentle waves of her light brown hair, her pale blue eyes, delicate features and the fresh colour of her skin were captured in an expression of pleasant contentment. I found myself taken aback at the sharp contrast with the wan complexion of the face I saw before me. The pained expression in her dull eyes gave me a pang of anxiety. I had not noticed the great change in her looks. "Aunt, forgive me, but are you not well?"

"Well?" For a moment the question seemed to puzzle her. "I find this place cold. The sun does not penetrate the castle's thick stone walls. The bishop's palace at Auckland has more comfort and we will go there shortly, but I confess I will be pleased to return to our home in Stene soon, or perhaps our apartments in London, if my Lord prefers it. The coming of autumn and winter in the North holds no pleasure for me. I will improve when we return."

I looked at my aunt and thought of my morning walk round Palace Green beside my uncle's magnificent cathedral and along the River Wear where I sought the shade of the trees to escape the heat of the day. Autumn was some six weeks away, and yet my aunt was shivering with cold.

Aunt Dorothy straightened her shoulders and composed herself, "Nathaniel wants to get back as soon as possible. It is better if he is not involved in things that are happening here."

I turned sharply to her. "To what things do you refer, aunt?" She pursed her lips, glanced round and murmured, "You must know of the demonstrations for the Stuart cause that broke out in early summer." I shook my head; I knew nothing of them. My aunt looked surprised but continued, "Oh, well I believe it was quite widespread; both sides of the Welsh borders and in Manchester and Yorkshire. These were easily quelled by the government, but there are rumours of more plots and preparations for undertakings across the land. Your uncle cannot be seen to favour such things, however much he might want James Stuart to come to his rightful throne. I do not know the full extent of Thomas's commitment, but if his loyalty to our King over the water is called upon, counsel caution. You and Thomas are my blood and those I care for most after my husband. Remember what we have to lose if we fail through hasty undertakings." She refused to explain further and nothing I could say helped lift her mood.

As I left the castle, Aunt Dorothy's parting words troubled me even more. My horse stumbled a little over the uneven cobbles of the castle courtyard and my Aunt rushed forward, a pained expression on her face, her hand raised. She came close and I detected an anxious urgency in her hushed tones. "Take care whom you trust, Dorothy, and heed my plea to you. Remember that my love and concern is always with you. Give my best and sincerest good wishes to all you may meet who are faithful to the true King."

I smiled and reined in my horse. "Of course, Aunt. 'Tis only a pity that they are not all faithful to the true Protestant religion." I looked down at my aunt, whose once statuesque figure seemed shrunken and frail. Again, I felt a wave of anxiety flow over me. I forced a smile. "My love and constant gratitude to you and my uncle and my sincerest wishes of health and happiness to you both. I will keep your words of love in my heart."

◆   ◆   ◆

I brought my thoughts back to the present as I ran down the hill from our castle of Bamburgh and walked along the road to the village. I felt a certain degree of resentment that next day I would have to leave the security of my well-ordered life in those pleasant surroundings. There was also the tedium of the long journey to Dilston and on to Blanchland, in all more than sixty miles away.

It was quite usual for us to make the journey to check that the collection of Lammas rents due to our uncle from his tenants in Blanchland had been duly recorded and to chase up those that were late in their payments and pay the estate workers. It was also usual to speak to the managers of Thomas's lead mines and to collect the revenues due to him. But what had come as a complete surprise was the news Thomas gave me on his return from Parliament and his consultation in Newcastle with the other Tory member of parliament, Sir William Blackett.

"In truth, Dolly, I've kept from you the full import of the point we've reached in our plans for bringing back our rightful King. Now things are moving apace and we must visit Derwentwater. The rents and such can be the reason if we need one, but you'll have to handle the business yourself."

I forced myself to smile sweetly, "That will not be unusual. In truth I should have left some time ago if you had not sent word asking me to delay. As to the other business, I'm sure we all want the return of our King, but please take care not to commit yourself to such a dangerous enterprise unless you are certain of success. Other plans have come to nought and Aunt Dorothy is fearful that you might act before the time is right."

Thomas's face set in a look of impatience. "I am fully aware of my aunt's opinion of me. But she knows only what her vacillating husband tells her. When it's been convenient for his health, he's been a puritan, a papist supporter and a fawner to that Dutchman William. Now he's for old blockhead Geordie from Hanover who cannot speak a word of English and flaunts his two ugly mistresses—the Maypole and the Elephant—about the Court. Aunt Dorothy insists that at heart Crewe is a Tory and a Stuart sympathiser as we are, but he manages to keep his wealth and position whoever is in power!" He took a breath. "Nay matter, he's turned a blind eye to activities in his diocese that could have embarrassed him and which we would have been sorry to have seen curtailed."

I was taken aback by his words. Much of what had been happening had passed me by. "Thomas," I began, "do not think badly of our Aunt. She may not approve of everything you do, but she cares a great deal about you and would not have you put your life in danger through some hasty undertaking. And neither, dear brother, would I."

Thomas smiled fondly at me. "There's no need to worry, Dolly. Our plans are well made and we have promises of such support throughout the country that when we do make a move, we cannot fail. It's just that I've received news that Bolingbroke is suggesting some changes to our plans, despite what was agreed with the Earl of Mar before he left for Scotland. I must speak with Derwentwater at Dilston Hall and I'm sure that you will be delighted to join me in enjoying his hospitality before we go to Blanchland."

◆ ◆ ◆

I smiled to myself as I took the fork to the right of the copse in the centre of the village and walked to the gate of our large, square manor house. That news had been a pleasant surprise. Our distant cousin James Radcliffe, Earl of Derwentwater, was well known for his generous hospitality. And I would most certainly enjoy the company of the extended Radcliffe family. James and his pretty wife were charming and his younger brother Charles was handsome and unpredictable, and always sent a shiver down my spine.

◆ ◆ ◆

I walked down the path to our manor house and was surprised to see the door flung open by Thomas, tankard in hand. "There you are, Dolly," he boomed, "I saw you from the upstairs window. I thought you'd be back for an early breakfast. You've been a long time. We've got much to do if we're to set off early the 'morra."

I stared in disbelief at my brother. He rarely left his bed before mid-day except to go fishing or shooting, and having consumed copious quantities of ale the previous evening, I had assumed this day would follow the regular pattern. Instead, his eyes were fired with impatience and he hustled me inside and thrust a paper and pen into my hands. He urged me to make a list of things we must do or collect together before we left.

As I sat down at the desk, he wheezed as if he had run some distance, but I was sure it was only his asthma, aggravated by the effort of heaving his increasingly large frame down the stairs. I remembered how handsome he'd been not so long ago, with his dove-grey eyes, strong, straight nose and angelic face. Now, at only thirty-two, his neck had thickened, his face was bloated and his fine and upright figure had become portly and slightly stooped.

I sighed. "I'm pleased that you are happy to help with the preparations and that you will be coming to Blanchland. You are not always so eager to stay there."

Thomas's eyes narrowed. "Damn draughty place, but needs must. I have people to see there as well. Business to discuss. Oh, and I would ask you to forgo the pleasures of taking your maid Jenny Lee with us. I have my doubts as to her leanings."

I looked at Thomas in surprise. "But she is cousin to your man Lee. Are you leaving him behind too?"

He shook his head. "No. I would trust him with m'life, but yon Jenny's side of the family are well known for their opinions. It might put us in jeopardy if she were privy to our dealings."

I felt a sudden wave of apprehension, but overcame my curiosity. This was not the time to demand further explanations.

Thomas sent for another small beer and we set about compiling a list of preparations needed for our trip. When all was completed to his satisfaction I stood up. "I will start giving the orders for looking after the manor while we are away and you can collect together the account books and the clothes you need to take. Give any that need a wash to Jenny. You can explain everything about your plans on our journey. I must ride my horse and take yours and Lee's to John Armstrong to be shod."

Thomas shook his head. "We've not much time; why not let Purdy do them here? He's nearer than Armstrong; it would take less time."

I stood my ground. "That may be, but Purdy is old and can be slow and slapdash and you know quite well we've used John since he first came as 'prentice to Purdy—why, it must be near eleven years ago. He knows our horses and they him. It may be some time before we return and I'd feel happier if he saw to it. Remind Lee we will need them ready saddled at first light in the morning. And see that Lee attends to our riding boots. Oh . . . and you must select some strong breeches yourself."

Thomas ambled away muttering to himself that he thought he was in charge, not me. I smiled; I knew it was just as well to have him occupied rather than give him time to add to what might already be a fuddled head come morning.

◆　　◆　　◆

I found John Armstrong hard at work in his smithy, but when he heard the clamour of our horses' hooves and looked up and saw me, he welcomed me with a broad smile. He put down his hammer, wiped his hands and took the leads of Midnight and Willow. He wrapped the leads round the post and helped me down from Chestnut. I did not need his help, but always enjoyed his strong arms lifting me down as if I were but a feather.

"What brings you here this fine morning?"

I looked up into his handsome face and played the fool for him. "Why, I thought I would come to teach you how to shoe a horse."

He raised his brows. "Well, if you can do that for me, I may teach you how to read."

"Done. We have a bargain!"

We collapsed in laughter and I searched in my breeches for a book I had brought.

He sighed. "Another book, Mistress Forster? I haven't finished the last you brought."

I stood with my hands on my hips. "Then I will take it away."

He put his head on one side and smiled. "If you read to me, it will pass the time while I work and be easier to read on my own later. Am I to understand you need all three shod today?"

"I do, and as fast as you can, please. We ride to Dilston tomorrow."

John led Chestnut into the smithy and turned and leaned his back against my horse's flanks. He pulled one of his hooves between his legs, inspected the shoe and nodded. He looked up at me, smiled a crooked smile and narrowed his eyes. "Please take a seat and begin."

I settled myself on one of the wooden benches, opened the book and looked up at him. "I may need a discount in return."

He laughed. "I will consider it. Begin!"

◆   ◆   ◆

On my journey home I reflected that there were few artisans I would allow to speak to me so, but our friendship had grown over the years and I knew there was not a bad bone in his body. He was illiterate when he arrived at Purdy's smithy eleven years previously, but I discerned a cleverness in his speech, sparse though it was, and made it my task to teach him his letters. He learned quickly and I was grateful it was so, for there were no others in my life with whom I could discuss the books I read.

◆   ◆   ◆

Next day in the early evening sunshine, as Thomas, Lee and I cantered through the forests of Rothbury, my mind was awash with all Thomas had told me and the number of people we had to see. The first surprise of the day had been to find Thomas up and almost ready when I entered the dining hall. Breakfast was hurried and we were on the road with unexpected haste. At Alnwick I discovered that no amount of reasoning could deflect him from the route he had planned.

"It makes no sense to choose a longer, steep and twisting road when we could follow the better, flatter and straighter one we usually do," I protested.

He persisted, "I ha' m'reasons to steer well clear of Newcastle for the present."

"And what might they be? Are you in some danger? Is it to do with parliament? Do they have intelligence of what you are planning?" Thomas shushed me; his eyes shifted uneasily and his head twisted and turned to see who might be near enough to hear me. He satisfied himself none had heard and rode on.

Not until we had left Alnwick and were alone on the road did he begin to explain. There were other people besides the Earl he needed to see.

Messages had to be sent from Rothbury—where we would spend our first night—to other parties across the county to alert them to the meeting in Dilston. The friends and associates who lived in the grand houses of Callaly, Wallington and Capheaton were on his itinerary. He planned to reach Dilston Hall in time for the mid-day meal on the third day.

I had to resign myself to accepting his plans. I also had to contain my eagerness to renew my acquaintance with the enigmatic Charles Radcliffe, and endure being excluded as Thomas partook of his meetings and hatched plans which I now saw might lead us into unknown and dangerous ventures over which I had little control.

CHAPTER 3

THE GREAT HOUSES OF NORTHUMBERLAND

1715

With a certain degree of resentment I cantered behind my brother and Lee and reflected that my usual route to Blanchland was less tortuous and more leisurely, with two nights' lodging and time to shop in Newcastle. Dilston was less distance than Blanchland, but this route was more tiring for both horses and riders.

During our visit to Callaly Castle on the first day, Thomas retired to the library with John Clavering and left me to wander aimlessly in the grounds. At Wallington Hall, on the second day, Sir Edward Blackett received us with a look of distrust. Thomas asked me to remain in the lobby while he talked to Blackett. I smiled sweetly at Sir Edward. "I'm sure you do not mind my joining you, since I have ridden this far to see you." He nodded, smiled and waved me into the drawing room. "My pleasure, Miss Forster. 'Tis a pity it cannot happen more often."

Thomas glowered at me as I sat down. He turned to Sir Edward. "Well, in the light of the latest news from the south, it's necessary we make plans at Dilston with all concerned, so I would ask you to join us there tomorrow evening."

Sir Edward frowned. "I'll give it some thought. I can say no more than that."

Thomas scowled. "I trust your thought will lead to action. All taking part must be apprised of the latest news and contribute to changing the plans." Sir Edward remained silent and Thomas's eyes flashed in anger. He stood up, indicated we should leave and turned on his heel.

James and Edward Swinburne showed no such reticence at Capheaton Hall where we stayed that night. Their welcome was warm and their hospitality generous; too generous for my liking.

◆   ◆   ◆

As I wearily guided my tired horse into the courtyard at Dilston Hall in the dusk on the third day, I looked on thankfully as servants rushed forward to assist us. Thomas's estimation of the time we would reach our destination was wildly inaccurate, mostly due to the previous evening he'd spent drinking and discussing matters with the Swinburnes at Capheaton. Despite my misgivings concerning the vast quantities of ale that were sure to be consumed, I was made aware when supper was finished that they wished to talk about more than their prowess at hunting and—after a glance from Lady Swinburne—was forced to follow her and leave them to their discussions. I retired to my room and fell into a troubled sleep, only to be awakened in the early hours of the morning as Thomas and the others stumbled noisily to their beds.

Even with Lee's help, I was unable to rouse my loudly slumbering brother before eight the next morning and it took us more than an hour to get him ready to depart. He had to make frequent stops on the journey pleading a sore head and gut, yet insisted on taking a mid-day meal at a small ale house en route.

To Thomas's delight and quite by chance, the Charlton brothers appeared and once more the talk turned to the uprising. I knew well that the rather dubious past of the Charltons meant that it would not be wise to get on the wrong side of them by brushing aside their inquiries. It was also true that they had shown their loyalty to the Cause many times before, but I was impatient to reach Dilston and resented yet another delay. I had to contain my exasperation by going for a walk in the rain. We eventually left at three and I stubbornly refused to make any further stops.

◆   ◆   ◆

Relieved we had at last reached our destination, I climbed the sweeping stone steps to the large oak doors of Dilston Hall and was greeted warmly by the Countess of Derwentwater, Anna Maria, Lady Radcliffe. She ushered us into the vast entrance hall with its warm, oak panelled walls and steered me past other guests towards the huge hearth where a roaring coal fire blazed. Even in August, balmy evenings are rare in the north and neither James nor Anna had quite become accustomed to the unreliability of our northern weather. I was grateful for the heat. As I began to untie my cloak, I became acutely aware of my mud-spattered and windblown appearance and hastily swept away the wet wisps of hair that clung to my face.

The Earl strode into the room and, after acknowledging those present, turned to me. "My dear cousin, you are most welcome. As beautiful as ever. We expected you at mid-day. You must be tired and hungry." He smiled and kissed my hand gently, and nodded politely in the direction of Thomas whose face was set in a look of irritation. "Dammed awful journey," he huffed, his red-rimmed eyes searching for a place to sit.

The Countess intervened. "I will get Betty to show you to your quarters where you can bathe and dress for supper. We were about to sup, but we will wait until you are ready." She glanced to her right, "Thompson, inform kitchen to hold supper awhile and to bring more refreshments for our guests in the hall." Her eyes fell upon the robust matron who was gathering up cloaks heaped on a wooden settle. "Ah, Betty," she said, "please show these good people to their rooms and see that they have everything they need."

"Aye, m'lady, that I will." Betty bustled over and turned to me. "Mistress Forster! You look like you've mebbies bin dragged through a hedge backwards! I'll take ya to ya room and bring some hot watter."

The countess looked taken aback and raised her eyes toward heaven and then me. "Sorry, Dorothy!"

I smiled at her. "Hot water's just what I need!"

◆   ◆   ◆

Seated a little later at the long, dark oak refectory table in the imposing
new dining room, I began to relax and was immensely relieved to see that
Thomas was deep in conversation and concentrating on the food rather
than the frothy ale in the wooden tankard in front of him. The other guests
seemed none the worse for the delayed meal but their mood was subdued,
though the conversation was urgent and, at times, animated. I caught
snatches of what they were saying but this only increased my curiosity to
know more of what had caused such seriousness in a place renowned for
its hospitality and good humour.

I noted with some disappointment that Charles Radcliffe was not
among their number. He always brought a somewhat high-spirited air
to any company and could be relied on to lift the mood. I mused that he
might be with one of his many rumoured mistresses. I had heard stories
of his wild life both here when he was younger and lately in London, but
usually dismissed them as the kind of falsehoods often bandied about
where well-connected, handsome young men were concerned.

I thought back to the time when I had been instantly attracted to
the good looks and gentlemanly ways of the Earl himself. He was not a
great deal taller than I, and slight of stature, yet bore himself so well that
his height seemed greater. It was said he had the grace and dignity of
his great-grandfather King Charles I, and the charm of his grandfather
Charles II, though his mother, Lady Mary, had been born the wrong side
of the blanket. She was almost twenty years younger than James's father,
whom she'd left at the age of twenty-four after bearing him four children.
Unlike James, his mother remained a staunch Protestant and would no
doubt have something to say about the education of her grandchildren.
She was renowned for her fiery temper, and I assumed it was her character
Charles Radcliffe had inherited.

James was altogether more gentlemanly, and his way of speaking was
most unlike people of the north. I had instantly noted the contrast between
his refined pronunciation and Thomas's Northumbrian burr. I knew of
no other who spoke quite like the Earl, for even Charles had acquired
something of the northern accent during his childhood. I found the Earl
pleasant and charming, and it was said he spoke French like a native. I

too had learned French from my governess—enough to read the small collection of books in the manor library—but I would not have trusted my ability to converse with him in that foreign tongue.

I had first met James when he returned to England from the court at St Germain-en-Laye in 1710. He had spent eight years there on the outskirts of Paris at the court of his cousin, James Edward Stuart, son of King James II who had died in exile. After a short stay in London, the Earl travelled north and came at last to his family home in Dilston. I was reluctant to admit that I was disappointed when, less than two years later, he had gone to Gloucestershire to marry Anna Maria Webb, a Roman Catholic heiress. He had never shown more than a kindly fondness for me; in truth, I had been sensible not to expect more. Not only was I almost four years his senior and a Protestant, but I was also poor, and the Radcliffe family was well known for its astuteness in choosing marriages which would enhance their considerable family fortune. Nonetheless, when he returned to Dilston two years later with his pretty, dark-haired wife and young son John, I felt a pang of regret.

I shook my head and berated myself for recalling such thoughts. I knew in my heart that I had to be content that my life was, for the foreseeable future, with my brother. Eleven years previously, I had been pursued by the heirs of many of the great Northumbrian families, some of whom were seated in this room.

I glanced round; how their interest had faded as my circumstances had changed. I no longer had an adequate dowry and although belonging to one of the chief Anglican families in Northumberland, my father's fortune was greatly reduced and my harsh step-mother had seen to it that he wasted no money on a daughter past her prime. If my present circumstances changed and I ever had need to find a husband, I would have to rely on something other than money and youth.

CHAPTER 4

TOWARDS THE
NORTHUMBRIAN MOORS

2005

Cathy gripped the steering wheel, her lips pressed tightly together, appalled by what she'd said and done. She had saved herself and left Tom when he'd needed her most.

Weighed down by an overwhelming certainty that guilt and regret would live with her forever, she was suddenly desperate to quit the endless roaring race of the motorway. She spun the steering wheel, turning onto an exit route still hitting seventy.

She slowed down and blinked, dazzled by the sudden glare of the sun, and glanced to her left in a frantic search for her sunglasses. She scrabbled one-handed in the bag she'd thrown carelessly onto the passenger seat. They weren't there. A frustrated groan escaped her lips as she narrowed her eyes and drove on. The new road was level, empty and undemanding and Tom's last words echoed in her head and she saw again her last image of him. She shook her head, "Idiot!" It didn't help to relive it.

Suddenly, she swerved to avoid a dark shape on the road ahead. She peered at it as she passed by and took a deep breath. It was just a shadow on the road. She punched the wheel, instantly aware it was a futile, painful gesture and tried again to regain control of her emotions and her driving. She leaned forward, pushed away a lock of hair, and focussed her eyes on the road ahead. After a few minutes she saw twists and turns as the road began to climb and narrow. It was a relief to have to concentrate on walkers, cyclists, oncoming traffic and deep ditches: anything but Tom.

Sinuous fingers of painful cramp enveloped her right hand. She flexed and shook it, weaving slightly across the road. A horn sounded from behind and a car swung past, the driver glaring at her. She cursed loudly, glanced in the mirror and saw she was alone on the road again; up ahead, a corner had already swallowed the speeding car. She pursed her lips and drove on, determined to beat the unwanted images.

Half an hour of determined concentration brought her to a straight road on top of open moors; no apparent bends or deep dips that required a gear change, no cars, no cyclists and no walkers; nothing but an empty road. She searched for a happy memory to relive. Every avenue of thought came back to Tom, their lives together full of memories that outweighed their time apart. His contorted face swam into her vision and was as chilling as the flood of memories she knew she was incapable of resisting.

"No!" She jumped on the brakes and the car came to an ear-piercing stop. Her hands grasped the steering wheel as panic overwhelmed her and she turned and fumbled for the door handle. Her cheeks felt tight and numb and black shadows crossed her eyes. She tried desperately to hold on to the light and resist the pictures she didn't want to see, but she was helpless to fight them; she could see him again and her own words came flooding back.

"Oh for God's sake Tom, you always manage to get your own way. You're so bloody selfish!"

The explosion—the squeal of brakes—blinding lights sweep across the rain-spattered windscreen as a huge shape bursts through the barrier and flings itself across their path.

"Look out Tom!"

He turns the wheel, jams on the brakes and the car judders, slews across the road and comes to a bone-shaking stop as it crashes against a wall of metal.

She screams as the seat belt cuts into her and Tom gasps. They sit for a moment, unable to grasp what has happened. Tom's breathing is laboured as he turns to her. "Get out Cathy . . . it's a tanker. My door's blocked. Get out!"

She opens the door and starts to climb out. She hesitates, half turning to him to speak and feels a hand shove her firmly out of the car . . . on her knees in the road. She stands up and turns back. "Tom . . ."

"Get out of here Cathy. I can't move, my legs are . . . Oh run, for God's sake, Cathy. Get help."

"But Tom . . ."

"Go Cathy. Run!"

Get help. He's all right but he can't move. Get help. Run, run to the lights; moving lights . . . cars . . . wave arms.

An explosion of heart-stopping magnitude. A powerful force of wind and heat hits her back. Blackness.

Cathy took her hands away from the steering wheel and dug her nails deep into her palms. Opening her eyes, the light pierced them like shards of ice. Her heart was pounding and tears rolling down her cheeks and she felt again the helplessness of being unable to stop reliving the whole terrifying nightmare. She'd lost count of the times she'd replayed the scene. She wondered miserably how many more times it would invade her thoughts and waking dreams.

She looked around. The road was still empty and to the distant horizon of rolling hills and hazy mountains, there was nothing but coarse grasses, bracken and heather moving gently in the autumn breeze. A handful of black-faced sheep near the roadside regrouped, looked emptily at her and skittered towards the rest of the flock.

She shoved the door open, took a gulp of air and stared ahead, seeing nothing and yet seeing clearly she'd been fooling herself. Her parents had been right when they said she shouldn't be driving, but it was hard to stay and watch their grief-stricken faces and know she was to blame.

She stepped out of the car, jumped across a shallow ditch at the edge of the road and tramped through the purple heather. A cairn of heaped stones on a hillock on the horizon promised some sort of ephemeral hope and she headed for it. She reached the stones and sat on the ground with her back to them, knees hugged to her chest. Her pulse was still pounding and the blood rushing in her ears but she closed her eyes and concentrated, willing herself to focus on the sounds of the countryside around her. Slowly, she became aware of the bleating of sheep, the songs of birds and the drone of a plane high in the sky. The sun began to warm her face and ease the numbness in her cheeks. She opened her eyes and saw her rented car; her thoughts crowded back and her vision blurred with tears.

The truth was, it didn't matter that the crash wasn't her fault, nor Tom's. It wasn't even the tanker driver's fault, yet he felt the need to try and explain what happened.

"I'm so sorry lass. I couldn't do nothing when the tyre went. It were like fighting wi' a wild animal. I'm so sorry." His face was pale and full of anguish. She couldn't find the words to comfort him; she couldn't speak. She closed her eyes and he went away.

"Oh for God's sake Tom, you always manage to get your own way. You're so bloody selfish!"

Almost the last words he'd heard.

"My words! And then I left him! Saved myself and left him to die . . ."

Her voice rang out in the emptiness of the rolling moors and surprised her with its tone of bitter condemnation.

She put her head in her hands and wondered again if she could have got him out. Everyone tried to make her feel better by saying she'd done the right thing, but she suspected it was just well-meant, misguided kindness.

The sound of a car forced her thoughts back to the moors. She watched as it sped towards hers. As it came close, it stopped and the driver got out. He looked around and saw her. She stood up reluctantly and walked quickly back. As she got near, it was clear why he'd stopped; her car was skewed across the narrow road and the door was open. There was no room to pass.

The man's eyes were on her as she approached and he looked anxiously at her. "Are you ok? Did you crash into something?"

Her insides churned. "Yes . . . I mean no! I just had to . . ." She blinked as her head swam and her body swayed and she felt his firm grip as he steadied her.

"You don't look too good. Was it those sheep? Stupid animals." He guided her to his car and opened the passenger door. "I've got some hot coffee. Sit down and I'll get it for you."

She sat down and watched him take a flask from the boot of his car and pour the coffee into a plastic cup. He offered it to her. "Sip it slowly, then I'll have to get your car out of the way before someone else comes along."

She began to drink in silence and wondered why she was allowing herself to be told what to do. He looked down at her. "Where were you heading for?" Such a simple question, but she had no answer. She shrugged her shoulders. "I don't know. Nowhere in particular."

"Well, Blanchland's not far. I'm staying at the Lord Crewe Arms. I'll take you there after I've moved your car to where the road widens ahead. I'll get someone to come back for it later."

She shook her head. She didn't want this attention. "It's very kind of you, but I'm fine now. I'll drive my car out of the way and you can go to your hotel."

He glanced at her and frowned. "I really don't think you should. Your hands are shaking and you're very pale. Are you sure you didn't hurt yourself?"

"No!" She choked, scrambling out of his car and handing back the coffee, "I didn't hurt *myself*. Not *me*. *I'm* fine!"

She ran to the car, jumped in and started the engine, drove speedily to where he could pass and braked sharply. She sat staring into the distance, angry at herself for her bizarre response to his understandable concern.

Moments later his car drew up beside her and he got out. Before she could think what to do, he'd opened her door, taken the keys out of the ignition and she watched in detached amazement as he took her case out of the boot and loaded it into his own.

"Hey!" she finally shouted, unsure whether it would be foolish to get out and wrestle it back. "What do you think you're doing?" He opened his passenger door, came back and stood silently beside her for a moment. "You're in shock or something. You're not well. Please get out and come with me."

She shook her head. "No way, I . . . please . . ." She couldn't find the words to make him go away, glanced at him and found his gaze unsettling. He began again, "There's no point in refusing. I'm not giving you your keys back."

She shook her head again and clutched the wheel. "Please go away and leave me alone. And bring my case and keys back!"

He didn't move. "Not a chance; you're not well enough to be driving and I'm not leaving until you're in the car with me, so come on, please get out. No point in being stubborn about it."

A lost memory pushed its way back into her consciousness. Tom's words.

"Oh come on Cathy, you might as well give in. Don't be stubborn about it."

"Oh for God's sake Tom, you always manage to get your own way. You're so bloody selfish!"

A cold panic swept through her as she tried to resist the words and pictures flooding back. She covered her ears and shut her eyes tightly.

She opened her eyes in surprise as the man eased her round in the seat and swung her legs onto the road. He took hold of her hands. "Please stand up."

The compassion in his eyes and gentleness of his voice overcame her surprise that he'd manhandled her so skilfully. Tears sprang into her eyes. She shook her head in silent protest, but he pulled her to her feet. "Come on; it's ok." He guided her to his car. She protested feebly, but without conviction, suddenly relieved that someone else was taking responsibility for her. She looked back at her car.

"Don't worry. I'll lock the car up." He eased her into the passenger seat and fastened the seat belt. She sat there meekly, disturbed at her lack of resistance and confused at her inability to find words to voice her resentment that he'd taken command despite her plea to be left alone.

She closed her eyes and sat back, taking in the sound of a door being shut and the click of a lock. The car shook a little as he got in, put her handbag on her knee and started the engine. She opened her eyes and tried to think what she should say to protest at what he'd done, but it was too much effort. It was easier to let someone else decide what she should do, even though she knew she was taking a risk. If something bad happened, she knew she probably deserved it.

CHAPTER 5

UNWELCOME HISTORY

2005

The car moved smoothly along the gently undulating road over the empty moors and Cathy began to relax and tried to rationalise what she'd allowed to happen. She closed her eyes. It had been stupidly irresponsible not to refuse to let this man coerce her into his car. But it had felt too difficult to resist; simpler to let things happen.

She opened her eyes and turned to face him. He glanced at her and back at the road. "Look, I know what I did might seem controlling, even scary, but I'm a doctor and . . ."

"A doctor? Well, that's a great excuse for practically kidnapping me!"

"Fine. Shout at me if it'll make you feel any better. I'd rather get an ear bashing than leave you there and have you on my conscience."

She swallowed and tried to think more clearly. *Leave you there. On my conscience.* It seemed as if every word he used triggered more unwelcome memories and guilt. She'd forgotten Tom's words until a few minutes ago. Blanked them out in some way.

"Oh come on Cathy, you might as well give in. Don't be stubborn about it."

What had he wanted? Was it so important? *Leave you there. On my conscience.* She shook her head and tried to block it from her thoughts.

He turned to her again. "If you don't want to tell me what's wrong, that's fine, but you need to see your doctor." She glanced at him and turned back to the road. He continued. "When we get to the top of the hill above Blanchland, we'll stop. You can sit in the sun and have another drink. All of it, this time."

She sat silently, knowing she ought to say something but unable to find the right words. She turned and studied his face. His skin was deep olive-brown and stretched smoothly over fine cheekbones. His nose was strong and straight, his heavy-lidded eyes fringed with dark sweeping lashes, his hair black, and so short that it looked as if it would feel like velvet. There was a suggestion of a dark moustache and beard caused by neglect rather than design. So unlike Tom with his floppy blonde hair, pale pink cheeks and piercing blue eyes. "Looks like an angel," she remembered her father saying, "and a bit of a devil half the time."

The man cleared his throat. "My name's Simon Wood, but I'm known as Jack."

She frowned and glanced at him. "Why Jack?"

"My middle name's Jackhu. It's my mother's family name. She's Indian. Apparently, when I was very young an uncle called me Jack and it stuck. Yours?"

She caught her breath. "Oh . . . Catherine Adams . . . Cathy."

He glanced at her with a grin. "Hi, Cathy."

"Um, hi."

She stared ahead, unable to believe she was responding to him as if it was an everyday happening to let herself be persuaded to get into a stranger's car. She'd also accepted his word that civilisation was near, despite the loneliness of the landscape, but still couldn't summon the effort to worry too much about it.

The car climbed a gentle incline and levelled out when it crested a hill. After a while Jack pulled off the road and parked. He looked at Cathy with a reassuring smile. "Come on." He climbed out of the car and got the thermos from the boot. After a moment's hesitation when she wondered if she should, she climbed out obediently, unable to find the energy to resist and wondering vaguely why she suddenly felt she could trust him.

They walked in silence to a point where they could look down on a village in a valley. It spread out below them, contained in a hollow and protected by fir trees on a hill to the north. It looked unnaturally peaceful, with only a sprinkling of people wandering past its imposing old buildings and the neat rows of fawn stone houses that formed a large square; buildings so perfectly placed that it looked like a model village suspended in time. It didn't appear to belong to the twenty-first century.

Jack stood silently for a moment. He turned towards her. "What do you think of it?" She couldn't think what to say. He began again, "It's my favourite village. I first found it when I was a medical student in Newcastle. I work in a busy hospital in London now and it can be very stressful. This is one of my bolt holes; where I come when I need peace and quiet. Out of season, that is."

She couldn't stop herself from sighing. "And I've got in the way."

He glanced briefly at her. "Not at all . . . I . . . shall I tell you how it got the name of Blanchland?"

She sat down and hugged her knees. "If you want." She didn't care and couldn't pretend she had any enthusiasm about anything anymore, but listening politely to him seemed to be the easiest option.

He sat down beside her and poured them both some coffee. Cathy nodded her thanks and sipped it slowly, staring into the distance. He pointed to the centre of the village.

"Can you see a large building with a tower at the far end?"

She ran her eyes over the buildings, trying to feign interest. "Near the archway?"

He leant closer to her and pointed again. "Well, the tower next to it." She nodded and glanced at him. He smiled, his eyes resting on her for a moment. She felt a twinge of discomfort and turned away.

"Well that's the Lord Crewe Arms, where I'm staying. It's what used to be the Abbot's house, part of a twelfth-century abbey built by monks who originally came from a place called white glades in north-eastern France. They wore white robes, and in the early thirteenth century they kept the French word for white in the name and the Abbey was called Blanchland. When the village was built on what was left of the Abbey, it took the same name."

Cathy sat silently and felt him glance at her. "Shall I go on, Cathy?" She nodded. It was easier than talking. He remained silent and she turned to him and saw a look of uncertainty on his face. "You're sure?"

She nodded again. "Sure."

"Ok. There's an old Northumbrian folk tale that says that in the fourteenth century, a band of Scottish raiders—looking for the abbey so they could loot it—got lost in the thick mist that sometimes settles on this village. The monks had been warned of a possible attack. Well, after some hours with no sight or sound of the raiders, the monks thought that the mist— that they were convinced God had sent—had saved them, and rang the bells to celebrate their miraculous escape. The Scots followed the sound, sacked the Abbey, burnt part of it down and slaughtered the monks who didn't manage to escape."

The story touched Cathy more deeply than she felt it should. She sat for a few moments, seeing the mayhem, the fear and the carnage. She felt sick at the thought of a base human instinct that drove some people to such senseless, violent acts. She turned to him. "That's so sad. Do you think it's true?"

A worried expression flitted across his face as he looked into her eyes. He shrugged his shoulders and gave a quick smile. "Who knows? You probably won't find the story in history text books, but local people know it. There are some great stories about this area, but it's hard to know what's historical fact and what's just folk tales. But I like to think that even the folk tales usually have a grain of truth in them."

A deep sigh escaped her lips and she ran her hands through her hair. Jack looked at her and frowned. "I'm boring you. Sorry. I expect everyone to be as interested as I am. I'm a bit of a history freak, I guess. Comes from wanting to know my roots, I think: my father's from round here. Met my mother when he was on a business trip in Bedford. I wish I'd asked him more before . . ." He looked away and picked up the flask. "Do you want some more coffee?"

"No thank you, and you're not boring. It's me, not you." She leant her forehead against her knees, unable to explain further.

He rested a hand on her shoulder. "Can I help? I'm good at listening as well as talking."

She looked up, attempted a casual smile and shook her head. "No. There's no way anyone can help. I'll get through it. Please could you take me to the village? I'd like to see if the hotel has a room."

◆　　◆　　◆

Dorothy Catherine Adams, Harrogate, North Yorks, Cathy wrote in the register. The receptionist smiled. "That's quite a famous name round here."

"What, Adams?"

The receptionist laughed. "No, Dorothy. Dorothy Forster. The 1715 Jacobite Rebellion?" Cathy shook her head. The receptionist seemed baffled. "Go into the Hilyard Room and up the stairs. There's a room at the top with her portrait inside. That used to be her bedroom and her ghost is supposed to haunt the hotel."

Cathy forced a smile. "Oh." She realised she was expected to show some interest. "I might have a look later."

Delving any further into why the woman's name should be famous in this particular area was not in her plans. She had a vaguely uneasy feeling she didn't want to know, but as she lay on the bed with the reflected sunlight streaming through the open window after a long and leisurely bath, she felt more relaxed and composed than she'd been for what felt like a long time. Perhaps Jack was right to come here when he needed a bolt hole. Perhaps this place would work its soothing magic on her too.

She sat up abruptly, remembering she'd forgotten to thank Jack for what he'd done for her. She'd disappeared up to her room while he was outside collecting his own luggage after bringing in hers. She bit her lip and knew she would have to go and thank him.

It was unusually warm for mid-September, so she flung on a cotton top, shorts and sandals. As she left her room, the door next to hers opened and Jack emerged. "Cathy. How are you feeling?"

She smiled. "Much better. I'm going to look for Dorothy Forster's room. Apparently she's famous round here. The receptionist noticed that Dorothy was one of my names. I don't usually tell anyone, but for some reason I wrote it in the book."

She frowned, remembering that Tom used to tease her about her first name because she'd been unable to pronounce it properly when young and had taken a dislike to it.

She was suddenly aware they were standing in silence and Jack was studying her face. She forced her expression into a smile. "Oh, I forgot; thank you for bringing me here and for looking after me."

He smiled and shrugged his shoulders. "That's ok. Someone had to. You certainly look a lot better. Would you like me to show you the room? I think the receptionist meant the one that's now the residents' sitting room."

She hesitated for a moment, wondering if it was right to prolong her monopoly of his time, but he looked so eager that she nodded and watched his face break into a smile. She felt an unexpected rush of comfort from the warmth of his gaze.

He put a guiding hand on her back. "This way. It's a bit strange that she's more famous than her brother, Tom Forster. It was him who led the rebel Jacobite army and as far as I know, she didn't have anything to do with it. Although I vaguely remember something about her having hidden him when the soldiers were looking for Jacobite sympathisers."

Jack's words echoed round Cathy's brain. *Tom: her brother, Tom.*

"Why no, man, that's not the reason!"

She turned, struggling to keep her emotions in check, and saw a white-haired old man sucking a pipe. "No, no. She was a heroine. Saved her brother from certain death. That's why."

CHAPTER 6

DILSTON HALL

1715

I quickly dismissed my musings on my unmarried status at the advanced age of twenty-nine, as I became aware that someone was speaking to me. "I beg pardon, sir, I was lost in my thoughts."

"I was just wondering, Dorothy, how your old uncle Crewe was faring is his chilly castles?"

I took in Lord William Widdrington's sneering smile and strong features. I attempted to smile alluringly at him. "He is well, sir, and very busy about his work. He has done much to improve the comfort of his castle apartments at Bamburgh, Auckland and Durham and is well pleased with the results. I think you would find as much warmth and comfort as you find here."

Widdrington's look softened and I noted with satisfaction that his eyes showed more kindness than before. He downed a goblet of port and rubbed his left knee. He leaned closer to me: "I suffer badly with the gout, y'know. I can be a bit choleric at times, but a bonny lass like yourself sitting next to me at supper can do wonders."

I acknowledged the compliment with a nod of my head and marked that, despite the fact I was in my thirtieth year, he had the gall to call me a lass. Like my brother, high living had aged Widdrington beyond his years, though I did not wish to judge him too harshly knowing that the loss of his wife the previous year had grieved him deeply and left him with five children to rear.

When supper was over, Lady Derwentwater indicated to me that we should not linger. We withdrew to the drawing room and I felt a degree of frustration at our exclusion. I wondered how much the Countess knew of the forthcoming enterprise and, as we seated ourselves on the lavishly upholstered sofa, I seized the moment. "Why such low spirits?" I inquired, "has something gone amiss?"

Anna Maria sighed, rose and began to pace up and down in front of the fire. "The plans are well thought out and bound to succeed, but it is rumoured that Bolingbroke wishes to change them and intends to put those changes to our King in St Germain. James only learnt of this earlier today when Clavering arrived. Surely you knew this much, for it was your brother told Clavering when you called on him? I believe it was Sir William Blackett's spies who informed your brother of the changes when he was in Newcastle, though they refused to ride to Wallington, pleading exhaustion, and so are waiting for Blackett at his house in Newcastle."

"I don't think he would be of a mind to risk his person there for the present."

Anna Maria frowned. "Nor has he arrived here. James is discomforted at his absence."

"Go on with your news; I am all ears."

"Well, the difficulty is that the Earl of Mar had already left for Scotland before the news of the changes was known. He must be informed before he raises the standard of rebellion there." The word rebellion struck fear into my heart. It seemed so much more dangerous than talk simply of restoring the Stuarts to the throne. I joined Anna Maria in front of the fire, full of anxiety.

"In England," she continued eagerly, "the greater part of the uprising was to have been here in the North East. The Scots and the Lancastrians have huge numbers waiting to join us but there are perfect places along the north-east coast where the fleet from France—and, pray God, our King—can land and join with our forces. First Tynemouth and then Newcastle is to be taken and the huge stocks of coal withheld from London." She smiled conspiratorially at me. "You see, the loss of the vast revenues from the coal will paralyse the capital and with the coming of winter, the lack of coal will also make the populace more uneasy at the deprivation of their warmth. They will be more welcoming to a King who can restore their wealth and comfort." She smiled ingenuously as if the mischief caused could be excused and could only lead to the success of the venture. I was unsure that their thinking would achieve the outcome to which they aspired.

I opened my mouth to speak my concern but she waved an arm and continued. "Let me finish. My dear James is hoping the main force from France will still land on the Northumberland coast in September after they have secured Holy Island, but he is not happy that some of the forces might now land in the south. Your brother had been given the final plan of action from the Earl of Mar and all are most distressed at the changes."

I felt disturbed that the preparations for the rebellion had become so advanced. Thomas had talked in general terms about meetings being held and plans made, but he had not mentioned how detailed they were and how close their inception, nor had he admitted to his close association with the Earl of Mar.

The Countess gave a gentle smile. "I see you are surprised that James has seen fit to discuss matters of such import with me. We have no secrets. I was brought up to understand that our loyalty to James III and thus the restoration of a Stuart to the throne is the most important objective we can have in life." Anna's eyes sparkled and her face flushed. "It is partly why James and I are so suited, so strong in our resolve. Our years in St Germain gave us a special love and respect for the House of Stuart and we were grieved and shocked when the people of England accepted George of Hanover. We thought at first it was mere apathy but we came to understand it was a matter of religion. When we show them that our two religions can live in harmony and that King James will not force his Catholicism on his subjects, we believe they will flock to our Cause. That is why it is so pleasing that we have two influential Anglican Tory Members of Parliament among our supporters in Sir William Blackett and your brother. Who better to share the leadership of the rebellion with my dearest husband?"

My heart skipped a beat and I clasped my hands together. "Does Thomas know that is what is intended?" The Countess looked puzzled. "I would presume so. They are discussing it now, I believe."

I shook my head in disbelief. "Share the leadership of the Rebellion? How could Thomas do that? He is and will always be a loyal servant to the Cause, but he has no knowledge of soldiering. He is a squire, a countryman, a politician. He is the kindest brother and most loyal friend one could have . . . but one of the leaders of an army? He has no experience of such things."

I saw a look of doubt flicker across Anna's face. She composed herself. "Dorothy, that may be true, but he will not be alone. There will be experienced soldiers to help plan the strategies. And my James studied such things in France with our King himself. There will be counsel enough to supplement any lack Thomas may have."

I felt I could say no more. I had grave doubts concerning the wisdom of trusting Thomas's capabilities in such an enterprise, but felt it would appear disloyal to him if I elaborated any further on the reasons for my opinion. I knew I would have to talk to him. He must see that it was not sensible. I smiled at the Countess, trying to convey my acceptance of her words. I stifled a yawn. "My Lady, would you excuse me? I am a little tired after such a wearisome journey."

Anna clasped her hands together. "Oh, my dear Dorothy, forgive me." She ran to grasp the brocade pull. "My housekeeper Betty will fill the bed pan with hot coals for your bed. It has not been slept in for some time."

I shook my head and waved my hand. "There is no need. There was a fire in my room when I bathed earlier. That will suffice."

The Countess stood her ground. "I would not hear of it."

Betty bustled in and began to unhook the copper bedpan from the wall even before she was given her orders. Anna smiled, "You see, Dorothy, I have her well trained."

Betty bristled as she scooped the hot coals into the pan. "More like y've mebbies larned a little northern hospitality from me yersel, ma'am," she said with a wink at me. Anna laughed a little nervously.

When Betty left the room Anna turned to me. "I don't think I shall ever become used to the irreverence of northern humour. But she's a good woman and so clever at organising the servants." We passed through the dining room where the men were still deep in conversation. Anna took her leave and left by the door to the nursery. I took the door to the entrance hall and reached the foot of the stairs.

A thunderous knocking made me pause and brought Thompson scurrying to the door. It creaked open and Charles Radcliffe swept through, throwing cape, hat and gloves in Thompson's direction. His gaze settled on me and a quizzical, but interested expression spread across his face. "Well, what have we here? Bonny Dolly with your teasing eyes and rosebud mouth. Where's that sot of a brother of yours?"

I composed the features that had just broken into a smile and spoke curtly to him.

"With your brother and the others, discussing the business that brought us here post haste. He may be fond of the drink but at least he does not waste his time bedding any young girl he can find!"

Charles stiffened and his expression changed to one of indignant anger. "So, you have been listening to clacking tongues. I'm disappointed, Dorothy. I had thought you were not one of those ready to listen to tittle-tattle or make hasty judgments. I must tell you that since I returned from London, I have had more pressing things to fill my time."

I lowered my eyes. "Forgive me, sir. I have a quick tongue sometimes. But you should not have abused Thomas's character. Anyway, it's your own business what you do with your time."

"True. And perhaps I should have spent more hours with the ladies, not less, as there'll be little time for such things for a while if all goes to plan."

I scrutinised his excited face. "What do you mean by that? How soon will it begin?"

Charles looked at me for a moment, seeming about to answer, but his attention was taken by a servant entering the hall with more coals. He hesitated and shook his head. "Go to bed, Dorothy; you look weary." He leant forward, took my hand and kissed it lightly. "Good night." I stood for a moment watching him stride away and turned slowly towards the staircase.

The evening's revelations troubled me. I wondered if all the fervour on the faces of the guests and hosts had clouded their judgment of the numbers who would rally to the Cause. I had heard that many citizens in the north—despite their loyalty to the Stuarts—had accepted that the true King would remain in France for the foreseeable future, probably until

George died. They wanted a peaceful restoration. And there were whispers, particularly in Newcastle, that there were many who had prospered in the years of stable protestant rule under William and Mary and later Queen Anne. And now they seemed quite happy with George. I wondered what would be their answer if they were asked to risk all for the sake of the Cause.

I climbed the huge curved staircase and took the right hand branch along the stone corridor which led to my room. A sudden draught caught the flaming wall candles and sent eerie shadows flickering across the walls. A shiver of apprehension coursed down my spine.

I entered the room and was thankful to find that Betty had laid out my night garments on the large, curtained bed. I undressed quickly, climbed in and succumbed gratefully to the comforting cosiness of the down-feather mattress. Despite my anxieties, sleep overwhelmed me before I could review what I had heard, or think what I might say to make Thomas reconsider the dangerous path he was taking.

CHAPTER 7

BLANCHLAND

1715

I had little time to speak to Thomas about my doubts concerning his part in the proposed rising. He was so eager to be elsewhere that he sent me back to Blanchland with Lee while he went to Beaufront to see his friend Mr Errington. Thomas told me he intended to go on from there to other meetings at Lodges across the north country. He promised to keep me informed as to his whereabouts and bid me see that Uncle's unpaid rents were collected and the missing revenues from the lead mines chased up. "We will need the money more than ever now, so you must see that there is no unnecessary expense. Frugality, Dolly, frugality."

"Of course, dear brother," I said with a smile, "I will follow your example, shall I?" Thomas laughed and pinched my cheek. "Naw, just follow my orders!"

◆　　◆　　◆

Lee cantered for most of the journey and I found it difficult to keep up with him. We had barely arrived when he announced that he could not linger and must now join his master. I was suddenly alone again, left to fret over what Thomas might do next and ponder when I would see them again.

The following day I sent a messenger to chase up the revenue from one of Thomas's lead mines and summoned Wilson, Uncle Crewe's estate manager. I ordered him to send for those tenant farmers who were late with their payments and require them to settle their rents that afternoon.

I also wanted to check that the estate workers, due their wages a few weeks previously, had received their full amounts. I demanded the receipts from Wilson. He had been known to short change them and excuse his actions by citing their lack of hard work if he could get away with it.

I found the revenues from Thomas's other mines locked up in the office and set about checking the figures, for I knew that the managers were not entirely trustworthy when they thought that Thomas's attention was elsewhere.

After luncheon I sat at the desk in the hall, and resigned myself to a long afternoon of excuses and the unwholesome presence of Wilson at my side. My uncle had replaced our long-time, faithful and trusted manager with a man of his own choosing and I neither liked him nor had faith in his honesty.

Later in the day I looked up as yet another overdue purse of money was proffered across the mahogany desk. The thin outstretched hand that held it, though clean, was ingrained with dark streaks and calluses covered the palm. I undid the string and tipped the money onto the desk. I counted it quickly. "It's short, William."

"Mistress, forgive me, my son is sick. We canna' spare more."

I could see the pain is his eyes and knew he was not one to lie. "I am sorry to hear it. What ails him?"

William looked uncomfortable and tossed the sandy-coloured hair from his face. "He was unconscious for many days wi' a clot on his brain. The doctor put the leeches to his head. You should've seen 'em roll off geet big and fat with blood. He's awake now but he'll need a lot of care and potions to help him get his strength again."

I gathered up the money, piled it into the cloth and tied it up. I offered it back. "Pay us a little more than usual next time, William."

He hesitated, then took it with a nod. "Thank you, mistress. We'd've struggled. I'll not let you down next time."

As he left the room, Mr Wilson tutted. I glanced briefly at him and returned to my list. "That seems to be all the late payments except Bisset. Is there a problem there, Wilson?"

He twisted his bulbous lips. "P'raps he was outside waitin' to come in and William told him how free you are to waive the rent at the first sob story y'hear."

I stood up abruptly, "Take care, Wilson, or you may find it's yourself with a sob story to tell!" I flung the list at him. "See this all tallies and lock the money up. I will check it first thing in the morning." I smoothed my workaday frock down with my hands and walked briskly towards the kitchen to revise the order for supper.

We employed a temporary cook and kitchen maid, who both came in when Thomas and I were in residence. Often, we ate only two or three courses for supper. I knew that the farm hands and lead workers in the area had little to spare and I didn't wish to appear profligate. I visited the homes of the poorest workers on the estate with gifts of vegetables and flour whenever we stayed in Blanchland and never failed to return home without feeling guilty that Thomas and I should ever have felt badly done to.

I reflected that James Radcliffe had shown even greater generosity to all his estate workers and tenant farmers from the time he first arrived at Dilston. When I said this to Thomas, he laughed. "His butler Thompson gets five pounds a year and his cook ten, but the Countess's yearly dress allowance is two hundred pounds!"

I shook my head. I must not think badly of James. The Countess had her status to maintain and all the servants' quarters were comfortable. They had more than generous food and drink supplied and were given more holidays than most. And James had made sure that even during his two years away in the south, his estate manager did nothing to cause any of his workers to doubt his continued kindness. His generosity and good-natured manner towards them assured him of their loyal support. I preferred to think these actions were the natural inclinations of a genuine philanthropist and it was only a happy accident that it might now benefit the Cause.

"Mistress?"

I was startled from my musings, my hand on the open kitchen door, to see the questioning expression on the face of Mary Liddell. "Oh, Mary, I forgot to tell you, there is only myself this evening. My brother will not return for a few more days."

A disapproving look spread across Mrs Liddell's podgy face as she surveyed the pile of vegetables already prepared and the meats cooking on the stove. I sighed, "Ah, you will all eat well tonight, Mary. Distribute anything that is left." I smiled apologetically and went to find Joe.

The permanent staff consisted of a housekeeper, Cissy, and her husband Joseph, a Yorkshire man. Cissy kept the rooms and linen clean and Joseph did all manner of jobs about the house and kept it secure. I felt it would not be economical to employ more. Gardeners could easily be found when needed and if Thomas had need of beaters for shooting or helpers with hunting, there were ready and willing workers to be had for a few farthings.

I went outside to take a turn round the cloister garden. It was not much more than a kitchen garden but I loved to wander among the herbs, sniffing their scents in the early evening. I bent down and picked some lavender that had been left to die but still held its perfume. It grew better here than in our garden in Bamburgh, which was exposed to the cold north-east winds that often blew across the North Sea. Here, the garden was protected by the buildings and the hills that encircled the hamlet.

I had ordered a wall to be built around the garden in Bamburgh in an effort to give it more protection, but when the winds swirled from the north there was nothing could stop their awesome power. The Bamburgh manor walls were on the lower part of the garden, but not so high that they would block the view of the sea which I loved so much. Even on a cool evening in spring or autumn, I wrapped up warm and sat with my back against the wall and sea to watch the sun go down behind the manor house, straining my ears to hear the waves and the plaintive cries of the gulls as they swept over the sea.

In Blanchland, the stones of the buildings seemed to hold the warmth of the day. On the garden side of the house, muffled sounds of carts and horses passing over the cobbles on the street side of the house could be heard. I missed the sea, but the banks of trees, the sparkling river, the circle of hills and even the blanket mists that sometimes descended unexpectedly, made me feel secure. I loved it almost as much as my home in Bamburgh, yet tonight there was a feeling of foreboding I could not quell. My aunt's words kept coming back to me, as did the whisperings about government spies I'd overheard as we left Dilston. It made me feel cold inside and all the excitement of Anna Maria could not counter my anxiety.

After supper I sat for a while on the small leather-covered box-seat within the confines of the great fireplace in the parlour off the entrance hall. The stone staircase that led to my bed chamber rose directly from the room and all the windows, including those beside the stairs, were ill-fitting and draughty. But the space to either side of the fire, contained within the carved stone lintel above the fireplace and the stone pillars at the side, was a haven in which I could sit for hours, even in winter.

I gazed at the crackling fire and mused over what the Countess had told me. I wondered again what the future would hold for myself and Thomas. I resented the fact that it seemed to be a woman's lot always to be left at home, waiting and fearfully thinking of all manner of dangers that might befall her loved ones. At least I didn't have a child to protect as the Countess had, but it was irksome that the women were never able to do anything that would affect the outcome of their men's exploits. And this time, without Jenny, there was not a soul to talk to. I felt the lack of a female companion to share my concerns and discuss my thoughts. Anna Maria could never be my close confidante, her status being so far above mine. And yet Anna had no one but her maid and her son's nurse. They seemed devoted to her, but she must be fearful lest she let slip something that might endanger her beloved James.

I sighed and picked up my book. I felt it fortunate that I found solace in reading and hoped my book might engage my concentration and chase away my wandering thoughts, but it did not. I wished that John Armstrong was nearby to discuss it with me and to reassure me that all would go well for Thomas. Many's the time I would sit pondering a problem on the window seat in my bedroom in Bamburgh and delight to see John riding towards the beach. I would find some reason to take a brisk walk and join him on the rocks where he sat looking out to sea. He never asked why I had come and merely listened while I unloaded my problems and in a while made decisions after a few wise words from him.

I leant forward with my elbows on my knees and read by the light of the flickering flames until I heard the clock strike ten. Reluctantly, I called for Joseph to dampen down the fire and said good night.

The morning brought news which both pleased and disturbed me. Lee arrived and announced that his master was to return later in the week with a gentleman called Henry Oxburgh. "A soldier, mistress. He is well known to Lord Widdrington and is a very pious man. My master would have you be prepared for Colonel Oxburgh and his man to stay a day or two before he returns to Newcastle."

I knew well that this was a veiled message from Thomas that there must be not only a good supply of food in the larder but also enough drink in the cellar that they would not be in danger of running dry. Thomas had told me about Oxburgh and his associates as we left Dilston Hall. "Irish, he is, and has contact with other Irish soldiers and also our fellow Northumbrians Shafto and Hunter and more on the Borders. Their intelligence gives us a link with the Earl of Mar in Scotland and also with London, so that we are not caught unawares if there should be any change of plan in the future."

"And how soon is this future for which you are planning?" I asked.

"Not yet, not yet," was all he would answer.

◆　◆　◆

Although Oxburgh's stay was longer than anticipated, I was pleased that he and his servant proved to be lively company. They were full of stories and would sometimes regale Thomas and me with amusing ditties that passed away the evenings pleasantly enough.

It was just into September when Oxburgh and Thomas left, having received news that dispatches from James Stuart had been brought from London. They had been taken to Derwentwater's town house in Newcastle, and the courier would only hand them over to one they could trust. Oxburgh persuaded Thomas that his face was less known to the populace of Newcastle and he should be the one to collect their instructions. Thomas agreed to stay at the house of his friend William Fenwick of Bywell while Oxburgh collected the dispatches.

◆　◆　◆

When Thomas returned three days later, he was both excited and disappointed. His news came tumbling out in such a rush that I found it hard to concentrate on all he said and to weigh up its significance.

"Bolingbroke has got his way, damn it! He'll land in Portsmouth and there'll be another group landing in Plymouth to divert King George's army from us. There's to be other risings in Bristol, Worcester and Shropshire."

I gasped. "Please, Thomas, tell me how you are to be involved."

He frowned. "Well, as planned, we are to capture Tynemouth and Newcastle and disrupt the coal trade. We think the keelmen will come out for us with a bit of persuasion from Blackett and he's also expected to persuade the merchants and political establishment in Newcastle to aid us. Mind you, I have my doubts about the man. He blows hot and cold." He removed his wet cape, "Well, no doubt he'll come right when we get word to rise."

I shivered with a mixture of excitement and apprehension as I ushered Thomas into the parlour. I made him sit in front of the fire while I went to order some hot broth. I returned to find him staring into the fire and holding his hands out to warm them. He looked up at me and smiled. "Come sometime in October we'll sweep the country and have our King chase that usurper from Hanover out. Are you not excited, Dolly?"

"Of course, Tom; it's . . . it's just that I'm anxious that you will get the support you need to overcome the government's army. They have such numbers; they are well-armed and organised. Where will you find such arms?"

"The Earl of Mar is to send men and arms from Scotland and those that land on our coast from France will bring more. We have swords and muskets hidden, and Oxburgh says we are promised thousands of men from the west to add to those who'll rise in Northumberland. And just think of the goodly number of Catholic and Tory Anglican families that live between Berwick and Newcastle. We are sure they will support James Stuart and are all waiting to join us."

I smiled and hugged Thomas. That did indeed sound promising and at first I felt greatly relieved to hear it. On reflection, lingering doubts remained and made me anxious that they were relying on vague expectations and too few firm pledges of support.

CHAPTER 8

DEPRIVATION AND DECISIONS

1715

Within a week, in mid-September, Oxburgh returned to our home in Blanchland to report his having heard that the Earl of Mar had raised the standard of rebellion at Braemar on the sixth day of the month. This information was received with glee by Thomas but Oxburgh's second piece of news was not.

The Privy Council had issued an order for the seizure of all horses and arms belonging to Catholics and others suspected of abetting a possible invasion. All papists' movements were to be confined.

Oxburgh's expression showed an excitement I found hard to share. His eyes glittered. "I called at Stella Hall to warn Widdrington. He was not at home and his servants would not reveal his whereabouts. Others have gone to Dilston and yet more, north and west from Newcastle to warn other parties. When I have taken some refreshment, I plan to return to Dilston. I think, sir, you should accompany me."

Thomas seemed spurred on by the sudden flurry of activity and immediately set about planning a visit to see James at Dilston. After issuing instructions to Lee, he turned to me. "I think that you should accompany me so it will seem to any onlooker that it is an innocent visit by one well-known for his fondness of a good social calendar . . . and his loyal sister."

I accepted his suggestion without comment, aware I would be less anxious seeing for myself what was happening than if I stayed at home. Indeed, I hoped that the visit would reassure me that my lingering doubts about the timing and likely success of the whole enterprise were unfounded.

But it did not.

As we left, the clouds gathered and we rode across Blanchland Moor in a fine drizzle which quickly became a relentless deluge. The earth and stony bridleway was soon reduced to a quagmire. I deeply resented the laughter of the warm and dry occupants of a small equipage as its wheels and four horses splashed passed us. Our progress to Dilston was greatly impeded by the difficult conditions and almost an hour and a half later, as we approached the Devil's Water, the stream sounded more like the River Tyne itself than the small tributary it was. It had been unusually wet in the past week and the rain continued its dreary downpour as we rode down the hill and along the track beside the stream.

I paused by the stone bridge that crossed Devil's Water near the track that led up to the Hall and listened to the roar of the gushing stream tumbling headlong towards the Tyne. I was not, and still am not, one to place much importance on superstition, but it seemed to me that it was a warning not to run out of control into deep waters. "Thomas," I began, but he was out of earshot and his horse beginning to climb the slope away from the stream.

I rode up through the dripping trees and emerged onto the slope where the carriageway led to the north side of Dilston Hall. It seemed to me that the building looked more like a dismal prison than a splendid home. James had tried to build a place that would rival the best of the great Northumbrian houses at Wallington, Capheaton and Callaly, but at this moment it had a bleak, unhappy look.

Much of the building work on the Hall had taken place during the two years of James's absence in the south. He had deemed the original, and to my eye more splendid, timbered hall as lacking in modern taste. "I wanted," he said, "a grand, spacious building more suited to entertaining in the eighteenth century."

From this approach it looked complete, but as I trotted round to the south side towards the main entrance, the proposed reception rooms yet to be built on the left-hand side were merely forlorn-looking, abandoned piles of uncut stone, and they added to my uneasy feeling.

Thomas and Oxburgh made straight for the drawing room, but I collected their cloaks and gave them to Betty to be dried. "Please bring me a towel to dry my hair and face and find a woollen skirt so I can remove my wet riding breeches, Betty." She bobbed her head. "In a trice, bonny lass!"

When I joined the assembled company I was surprised to hear a great deal of resentful talk about the insulting deprivation of their horses, the need to hide their arms and restrictions on their movements. It seemed to me that when the government had suspicions about their intentions, it was the very least they could expect. In any case, James's favourite grey horse was safely stabled by his friend Mr Hunter and Charles's horse was being cared for by the blacksmith in Dilston village.

The discussions turned to the Earl of Mar's activities and the preparations that must be made. Charles and James listened eagerly to Oxburgh's news of promises of support from various families in the northern counties, but I thought there seemed to be few firm offers to join. I was pleased to hear Thomas counsel they should not change the instructions they had been given and should bide their time. "Mar told me our King is not expected to arrive from France until the end of September or perhaps early in October. The uprising in Northumberland is not expected to begin until then."

Charles, still angry at the threat to their horses and the rules of their confinement, looked scornfully at Thomas. "I see no reason to delay longer than the time it takes to assemble our forces. I'm sure Blackett will not dither like you Thomas. Perhaps you lack the courage to commit to such a decision."

Thomas looked greatly angered at this insult and I was relieved when James intervened to say he saw the wisdom of not acting hastily. James held his ground despite Charles's protests, the look of disbelief in Anna Maria's eyes and the outrage of his aunt Lady Mary Radcliffe who was visiting from Durham City. She snorted and waved her arm at Thomas, "I hope, James, that you will not be influenced by this hesitant heretic, when what is needed, is action!"

I had not met this rude and domineering woman before and despite her status felt unable to excuse her sudden tirade against Thomas.

"I think, my Lady," I cried, "that one cannot fight for a cause without soldiers or replace a King without a successor."

Lady Mary's face froze in a look of sneering superiority. "I think, Miss Forster, that your opinion matters not a jot. It ill behoves a landless spinster to think she should have anything to say worthy of notice on matters of such import."

"My Lady!" James fixed his eyes on Lady Mary and spoke angrily, "I would beg you to remember that Dorothy is not only our kinswoman but also our guest! I think there is truth in what she and Thomas have said. When the time is right we will follow the plan that was agreed upon. Mar has raised the standard to send a message to clans scattered throughout Scotland that they should come together in preparation for joining us. If we move now, the government has an excuse to come north and quell the movement before it is a well-armed force ready to take Newcastle. We must lull them into thinking that their suspicions are unfounded and their problems lie only with the Scots."

He looked round at the assembled company and his eyes alighted on his pretty wife and sleeping child. He smiled at his wife briefly with a hint of sadness in his eyes.

"Meanwhile," he continued, "we must alert those we can trust and gather arms and horses where they can be hidden safely. Take great care to steer clear of William Cotesworth and his cohorts. We believe his interests do not conform with ours and he is almost certainly working for the government. Our housekeeper Betty had cause to be wary of our regular cheese monger who is known to be an associate of Cotesworth. She was suspicious at the number of questions he asked and later discovered him to be in his pay."

I knew about Cotesworth, the Tyneside merchant, having heard a great deal from one of the pastors who regularly visited St Aidan's Church in Bamburgh. Cotesworth was fervent in his Low Church Protestantism and had an irrational hatred of all things Roman Catholic. Being a rich coal owner and a magistrate, he also had the resources to finance spies. I felt the sudden shock of realisation that there must be many friends and acquaintances who might be potential enemies to the Cause. It was an unpleasant thought that we must now be wary of trusting anyone until they proved their loyalty to the Stuarts.

◆   ◆   ◆

I passed a sleepless, troubled night at Dilston before Thomas and I returned to Blanchland. As we left early next morning, James assured Thomas that he was happy to wait until they received word from their King's messengers that the uprising should begin.

"Now that we are close to our goal," he said with a sad smile and out of earshot of Charles, "I confess that any stay of action is welcome to me. I have much to lose if we fail. My dearest wife, my darling son and heir, this lovely home . . ."

He turned away with a wave of his hand and I felt an overwhelming surge of sadness as I watched him enter the Hall without bidding us farewell. His dejection was as chilling as Charles' reckless impatience.

Charles had swept out of the room after the evening's deliberations and left muttering that an ale house in Corbridge would provide some solace. I had not felt inclined to offer it, despite his pausing to glance in my direction with an inquiring look and raised eyebrows before he left.

CHAPTER 9

THE LORD CREWE ARMS, BLANCHLAND

2005

"Saved her brother from certain death." The phrase echoed round Cathy's mind and the shock of the old man's words sent an icy knife of guilt that struck deep beneath her ribs.

In one swift movement, she spun round and began to run along corridors, down stairs into the oak-panelled entrance hall and out into the wide street. She ignored a distant voice calling her name, ran though the square and kept running until she came to a bridge. She turned along the riverside and ran along its banks until her lungs felt ready to burst. She had no idea where she was going. She only knew she had to be alone.

When she felt too exhausted to go on, she stopped, sat down beside the river and breathed deeply. She stared into the rapidly moving, clear water. She refused to let her mind think of anything except the shallow water speeding over glistening pebbles and swirling round huge rocks. The noise of rushing water blotted out all other sounds and she let herself drown in its enveloping roar.

A painful soreness in her foot pierced her concentration. Her left foot was bare and bleeding, yet she couldn't remember losing her sandal. She climbed carefully down to the water and sat on a rock with her foot submerged. It was icily cold. As the water swirled round her ankle, the numbing pain dominated her thoughts and she wondered briefly how it would feel if she was totally submerged.

"Your shoe, Cinderella!" Jack's voice startled her. He was standing on the path, panting. "You're not an Olympic athlete by any chance, are you?" He was smiling but she could see the concern in his eyes and knew he wanted to help and would ask questions.

She was about to tell him to go away but he climbed down and sat beside her. She turned away from him and drew her foot out of the water. The pain was in her thoughts again and she shivered and folded her arms around herself. She waited, scared he'd ask why she'd run away.

In silence Jack picked up her foot and dried it with the edge of his t-shirt. The cold water had stopped the bleeding. She watched without comment as he rubbed some feeling back in her foot and replaced her sandal. He looked up. "I really think we should go back to the hotel. The sun will soon disappear behind that hill and you're cold enough as it is."

She shook her head. "No, I can't. Could you please take me back to my car? I'd like to leave here."

His expression changed. "That's not a good idea, Cathy. You shouldn't be driving right now. And you can't keep running away. Whatever it is that's upsetting you has to be dealt with, sorted out."

She stood up, suddenly angry. "You don't know what you're talking about! There's no way it can be 'sorted out'. Not ever! So why don't you just go away and leave me alone!" Anger clutched at her throat as she scrambled up the river bank, and set off along the path.

He followed silently, caught up and walked beside her. After a while he sighed, "Ok. I put that badly. Of course I don't know how you feel or what's happened to make you so upset. If you really want to leave, the local garage brought your car back when you were resting. I gave them the keys because I didn't want to leave you alone. I thought you might want to talk. Obviously, I was wrong. But Cathy, please think about it; at least have something to eat before you leave. Dinner's in less than an hour. But, to be honest, I really think you *need* to stay the night."

Cathy lessened her pace and forced herself to think about what he'd said. Perhaps he was right. An overwhelming tiredness swept over her and the thought of driving off into the night was suddenly too much to cope with. She knew she'd been unkind and unfair. He didn't understand, but that wasn't his fault.

As they walked up the street and into the square, she turned to him. "I'm sorry I shouted at you. I'm a mess right now."

He looked straight ahead. "It's ok. Forget it." His voice was controlled but there was something in his tone that sent an uncomfortable shock through her body. She kept her eyes on him and he returned her gaze. There was no anger in his expression, but she felt he wanted to say more but was holding back.

She continued, "I'll stay tonight, but I don't want dinner. I'll have a sandwich or something in my room . . . get an early night and leave in the morning."

She was unable to tell him the truth; she didn't want any more conversations about the famous occupant of that room.

◆　　◆　　◆

She ate the sandwiches and drank the coffee. She watched a television programme without registering much about it. She decided to do the packing so she would be ready to leave early the next morning and tried to make it last as long as she could, but she'd brought so little that it was done in ten minutes. She heard Jack's door as he returned from dinner.

She began to pace the room. It was quite large, yet she felt breathless and a little claustrophobic. She flung the window open and leant out. Jack's window was open too and she pulled back into the room, afraid he might look out and she would have to speak to him. There was nothing more to say.

She undressed, flung on her night slip and climbed into bed. She lay with the curtains open, the stars bright against the pitch black sky. For a while she managed to keep her mind blank, but it was an unequal struggle. She pictured Tom's anguished face and moaned as she hugged the pillows for comfort. Despite her earlier determination that it wouldn't defeat her, she knew she would never be without the guilt and anxiety that gripped her with an intensity she found hard to bear. Tears forced their way out of her tightly shut eyes and she couldn't stifle the loud sobs that came from deep inside.

A few seconds later there were two loud knocks on her door. "Cathy, please open the door." Jack's voice. She sat up and stared at the door, trying to control her sobs and shaking body.

"Cathy, please!"

Her need for comfort overcame her caution. She climbed out, unlocked the door and ran back to bed, pulling the duvet up to her neck as she tried to stop the flow of tears and control the spasms that shook her body .

Jack walked quickly to her bedside and looked down at her. "Oh Cathy, you can't go on like this!" He sat on the bed beside her, pulled her head and shoulders against his chest and wrapped his arms tightly around her. She didn't resist. His actions acted like a trigger and she wept noisily, her imprisoned body convulsed with shuddering breaths.

After a while he began to talk quietly to her, still holding her and occasionally stroking her back. "Maybe if I tell you a bit about myself, you might feel able to trust me enough to tell me what's wrong." She shook her head and tried to tell him no, but he ignored her muffled rebuff and began. "I told you my mother is Indian; well, my grandparents came to England when she was ten and they had big ambitions for her. Her twin brother died of malaria in India the year before and they didn't want it to happen to her. It's a good thing she wanted what they wanted: to be a doctor. In fact, her mind was already made up the day her brother died, and she never wavered. She said she had to work hard and face quite a bit of prejudice both about her colour and her sex, but never once thought about giving up. She wanted me to do the same, and it never occurred to me to think of doing anything else. I think I get my stubbornness from her. Once I've decided what I want . . . Fortunately, after practising for, um, quite a few years, I still wouldn't want to do anything else, despite the frustrations of working with some managers who haven't a clue about the practicalities of medical care. Sometimes I get so mad, I feel like punching them!"

Cathy looked up at Jack, smiled through her hiccoughs and wiped her wet cheeks. A smile transformed his face. "Do you want me to go on, or are you just being polite?" She sniffed and nodded, her breathing still a little ragged, but beginning to feel calmer.

"Ok, since I've got a captive audience." She leaned her head against his chest again and was relieved he hadn't taken away his arms. He was silent for a moment and then began again. He described some of the things that had happened during a year he'd worked in India with his friend Charlie and said he would like to go back sometime. He told her where he was working, where he was born, stories about his sisters, uncles, aunts and cousins and continued until her breathing was more regular. She listened without comment and avoided his eyes, wondering if he'd be so kind and caring if he knew what she'd done.

He fell silent, released her gently, lifted up her chin and looked into her eyes. "Do you want me to go now?"

She shook her head. "No!" She said it before she even considered the question, but it was true, she didn't want him to go; there was too much darkness to get through. "No, please stay and tell me more about yourself."

He sat for a moment, his eyes fixed on her so strongly that she was afraid he could read her guilty thoughts.

He took his arms away, shuffled further on to the bed and rested against the pillows with his hands behind his head. "Well, I don't usually get the chance to talk about myself this long without being interrupted, so I'm running out of things to say. I suppose I could tell you the kind of music I like or my favourite films . . . I . . ."

With no conscious thought, she moved instinctively towards him, put her head against his chest in the crook of his arm and slid her arm across his waist. His chest heaved as he took a breath and swallowed. For an anxious moment she was afraid he'd stop talking and leave. He moved slightly and she felt him draw his arm around her. Relief flowed through her body. He started talking again and continued in a quiet, soporific voice until she fell asleep.

CHAPTER 10

LIFTING THE BURDEN

2005

The light and silence woke Cathy. For a brief moment she couldn't make sense of her warm, hard pillow or her inability to move, but Jack's rhythmic breathing shocked her into remembering. Her eyes snapped open and she lay, hardly daring to breathe, and wondered how to get out of bed without waking him. Very slowly and gently she began to disentangle herself and wriggle, bit by bit, to the side of the bed. He stirred, but didn't wake. She swung her legs out into the beams of sunlight streaming through the window, grabbed her clothes, tiptoed to the bathroom and quietly locked the door.

She lay in the bath and grimaced to herself, unable to believe what she'd done. Her ability to look at things in a logical and detached way seemed to have returned overnight, perhaps because it was the first full night's sleep she'd had since . . . she shook her head; she didn't want to think about that.

She replayed the events since Jack had arrived on the scene and wondered what had happened to her usual caution, her distrust of people's motives— particularly men—and her common sense. They seemed to have deserted her and she imagined trying to explain how she'd shared her bed with a complete stranger, even though he was on top of the duvet and she beneath it. It wasn't like her to do something like that, and she didn't even have the excuse of being temporarily irresponsible while under the influence of alcohol. She decided her emotions had been in a mess and she hadn't thought it through. Jack offered her comfort and he was just someone to cling to. Nobody would believe how innocent it all was.

She soaped her hands and imagined her friend Liz's reaction. She'd be incredulous that having got such a good-looking man into her room, she'd just fallen asleep. It would confirm Liz's opinion that she was naïve and impossibly puritanical.

She remembered the last conversation they'd had after a party more than a month before. As usual, Liz had been both damning and incredulous. "You're unbelievable, Cathy. I don't know how you get away with it; flirting quite outrageously and then keeping them at arms' length. I'm surprised they still keep coming back. See you as a sort of challenge, I suppose. You should loosen up a bit. There aren't too many men who'll stick around and not expect anything more than a platonic kiss and cuddle. Although, when I think about it, look at poor David; he takes it and comes back for more. He must be so frustrated!"

"Look Liz, that's his problem. And all the rest. It seems to me there are too many men who think sex is all relationships are about, and women who think they've got to go along with it."

Cathy gently soaped her arms. Had she really been so dismissive and opinionated, so sure of herself? She wasn't sure of anything anymore. Perhaps Liz was right. Maybe she was asking too much of a relationship, wanting love and commitment before she went that far. And yet that's how she'd felt, no, still did feel. Twice, she'd believed someone and been fooled. But it wasn't going to happen again. She knew David loved her, but she felt nothing, so it was over.

She leaned back and closed her eyes. Twenty-four years old . . . and she could count the times on less than the number of fingers on one hand. Well, Liz was wrong about one thing; they weren't all driven by the uncontrollable male libido. Last night she couldn't have worn anything more flimsy and provocative and she and Jack couldn't have been in a more ideal situation. And nothing had happened. And now, she thought, with a tinge of unexpected regret, perhaps it never would.

Jack was still soundly asleep when she went to pick up her suitcase and bag. She looked at him and remembered how kind he'd been. She felt a surge of indefinable feeling for him which made her hesitate. It would be mean and ungrateful not to thank him somehow and say goodbye. She put down the case and searched for a pen and paper.

The scribbled note seemed inadequate. She moved across to where a tray had various tea and coffee sachets in a bowl and switched on the kettle. She needed a drink before setting off, so why not make two?

She stood by the window and stared across the neat lawns and onwards in the direction of the hills. She could see a road winding up to the horizon. A large motorbike snaked its way along the road. The silver-white metal caught the sun and she thought of Tom. His words slammed into her thoughts; he'd wanted to borrow her car to go away the following weekend with his girlfriend who hated bikes. It didn't matter to him that she'd booked a short holiday in Scotland and needed it.

He'd persisted. *"You can take the train, Cathy, you love trains."*

"No, Tom, you had my car at Easter. If you need a car, sell that monstrous bike of yours. I saved for two years to buy my car and I'm using it to go on holiday." Tom's voice had become softly persuasive. *"Oh come on Cathy, you might as well give in. Don't be stubborn about it."* She'd sighed and felt her resolve slipping and was cross. *"Oh for God's sake Tom, you always manage to get your own way. You're so bloody selfish!"*

Her heart leapt. Did he realise that was a reluctant yes, or did he die thinking about her damning opinion of him?

The boiling kettle clicked into her thoughts and she moved across to make the tea. Jack was still soundly asleep despite the increasing volume of the early morning sounds of the hotel and rousing village.

She noticed he was still wearing his trainers, carefully loosened the laces and eased them off his feet. She poured two cups of tea, put one down on the table beside him and sat on the bed sipping hers. He stirred but still didn't wake. She shook his shoulder. "Jack, please wake up. Jack, I'm going now, but I wanted to say good-bye and to . . ."

"What?" Jack opened his eyes, wrinkled his brow and swallowed. "Cathy! . . . I, what did you say? Goodbye?" She nodded. He sat up. "How are you feeling?

"I'm fine. I'm going when I finish this drink, but I wanted to say goodbye and thank you for last night." She giggled. "That sounds terrible! I mean for staying with me and being so kind. I hope you weren't too uncomfortable,

I mean with me . . . being . . ."

"Not at all," he yawned and a smile flickered across his face. "No problem. It was . . . um . . . it was fine." He sucked in air and stretched. "Where are you going?"

She turned away. She didn't want him to ask questions and didn't know where she was going. "I'm not sure. To the coast perhaps." She turned back to him and forced a smile. "So, I just wanted to say thanks and let you know I'm leaving."

He stretched again and looked thoughtfully at her. For something to do, she handed him his tea. He put it down again. "Cathy, it seemed yesterday that I kept saying the wrong thing; that old man too. Words that triggered bad memories. Is that right?"

She felt her face freeze, stood up, took her unfinished drink to the table and picked up her suitcase. It wasn't a question she wanted to answer. "Bye Jack," she said, moving towards the door. "And thanks."

"Hang on! You can't just calmly walk out like this and expect me to forget it all!" He swung off the bed, moved across and took hold of her shoulders. She suddenly found it hard to breathe. She looked warily at him and wondered if Liz had been right after all. Did he think she owed him something?

"Why not?" she stammered.

"You just can't. Look, sit down and tell me about it. Whatever you've been through, avoiding talking about it isn't the answer. Putting it into words is sometimes the only way you can begin to come to terms with . . . whatever it is."

A feeling of uncertainty made her stand there mutely.

He continued, "If you go now, there'll be other words and other situations that remind you. Tell me about it, Cathy. I want to help."

She shook her head miserably. "It's no good. I've lived through it over and over again. It gets worse, not better. I don't want to talk about it! I don't even want to think about it!"

Jack looked steadily at her. "Can you stop yourself thinking about it?"

Cathy closed her eyes. "No! I can't!" She dropped the case and sank onto the bed. "I hate myself and if I tell you what I did, you'll hate me too."

Jack sat down beside her. "Try me."

The urge to stand up and leave was great, but an even greater need to find some relief from her pain kept her sitting there. She forced herself to look into his eyes. "All right. I saved myself and left my brother to die, horribly. Shall I continue?"

She watched the quick intake of breath and the widening eyes. She'd seen it all before. Jack swallowed. "Yes," he said quietly. "From the beginning."

She sat for a moment, torn again between the need to run away and a desire to stay and perhaps rid herself of the impenetrable black cloud that refused to leave her. She looked at the floor. "Ok, I'll try. My brother Tom . . . was driving us in my car to his girlfriend's house for a party . . ."

She tried several times to find the right words to continue. It felt almost impossible to put into words what little she could remember of what happened before the crash. It wasn't a long story and she could see much of it in her mind's eye and hear Tom's voice and her own, but saying it out loud was hard. She stopped several times, trying to clear the pictures that invaded her thinking and made her incoherent. Jack's eyes never left her face and he listened silently and waited patiently when she faltered. She knew his interest and concern was purely medical and it distressed her that what she was saying would add to his poor opinion of her. She got through it at last and told him what the driver and her parents had said.

She sat back and looked at Jack, "So now you know what a despicable person I am! I saved myself and left him to die."

For a moment she thought Jack was too shocked to speak. His eyes closed briefly and then focussed on hers. "Cathy, you're not despicable. You didn't know what was going to happen. What else do you think you could have done?"

That was the question she'd asked herself many times; that, and the question why she'd done nothing at all.

"I don't know," she whispered, "but I should have tried to get him out. Something had trapped his legs; the door, I suppose. Perhaps if I'd stayed, I could have freed them. He must have been in such pain . . . but he didn't say . . . and I just left him there!"

She looked up and Jack's face began to swim before her eyes. She got up and walked to the window trying to choke back the tears. Talking hadn't helped. She felt more wretched than ever.

Jack got up and joined her. "Cathy, if you'd tried to help, you'd have been killed too. I think Tom could probably see that. You did what he wanted. I'm sure it was obvious to him that his chances of getting out alive were pretty slim. I think he ordered you out so you wouldn't question what you should do. You've got to accept that it was his way of saving you."

Cathy spun round. "But you don't understand, it was *my* job to look after *him*," she shrieked, "not him *me*. *My* responsibility. Even if I'd died trying!"

Jack frowned. "And then your family and friends would've had double the grief they're feeling now? Is that what you would have wanted? Because that's what would have happened. There wasn't time to get him out, was there?"

"But I didn't know that! I should have tried to help him."

"Even though he ordered you to go? Oh, Cathy, why on earth do you feel *you* were more responsible for him than he for you?"

Cathy walked slowly round the bed knowing it was impossible for him to understand and suddenly feeling too exhausted to say more. Her legs felt weak and she sat down again. "Because I am. Was. Oh God, I knew this wouldn't do any good. I don't want to talk about it anymore."

Jack sat down next to her, took hold of her hands and looked into her eyes. "Ok. Let's leave it for the moment. But think about what Tom wanted you to do. Out of his love for you, I imagine."

She knew he thought that would comfort her, but it didn't and she couldn't stop the trickle of tears from her eyes. Jack brushed them away with his thumbs. "Oh, Cathy . . ." Suddenly he stood up, turned away and ran his hand over his head. "I think we should go and see if there's any breakfast left. Just give me five minutes to have a wash." He disappeared into her bathroom.

She blinked; obviously he'd decided she wasn't leaving immediately. She stood up, stared blankly at the bathroom door and was hit by a wave of disbelief at what she'd just done. For perhaps the first time in her life she'd opened up and shown her emotions and her vulnerability. To a stranger.

She frowned. She'd never done that before; not even to Tom, and certainly not to her parents. Yet it had all come pouring out to Jack. And now he expected her to behave as if everything was normal and go into breakfast with him.

She sat down in front of the dressing table. She wasn't sure what she wanted to do, but hunger—though the least of her pain—was gnawing at her stomach and she realised she'd eaten only a few sandwiches in almost twenty-four hours. She caught sight of her wet-lashed eyes staring out of her pale face and peeled a strand of damp hair from her cheek. She looked a wreck.

She rushed into the bathroom to splash her face with cold water. Jack was stripped to the waist rubbing himself dry. She was surprised that the skin of his muscular shoulders and back was darker than she'd expected. His reflection grinned back at her. "You'd have had a bigger shock if I hadn't decided against a shower."

She blinked. "I . . . I'm sorry, I didn't mean to . . . I, um, I wanted to wash my face." She stopped and chewed her lip, aware she was stating the obvious, and knowing she must look and sound an idiot. She looked through the mirror into his eyes, attempted an apologetic smile and shrugged her shoulders.

He turned round and stepped aside, with a quick laugh. "It's your bathroom, you don't have to apologise. Well, before we go to breakfast, I think I'd better go and look for a shirt. Don't know why I didn't go to my bathroom in the first place. Back in a minute." He raised his eyebrows over his deep brown eyes. "Ok?"

Cathy felt a sensation in her chest, took a breath and nodded. It was the only answer she could make.

CHAPTER 11

EMOTIONAL COMPLICATIONS

Jack tossed his napkin onto the table and leant back in his chair. They'd made small talk during breakfast, but now Cathy felt his steady gaze and knew he was going to get back to his job of counselling the pathetically disturbed woman he'd picked up on the moors.

She looked at him for a moment, wondering how to pre-empt his questions. "Before you start," she began, "I really do appreciate all you've done for me, but you don't have any more responsibility for me. I'm fine now. I'm going to drive to the coast and . . ." She searched for something to say that would convince him she'd got herself together and made plans.

"Yes, go on," he said, "it's not exactly weather for lying on the beach, so what *are* you going to do?"

Cathy panicked and suddenly felt rebellious. "I don't have to explain my every move to you!"

He held her gaze and she felt like a petulant child who has told lies and is frantically trying to talk her way out of it. She took a breath and tried again. "Oh, I don't know . . . I'll find out about this area, like you have. Visit churches and . . . things." Her words hung limply in the air. She knew it didn't sound convincing.

He raised his eyebrows. "Ok. We'll start here."

"We? Don't you think I can do it on my own?"

"Sure, but I've got some time to kill too and I know the area." He paused. "I also think it would be good for you to find out more about that woman Dorothy and her brother so it isn't left as an unresolved issue. And I think it would help to have someone around."

A wave of panic threatened to engulf Cathy and she was powerless to stop it turning into anger. "Find out about that woman?" she repeated incredulously. "I really thought you understood the effect it had on me. How can you say it would be good for me? Why would you want me to?"

Jack leaned forward. "I . . ."

"Forget it! I know what you want to do! You want to practise your counselling technique on me and . . . and maybe write me up as a case history about how you solved my pathetic problems!"

Jack reeled back in his seat as if caught by a punch from her fist. He took a breath. "Is that what you really think, Cathy?" His voice was calm and quiet. She tried to avoid his eyes but his hurt expression held her attention. She closed her eyes, knowing she'd made an unfair judgement. She looked at him again. "Oh, Jack, I'm sorry. That was an awful thing to say. The idea just freaked me. Of course you wouldn't."

He frowned. "No, you're partly right. I do have a bit of a clinical interest in the effect of what's happened to you. One of the reasons I became a doctor is because I'm interested in the psychology of illness." He leant forward. "But I haven't that sort of ulterior motive for suggesting that you do this or that I stick around. I just think it might be therapeutic for you to spend some time researching her story because until you know what she did, you're going to assume that what she did was somehow better than what you did. But it won't be easy, whatever you find out, and I think it would help if I was around."

Cathy thought for a moment and looked into his eyes. "I don't think I could handle it."

"Cathy, I really think it would be good for you to have something else to concentrate on." Suddenly, he grinned. "With a little help from your friend."

He paused, put his elbows on the table, rested his chin on his hands and looked into her eyes. "I promise not to write you up." There was a trace of amusement in his voice and a gentle but mocking smile on his face.

Cathy gave herself a metaphorical kick. "Oh Jack, I really am sorry. I don't know why I said that, it was so wrong after all you've done for me, but I don't think I would be able to . . ." She looked into his eyes and expelled a breath. "I'll think about it."

She picked up her coffee cup and took a sip, trying to avoid his eyes, but was drawn back to the comfort of his smiling face and couldn't resist smiling back. They sat in silence for a few moments until Jack took a breath and his expression became serious. "Look, I don't mean to be patronising but have you rung your parents to tell them you're ok?"

Cathy frowned, "No. I suppose I should, but . . . oh Jack, they'll try to persuade me to go home; they didn't want me to leave. It's just too much of an effort to explain it all: where I am and why I'm not ready to go back."

"And meanwhile you add to their grief by disappearing without trace." Jack's tone jolted her. He continued, "You're not the only one suffering, you know. Did you even tell them where you were going?"

"I didn't tell them because I didn't know myself!"

"Cathy, they'll be worrying about you. And they don't even know what a dangerous situation you were in. They can only imagine and I bet they have been! You were in a hell of a state when I found you. Things happen to beautiful young women lost, alone and vulnerable on empty moors. I could have been anyone."

"I wasn't lost."

"You knew where you were?"

"Not exactly. Oh, stop. You're making me feel even more guilty." She heaved a sigh. "Ok. I accept that I was foolish and lucky it was you who found me. And that I should have let them know where I was. I didn't think. I'll ring them. I don't have my mobile with me, so I'll have to go back to my room and use the hotel's phone."

Jack smiled, produced a phone from his pocket and offered it to her. She couldn't stop her face breaking into a questioning smile. "Why is it that I have this feeling that I'm being manipulated?"

He shrugged his shoulders with an innocent expression on his face. "Can't think."

◆   ◆   ◆

Cathy walked slowly back from her stroll in the garden. Her parents' relief had been overwhelming and she cursed the self-obsession that had blinded her to what would have been an obvious thing to do, had she been her usual self.

She found Jack in a side room looking at a table covered in books and leaflets. As she approached him, he seemed to sense her presence and looked up. "Sorry, I had no right to tell you what you should be doing. Forgive me?"

"You don't need to be forgiven. You were right. I've told them I'll be here a couple of days and I'll let them know where I'm going next."

"So, we're going to do a bit of research?"

"Maybe. What are those?"

"This leaflet is about the hotel and those others are various books about the area. I think I'll buy this one. I bought a book of traditional north country tales and a booklet about the history of Blanchland ages ago and started reading it—in fact it's where I got my story about the Scottish raiders from—but I didn't get past the sixteenth century because the other book was more what I wanted. I was hoping to find the booklet here but they must have run out. This one'll do for a start. I've had a flip through and it might be quite useful. And I spoke to one of the staff who said that the Forster family also had a castle in Bamburgh on the coast and a large estate at a place called Adderstone, not far from Bamburgh. And Lord Crewe, Bishop of Durham at the time, was Dorothy's relation."

"And, obviously, this place was named after him?"

"Yup."

"And Dorothy lived here with her brother before it was a hotel?"

"Yeah, apparently."

"'Saved him from certain death,' that old man said, didn't he?" The chill of unwanted memories crept through her body and she turned away. Jack walked round her and put his hands on her arms. "Cathy, you weren't responsible for what happened. It was an accident."

A young woman strode into the hall. "Dr Wood. Your packed lunches will be ready in about ten minutes." Cathy raised her eyebrows at Jack. He smiled. "Have you seen the blue sky and blazing sun? We don't get enough of it to stay inside on a day like this and we can read outside just as well as in."

◆   ◆   ◆

As they climbed a hill and struggled through the dense, purple heather, Jack turned to her. "Watch out for adders; they're poisonous. I think the nearest hospital to get the antidote would be Hexham, so keep your eyes peeled and be careful near any rocks, especially those close to water."

She glanced round, suddenly alert. Fear of snakes had been drummed into her when she was eleven and she and Tom had gone with their parents for a holiday in Botswana, just before her father took up a job in South Africa. Spitting cobras had been high on the list of those to avoid and she remembered being told not to leave any naked skin for them to aim at. She glanced at Jack and herself and their bare legs made her uneasy. Suddenly, Jack stood still and expelled a sharp breath. Her heart missed a beat.

"Have you seen one?" she whispered, her pulse racing.

"What? Oh no! I just had a thought. Adders, Adderstone—the Forsters' house near Bamburgh. I wonder if the name has anything to do with snakes."

"Oh, Jack! Don't do things like that to me! I was frantically wondering how I would get you back to the car and find the road to Hexham!"

Jack flashed her a smile that hit her like a blow. She gasped and turned away, hoping he hadn't noticed.

He continued walking until he reached a pile of huge boulders near the brow of the hill and turned to look at her. "Is this ok?" She nodded, unable to say anything coherent for the moment.

The sun had already warmed the rock and they settled themselves on a cushion of heather in front of it, leaning against the rock's warmth. While Jack skipped through the book, she began to look at the leaflet. It had pictures of various rooms in the hotel including one entitled "The Hilyard Room", where General Forster was supposed to have hidden in a priest hole to evade capture during the uprising of 1715. A verse printed to the left of the pictures mentioned the place above the inside of the fireplace "where sister hid brother to save him from doom". Cathy frowned and wondered if that was all Dorothy had done to save her brother.

Jack suddenly let out a sigh. "I don't think this is going to tell us much. It's mostly about the village and the area around it, although it has a bit about Lord Crewe, Bishop of Durham, who married Dorothy Forster."

"The same Dorothy Forster whose brother was the Jacobite General?"

"I don't think so, but this might say."

She watched as he continued to read silently. A surge of warm feeling for him took her by surprise. She couldn't remember feeling so relaxed and content when out with a man. But this was not a date. Jack was just someone who'd taken the time to listen and what she was feeling was gratitude. He'd been kind, so it was natural to feel gratitude. And it was good to feel something, anything, rather than the pain of the last weeks. She lay back against the rock and closed her eyes.

Jack sat up. "Well, that's interesting. The Dorothy that Lord Crewe was married to was their aunt. The book mentions a novel called *Dorothy Forster* by Sir Walter Besant published in the nineteenth century, which is about the younger Dorothy, her failed love affair with the Earl of Derwentwater and her exploits with Tom's tutor Anthony Hilyard in rescuing her brother."

"Ah, the Hilyard room in the hotel. There's a picture in this brochure. It says it's where she hid him 'to save him from doom', but it doesn't actually mention Hilyard or say what kind of 'doom'."

"Ah yes, I vaguely remember reading that." Jack fell silent again and continued to read.

Cathy leaned over, trying to see where he was on the page. "Is there more?" He glanced at her and she felt his breath on her cheek as he spoke. "Um . . . well, no. Very annoying really. The rest is about walks and drives around this area." His eyes locked on hers for a moment, a frown crossed his brow and he turned away. "Damn; I just bought a lap top. I wish I'd brought it with me. Perhaps we should go to Hexham Library. I don't know much about the Jacobite Rebellion, do you?"

"Not a thing. I wasn't interested in history. We did a lot of twentieth-century stuff at school. I couldn't get interested in all the boring wars and treaties."

Jack smiled and shook his head. "History is more interesting when it's about people. If you can find out what influences their lives and the motivation for how they think and what they do, it's fascinating."

Cathy raised her eyebrows, a smile hovering round her lips and trying hard not to react to the look in his eyes. "I think we're getting back to psychology, Dr Wood. Let's stick to the Forsters."

CHAPTER 12

MIXED SIGNALS

Jack drove north over the moors towards Hexham and the Tyne valley as Cathy tried to untangle the unexpected feelings he'd caused that had thrown her off balance.

She wondered if he intended having such an effect on her; perhaps trying to take her mind off the accident. If so, it was a dangerous game to play and she realised she could easily get hurt, because she wanted him to like her and not merely be involved because of the mess she was in after the accident. The accident: she hadn't really thought of it as an accident until Jack called it that.

She unpacked lunch. It wasn't yet mid-day, but they agreed they were ravenous and began to devour the sandwiches. Jack dropped a triangle of sandwich as he rounded a corner and Cathy picked it up and fed it to him. As his lips and tongue touched the tips of her fingers, his mouth curled up in a smile and he glanced at her. "Thanks." A warmth spread through her and she wondered if he'd felt anything. If he did, he wasn't showing it.

They finished the last of the sandwiches as they crested the hill from where the road dropped down towards Hexham. A wide, gently meandering river in the distance sparkled and glinted through a mass of gold, red and rust-coloured leaves, and the town stretched to the east on the south side of the river, basking in the autumn sun. "The River Tyne and Hexham," Jack announced proprietorially.

They found the library and asked a librarian to help them find books about Dorothy Forster and the Jacobite Rebellion. She paused thoughtfully. "There's a book from way back called *Dorothy Forster* by Walter Besant, but if I remember rightly it was pure romantic fiction. All about a love affair between General Forster's sister and the Earl of Derwentwater who was also one of the leaders of the rebellion. Also about her supposed rescue of her brother. Anyway, the love affair was all in the author's mind, but it's very descriptive and gives a wonderful picture of Northumberland in the early eighteenth century. I could send for it, if you're a member."

Cathy shook her head. "We're here on holiday. Do you think I could order it from my own library in Harrogate?"

"I'm sure you could."

"But we'd like to do some background reading on the Jacobite rebellion while we're here," Jack said.

The woman disappeared round the other side of the shelves and reappeared, moments later, a look of satisfaction on her face. "You might find something in this one." She handed over a large tome to Jack and he carried it to a table. She beckoned to Cathy, who was eventually rewarded with another large book carefully placed in her hands. "Might be more meaty, this one," the librarian said, smiling enthusiastically. Cathy staggered a little under its weight and went to find Jack.

She found him already absorbed, scribbling in a small notebook and sat down silently and leant close to him. "I didn't bring anything to write with or on," she whispered. He started at the sound of her voice and looked at her, a frown on his brow and a confused expression on his face. It felt as if she'd posed him an insoluble problem. "Oh, right. I've only got one pen. If you find anything relevant, give me a nudge and I'll make a note of it." He continued to look at her as if he had more to say, but with a sudden movement, turned away and resumed reading.

Cathy tried to settle down to her book but found his nearness a distraction, took it to a seat by the window and saw that Jack seemed relieved too.

◆　　◆　　◆

As they drove away Cathy looked back at the magnificent cathedral and thought about Tom's funeral service. She couldn't remember much about what had been said or sung. It remained an upsetting confusion of forgotten words and sad faces. She closed her eyes and wondered if researching the story of Dorothy and her brother could do anything to stop the memories that forced themselves on her so devastatingly. Could it distract her from thinking about the accident? And if she could be, *should* she be? And was that the sole reason that Jack was encouraging her to continue? She opened her eyes and sat silently, wishing they could return to their easy conversations on the drive over.

Jack's voice jogged her out of her reveries. "Shall we leave my discoveries until later?" She nodded. He glanced at her and smiled. "Ok. Your turn to tell me about yourself. I have no idea what you do or anything about you really. You mentioned Harrogate to the librarian; that's where you live?"

She nodded and began to answer Jack's questions rather distractedly. "We lived with my grandparents . . . I was going to do a degree in geography or travel and tourism . . . I thought about lecturing in it . . . or something. But after a term, I decided I needed to be there when Tom came home for the weekends. My parents were abroad, my grandfather had died and my grandmother couldn't cope too well. So I dropped out and started working as a travel agent and just sort of . . . I'm deputy manager now."

Even to herself, her voice sounded boring and detached. Jack tried to keep the conversation going but there were long silences when her thoughts became jumbled as her mind returned to the funeral and she found it hard to concentrate on his questions.

Jack looked at his watch and switched on the radio. Cathy tried to think of something interesting to say, but nothing came to mind. She shook her head. "I'm sorry, Jack; I can't seem to . . ."

"It's ok, Cathy. Relax. Just listen to the music." She wasn't sure, but she thought there was a touch of impatience in his voice. She felt impatient with herself, so he had every right to feel the same, but she could do nothing more than close her eyes and try to lose herself in the music.

The setting sun cast long shadows over the road as they swung into Blanchland's main street and stopped in a parking space in the middle of the wide road in front of the hotel. The fawn stone walls of the building had a rosy tinge as Jack ushered Cathy in through the heavy wooden door, through the porch and into the dark oak reception hall.

An overbearing voice startled her. "Cathy, darling! I was beginning to wonder where you'd got to." Her eyes opened wide with surprise as they locked on to an uncomfortably familiar face crowned by precisely cut hair, grey eyes and thin lips. He strode forward and wrapped his arms round her. "You'll have to start packing straight away or we won't be back until late."

Cathy struggled out of his arms, an instant irritation surging through her. "David! What are you doing here? And what do you mean, start packing? I have no intention of going back right now."

David managed to look both perplexed and concerned. He glanced briefly in Jack's direction and turned his back on him. "Come on Cathy, don't mess me about. I couldn't get through to you before; your mobile's been switched off, so I called at your parents' house to see how you were. They said you'd left it behind and told me about your phone call and I decided I would bring you back. Look, we need to talk, but not here. Let's go to your room." His hand grasped Cathy's arm and he began to propel her towards the door.

"David, please!" She tried to shake herself free, but his painful grasp was too strong.

"Let go of her." Jack's tone was calm but his voice was firm and she saw a look of controlled anger on his face.

David glared at Jack and turned back to Cathy. "Who the hell does he think he is?" He swung round to face Jack. "Get lost! This has nothing to do with you."

Jack stood his ground. "It's obvious Cathy doesn't want to go with you, so let go of her arm. I won't ask you again."

"Are you threatening me?"

"Warning."

Cathy's fear for Jack's safety turned to anger. "For heaven's sake, David, there's no need for this! I'm sorry you had a wasted journey, but I'm not ready to go back yet. This is Jack and he's been very kind to me. He helped me through a very difficult time."

"Really?" David's tone was heavy with sarcasm. "Cathy, I was worried sick when they said you'd taken off yesterday. Why didn't you come to me if you needed help? Instead you rush off without a word and fall into the clutches of a . . . a . . ." He looked Jack up and down. "A stranger!" he spluttered. "I know you're in a bit of a state, but that's no excuse."

Cathy opened her mouth to protest but David continued. "Don't try to deny it! I'm right, and you know it. The way you were, you could have got yourself into real trouble. Look, it wasn't easy for me to drop everything and come looking for you. You're damned lucky I could arrange to be free this afternoon. Now go and get your things!"

Cathy flushed with anger. "Don't order me around! I'm staying here." David's eyes flashed from her face to Jack's, and back. He leaned forward, "I'm warning you, Cathy, if you're not careful, we're history."

She stuck out her chin and looked him straight in the eye. "That's fine by me, David. As I said, I'm sorry you had a wasted journey and I'm sorry that, apparently, I didn't make it clear enough when I refused to see you before and after the . . . the accident. I thought it might have given you a clue just how much I didn't want to see you again!"

David's mouth fell open and an expression of malevolent anger clouded his face. "You bitch!"

Jack moved swiftly forward and grasped David's lapels. "Out! Now! Before I lose my temper completely!"

David shook off Jack's hands and for a moment Cathy thought he was going to hit Jack. David looked back at her and his face was full of fury. "Go to hell. The both of you!" He strode angrily through the door and left it crashing behind him.

Cathy closed her eyes and breathed deeply. She opened her eyes as she felt the reassuring touch of Jack's arms as they closed round her. "I'm so sorry about that," she said quietly as she rested her head against his shoulder.

"Don't worry about me. Are you ok? I nearly thumped him when he called you a bitch."

She raised her head and blinked away tears, determined not to show Jack how upset she felt. "I'm fine. Thanks for sticking up for me."

"No problem." He took his arms away and held her face in his hands. "Are you sure you're ok?" She nodded, but wanted the comfort of his arms round her again.

"Was he your boyfriend . . . partner?"

"Yes, sort of. On and off for about six months. More off than on. He used to accuse me of giving off mixed signals. If I was, I certainly didn't mean to."

Jack smiled and put his hands on her shoulders. "Right. Well, if you're sure you're ok; dinner's in an hour. I need to take a shower. How about you?"

"A relaxing bath, I think."

He nodded. "Good idea. I'll call for you just before seven thirty. Ok?"

"Fine."

Jack hesitated, took his hands away and she felt vulnerable again. She looked into his eyes. "Um, do we have to dress for dinner?"

He frowned. "I'm not sure. I didn't really look that closely last night; perhaps you should cover up those long legs of yours. You might distract the diners; well, the men anyway." He smiled and winked. "Can't have you causing friction among the guests."

CHAPTER 13

THROUGH A GLASS CLEARLY

At dinner Jack described what he'd found out in the library. "There was a bit about the make up of the Jacobite rebel army. From what I've read so far, it appears that the reason the Roman Catholic rebels included Dorothy's brother in their number was more to do with giving the rebellion wider appeal than any qualifications or ability he might have for the position. He was Member of Parliament for the area and from a prominent Protestant family. Their uncle, Lord Crewe, was a very wealthy man. I'll bet they thought his money would come in handy when they needed it. Tom and Dorothy seem to have relied on their uncle for everything as their ancestors had somehow lost all the family money. It said that Forster was useless as a general and also partly to blame for the family's financial problems; a compulsive drinker and gambler my book said. Quite a waster, this Tom."

Cathy couldn't stop a sharp intake of breath. Jack glanced at her as she swallowed and bit her lip. He frowned. "Sorry, that was thoughtless. Oh Cathy, it's going to be difficult to do this without mentioning his name. Perhaps I was wrong asking you to do this. Shall we give it up?"

A swirl of panic that giving up would mean losing Jack and she would have to face her failure alone left Cathy unable to think what she should answer. She looked at him and made a decision. "No, I don't want to give up, but perhaps if you call him General Forster it would be . . . better."

"Sorry. I should have thought about that."

"No, I know I can't avoid the name forever and I think perhaps I do need to find out what she did, but right now the mention of his name hits me like a blow and the guilt comes over me again. My Tom wasn't exactly a waster, but I think I went wrong somewhere in his upbringing because he could be terribly selfish and self-centred."

"What do you mean *you* went wrong? How did you have any responsibility for his upbringing?"

"Well, I'm exaggerating a bit, but the time we spent in expat school in Hong Kong—where we both went until I was eleven—was tough on him. He was very small for his age and for three years we were in a school that had some very large Dutch and American children. He was only five when we first went there. My instructions at the ripe old age of eight were to take care of my little brother. I took that very seriously. I fought his battles in the playground; I picked him up when he fell down and patched him up. I also helped look after him when he was ill, even though we had a Chinese Ayi: ours was like an au pair and maid all in one. Mum and Dad both worked for the Foreign office and always seemed to be very busy and have lots of occasions to go to. Then, when I was eleven, I was sent to boarding school in England. When I was fourteen and Tom eleven, Mum and Dad were working in South Africa and Tom joined the same weekly boarding school as me back in England. He'd also had a bad time in the school in Pretoria without me to stick up for him. It had changed him."

"Ah, so that's what you meant when you said you wanted to be there for him when he came home for weekends at the time you should have been going to uni?"

"Sort of, but that was for a different reason. He was a bit of a rebel by the time he was fifteen and big. Mum didn't seem to think me going to university was that important—she'd done well without a degree—and thought Gran was too old to cope. She said it was up to me to keep an eye on him and after a term away, I realised she was right. My mother was the youngest child of five and my grandmother was in her late twenties when her first child, Uncle Tom, was born, so by the time we turned up, she was in her late seventies and a bit frail." Cathy sat back in her seat, a slight frown on her face. "I never knew Uncle Tom. He died young too."

"Your brother was named after him?"

"I suppose so." It was a shock to realise she hadn't made the connection. "I never really thought to ask. My mother idolised her brother. He was very clever. After his degree he did a trip round the world, caught cerebral malaria in Africa and died. My mother told me about him when I was old enough to understand. His death was a great shock to her."

Cathy stopped and the enormity of what she'd said hit her. She covered her face with her hands. "Oh, Jack! I've been so obsessed with myself, it never occurred to me that Mum's grief over Tom must have seemed like a recurring nightmare. All I've thought about is my own part in his death, and there's Mum who's lost her only son who was named after the brother she adored."

Tears sprang to her eyes and she bit her bottom lip. "I can't believe how insensitive I've been."

"You were in a state of shock and suffering from grief, Cathy; you still are."

Cathy sat, her hands against her mouth, trying to unravel the implications. She looked up. "Oh, Jack, what must she be going through? How could I have been so wrapped up in myself that I couldn't see . . . and then I give them more worries by taking off . . . I've got to go back and somehow make it up to her."

Jack reached across the table and took her hands in his. She looked into his eyes. "I'm sorry for messing you about. Perhaps I'll come back and take this up again, but right now I've got to be with my mother and do what I can to help her get through this awful time. It's less than three weeks since he . . . since the accident. What was I thinking?"

Jack squeezed Cathy's hands. "You had a lot on your mind. For what it's worth, I think you've made the right decision, but it's a bit late to go right now. I'll drive you there in your car in the morning. I don't think you should drive yourself. I'd be a nervous wreck thinking you might have one of those flashbacks again."

She sat for a moment. "I don't feel as if I'm going to have one, but I suppose I can't be sure I won't if I start thinking about it all again. I don't want to give them anything more to worry about. But are you sure you can spare the time? It'll be quite a complicated journey to get back without a car."

Cathy was aware that Jack was still holding her hands as he shrugged his shoulders. "My friend doesn't arrive until Tuesday and I can get the train and bus back. Next question?"

She smiled and put her head on one side. "Are you always such a wonderful person?"

He laughed and raised an eyebrow. "Always. Hadn't you noticed?"

"As a matter of fact I had."

He shook his head dismissively and smiled. Cathy tried to keep her expression serious. "No really, I mean it. Thank you. I've been a pathetic pain. I don't know why you bothered."

He released her hands, raised his dark brows over eyes she suddenly felt she could drown in and waved his hands in a gesture that suggested he was baffled too. "Well, Dorothy Catherine Adams, I had nothing better to do. Had to fill my time somehow." He grinned and leant forward. "And anyway, I'm a sucker for deep blue eyes."

◆　　◆　　◆

They drove away from the Lord Crewe Arms in the early morning sun and Cathy felt a sudden compulsion to turn round and remember the atmospheric village where something significant had happened to her as well as Dorothy Forster. Hiding her brother in the priest's hole must have been an anxious experience for Dorothy, but Cathy wondered if Dorothy had ever felt the intense pain and grief that Tom's death in the crash had caused her.

As the car turned a corner and the village receded into the distance without her thoughts about Tom causing her to relive the accident, Cathy suddenly knew that a little of the burden had been lifted from her. It was Jack's sympathetic ear that had helped and she felt that the black cloud had receded a little. The future was less bleak.

She began to read through more of the notes Jack had made. They were mainly about the Jacobite army wandering aimlessly throughout Northumberland, trying vainly to raise more soldiers and meet up with groups from across the Scottish Border, or trying to liaise with ships from France carrying their Stuart King. She read on, hoping to find something about Dorothy, but found nothing. She looked up as the car swept round a curving road and down onto the A1.

"Dorothy doesn't get a mention. It's all about plotting, marching, raising standards and arguing—particularly with the Scottish rebels. If you find more info, will you let me know?"

"Sure."

Cathy put the notes down and turned to Jack. "Where do you live?"

He glanced at her with a faintly amused expression on his face. "Well, I come from Bedford, though I'm living and practising in London."

"Oh, yes, of course; I remember now. Sorry, I think my concentration wasn't too good when you told me. That was only two days ago wasn't it? It seems so much longer."

He nodded. "Mm, it does."

Cathy looked out of the window and tried to think of a question she didn't already know the answer to. "How long are you staying in Blanchland?"

"Until Wednesday; then my friend and I were thinking of going to the coast for a couple of days. I think now I'll suggest Bamburgh. You never know what I might dig up."

They were soon in heavy traffic and the rest of the journey was spent in a companionable silence with only a few casual comments as Jack negotiated his way through traffic jams or asked her to repeat what she'd said if he forgot her directions. From time to time he glanced at her and smiled but it was as if he was already gently distancing himself from her. He asked nothing that required any personal answers and she found herself wishing she could do or say something that would rekindle his interest. When her parents' bungalow finally came into view, she was jolted into giving up her preoccupation with herself and instead focused her mind on her parents.

◆   ◆   ◆

She spent the rest of the day trying to comfort her relieved and grieving mother. She hugged her with a passion she'd never felt before; she talked, listened and at times found silent tears on her cheeks as her mother wept.

For the first time, Cathy saw the change in her mother's face. A mixture of fear and pity gripped her as she looked into her mother's anxious, pale blue eyes and her tautly-stretched pallid skin.

It was clear her mother was not the strong, confident, rather distant woman she'd always thought her. From time to time she held on to Cathy as if she feared someone might take her away. There were times when Cathy had to make an excuse to leave for a moment so she could be alone and look out of a window whose view was so familiar, it required no thought.

She found it strange that neither of her parents seemed to think she needed the same degree of comfort or reassurance any more. Perhaps their need was greater than hers or perhaps they were aware that, for her, something had changed: the grief and guilt remained, but she felt more in control. Her parents needed her as they'd never done before and somehow Jack had given her the strength to cope. Jack had listened, counselled and consoled as only someone detached from it all could. She didn't like the idea of his being detached from it or her.

After supper Cathy stood alone in the kitchen and for a few seconds the image of lights in the darkness and the thundering black shape coming towards her car swam back into her vision. She shook her head, grabbed the kettle with grim determination and turned on the tap.

No, she thought, *I can't change what happened by reliving it. I won't think about it. I did what I could; what Tom wanted me to do.*

A shock of recognition ran through her body. They were Jack's words. But he was right; at that moment she'd thought that getting help was the right thing to do. It was only when the unthinkable happened that she decided she should have stayed with him. If she had, she'd have been killed too. They'd have lost both their children. She wanted to believe they thought the same.

Cold water splashed over Cathy's face. She looked down to see the stream of water from the tap overflowing the wide kettle spout and hitting a spoon in the sink. She turned off the tap and sat the kettle back on its base. As she reached for mugs and coffee, she realised with a sense of achievement that this was the first time she'd been able to rationalise her way out of going through the whole frightening flashback.

She leaned against the counter as the kettle's noise increased. She knew it was a different kind of nightmare her parents were going through—second hand. They'd only heard what happened to Tom from the tanker driver. Until today, what she'd been able to tell them had been very little. She spooned the coffee into the mugs and closed her eyes, waiting for the kettle to boil. No wonder she'd returned to find her parents in a nightmarish limbo. Not until these last few hours had she been able to be for them what Jack had been for her.

She made the coffee and returned to her mother's side. Her mother accepted the mug with a look of disapproval. "We do have coffee cups and saucers, you know. I'm still not comfortable with using mugs. Such ugly things." Cathy shrugged her shoulders. It seemed such a trivial matter.

Her mother sipped her coffee slowly and recalled the day Tom had rung to tell her he'd got a place at university. "I was so proud. I do wish he'd stuck at it." She began to dwell on the years abroad when she'd missed being with him. "Perhaps I was wrong, but when we finally came home I didn't want to nag him. I felt I needed to indulge him a little after so many years of not being there during his teens. Holidays are such a poor substitute for lack of day-to-day care. But besides my job, which I loved, I felt your father needed me out there and thought it best." She looked up. "Did you feel neglected? I never thought to ask."

Cathy instantly saw the little girl she'd been and remembered the times she'd wondered what she'd done wrong to make her mother leave their care to the Ayi in Hong Kong and later send her away to boarding school in England. She'd never felt able to invite friends home at weekends or half-term as others could. Her grandmother found it hard enough to deal with one and then two teenagers, let alone their friends.

"No," Cathy lied, "I didn't feel neglected."

Her mother nodded. "Oh good, I'm glad. You always seemed much more able to cope than Tom." She stared ahead. Mention of his name had triggered some memory and she sat silently.

Cathy's father drifted into the room with vague suggestions of making lists of shopping they might need. "If we make a list now, I can get an early start in the morning."

He seemed to need things to do and it was clear he couldn't stay for any sustained discussion about Tom. He looked distracted, his clothes uncharacteristically crumpled. Cathy could see the pain in his deep blue eyes; it wasn't that he didn't care, he just dealt with it differently to her mother.

Cathy sat at the table with him while he wrote down suggestions that each of them made to buy things they didn't really need. Satisfied with his list, he said good night and kissed them both on the cheek. To Cathy, this gesture seemed out of character, but her mother took it as if it were nothing out of the ordinary.

She sat and talked with her mother until late in the evening, yet when she eventually got to bed, she couldn't sleep. Through a chink in the curtain she could see the same stars she'd seen the first night in Blanchland, but this time there was no Jack to comfort her. Her father had driven him to the station as soon as they'd eaten lunch.

As he'd ushered Jack through the front door, an anxious frown had clouded his face. "The trains are quite frequent from here to York and there are plenty from there going north. After that it could be more difficult. Hopefully you'll get a bus connection from Durham . . . or would Newcastle be best? Oh dear, I hope you get one. I don't think there'll be many going that way."

"Don't worry, Mr Adams, I'll ask at the station."

Jack flashed a smile in Cathy's direction and she ran over to him to say goodbye. He hugged her briefly, kissed her lightly on the cheek and was gone without a backward look before she had time to thank him properly.

◆　　◆　　◆

Cathy lay thinking about the last few days and wondered about the friend he mentioned. He hadn't said a name and she hadn't asked; probably his girlfriend. A pang of irritation, regret and something more she didn't want to admit to, took hold of her; his amazing self control would make sense then. He didn't make a move on her because he already had a girlfriend; that was the kind of man he was. She felt empty and miserable. He hadn't even given her his home address. She sat up, plumped up her pillows and leaned against them.

She frowned, wondering if her interest in Dorothy's story was genuine or merely an excuse to keep her link with Jack. Would she be continuing if she had to do it on her own? Perhaps. But the truth was, she wanted Jack's support; she wanted them to do it together.

Cathy clenched her fists and sighed, remembering her distress when she realised she would have to give up her course at university. Another thwarted dream? How typical of her life if he was seriously attached to someone else when, once more, she knew what she really wanted.

CHAPTER 14

DOUBT AND DETERMINATION

Cathy woke to the sound of a tap on her bedroom door. Her father's apologetic-sounding voice called her name and she sat up. "Come in, Dad." He entered carrying a tray and put it down beside her. "A little breakfast. Your mother thought you looked as if you hadn't been eating properly. And there's a message on your phone."

Cathy snatched it from him and pressed the keys. She scrolled down the message and looked up. "It's from Jack."

"I thought it probably would be."

"But how did he know my number?"

"Oh, he asked me for it and I have it in my diary. You don't mind do you?" Cathy smiled. "Oh no."

"I thought not." He walked to the door and with his hand on the knob, turned back. "Thank you for the time you spent with your mother yesterday, particularly last night. It helped her a great deal."

"Good. I'm just so sorry I didn't think things through before I rushed off."

"Don't feel guilty about that. You had so much to resolve yourself. Um . . . if you don't mind me asking, did Jack help?"

"Yes, I really think he did. But I still feel terrible guilt . . . leaving Tom."

Her father ran his hand through his tousled grey hair, looking puzzled. "You have absolutely no need to. We are so grateful that, for once, Tom did the unselfish thing. We knew that, deep down, he was a good boy. Just a bit wayward. His death was a terrible, tragic accident, but now we know that the result of his last words is that we still have our dearest daughter. Our grief is mixed with a great thankfulness that we didn't also lose you."

Tears welled up in Cathy's eyes. "That's sort of what Jack said. But I couldn't be sure. I felt you were just trying to be kind when you said you didn't blame me. Thank you, Dad, for saying that." She ran to him, put her arms on his shoulders and kissed his cheek. He smiled and nodded as he left the room.

Cathy re-read Jack's message. 'Hi. How are you? No problems on journey. Boring without you. Take care of yourself and keep in touch. Jack xx'

She sat down on the bed, focussed on the two kisses and thought about the words he'd used.

He wants to keep in touch and there are two kisses and he's finding it boring without me; that's cool. She sat back against the pillows and closed her eyes. *Who am I kidding? Liz could have sent a similar text and signed in exactly the same way. In fact, she would have put 'love'. Damn.*

She scrolled to 'text reply.' She stared at it and her mind went blank. She felt her old reserve telling her not to admit to anything she might regret later. There was no doubt that she felt more deeply about Jack than any other man she'd met and wanted to see him again. But what if his interest were merely as a friend? He'd find it embarrassing if she hinted how she felt when he only had a friendly interest in her state of mind; just filling in time while he waited for his girlfriend.

She got up and paced the room, creating different messages in her mind and finally decided she should say something that was encouraging without being too keen. She sat down and took a breath.

'Hi! I'm fine. Glad journey was ok. Miss your support.' She stopped, wondering if that was the same as saying 'missing you'. No, that was all right. She began again, 'Hoping to hear latest info when you get to Bamburgh. Cathy xx'

She pressed 'send' and the message was gone. She saved his number and suddenly had a great urge to hear his voice. She stared at her phone, shook her head and put it down. Perhaps later, but not yet.

She phoned work to say she would be back a week on the following Monday. She hadn't yet reached the stage when she could ignore the thoughts that crowded unbidden into her mind, and she wasn't ready to answer the questions or handle the concern she knew her colleagues and clients would send her way. She dressed quickly without giving it much thought and found her mother quietly puzzling over a crossword.

She looked up. "Your father's gone for the groceries. I thought we might have a walk and go to the library to return my books. I haven't read them. I just couldn't seem to concentrate while you were away. They weren't my usual kind of books anyway; I'm not sure why I took them out . . ." Her voice trailed away and she stared at the floor. She looked up and forced a tight smile. "I'd be quite glad of the company. Do you mind?"

"No. As a matter of fact I'm going to look for a book about a famous Northumbrian woman we began finding out about in Blanchland. At least, she's famous there. I'd never heard of her. I don't particularly want to buy it or I'd order it online, if that's possible."

Her mother looked at her with narrowed eyes. "You said 'we began finding out'. Would that be Jack you're referring to in the 'we'?"

"Yes."

"How did you meet him?"

"He came across me when I'd parked my car badly on the moors and sort of took care of me."

"Took care of you? How do you mean?"

Her voice was suddenly sharp and there was deep anxiety in her eyes. Cathy regretted her hastily chosen words. "Oh, I was upset, thinking about . . . Tom and the accident. Jack's a doctor. He was very kind and got me through a particularly bad time. It was him who brought me to my senses—me rushing off and not contacting you. I'd forgotten my mobile anyway, but it didn't occur to me to phone you. All I was thinking about was myself. I'm so sorry."

Her mother relaxed and shrugged her shoulders. "We were a bit worried but we felt better when you rang. I was wondering why he drove you back. It was nice of him to help, but don't get too, um, too reliant on him, will you?"

"Why not?"

"Well, when one's emotions are near the surface after the kind of thing you've been through, one can attach oneself to a person who shows kindness. One can get hurt."

"I don't believe Jack would hurt me."

"Perhaps not, but it can be too easy in these situations to feel gratitude which can sometime result in, well, falling for someone inappropriate when one isn't oneself."

"Inappropriate?"

"Yes, well . . . they're different, you know."

"Who are?"

"Asians."

"Mother!"

"Oh, now you're going to say I'm prejudiced, but I've lived all over the world and almost all of them have a different way of looking at things, different customs and behaviour; you know what I mean."

"So do Americans and Australians, but I bet you wouldn't mind if I married one!"

"Married! Good grief, I hope it hasn't gone that far."

"I'm talking hypothetically."

"Thank goodness for that."

"You can't think the colour of someone's skin is a problem!"

"In my experience, it can be. I'm just saying it's something you have to think carefully about. Would you want any resulting children finding themselves having to cope with explaining the colour of their skin against yours?"

"Mother! That's enough!"

"It's not nearly enough, but I suppose I'll just have to hope you come to your senses. By the way, was it you who disposed of the bunch of roses David sent? The cellophane was still on them when I found them in a bucket in the garden."

"Yes. I put them there."

"How ungrateful. And he must have spent a fortune on the wreath he sent for Tom. Now he's the kind of man you should hang on to. Earns over a £100,000 a year, his mother said. Right. I'll get my coat."

"I'm not sure I want to go with you now."

"Don't be silly. I'm just saying how things are and if one can't say how one feels to one's daughter, well . . . oh, go and get your coat!"

Cathy pursed her lips and went for her jacket, amazed at her mother's ability to switch moods and move on abruptly despite the grief she was feeling. If she hadn't been part of her mother's emotional outpouring the previous night, she would have thought her indifferent as well as judgemental and infuriatingly prejudiced.

◆   ◆   ◆

The library's computer brought up a long list of books about the Jacobite Rebellion, including the one called *Dorothy Forster*, which was in a county reserve store and had to be sent for. Cathy selected it and a couple from the shelves. Two others also had to be sent for and she felt frustrated at the delay and wondered why her quest seemed to have taken on a greater urgency and importance in her life. It seemed illogical that she wanted to know why Dorothy was able to do what she'd failed to do.

She stared at the screen. Perhaps she was intrigued that a woman had achieved more fame than a brother who'd taken part in a historical event. She'd presumed an eighteenth century woman's role centred on home and family, but so far she'd read nothing about Dorothy being married. The only information had been her alleged love affair with the Earl of Derwentwater and her supposed part in Tom Forster's escape. Perhaps it was all pure romantic fiction whipped up to attract the tourists; perhaps none of it had ever really happened.

CHAPTER 15

KEEPING IN TOUCH

Jack rang the next morning at eleven. Cathy's phone was lying on the kitchen counter and her father answered it. "Yes, oh hello . . . yes, she's here. Cathy, dear, it's Jack."

She ran over, grasped the phone and walked to the sitting room. "Hi, Jack."

"Great to hear your voice. How are you doing?"

"Fine . . . you?"

"Fine; I'm glad you're feeling . . . fine . . . Cathy . . ." He paused and began again. "I rang because I wanted to tell you I've arranged a session in Newcastle University's Special Collections library—I think I told you I trained in the medical school—anyway, I remembered about it. I couldn't look at the books straight away but I filled in forms and selected some books on their list about the Forsters and the rebellion. I'm going back for a couple of hours to look at them on our way to Bamburgh."

Cathy registered the 'our' in his sentence. "Your friend's arrived?"

"Yes; very late last night. He had a hellish journey from London after a really busy day at work. A problem on the line somewhere near you actually, and there was no refreshment coach. I had to wait for hours in Newcastle Central. I think I told you about Charlie, didn't I? He's still asleep."

Cathy smiled to herself and sank gratefully on to the sofa. "Yes, the friend who went to India with you. You see, I was listening. Anyway, I've got a book from the library myself, and it has a bit about various members of the Forster family, their history and titles, birth dates and some deaths and the reason Thomas and Dorothy ended up in Bamburgh. Some more books are on order, including the Walter Besant novel on Dorothy Forster."

"So you're still interested?"

"Oh yes, in fact I might come up in a couple of days myself. How long are you going to be in Bamburgh?"

"Oh, only a couple of nights and then we have a reunion in Newcastle on Saturday night. Guys' night out and then it's back to London."

"Oh, well . . ." She frowned; was he ruling out meeting up again?

"I could call in on the way back."

"That would be nice." Cathy rolled her eyes at her pathetic response. "I mean, please do. We could have lunch here or something."

"It might be a late lunch depending on how hung-over I am."

"I'll make sure it's something that doesn't ruin no matter how late you turn up."

"Great. Cathy . . . any more flashbacks?"

"Just one, but I fought it and talked sternly to myself and sort of found my way out of it."

"Great stuff, but don't worry if they still come back occasionally, sometimes when you're least expecting them. Give it time. Right, got to go. Take care of yourself."

"You too."

"See you Sunday."

"Yes, Sunday; I'll look forward to that." She screwed up her eyes, hoping she hadn't seemed too keen.

"Me too. Please keep in touch, Cathy."

"Right."

"Bye."

"Bye, Jack."

His phone clicked off and Cathy bit her lip, her heart beating harder than she could remember happening before. She felt like a teenager reeling from someone she had a crush on noticing her at last. She sat down and replayed their conversation in her head. He obviously wanted to see her again and talked like a friend who cared, but she wasn't sure it meant much more than that. Her shoulders sagged.

Her father's voice penetrated her thoughts. "I didn't mean to eavesdrop but I couldn't help but overhear a bit of your conversation as I came in just now. You said, 'Sunday, I'll look forward to that.'"

"Yes. I invited him to lunch. That's ok isn't it?"

Her father sat down beside her, a fond smile on his sun-wrinkled face. "Quite all right. I might have to do a little work on your mother, but he seems to be a nice young man. You really like him, don't you?"

Cathy looked up. "Yes, very much. But I'm not sure he feels the same."

"Well, after he brought you home he could have easily let it go at that, couldn't he?"

"Yes, but he's a doctor and maybe he just wants to make sure I'm ok."

"Perhaps, but I have the feeling it could be something more."

"Really?"

"Yes. Cathy, it's not like you to doubt yourself so much; you're usually the strong, confident one of the family."

She blinked. "Is that how you think of me?"

"Oh, yes; you were so capable, even when you were young. I was very conscious of how much we relied on you over the years and, to tell the truth, a wee bit guilty, but you always seemed to know how things should be, what needed to be done. I was a natural at my job, but a pathetic creature without your mother. Thank you for what you did."

Cathy looked at her father. She could have told him how many times she'd felt lost, unwanted and alone and how much she'd needed them, but it was too late and would have devastated them both. She smiled at him. "You're welcome. Right; well, I'd better get my act together, hadn't I?"

◆   ◆   ◆

She was drifting off to sleep after a day of reading and making notes when her phone bleeped. She blinked her eyes wide open to read Jack's text.

'Sleep well xxx'

Three kisses. Things were getting better. She tapped in her answer. 'You too xxx'

◆   ◆   ◆

A librarian rang the following morning to say that a couple of the books were ready for collection. *Dorothy Forster* was one of them. Cathy dressed at full speed and walked briskly to the library. The weather had turned colder and as she left the library the clouds were gathering. It was a perfect day for curling up with a book or two. Jack hadn't rung or texted that morning and she needed something to take her mind off him. Her parents were sitting reading in the conservatory when she arrived back and put the books on the side table.

"I'll join you both in a minute. I'm going to make some coffee. Would you like some?"

"That would be nice, dear. Ground coffee, please." Her mother had some colour in her cheeks and was smiling. "We had a little walk to the Valley Gardens and we just flopped down exhausted when we got back."

Cathy went to the kitchen, switched on the kettle and reached for the cafetiere. She couldn't remember seeing her mother smile in a genuinely happy way for some time. In fact it was the first time since the day before the party . . . A cold panic swept over her and she looked blankly out of the window. She was in the car again and the tanker was bearing down on them.

"No!" she screamed. A sudden crash shattered the picture and she looked down to see the fractured cafetiere on the kitchen floor. Splinters of glass were scattered across the tiles and she bent down and frantically began to pick up the larger pieces. The kitchen door opened.

"Leave them, Cathy! You'll cut yourself."

"What? Oh Dad I'm so sorry, I've broken the . . ."

"It doesn't matter. It's only a thing. I'll get the brush and shovel. But why did you scream? That was before the crashing sound."

Cathy sat back on her heels and gulped. "It's ok; it's gone now."

"What's gone?"

"The flashbacks I get. The crash. Tom."

"I didn't know you were getting flashbacks. Did you tell the doctor?"

"I didn't get them until after the funeral, not long before I left. I was sort of numb until then and couldn't really remember much of what happened except that I'd got out and left Tom. Oh, Dad, I thought it was getting better. Jack said it might come back but I thought that I'd dealt with the last one so well that it might have gone for good."

"From what I've heard about these things, I think it might take quite a bit longer. Cathy, you have to keep telling yourself you were not to blame. Hopefully it will gradually be easier to deal with and less painful."

"That's more or less what Jack said."

"Have you heard from him today?"

"No."

"Ah. You go and sit down and I'll clear up and make us some instant."

Cathy walked slowly out of the kitchen and into her bedroom, sat down and stared out of the window, annoyed with herself. She'd upset her father and he didn't need that. She had to distract her mind with the research. Jack was interested enough in Dorothy's story to be going to Bamburgh to find out about her. She had to do the same and show Jack she was taking control of her life. She couldn't let him think she was incapable of building on the help he'd given her.

She stood up, suddenly determined not to add to her parents' distress. She would continue with the research and do all she could to make sure she didn't lose contact with Jack. If nothing came of their relationship, it would be his fault, not hers.

CHAPTER 16

CONCENTRATION AND EXPLANATION

Cathy spent what was left of the day trying hard to immerse herself in the Dorothy Forster novel. The nineteenth-century style was very different to the kind of novel she usually read and about a world she didn't recognise: a world where supernatural happenings, herbal potions and gypsies' warnings were everyday events. Enjoyment seemed to come from simple pleasures such as bonfires on the beach, hunting, shooting and fishing, fairs and celebrating saints' days. The story was written in Dorothy's voice and was a fierce defence of her brother, Thomas; praising his character and showing her pride in the work he did in Parliament as well as what he'd done in the rebellion.

Cathy laid the book on her knee. Dorothy's defence of her brother struck chords of empathy and her childhood memories came flooding back. She'd done the same many times and sometimes it had cost her. She'd earned punishments from teachers for causing heated arguments at school in Hong Kong and sometimes for physically defending Tom. Often, it had resulted in taunts and once, a roughing up from pupils on her way home. Not until her father got the truth out of her about the reason for her bruises and talked to her teachers, had her troubles lessened. She'd learnt that discussing problems calmly was sometimes a better way to stop them; until later when Tom's teenage stubbornness and refusal to discuss things made it difficult. For a while, it was boys who were his targets that she had to defend.

Cathy walked through into the garden and stood in the misty rain, the drops catching on her lashes. She shook her head.

All that effort. Everything I did during those years is wasted; ended with my words accusing him . . . and then . . .

"Cathy! Come in out of the rain, or at least put a coat on." Her father came out of the conservatory and took her hand. "Come on. No point in staying out here. We'll have a cup of tea and a chat and then you can get back to your reading. Jack will be interested to hear what you've found out, won't he?" She nodded and allowed herself to be led back inside.

◆ ◆ ◆

She went back to the novel and it fell open on a page that described a learned but physically unattractive man called Hilyard who was Thomas's tutor. 'Dorothy' wrote that he'd stayed on to live with them as a kind of advisor and book-keeper after his role of tutor was no longer needed. So this was the man the Hilyard room was named after. Cathy ran a finger over his name and wondered why.

She skipped a few chapters that didn't appear relevant to the Rebellion and hit on a chapter that began to describe the love affair between Dorothy and James Radcliffe, Earl of Derwentwater. She remembered what the librarian had said, "all in the author's mind". If that was true, it was sad. Dorothy didn't seem to have any man in her life except her brother.

A cold fear gripped her again. She stared at the book and wondered if reading it was a mistake. Was she trying to punish herself? A few hours ago she'd been full of resolve, but now could easily give it up, if it were not for Jack. She shook her head. *Jack thinks it might help. I have to keep going.*

She went back to the chapters she'd skipped. Long, repetitive, descriptive passages took the story no further and she found her mind wandering and had to reread whole pages she couldn't recall. Normally she zipped through novels and it frightened her that she seemed to have lost her ability to concentrate. It wasn't the book's fault; her attention seemed to wander whatever she was doing. She gripped the book and tried again.

Supper appeared on a tray and she ate it with the book in one hand, hardly aware of what she was eating. A profusion of names and families confused her and at times she had to look back to remind herself whose side they were on. It was disturbing to realise how long it was taking to read and remember what she read, but she pressed on, determined it wouldn't defeat her.

Only when her father leant over, tapped the book and said they were going to bed, did she look up and ask what time it was.

"Getting on for eleven. Quite late for us."

"Oh heavens! I didn't realise it was that late. I might read a little longer."

"Night, sleep well."

They disappeared and she picked up the book again.

Two hours later she put down the book and yawned. Although Dorothy was telling the story, there'd been no mention of her actually doing anything for a long time. Cathy suddenly felt an overwhelming tiredness and didn't have the energy to continue. And Jack hadn't rung.

◆   ◆   ◆

She slept late the next morning. Still unable to push Jack's silence out of her mind, she mowed the lawn and wandered aimlessly round the garden until it was time for lunch. She found it difficult to appear interested as her father began to discuss what he should buy for Sunday lunch.

"We could have a roast—say at one—and if Jack's later than that he could have cold meat and we could make some salads. Potatoes in mayonnaise, tomato and peppers. That sort of thing."

She nodded. "I suppose so, or we could go for a pub lunch instead when he arrives; *if* he arrives. Let's not make any plans until we're sure he's coming."

"But he said he would."

"Yes."

"I wouldn't have thought he was the kind of person to say he was going to do something and then not do it."

"No, I suppose not."

"Have you heard from him today?"

"Not so far, and not yesterday, either."

"Ah. Why don't you ring him and put yourself out of your misery?"

"He's on holiday with a friend. I don't want to call him when he's got other things he wants to do with his time. Obviously he's too busy to ring. Or text."

Her mother looked up from her book, a "told-you-so" look on her face. "I'm not surprised. Just relieved. Can you imagine family gatherings if it had got serious?"

"Alice! Do you remember how angry you got when your mother said I was too old for you? I think your phrase was: 'my decision, mother!'"

"This is not the same at all!"

"Maybe not, but it *is* Cathy's decision!"

Cathy stood up, her soup half eaten. "Please, don't argue about something that might never happen! I'm going to go and read some more." She went to her room and glanced at her phone, willing it to have a message waiting. It sat there, annoyingly displaying the time and nothing more.

She made another attempt to concentrate on the book. The details of the Jacobites' battle tactics and their disagreements didn't hold her interest and after a few minutes she gave up the struggle, closed the book and decided to come back to it later.

She went for a walk in the park, found an empty seat and sat in turmoil trying to decide if she should be the one to make contact and wondering why she swung from happy determination to miserable indecision.

A misty dusk began to fall and she had to run down the sloping path and leave before the gates were locked. On her walk back she wondered briefly if she should go back to her own flat where she had the internet. She decided her parents might be unhappy if she did and perhaps she wasn't ready to live alone just yet.

She settled down for an evening slumped in front of the television with her phone beside her. The clattering dishes and chattering voices coming from the kitchen reinforced her loneliness. Sitting in the gloom with the early evening news babbling in the background, she was thinking of Jack when the phone rang.

She fumbled with the buttons in a panic and almost dropped it. It was Liz. She took a long breath to stop her heart beating so hard.

"Hi, Liz."

"Oh hi! So you're back. Where the hell have you been?"

"I went to Northumberland."

"Northumberland? Why? And since when have you travelled without your trusty little mobile? Were you trying to avoid me?"

"No, I forgot it and I just wanted to be alone for a while."

"Fine, but you had me worried. So, how are you?"

"Ok I suppose. It's getting better."

"Come and have a drink." It wasn't a question. Liz was hard to deflect once she'd decided something should happen. She was the one person Cathy always found difficult to refuse.

"I don't think so."

"If you don't say yes, I'll come over and get you."

"I'm waiting for a call."

"So your mobile's suddenly too heavy to bring with you?"

"No but . . . "

"No buts. Are you coming or do I have to come and get you?"

"Ok, ok. Where?"

"Have you eaten?"

"No."

"Meet you in our usual Italian. Whoever gets there first, grabs a table and has two cool Pinot Grigios waiting. See you later."

◆　　◆　　◆

Despite severe doubts she was doing the right thing, Cathy felt happier and more relaxed by the time they reached dessert. She'd given Liz a heavily censored version of her time with Jack and a full account of David's behaviour.

Liz groaned. "Poor David. He must be terribly thick skinned if he didn't get the message after you refused to see him. Perhaps he thought it was just because you were upset. Guess he must have got it bad. No need to try and bully you into coming back with him, though. Serves him right—what Jack said and did. He sounds gorgeous; very protective. When are you seeing him next?"

"He's supposed to be coming for lunch on Sunday, but he hasn't been in touch for two days and I'm wondering if he's gone off the idea."

"So ring him."

"I don't want to hassle him if he's having second thoughts."

Liz sat back in her seat and hooted with laughter. "Cathy, you idiot, you're obviously a bit gaga about him and you're letting two days go by without saying hi. What kind of message do you think that gives?"

"What makes you think I'm 'gaga'?"

"Your eyes when you talk about him. Dead giveaway. Anyway, why haven't you rung him?"

Cathy shrugged her shoulders. "It would be so awful if he was trying to hint that all he was interested in was improving my mental state . . . and . . ."

"And if he's waiting to see if your interest is anything more than being a very grateful bunny, he must be deciding right now that you couldn't care less."

"Oh Liz, do you think so? I didn't think of it like that. I suppose you could be right. He did say, 'keep in touch'."

"Doh! The message is in the words, Cathy. Ring him before you lose him."

Cathy's cheeks suddenly felt hot and somewhere beneath her ribs, a bubble of panic was rising. "Yes, you're right, I'll call him . . . but I've drunk too much wine, I need to go to the loo first."

"Me too!"

◆　　◆　　◆

They returned to the table and a waiter come forward, Cathy's phone in his hand, "Madam, your phone rang. I switched it off." He pointed to a sign that said they respectfully asked their customers to switch off their mobile phones. "You can use it in the ladies if you wish."

Cathy snatched the phone, ran outside, switched it on and it came up with Jack's phone number. She rang it and found he'd switched off too. She realised, with an almost hysterical dread, that unless he switched back on she had no other way of contacting him. No home or work number.

No address. Nothing. She walked slowly back into the restaurant and sat down. Liz looked at her and raised her eyebrows.

"Well? What's wrong?"

"He's switched off."

"Jack?"

"Yes."

"So what's the problem?"

"It's the only way I can contact him and . . ."

"So leave a voice mail or text him. When he switches back on it'll be the first thing he sees."

Cathy leant her elbows on the table and covered her face with her hands. "Oh Liz, how stupid can you get? I can't believe I jumped to such a weird conclusion. What's wrong with me? I just panicked." She looked up. "Oh Liz, you're right. I can't seem to think straight at the thought of not seeing him again. I felt like this when he left me to go back north. I'm a mess. I just can't seem to get him out of my mind."

"Wow! Come on, you've got to tell all. Is he a good kisser?"

"Um, we haven't actually kissed."

"Whoa! Wait a minute. He has this effect on you and you haven't actually kissed?"

The waiter came over and hovered by the table. Liz turned to him with an impatient look on her face. "What?"

"Coffee?" he said tentatively.

"Look, you've just caused a minor crisis here and we're trying to sort it out . . . Um, yeah, we'll have two Irish coffees." She waved him off and turned back to Cathy. "Just what makes you think you might have gone slightly crazy about a guy you haven't even kissed? He might be the pits. Good sex is so important and you don't even know if you'd enjoy kissing him!"

"He held my hands and kissed me on the cheek."

"*There's* a first!"

"Well, actually . . . we spent the first night together."

"What!" Liz shouted, "You spent the night together but just didn't bother to tell me? Well, he sounds a bit of a weirdo if he didn't kiss you when you were making love, but . . ."

Cathy felt the colour rush to her cheeks. "Liz, for heaven's sake keep your voice down. All I said was, we spent the night together. Nothing happened."

"Yeah, right."

"Honestly. I was very upset and he just lay with me and talked to me until I fell asleep."

Liz rocked back in her seat. "Then he's either a saint or gay!"

"Liz! He's neither. He's just very kind and patient and understanding. And he's just tried to get in touch and been switched off, so if you don't mind I'm going to text him."

Cathy looked down at her phone and back at Liz. "I'm not sure what to say, I think I'll go home and do it. Drink my coffee for me, will you? I'll call you tomorrow."

CHAPTER 17

CONTRADICTIONS

Only the lights in the hall were on when Cathy let herself in. She grabbed a bottle of water from the 'fridge and sat down in the conservatory. She looked up at the stars and tried to compose a message, but the explanation took too long for a text and no matter how she phrased it, seemed too impersonal. On impulse she tried his number again. It rang. Cathy closed her eyes and prayed he'd answer when he saw it was her.

"Hello Cathy." His voice sounded flat and cold.

"Oh Jack, I'm so sorry, the waiter turned it off while I was in the loo."

"What?"

"My phone. I was having a meal in a restaurant with my friend Liz and left it on the table. It's their policy that mobiles should be switched off and I didn't and he switched it off."

"Actually he pressed the answer button first. I heard him mumbling angrily before it went off. I thought it might be David."

"David? But Jack, you know he's history."

"Well, when you didn't contact me for two days, I was beginning to think I was too."

"Oh Jack, I'm sorry. I was waiting for you to call or text but I thought you must be too busy or enjoying yourself too much to find the time."

"Cathy, I asked you to keep in touch because I wanted to be sure I wasn't pushing you into doing something you didn't want to do. You didn't call. I thought perhaps you didn't . . . need my support anymore."

"I do!"

"Oh. Right. I wasn't sure how you felt. I didn't want to keep calling without some encouragement."

"Oh Jack, I really am sorry. I didn't want to assume you'd want to hear from me when you were doing things with Charlie."

She heard him heave a sigh. "So we both got it wrong. Shall we start this conversation again?"

"Absolutely."

"Would you like to know what I found out in the university library?"

"Of course I would."

"Right. I read part of a contemporary account about the Jacobite rebellion and Forster's part in it. It was written by a curate called Patten who was Forster's chaplain in the rebel army and later blabbed all about it in order to get a pardon. He didn't mention Dorothy and I didn't manage to get through much of it. I was a bit pushed for time. But I flipped through it, and guess what I found near the end of it?"

"I haven't a clue. Don't keep me in suspense."

"Well, at the end of Patten's account there's a list of captured Jacobite followers or servants, mostly Northumbrians. Hilyard gets a mention; d'you remember the Hilyard room in the Lord Crewe Arms?"

"Yes. He's a character in the *Dorothy Forster* book I'm reading: Thomas's tutor, then later his book-keeper and the man who helped Dorothy after the rebellion . . ."

"What? Impossible. Hilyard's described in Patten's book—and this is a record, not a novel—as 'Gentleman to Lord Widdrington', which means he was his valet. He was in the list of people captured by the government after a battle in Preston, Lancashire, so he couldn't have been with Dorothy and I don't know why on earth he should have a room named after him."

"Oh, well probably because of the Besant novel. He really was made out to be a central character in their lives. And there could be more; I've a long way to go."

"Well, he mightn't even have met Dorothy if he was a servant to Lord Widdrington as Patten says."

"No, I suppose not."

"Anyway, when I said I was interested in the Jacobites, one of the staff in the university library recommended another book called *The Annals of King George*. I couldn't see it then because I hadn't ordered it. She said it was written in 1716 about the aftermath of the rebellion. There's also the university's website which they said has something about Dorothy. Oh, and there was another book I did see. It was a fairly short account of the uprising but all I did was scan through the pages for Dorothy's name and didn't find it. I might have missed it in my panic not to overrun my parking time and get a fine, but I don't think so. The trouble was, neither of the books I'd ordered had the kind of index where you could look up a name, so it wasn't easy to find her."

"You sound a bit frustrated."

"Well, I was, but that's not all I found out. I haven't mentioned that we stayed in Bamburgh last night at The Lord Crewe Hotel and that's where I am now, have I?"

"You did say you'd probably go to Bamburgh but I don't think you told me it was another hotel with the Bishop's name."

"Yep, and I've also been to Bamburgh castle."

"You *have* been busy!"

"Uh huh, I'll overlook that touch of sarcasm and continue, shall I?"

Cathy laughed. "Sorry. Actually, I can't believe how much you've packed into two days as well as the travelling. Your friend must be very tolerant."

"Charlie? Oh he's no problem, as long as there's a bar handy."

"Go on then."

"Right, well, the castle's a fantastic place. Huge. More impressive in real life than the pictures I've seen of it. It's exactly how you'd hope a castle would be. It's up high on a massive cliff—made from ancient volcanic rocks called winsill I discovered—with the cricket pitch and village below and a wide sandy beach on the east side with the Farne islands in the distance. You'll have to see it some day. Apparently only the keep is from the original Norman castle but Lord Crewe did a bit of renovation and someone called Lord Armstrong completed it in the nineteenth century."

"Did you find anything about Dorothy?"

"Yes. I picked up a sheet of paper which gave a short history of Bamburgh Castle and one bit was called 'The Forster Family.'"

"And?"

"I've got it here. It's pretty damning about Forster's reasons for joining the rebellion. It says something about him being short of cash and that he did it, quote, 'with an eye to the main chance'. It also says that at the battlefield he took one look at the opposition and promptly surrendered."

"That's a bit harsh."

"Well, that's what it says and it also says that one of the reasons the Roman Catholics got into the Rebellion was that they had nothing much to lose."

"Really? Nothing I've read so far gives much about their reasons for being in it, apart from wanting the Stuarts back. Does it say anything about Dorothy?"

"Yes. It says she was living in the castle."

"That's not right; my book says they lived in the manor house next to the church in the village."

"Well, who knows which is right, but the more important thing is that it said that when Forster was taken prisoner, Dorothy and her maid went to help him escape."

"So it wasn't just hiding him in the priest's hole?"

"No."

"But it got some things wrong so perhaps it got that wrong too."

"Possibly."

"Anything more?"

"Yep; it says that after rescuing him, she hid him in the castle for two years until he left the country in a boat somewhere up the coast from here."

"She hid him in the castle?"

"That's what it says."

"For two years?"

"Yes."

"And the government didn't think of looking for him there?"

"Yeah; it does seem a bit unlikely doesn't it? I'll bring you the whole article and you can check it out. Anyway, in the first room you go into they have a display case with a dress worn by Dorothy. Going by the size of the dress, she wasn't tall: about five feet three or four at the most I would guess."

"What was the dress like?"

"Uh, um, sort of shiny, striped. I think it was pink and gold. Yes, and there was a pair of tiny gold shoes with quite high heels. From the portrait in another part of the castle she was quite pretty, twinkling eyes, greyish brown, I think, if the portrait's accurate, and chestnut-brown curly hair with a frilly white cap on her head and a sort of mischievous look. Her aunt's portrait was there too. Very good looking, but she had fairer hair than Dorothy. Nowhere near as fair as you, though. I think you must have Viking genes."

"Not a single one! I'm English through and through and proud of it. Oh, I mean, not that having other genes is . . ."

"A problem?" Jack laughed. "That's reassuring."

"Jack I was talking off the top of my head as I often do. I didn't mean . . ."

"I know. I'm kidding. I can see it in people's eyes at once if the colour of my skin bothers them. I tolerate people like that . . . but I definitely don't sleep with them."

Cathy couldn't stop a giggle escaping her lips. "My friend Liz wouldn't believe our night together was entirely innocent."

"You told her about it?"

A shiver ran through her body at the tone of his voice. "Well, yes . . . I was just explaining . . . I mean . . . I'm sorry, I didn't mean to say anything, but . . ." The silence at the other end of the phone was deafening. "Jack?"

"Yeah, I'm still here. It's just that I wouldn't even consider telling my own friends about that night. They might get the wrong impression."

"Oh, Jack, she knows I don't make a habit of sleeping with strangers or anyone else, if that's what you mean."

"Forget it. What time's lunch on Sunday?"

Cathy felt he was changing the subject a little too rapidly but let it go. "In theory, at one; roast beef, Yorkshire pudding and all the trimmings, but if you're late it'll be cold meat and salads."

"I'll do my best to be there at one." His voice still sounded strained.

"Jack, you're not angry with me, are you?"

"No. I just don't talk a lot about the more . . . private things in my life, and for some reason I thought you wouldn't either."

"We both did, Jack."

"That was to each other. And for rather special reasons. That was different."

"Yes, I'm really sorry. I was kind of explaining something to Liz and got carried away. I get defensive with her sometimes and the words just seemed to come tumbling out. I didn't mean to make you feel uncomfortable."

"Don't worry about it. It's fine. Um, Cathy?"

"Yes."

"Oh nothing. It'll keep. Don't lose sleep over what I said. It's the night out in Newcastle tomorrow and if I don't call you, I'm not upset, or angry, just mortal."

"Mortal?"

"That's what some people say here when they're drunk."

"Right." Cathy realised he was terminating their conversation. "Have a good time . . . and take care."

There was a short silence. "You too. Sleep well."

"Thanks. Night, Jack."

"Night, Cathy."

She felt wide awake and too stimulated by a mixture of excitement that Jack was obviously affected by what she said and did, but also anxious she'd upset him by telling Liz more than he felt comfortable with. She knew there was no chance she would sleep for some time. She logged on to her father's computer, read through her notes and began to write down what she knew so far about Dorothy's story and her rebellious brother.

After a few pages, she stopped and decided to go back to the beginning, change it to Dorothy's voice, and write it like a journal.

CHAPTER 18

CONFUSION

In the middle of preparations for lunch on Sunday morning, the phone rang and Cathy's father shouted for her. "Jack's on the house phone; he wants to speak to you." Her heart fluttered as she ran into the living room and picked up the phone.

"Hello."

"Hi. I rang your mobile but there was no answer. I had to ring directory enquiries to get this number. Is everything ok?"

"I was just going to ask you that. My phone's in my bedroom, on silent, I think. I was busy in the kitchen. I didn't expect you to call. Is something wrong?"

"Sort of; Charlie and another mate overslept—totally hungover—and missed their train to London. We're on duty this evening and their tickets were only for the booked journey, so going on a different train would cost them a bomb and they're skint at the moment. They've just asked me for a lift. So I wondered . . ."

"Bring them too."

"You're sure?"

"Of course, we'll just do extra veggies and roast potatoes."

"And extra Yorkshires too?"

She laughed. "Don't worry, you won't starve."

"Thanks, Cathy. I thought it was a bit much to ask and was going to have to say I couldn't make it. I felt miserable, so I thought I'd chance my arm and see what you said."

"You felt miserable?"

"Yes . . . well . . ." She hung on his words and waited for him to explain.

He continued, "the thought of missing a home cooked dinner and ending up at a motorway caf. No contest."

"Oh."

"And missing seeing you, of course."

"Right. Well, see you later."

There was a pause. "Cathy, are you sure everything's ok?"

"Everything's fine."

There was another pause. "Ok. See you later."

"Yes . . . bye."

Cathy rang off and sat down on the sofa, wondering if she was being too sensitive about him putting the home-cooked meal before missing her as the reason for being miserable.

◆   ◆   ◆

Her mother was taking the joint of beef out of the oven when the doorbell rang and her father smiled at her. "Everything's under control. Go and answer the door."

She ran into the hall and glanced at herself in the mirror. She was slightly flushed from the warmth of the kitchen. She smoothed her hair. It wouldn't be good to appear too keen; she had to be cool. She took a breath and opened the door.

The smile on Jack's face and the glow in his eyes was so overwhelming that she forgot to keep her expression composed. A smile she couldn't control beamed at him. He stepped forward and hugged her to him, his lips very close to hers. "Oh Cathy, it's great to see you. You look gorgeous." He frowned, released her and pulled back. "I mean . . . well. You look well."

Cathy stared at him, confused. He'd said what she'd hoped he would say and almost done what she'd hoped he would do, and suddenly, he'd changed.

"Jack?" she began, as he looked back at his friends.

A man with tousled, curly fair hair and startlingly blue eyes stepped forward. There was a pinkness round his bleary eyes and a tinge of grey in his complexion. He smiled at her. "And in case you're wondering, although you don't seem to be; I'm Charles." He leant forward, kissed her on both cheeks and raised his eyebrows at Jack. He waved his arm at the other man, "And this is my partner, Adrian." Adrian gave a shy smile and walked forward offering his hand. He was as dark as Charles was fair, and devastatingly handsome.

Cathy smiled at them. "Come in. Great to see you . . . all."

◆   ◆   ◆

"Well, well," her mother smiled at her as they ate dessert, "How very pleasant to be surrounded by three such handsome young men. I'll bet the girls hang round them in droves, don't you Cathy?"

Cathy opened her mouth and swallowed. "Um, yes, I suppose so." Charles winked at her as her mother picked up the cake slice. "Anyone for more apple pie?"

"Oh definitely me," said Charles. "Earlier this morning, Mrs Adams, I thought I wouldn't be able to eat a thing, but your cooking is so delicious, it's irresistible."

"That's very kind of you, Charles, but it was a joint effort and do call me Alice; Mrs Adams seems terribly formal. We're over all that." She smiled and tipped another slice into his dish.

He beamed at her. "Thank you, Alice." He raised his glass. "A toast to the cooks!"

Cathy watched as the three of them, Jack with a tumbler of tonic, toasted them. Jack turned to Cathy and his smile overwhelmed her. "And here's to further revelations about Dorothy Forster." She couldn't help but return his smile. She lifted her glass to his and their hands touched briefly and a shock ran through her body. Jack flinched. An invisible thread locked their eyes together for a split second. Jack frowned and turned away to look at her mother. "Can I make the coffee, Alice? We'll clear away; the three of you deserve to sit back and have a rest."

Cathy stared at him, wondering why he seemed to be sending out such confused signals; he seemed embarrassed at the electricity between them and apparently didn't even want to stay in the same room.

"Not at all," her father beamed at Jack, "That's my job. And you and

Cathy probably have a lot to talk about. Have you told Jack about the books you've been reading so avidly, Cathy?"

"Yes," she said quietly. Jack obviously didn't want to be alone with her, so she stood up and started clearing away the plates. "I think we've talked about most of what we've found out so far." She continued picking up dishes and walked towards the kitchen, avoiding looking at him.

◆   ◆   ◆

She could see Jack alone in the conservatory when she returned to the dining room with the tray of coffees. The urge to speak to him was stronger than her instinct to avoid him. She put the tray on the dining table, smiled briefly at the others still sitting chatting at the table, picked up Jack's coffee and walked through to where he was standing, staring into the garden.

"Your coffee."

He looked down at her and took it. "Thanks. You know, Cathy, for some obviously stupid reason, I'd actually hoped this visit would be more than just eating and drinking coffee. And I didn't realise our conversation had to be restricted to historical research. Am I allowed to ask how you've been?"

The hurt in his voice made her take a sudden gulp of air. "I didn't mean it to sound like that. Sorry. I've been fine. A few flashbacks. Well, often only the beginnings, but I fight them and it usually works."

"Good. Well, perhaps you don't need my help any more. And maybe you're quite capable of doing the research on your own, too. Am I right?"

His words had the effect of a heavy blow in the region of her ribs and she found it hard to reply. "I could, I suppose . . . but I thought . . . I mean, you seemed . . . I'm confused, Jack."

"So am I. I can back off if you want to cut me out of the Dorothy business." Her stomach lurched. "No! I would like us both to do it. I thought you were interested too."

"I was; am." His tone softened, and he touched her arm. "But if that's the only thing we have to talk about . . . I mean, you gave the impression you didn't want . . ." He took his hand away and sat down on the cane seat. "Anyway, from this evening, I'll be very busy at work and I don't have any more proper holiday till near Christmas."

Her eyes widened. "Christmas!" She heard her voice ring out and it sounded almost hysterical. She clenched her fists and tried to calm herself. "Don't you get weekends?"

He looked up. "It's hit and miss; on a shift system. Sometimes I do. Cathy, are you trying to say you'd like us to meet up occasionally or that you think I should do some research of my own during my time off?"

Cathy closed her eyes briefly, wondering if she should take the plunge and tell him how she really felt even if he didn't feel the same. "It's your choice," she said quietly. "If you'd like to meet up sometime, I'd like that too. If you prefer to do some research on your own . . . then I suppose . . ."

"You don't care either way."

"I didn't say that! I've told you, I'd like us to do it together. I just don't want to ask you to do what you don't *want* to do."

A suspicion of a smile flickered across his face. He stood up and moved towards her, touching her cheek with his hand. "Cathy, I do want to find out about her, partly because I think it would help you and partly, in a way, because of my father."

"Oh; you said he was from Northumberland, didn't you?"

"Corbridge, actually, though his job was in Newcastle." He looked away and she sensed there was something he felt uncomfortable about. She reached up and with her hand on his cheek, turned his face back to her. "*I* could help *you*."

He held her gaze. "Let's get the Dorothy story sorted first."

"Are you upset about something to do with your father?"

His eyes looked pained. "Let's leave it for now." He grasped her wrist, lifted her hand away from where she'd rested it on his chest and kissed her fingers.

Charles strode in and tapped him on the shoulder. "Don't want to break up this touching little scene, but Ade and I are on call at six. Don't you think it's time to make a move?"

Jack glanced at his watch. "Oh, dammit! Yeah, ok Charlie. I'll be there in a second."

She picked up his coffee and handed it to him. With his eyes on her, he started to gulp it down. "Trying to get rid of me?"

"No, of course not, but I don't want to make you late and worry about you speeding to get there on time."

"So we're friends again?"

"We've never *not* been friends, have we?"

He smiled, put down the coffee cup and put his hands on her shoulders. "I'll kiss my 'friend' goodbye then."

She smiled at him and offered up her mouth. He hesitated and kissed her cheek. "I'll let you know when I have some time off. Take care of yourself."

"You too. Drive carefully." She touched his arm. "I forgot to tell you. Dorothy was her brother's companion and housekeeper from the age of eighteen to twenty-nine, when the Rebellion began."

"And you looked after your brother from eight to twenty-two . . . three?"

"Twenty-two when my parents came back, but with a three year break."

"Almost the same, then."

"Yes. Spooky, isn't it? Um, Jack, please text me when you've arrived safely."

"Sure," he smiled.

Her heart skipped a beat and she smiled back at him. His smile deepened and he took her face in his hands and brushed his lips against hers. She gasped and they locked eyes. Suddenly he kissed her again, more strongly, and her lips parted. Abruptly, he pulled away. "Oh, Cathy, I'm sorry. Must go." He frowned, walked quickly across the room and through the door.

Cathy stood for a moment, in disbelief at what he'd said. She followed him into the hall. Her parents were saying goodbye to Charles and Adrian and Jack nodded to them. "Thanks a lot. Great meal. You've been very kind." He gave a quick wave to Cathy, ran down the path, jumped into the driver's seat and roared off down the road.

The three of them stood at the door and watched the car disappear into the distance. Her mother grasped her father's hand and frowned. "I do so hate goodbyes," she said quietly.

Cathy linked her arm through hers, her pulse still racing. "Jack's going to text to let us know when they get safely back."

"Oh, good; so thoughtful. Now, what about that Adrian, Cathy? He is *so* good looking."

Cathy looked at her father and they smiled at each other.

"Alice, dear, he's gay. Charles and he are partners, I think. Isn't that right, Cathy?"

"Yes."

"Oh, what a pity! Well just don't get any ideas about Jack, Cathy. He's not suitable."

Cathy pursed her lips. "I'll decide about that, Mother dear."

CHAPTER 19

REVIEWING THE PROBLEM

"He apologised for kissing you?" Liz spluttered. "Houston, we have a problem! Perhaps he thought that was what you wanted but didn't expect you to respond like you did." She frowned. "Cathy, isn't that a bit like how you got involved with David? A bit of an impetuous kiss when he gave you that gold bracelet out of the blue?"

"Don't talk about David in the same breath as Jack! Anyway, I just kissed David on the cheek to say thanks. I didn't kiss Jack. Although I suppose I did offer up my mouth but then he just kissed my cheek."

Cathy and Liz continued to eat lunch. Cathy chewed thoughtfully. "Oh, I don't know why Jack said sorry, but both kisses blew me away. *And* he almost kissed me when he arrived and then suddenly pulled away from me as if he might catch something. Then there was a moment when our hands touched and . . ." She shook her head, worried she'd already said too much. Jack seemed to have unlocked the lid on her Pandora's box of secretiveness and now she found it hard to close.

Liz put her head on one side. "I think there's something he isn't telling you and I wouldn't like to speculate what it might be."

◆   ◆   ◆

Cathy walked to the library from the tea rooms feeling more confused than when Jack left the previous day. She remembered she'd spent the rest of the afternoon reading about Dorothy and been pleased at the new information she'd discovered but distinctly jumpy that Jack still hadn't texted he was back. Then her eyes had wandered to a photograph of Tom and she suddenly remembered his excitement as he'd climbed into the car the evening of the accident. "After me and Ginny have had a holiday, I've decided I'm going to take off round the world. Stay in Australia for a while, perhaps. One of my mates went there and worked on a farm in the outback. He made enough money to spend a couple of months in Sydney living it up."

She'd seen a mixture of mischievous excitement and determination in his expression and knew there was nothing she could say to change his mind. The business course he'd promised his father he would do had, apparently, gone out the window.

Cathy tried to close her mind to thoughts about Tom and looked out of the window. She'd managed to think about him without reliving the nightmare and next week she'd return to work. At the end of that week she'd go back to her flat. Things were getting better. She had a future. Tom's had come to a premature and horrific end.

She'd leaned forward, elbows on her knees and run her hands through her hair. *Why should I have come out of it unhurt? He was almost three years younger. Why should I have been the one to survive?*

She'd stood up, another memory flooding back.

It was Tom who insisted on driving; I didn't ask him to. If I'd refused, it would have been me!

Suddenly she saw him switching on the car headlights because it had been raining and the clouds were dark and threatening when they set off. The quickest way to his girlfriend's house was up the motorway . . .

A cold wave of panic had spread through Cathy as she realised where her thoughts were taking her: she was in the car again and the black shape and blinding lights were bearing down on them. She'd shaken her head.

No! That's enough. No more. Think about something else. Think about Jack. She'd breathed deeply and concentrated on his face and jumped as her phone bleeped.

The text was brief. "Traffic bad. At work, filling in for missing colleague. xx". She'd thought for a moment, desperate to ask him to explain what he'd said after the kisses, but this wasn't the right time. Patients needed him more urgently than she needed him. She'd texted back. "Glad you're back safely. Ring me when you have time to talk. Didn't tell you what I'm doing with Dorothy's story. Cathy xxx."

His reply was short. "3-ish tomorrow afternoon. xxx"

She'd spent the evening feverishly reading and writing on her father's computer until midnight and slept fitfully until the sun flooded her room. She'd eaten breakfast and lost herself in her writing again until it was time to meet Liz for an early lunch.

◆   ◆   ◆

As she was walking into the library, Jack rang two hours earlier than he'd said he would.

"Jack, what's wrong?"

"Hi! Nothing's wrong. I just woke earlier than I expected and wanted to talk to you. Is that a problem?"

"No! But you probably didn't get home until early in the morning and I thought you'd still be asleep. That first night you told me you sometimes sleep for ten hours after a night shift and you can't have had that."

"Shall I ring off and go back to sleep, then? I'm still in bed."

"No, don't you dare. You can sleep later. There are some things I want to tell you and some questions I want to ask you."

"So ask me."

"Actually, I'd rather do the things I want to tell you first."

"Right."

"I've started writing a journal about Dorothy. I've been writing notes for four days, but the journal only since the early hours of Saturday. I don't think I told you, but I've got practically a library of diaries from when I was eleven to eighteen and a few short stories I did a few years ago, but nothing like this. I'm writing Dorothy's journal as if I'm her and using facts which are as accurate as I can find. I fill in the gaps with what I think is possible. I don't know where it all comes from, but it seems to flow out of me and I find it hard to stop. The *Dorothy Forster* book and another novel were great for getting an insight into the atmosphere and language of the time, although I'm not using 'thees' and 'thous' like Besant does. It just doesn't feel right. I've got a lot of information floating round in my head from all the histories about Dorothy's early life, her family and the people she knew and those who were involved one way or another in the Rebellion. I also searched the internet on Saturday and got a real feel for Bamburgh and Blanchland and for the Northumbrian countryside and Durham City. I looked at photos as well as maps. The beach at Bamburgh is fantastic, isn't it?"

"Yep. I wouldn't mind going there for a longer holiday sometime."

"Me too. Anyway, when I add in what I've found in the histories and novels I've been reading, I feel I can get inside Dorothy's head. It just seems to come tumbling out once I start writing."

"Wow. What a talented friend I have."

"You haven't read it yet."

"Email it to me."

"I'm not sure if I'm ready for criticism. Anyway, I've only finished two complete parts; the third is fairly rough and needs a lot of editing and the rest are notes that I keep adding to. Give me a couple of months. Though I hope I'll find out the truth before then!"

"So, what about your questions?"

"Oh, yes." She hesitated, wondering if she could find the right words. "Sorry, maybe I should leave it for now."

"Cathy. You can't do that to me. Ask me."

"Oh, Jack." She closed her eyes. "I'm not sure if this is the right time, but I want to know . . . I've been thinking about what you said after you kissed me goodbye and I'm confused. Please explain what you meant."

"Oh damn. What did I say exactly? I know I did and said something stupid but I was in such a panic, I can't remember the exact words."

"You said: 'Oh, Cathy, I'm sorry. Must go.'"

"I made a mess of that, didn't I? I just remember your lips parting and I panicked."

"Why?"

"Um, I didn't mean to kiss you at all; not like that, anyway."

"Oh. So it was a mistake."

"I suppose you could call it that."

"Right."

"Cathy. It's not what you're thinking."

"You know what I'm thinking?"

"I've got a good idea, yes. Look, you're still recovering from what happened and I happen to be the one who tried to help. I didn't want you to respond to me because you were grateful. Patients often attach themselves to staff who've helped them get through a tough time."

"You're not the first to tell me that."

"Well, it's true."

"So I'm a patient, and a dumb one at that?"

"That's not what I meant! After the trauma you've been through, it would be easy for you to develop feelings for someone who's tried to help. You need time to feel normal again. Can we talk about something else?"

"I suppose so; if that's all you feel you can do."

"Don't be mad at me."

"I'm not mad; just confused."

"Look, I've already said too much. Please don't push it. I'm finding it hard enough to be as objective as I should be."

"Well yesterday you had me totally confused at least three times when you were here and you've just implied that it would be bad to develop feelings for 'someone' who's tried to help me and that you knew you'd done and said something stupid."

Jack was silent for longer than was comfortable. "It was stupid. Bad timing. Look, I care about you, Cathy. Just let's keep it on the back-burner for now."

"Care *about* me, right." She took a breath, "Well, I've got some other things to tell you about Dorothy. Do you want to hear them?"

"Can it keep till later?"

Cathy suddenly felt she had to seem unfazed by this sudden rejection. "Fine."

"Now you do sound mad at me; please don't be."

"I'm not mad at you, but . . . oh, I wish I could see you and talk properly."

"Don't."

"I just mean like that first night."

"What! Do you remember what you were wearing? That night was agony. It took me ages to get to sleep with you dressed like that and draped all over me."

"But you didn't make a move on me, did you? I mean, some men might have."

"There are rules. What you needed then was comfort."

"You really are quite a man."

He laughed. "Speak to you later."

"Sleep well, Jack."

Cathy ran up the stairs in the library still feeling confused, but a little happier.

◆   ◆   ◆

Just before six, her phone vibrated. It was Jack.

"Hi. I'll ring back," she whispered. She ran to the library's café and rang back.

"Sorry, Jack, I'm in the library café now. We don't have the internet at home and my flat's on the other side of town and I wanted to do some more research that didn't mean I had to search through books."

"Right. So what have you found out?"

"Straight to business, eh?"

"Yep."

"Ok. Well, I skipped through to the end of the Dorothy Forster book and it's so sad. The last chapter is supposedly written by Hilyard—the tutor who wasn't a tutor, and couldn't have been with her—after she'd died alone in her early fifties, still grieving over the loss of her love, James Radcliffe—which was probably totally fictitious. The other books I've read so far say nothing about any affair between them; in fact they say nothing about her getting married at all. She seems to disappear from the history books, apart from the odd reference to her saving her brother. There is another possible man in her life who was around from when she was eighteen, but he wasn't her social level so it seems unlikely. And there's some suggestion that Charles Radcliffe, was a bit of a Don Juan, so who knows?"

"Well, if there's no juicy love affair, I hope the rescue turns out to be true and successful."

"Besant makes Hilyard out to be the one who organised and was the prime mover of the rescue, not her, but we know that can't be true. The other thing that niggles me is about the Roman Catholic rebels. You remember you read about them joining because they had nothing to lose?"

"Yes, it said they were impoverished by the government taking their lands, and their properties and horses."

"Well not according to the other novel I've read. It seems to concentrate more on Charles Radcliffe, but Dorothy certainly comes into it. They may have got swept up in the Rebellion accidentally, but the families don't seem to be impoverished. Along with lots of the other rebels, they had titles, large houses and estates and, I assume, plenty of money from their lands and farms, although debts keep getting mentioned in both novels. And they linked up with aristocrats from Scotland—like one called the Earl of Mar—and France. And Thomas seems to have had a high profile in the planning, as well as actually being the General."

"But that was just a novel; do the history books agree with it?"

"Not entirely. There are tons of contradictions between the four histories and two novels and also what you found out."

"But you're not giving up?"

"No way! I've been on the internet again this afternoon. I found a site about the Forster family and a list of email contacts. I've sent off a request for more information and written to an author who wasn't contactable by email."

"Great. I'll try and do a bit more when I can find the time."

"Oh, I forgot one of the bits of info I did find in the second novel."

"Right. Go on."

"It was about Charles Radcliffe going back to Dorothy and Thomas's home in Blanchland in 1723. It said he found the house was now a pub and Dorothy serving in it. By my reckoning, she was then thirty-seven. In the book she tells Charles she's married to a fisherman. I've forgotten what it said his name was. John somebody. My memory's really bad at the moment, but I'm going to follow that up."

"A fisherman? Blanchland's a long way from the sea."

"Yes. It does seem a bit unlikely, but I'm going to try and find out if it's true. Anyway, the novel has her serving in the pub every now and then for the sake of her Uncle Crewe's memory, so perhaps her home was somewhere nearer the sea and she was only there temporarily."

"I would have thought that was a bit of a comedown for her, working in a pub. Landed gentry, I thought."

"Yes, her family were quite prominent Protestants, with a rich bishop for an uncle, of course!"

"Yeah. So Crewe was dead by then?"

"Well, he actually died two years earlier in 1721 and left all the Northumbrian properties to a Trust; the Lord Crewe Trust, which still exists. Nothing at all to Dorothy or Thomas, so I don't see how she could have been there anyway. Did I tell you I found out quite a lot about Lord Crewe in a biography the library got for me?"

"No. Did it say anything about Dorothy or the rescue?"

"Not a thing. But Lord Crewe's marriage to their aunt was his second marriage. And he lived into his eighties."

"Have you found out how old Dorothy was when she died?"

"I can't find her death under her Forster surname, even on websites, so that's why I'm hoping the marriage bit was true. I don't really think it could be the John person, but when I remember his family name, I'll follow it up."

"Good luck! Oh, I forgot to tell you, I'm going to Bristol for almost a week from Thursday. I applied for a seminar about a research project they're doing there. Some other stuff that my . . . colleague and I are interested in follows on after that. So next weekend is out and the next one I'm probably working. Sometime the following week is a possibility for coming to see you."

Cathy smiled to herself. "Right. I'll be in my own flat then. It'll probably take me an age to clean it up."

"Your parents are ok about that, are they?"

"Fine."

"You might find it harder when you're alone, you know."

"Yes, I know, but I'm sure Liz will soon have me back into the swing of things."

"I'm not sure I like the sound of that."

"Why not? I thought you'd be pleased. I'm going back to work next Monday."

"Great, but don't overdo it."

"My boss, Maggie, has been brilliant. She's insisted that I do only a couple of weeks and then have one off. She said she didn't count these last few weeks as holiday."

"She sounds a good boss. What will you do with it?"

"I'm not sure."

"Well, the local history section in Newcastle Central Library has masses on the history of Northumberland. There's bound to be more about the Forster family."

"So are you suggesting I go there for my holiday?"

"Perhaps. If you're still interested and haven't got sick of her."

"I don't think I will have. I hope her story has a happy ending."

"What's your idea of a happy ending?"

"More than what I've found out so far. Someone to love and who loves her, I suppose. I mean, if she really saved her brother twice, she deserves . . ." She stopped and clamped her lips together.

"You did the right thing, Cathy, and what Tom wanted."

Cathy frowned and said nothing.

"Cathy?"

"Yes."

"I could join you for part of your holiday, if you'd like me to."

"Of course I'd like that! You could show me the sights. Believe it or not, I've never been to Newcastle, except for passing by on my way to Scotland."

"You're on! Right; have to go. Some of us are meeting up for a coffee in . . . ah, five minutes ago and then later on to a meal. Must go."

"Bye, Jack. Enjoy your meal."

"Yeah, I'll try. Give me a ring or text, soon."

"I will. Bye."

"Take care, Cathy."

Cathy smiled, her heart racing. Dorothy's journal needed updating, but first she had to investigate the latest possible love in Dorothy's life.

CHAPTER 20

PREVARICATION

Cathy leant back in her chair in the library. She reviewed what Jack had said again and again and found it hard to concentrate on her writing. She felt the kiss must have meant something and what he'd said when she'd asked for an explanation was a huge hint that he was holding back his feelings for some altruistic reason.

She got up and wandered round the room lined with computers, oblivious to those concentrating on their work. Perhaps if she didn't contact him for a couple of days it might make him worry about *her* feelings and be more open about his.

She rang Jack at seven on Thursday night. His phone was switched off, so she left a brief message. He rang back as she was about to put out the light. He sounded slightly drunk and she could hear others in the background.

"Hi Jack. Are you in a pub or something?"

"No. A friend's room. We had an evening lecture after supper. It ended about a couple of hours ago, I think. I don't know why I came here. I'm wiped out. Came for a drink, sounded like a good idea. But I'll fall asleep if I don't get back soon."

"Go to your room, Jack. We can talk tomorrow."

"Yessh. You're absolutely right."

"Jack?"

"Yessh."

"Is it far?"

"What?"

"Your room."

"Next floor down."

"Right, take care then."

"Mm. You too." He made a sound like blowing a kiss. Then the phone went dead. Cathy sat looking at the phone, hoping he'd be all right and that he really had blown her a kiss. She bit her lip and wondered why she'd been so cool with him for the last few days.

She was woken next morning by her ring tone. She struggled to switch it on in the gloom and couldn't focus on who it was.

"Hello?"

"Cathy, it's Jack. You sound half asleep. Did I wake you?"

"Oh, hi. Yes. Have I slept in?"

"Don't know what time you normally get up, but it's eight."

"Oh. That's ok then." She sat up and switched on the light. "You sound more with it this morning."

She heard him groan. "Oh God, so it wasn't a dream, I did ring you. I can't actually remember getting back to my room."

"Must have been quite a party."

"It just sort of happened after the evening group discussions. The trouble was that I came off duty at eight yesterday morning after working about sixteen hours non-stop, hopped on the train to Bristol and straight into lectures."

"That's crazy, Jack."

"Yes. It wasn't planned like that but one of the doctors didn't turn up and I had to cover for her."

"How do you feel now?"

"Fine. Amazingly. I've just been woken up and I feel fine. I don't think I actually drank that much. I was just shattered and hadn't eaten much and the alcohol wiped me out. Josie's just rung me from the dining room to tell me to get there soon if I want anything to eat. Apparently she had to wake me up last night before she could get me down to my room. I just can't remember."

Cathy swallowed and tried to sound vaguely disinterested, "Josie?"

"Haven't I mentioned her before?"

"No."

"She's a colleague and . . . a . . . friend."

"Oh. And you rang me from her room?"

"Apparently. Cathy, did I say . . . I mean, what did I say last night?"

"Not a lot. You did mention that you felt wiped out, but I thought you meant drunk. Your speech was slightly slurred."

"Sorry. Did I say anything else?"

"Like what?"

There was a long pause. "Oh, I don't know. It's a bit of a bummer having had a conversation you don't remember."

"It happened to me once, when I was at a party. Apparently I argued a whole hour with someone and got quite heated."

"About what?"

"Spending obscene amounts of money on wars when there were so many better uses for it. But then I would probably say the same without being drunk."

"Sounds ok to me. It's the kind of thing I might argue about. Anyway, I've heard it said that the truth of what you feel comes out, only stronger, when you've been drinking."

"In vino veritas."

"Something like that."

"So, were you afraid that's what might have happened last night?"

He was silent.

"Jack?"

"Yeah. I'm still here. I should have a shave and go and grab some breakfast."

"Don't change the subject. What did you think you might have said that you didn't want me to hear, Jack?"

"Cathy, I said enough on Monday. I really have to go."

She felt a sudden surge of frustrated anger. "Ok, fine!"

She pressed the key before he could answer and switched off the phone. It was suddenly clear to her what the problem was. He might be physically attracted to her, have feelings about her and care for her mental state, but it was Josie he was on the course with; Josie's room he'd fallen asleep in and Josie whom he was about to have breakfast with. Did he hope he hadn't told her the truth about their relationship and didn't want to upset her just as she was beginning to get herself together?

She forced herself to breathe deeply and stifle the need to scream. She decided she needed to be doing something physically demanding, probably to a background of very loud music.

She dressed quickly and ran into the kitchen. She downed a mug of coffee, demolished a piece of toast and told her father she was going to her flat. She raided the kitchen cupboards for cleaning materials and caught the bus to the other side of town.

She climbed the stairs to her first floor flat and a faintly musty smell greeted her as she opened the door. She switched on her DVD player and pressed the button; she didn't care what was on, just as long as it was loud.

She flung open the windows despite the cold and looked around. She walked through the rooms.

She'd left it in a mess the fateful night of the party and now it was abnormally neat. There were no unwashed dishes in the kitchen, no clothes scattered around her bedroom; merely a little dust here and there. Obviously her parents had cleaned and tidied the flat while she was away in Blanchland or perhaps when she was oblivious to everything in those first two weeks when she'd spent hours lying on their sofa after she checked out of hospital.

She heaved an exasperated sigh and felt thwarted. She stared out of her sitting room window across the wide expanse of grass and trees and looked back at her walls. They looked drab and dismal and she decided they desperately needed some fresh paint. She picked up her shoulder bag and went shopping.

Late in the afternoon as she cleaned the paint from her hands, she made a decision. She would stay in her flat and not wait until next week. She switched on her phone and saw two voice mails and was sure they'd be from Jack. She kept them for later and rang her parents. Her father's voice sounded concerned. "We couldn't reach you. Your phone kept saying you were unavailable and to leave a message."

"I switched it off."

"And the house phone?"

"I unplugged it."

"That's what Jack said you must have done, on both counts."

"He rang you?" She felt angry again.

"At lunchtime. He seemed upset. Wanted to talk to you, though he didn't say what about. That made us worried. I really would rather you didn't switch your mobile off or unplug the phone."

"Sorry Dad. I'll leave them both on. I forgot to plug the house phone back in after painting round the point."

"Why did you switch your mobile off? Have you two had a row?"

"I was painting. I didn't want to get paint on my phone if it rang," she lied.

"Ah. Well I think you should ring Jack and explain, poor boy."

"Um, I've decided I'm going to stay here tonight and tomorrow. I'll come for lunch on Sunday."

"Oh, right. If you think that's best. I'll tell your mother. See you Sunday."

"Bye Dad."

"I hope you won't be too lonely. Bye."

Cathy was in the shower when her mobile rang again. She let it ring and was tempted to switch it off, but decided that not worrying her parents was more important than getting an unwanted phone call from Jack. As she dressed, it rang again. She glanced at it. It was Liz. She didn't feel like talking, but answered it anyway.

"Hi, Liz."

"Will you please leave your phone on? Where are you anyway?"

"And how are you too!"

"Sorry, but I've got this invitaton to supper from this delicious man and I've been asked to bring a friend . . ."

"No, Liz."

"Look I know you're taken but . . ."

"I don't think I am."

"What?"

" 'Taken,' but I just don't feel like going out."

"So what's happened to the saintly Jack?"

Cathy sat down on the bed. "I'm pretty sure he's got someone else."

"What makes you think that?"

"Look Liz, I don't want to talk about it. Can we leave it?"

"Certainly not. I'm not going to leave you there moping when you could be out enjoying yourself and doing me the most enormous favour as well. Please, Cathy, I know I'm being a tinsy bit selfish, but let me explain. I really think that, given a chance, he might just be 'the one.'"

"Again?"

"Don't be bitchy, Cathy. It doesn't suit you."

"Look, I've been painting the sitting room in my flat and I was looking forward to an early night."

"You're twenty-four, not sixty-four!"

"I'm just not in the mood."

"We'll soon fix that. It'll be so much better for you than crying into your hot chocolate. I'll pick you up in twenty minutes. See you later!" She rang off.

Cathy gritted her teeth and went to get ready, annoyed she'd given in just when she needed to get back to her writing. It would have to wait until she could make an excuse to return home and finish the latest chapter.

CHAPTER 21

MISCOMMUNICATION

Liz's handsome target, Matt, was struggling to turn out a wayward mound of couscous onto her plate when Cathy's phone rang. She excused herself and went to pick it up from the shelf behind her. It was Jack.

"Jack, I'm sorry I can't talk to you. I'm out to supper and . . ."

"Please, Cathy."

Something inside her lurched as she heard the urgency in his voice. "Hold on." She looked across at the tricky operation going on in front of her and hardly dared to speak. "Sorry, Matt. I'll be as quick as I can." He murmured something noncommittal as he added a precisely delivered coulis to his carefully assembled meat, vegetables and couscous. Liz was mesmerised and hardly seemed to notice as Cathy went out into the hall.

"Well, Jack. What is it?"

"What the hell is going on, Cathy?"

His quiet, controlled anger hit her like a blow and she found it hard to answer. "I'm out to supper."

"That's not what I meant. You suddenly rang off this morning. Then you switched off your mobile. You haven't answered my call or my messages."

Cathy was silent, struggling to think what to say.

"Would you like to explain what's going on?"

She stared at the wall and knew she didn't have a good enough explanation. It would sound ridiculous if she confessed she'd felt jealous of a woman he'd explained was a colleague.

"Cathy, talk to me."

"Jack, I don't know what to say." She searched for an explanation and hit upon his anxiety about what he might have said to her the night before.

She could only tell him the truth; or part of it. "I suppose I was angry when you wouldn't tell me what you meant about what you might, or might not have said to me last night in Josie's room. I couldn't work out why you wouldn't explain; why you insisted on changing the subject."

"I thought that might have been it." He sounded relieved and she was glad he hadn't sensed her jealousy. "I'm really sorry, Cathy, if I sounded, um, well, evasive I suppose. When we meet up, it'll be so much easier to talk. I hate telephone conversations. It's too easy to read the wrong thing into what's being said."

"Yes, although even face to face you didn't find it easy to control what you said . . . or did."

Jack laughed. "It's your fault. I'm not usually so inarticulate or so out of control."

"I'll try to be less of a trial to you."

"Just don't get angry and cut me off. I can't take it."

Her shoulders sagged. "Oh, Jack, I feel really rotten now. I'm sorry. I'll try and be better."

"Oh, Cathy, don't! Now *I* feel bad. Look, I don't want to keep you from your supper, but I'd like to talk again soon. I just wanted to make sure you were ok."

"I'm fine."

"And Matt is?"

"He's the one giving the supper."

"Just the two of you?"

"Four of us, and it's getting cold."

"Sorry. We are ok now, aren't we?"

"Yes Jack. We're fine."

"Take care then."

"You too, bye."

"Um, bye."

◆　　◆　　◆

The next morning a letter was waiting for her when she got up. It was from the author she'd contacted who'd written a book about the Rebellion. His letter was brief but charming. He gave the details about a Jacobite website that mentioned his book and how she could order it. After she'd ordered it, she wrote a quick note of thanks to the author, dressed quickly and decided to take it to the main post office in the centre of town to be sure it got there by Monday.

◆   ◆   ◆

The letter posted, Cathy stepped outside the post office and surveyed the crowds of shoppers. She was suddenly overwhelmed by her loneliness. Everyone else seemed deep in conversations that absorbed them to the point of being unaware of those around them. She felt invisible.

A young couple passed by with their arms round each other, oblivious to everyone but themselves and she realised in that instant—with a force of desire she'd never felt before—that she desperately wanted to be walking along the street like them, but with Jack. A wave of negativity swamped her. She forced herself to ring Liz. She was about to ring off when Liz answered.

"Huh? Hi."

"Hi Liz, join me for lunch?"

"Oh, Cathy, um, sorry, but we . . . I'm not having lunch." Liz's voice sounded sleepy.

"We? You're not still there are you?"

"Well, actually, yes. Now standing in my bare feet on the cold kitchen floor."

"Right."

"Don't sound so judgemental! After you got your taxi, and your . . . Mike left, we sort of continued talking and . . ."

"Right. I get the picture. How's Matt?"

"Not bad. Pretty fit, really." Liz whispered.

"Right. Hope I didn't call at a bad moment. Bye!"

Cathy walked on and knew she had to fill the emptiness of a Saturday alone. Writing up her latest research seemed to be the only answer.

As she closed down her computer at nine o'clock, she wondered whether to send Jack a text before she went to bed, but he hadn't texted her so she switched it off and left it in the kitchen.

◆   ◆   ◆

She called him just before she was due to leave for lunch on Sunday. She felt a great need to hear his voice. It seemed sad and pathetic and he obviously didn't need the same crutch to get through his day. She phoned anyway and he answered almost immediately.

"Hi Cathy. I was hoping you'd ring. How are you?" The background noise was loud and boisterous.

Cathy grimaced. "Fine. This time you're definitely in a pub."

She heard him laugh. "Yeah. We're having a pub lunch. Just hang on 'til I go outside."

She heard a door bang.

"Right, that's better. Thanks for ringing. I nearly rang when I woke very early this morning. About six, I think."

"I don't think I'd have thanked you for that. I'm not a morning person."

"Me neither, but you didn't call or text yesterday and I think it was on my mind. Anyway, I eventually went back to sleep and the next thing I knew, people were banging on my door to go for a drink before lunch. I'm starving now."

"Right! Well, I wouldn't want you to miss your lunch. Perhaps you might find time in your busy schedule to talk tomorrow."

"Cathy! Sometimes you can be totally infuriating. And don't you dare have one of your strops and ring off. Tell me what you've been doing. How did the supper go?"

"You want to know about the supper?"

"Yes!"

"It just went! It was Liz's ploy to get her hands on the guy you heard me mention—Matt."

"Did it work?"

"Oh, yes. But I didn't terribly fancy the one she paired me up with!"

"Don't joke about something like that."

"Jack, I didn't want to go at all, but Liz twisted my arm."

"Yeah, well. Your holiday starts the weekend after next, doesn't it?"

"In theory, yes."

"I'm pretty sure I can get it off so I can join you."

Cathy flopped down on a chair. "Oh, right, good, I need your help. I've found a lot more about what happened to the rebels and what Dorothy did—I think the fireplace business we read about in the hotel leaflet was when the government messengers were trying to arrest the rebels before anything happened. Thomas was one of the main leaders and later they were really let down by people not turning up when they should have. Communication also seemed to be a problem."

"I can empathise with that."

"What? I think that having to send messages by horseback with government spies everywhere and soldiers waiting to intercept them is not quite the same as our being unable to say the right things to each other on the phone."

Jack was silent.

"Anyway, I've got a lot of new stuff about the Radcliffe family, but a lot of the information about the rebellion is still contradictory and I'm hoping that two of us can get through a lot more than I can on my own. Look Jack, I'm due at my parents' for lunch and you . . ."

"You're not still living with them, then?"

"No, I thought I told you I was going back."

"I hoped you might change your mind."

"I needed to be on my own."

He was silent for a moment. "Right."

"I have to go."

"Yes. I'll ring tomorrow to see how your first day back has gone."

"Oh, gosh. I'd forgotten. It's amazing how easily I've slipped into idleness."

"You've been far from idle, but I think you're probably ready to go back."

"Ok Dr Freud. What makes you think that?"

She heard Jack laugh. "Cathy, darling I . . . er, I mean . . ."

"Don't worry, I'll ignore the 'darling'. I suppose you call all your women friends darling."

"Actually, I don't think I've ever called anyone 'darling' before. Don't know where that came from."

"Oh. Right. Well, we'll 'put it on the back burner', shall we?"

Jack groaned. "I wish I'd never said that!"

She laughed. "Ok. Let's get back to you thinking I might be ready to go back. I think I am. I still think a lot about Tom and the accident, but most of the time it doesn't affect me quite so badly as it did."

"Good. Great stuff. Right; lunch. Give my best wishes to your mum and dad. I'll call you tomorrow."

"Right. Bye, Jack."

"Bye, take care."

"You too."

CHAPTER 22

"WHERE SISTER HID BROTHER TO SAVE HIM FROM DOOM"

1715

I was exhausted when we reached Blanchland. I took a bowl of broth and retired to my room leaving Thomas to deal with any household matters that might need attention. I felt I could not listen to any further discussion on matters relating to their plans and strategies. Thomas had talked of little else as our horses picked their way through the mud and pools of the bridleway on our way home. I felt strangely low despite his obvious delight that he should be at the forefront of such an enterprise.

"I confess," he said proudly, "that I'm greatly honoured Mar and the rest should see me as one of their top confidants and prime movers in this business. I've worked hard at the planning and persuading and I'm sick of being seen by the family as the poor relation who's only fit to collect rents and attend Parliament now and then when not passing m'time hunting and shooting."

I refrained from pointing out that there was some truth in this summation and fervently hoped he had at last found a path that might fulfil both his potential and his expectations. I knew he was capable enough when he set his mind to something; it was just that he could be easily distracted when tempted by more agreeable pursuits.

Almost a week passed before I received the next piece of shocking news. Thomas returned home from Newcastle late one afternoon to report that an urgent warning had been received from Lady Cowper by her kinsman

136

John Clavering of Callaly. Despite her being the wife of the Lord Chancellor, she'd sent a secret messenger to bring him news that the government had issued warrants for the arrest of those thought to be conspiring Jacobites.

Thomas, Derwentwater, Widdrington, Blackett and two others were named. There was a degree of pride in Thomas' voice as he told me. "The messenger passed through Newcastle with the news on his way to Callaly and Blackett got wind of it when he was staying in Yorkshire and left Newby just in time to elude the messengers. He's not in Newcastle, so no doubt he's back in Wallington Hall. I called in at Dilston on m'way home. Derwentwater and Charles mean to hide in Sir Marmaduke's hunting lodge at Farnham, though they didn't seem in too great a hurry when I left. Widdrington's still not back to Stella Hall so I may have to seek him out and warn him." He patted his stomach and smiled at me, "I'll get rid of m'belly at this rate, Dolly."

I stared in disbelief at Thomas. "How can you make light of this news? The messengers might arrive at any moment. Where can you go to be safe?"

"Worry not, Dolly, they hadn't even reached Newcastle when I left and I've wasted no time at all. As for looking for me, they'll probably try Bamburgh first. And I think Derwentwater is regarded as being a bigger fish than I am. William Fenwick's house at Bywell is a safe enough place for me to hide when the time comes. Sister Margaret's house in Low Staward could be another. Only ten miles from Hexham but it'll seem like the back o' beyond to southerners."

"Blanchland might seem like the back of beyond to southerners, but everyone knows you stay here regularly. Surely they're more likely to come here, knowing how close it is to James at Dilston?"

"Mebbies, but they don't know their way around and I'm staying here for now. Now then, Dolly, I have a great hunger on me and some ale would be welcome."

I sighed and resigned myself to accepting his decision. I felt he was being overly optimistic about his situation, but I could see that on this occasion I was unlikely to change his mind. I set about organising refreshments for us both and after supper we retired to bed early.

Thomas slept late the next day and it seemed so quiet and peaceful that I refrained from disturbing him until breakfast could be delayed no longer. After we had eaten, Thomas sent Lee out with messages to several people, including the Charlton brothers and the Swinburnes. They had contacts across the north-east and knew safe places where people could hide and secret messages be hidden.

Quite unexpectedly, Thomas decided to go fishing, stating pointedly to me that it might be a while before he had the luxury of doing so again. He returned as the shadows lengthened and was just settling down in front of the fire with a mug of ale when the sound of a single horse came down the street, followed by an urgent knocking on the door.

Joseph harrumphed noisily, put down the coal scuttle he was bringing to the fire and raised his eyebrows to Thomas. Thomas nodded. "A single horse is no threat." Joseph shuffled away to the hall. The knocking became louder and more insistent. "Hold tha' noise!" shouted Joseph. "Tha'll wake the dead and scare the living."

I heard the groan of the rusty hinges as Joseph opened the door. I looked up from my sewing and turned towards the door as the small, rotund figure of Anthony Hilyard burst into the room. "Beg pardon, sir, but Lord Widdrington sent me to warn you. We were coming back along the Hexham road when we met with the Earl of Derwentwater and his brother Charles. They were nearly arrested and had to escape Dilston Hall through the secret passage from the dungeons. When we saw them they were on their way to Sir Marmaduke's shooting lodge at Farnham. You must also find a safe house to hide."

I dropped my sewing and rose from my seat. "Thomas, you must leave at once. Joseph, Lee might not return for some time, so you must gather together your master's clothes and musket and sword, oh, and a stout doublet to protect his vitals. I leave you to add any other things you think my brother may need on his journey." I turned to Thomas. "Get up, for heavens sake, the King's messengers might arrive at any moment."

Thomas seemed frozen to his seat. He had gone pale and was biting his lip. He swallowed and stood up. "Right now, right. I suppose this is it, Dolly. Erm, Hilyard, you can accompany me, so see to your horse. Oh, damnation, with all m'travels mine needs to be shod and our blacksmith is sick."

"Peter Cumin has come from Hexham to help out," I said hurriedly, "I'll see to that. You must look to your needs and seek your hidden arms. It could be some time before you will return."

I picked up my skirts and ran to our stables. I collected Tom's fine black charger and ran him across the wide expanse of grass to the narrow winnel that led to the forge. I turned the corner and could see the sparks flying as Peter Cumin hammered a red-hot shoe on his anvil. He looked up as he heard the ring of horse hooves across his yard.

"Peter, we have urgent need of your help. My brother must leave as soon as possible and his horse must be shod."

The smith nodded and laid the shoe aside. "So it's come?"

I feigned incomprehension. He continued as he manoeuvred the horse, "You've nothing to fear from me, mistress, I mean to join the rising. Tell Mr Forster I'll be waiting in Hexham and will warn others to be ready. Tell him not to expect much from his lead miners though; dissenters the lot of them. You go back and see to him. I'll bring his horse across when I'm finished."

I smiled at him. "Thank you. I'll bring the money later."

He shook his head and smiled back. "Your smile's enough thanks."

"Thank you Peter. I'm most grateful."

I scurried back to the house in the gathering dusk and found Lee had returned with news that the messengers were still trying to track down James and Charles, and were last seen riding north of Corbridge. Thomas was standing talking to Lee and Hilyard in the hall.

"It's almost dark; we need light and sharp eyes for identifying other travellers on the road and we've none of us eaten since well before midday. It's my thinking that we should sup, get an early night and leave at five on the morra. D'y'agree?"

I felt the others were in no position to disagree, so I stepped forward. "We do not know if there is more than one group of messengers. The longer you stay here, the greater the chance that they may find you. You could go west to sister Margaret's at Low Staward if you think going north is more dangerous in the dark."

Tom clasped his hands and thought for a moment. "No. Will's place at Bywell is closer to Dilston and is a much better place to keep in touch with events. We'll have to trust that an early start will outwit Geordie's lackeys."

As the evening unfolded and our small company ate and drank their fill, I felt an increasing unease. It seemed to me that the amount of ale that was being consumed did not bode well for an early start and I was still not convinced that delaying was the right decision. There was a bright moon and they could have made the journey with ease. Joan, the kitchen maid, cleared the table but Thomas insisted that the wooden tankards and replenished jug of ale must remain.

Just before eight I rose from the table. "I am retiring now in order to get a good night's sleep as you, dear brother, suggested you must do in order to make an early start. I think you should all do the same."

Tom stood up, "Night, Dolly, we'll follow shortly. Sleep well." I hesitated, but felt there was nothing more I could say. Reluctantly, I took leave of the drinkers and climbed the stone stairs to my room, all the while feeling distinctly uneasy.

Half an hour passed and I remained sleepless as I listened to the talking and laughter below. A new sound of muffled horses' hooves in the distance and coming closer caused me to sit up. The noise of the hooves echoing through the arch and clattering across the cobbles sent me leaping from my bed. I threw on a woollen dressing gown and went out onto the landing. I peered down through the window and saw five riders. On one of them, the outline of a distinctive plumed hat could be discerned in the moonlight and I knew at once who he was.

I ran down the stairs and hushed the startled company. "They're here, and Brown the bailiff as well."

All rose to their feet as a thunderous knocking began on the door. Joseph entered the room. "Shall I answer the door, sir?" Tom shook his head and looked helplessly at me.

I took a breath, "Joseph, gather up your master's clothes and arms. You and Lee must carry them all to the chapel ruins and hide them in the crypt before the messengers find the way round the back. After that, go to bed, Joseph. Lee, when you've dealt with the arms, go—at a run—by the back ways to Mary Liddle's cottage and stay there until you hear from us." They scampered around doing as I'd bid. I turned to Thomas, knowing that running anywhere was impossible for him.

"Thomas, you will have to hide in the priest's hole."

"But the fire's on Dolly. I'll either roast or choke." The thunderous knocking began again and this time was accompanied by loud calls demanding entry.

"Would you rather be imprisoned and the Cause die?" I hissed. "Hilyard, get a chair and come help me get him up the chimney."

Hilyard looked startled but did as he was bid. He placed the chair inside the wide fireplace next to the burning coals and Thomas climbed gingerly onto it. He reached up to the wide shelf above and tried to pull himself up. He puffed and panted but his arms gave way. "I cannot do it, Dolly, I cannot do it." Hilyard saw a foothold and guided Thomas's right foot into it. "Pull up when I say 'now', sir."

I watched in great agitation as Thomas reached again and Hilyard pushed Thomas's ample behind with a tremendous shove. There was a grunt and groan and Thomas's feet disappeared.

I heaved a sigh of relief. "Bring the chair out, Hilyard, take the tankards and jug to the kitchen. Bring brush, shovel and bucket back here and make as if you are settling the fire for the night."

I glanced round the room, my stomach churning. I heard a muffled cough from the chimney and rushed over to the fireplace. "Stuff your kerchief in your mouth, Thomas," I whispered, "I'm going to let them in."

CHAPTER 23

FLIGHT

I glanced quickly round the room and decided all was normal and showed no signs that visitors had even entered it. I pulled my dressing gown about me, picked up a candle and hurried to the door. I levered the wooden bar out of its rests and swung open the heavy, creaking door.

"Now then sirs, what brings you to my door so late at night? I was in my bed until you roused me so rudely."

Brown pushed past the others, musket in hand, and I had to step aside or he would have knocked me off my feet. "We're on the King's business, Mistress Forster, and would speak with your brother. Show me to his room."

I looked straight into his eyes. "It would be a wasted effort to do so, for he is not there."

He looked at me, his mouth working and his face a purplish-red, no doubt in his fury that he had been kept waiting so long. He turned to the messengers. "Two of you search the place from top to bottom, and you two, the stables and land." He grabbed me by the arm. "You can show me to the bed chambers, mistress."

I shook my arm free. "Take care, Brown, I will not be brow-beaten into doing your bidding. Find the stairs yourself if you wish to waste your time looking for my brother!"

As the messengers ran off, the bailiff grabbed the hall candlestick and stormed off in the direction of the kitchen. I smiled at his mistake and walked into the parlour. Hilyard had snuffed out all the candles and was on his knees in the fireplace, with a lamp at his elbow, shovelling up red hot coals into a bucket. One of the messengers was questioning him about his master and trying to light a candle from the dying embers. I was astounded to see Hilyard turn to him with a stupid, vacant expression on his face.

"Mister Forster?" he said, painfully slowly, "Now then, when did I last see him? Now then . . . "

"Come on, man, where has he gone if he's not here?"

"The master doesn't tell me where he's going. He likes to hunt and shoot so he might be off stayin' wi'is friends . . . mmm." Hilyard looked blankly around the room as if he expected his master to appear at any moment. I found it hard to contain my amusement. The messenger lit his candle at last, peered at both of us with an irritated look on his face and ran up the stone stairs.

Mr Brown burst through the door and surveyed the room angrily. Seeing the stairs, he pushed his way between me and the chairs so recently occupied by my brother and the two servants.

When we were alone again Hilyard picked up the bucket. "I think, mistress," he whispered, "You should not stand there looking alternately amused or worried. Rather sit down and look sleepy and, perhaps, a mite irritated. I shall return to the kitchen and be about my servant duties should they wish to check up on me again."

I nodded and smiled briefly. I whispered, "I'm sure you will play your role well but I find it harder to play mine and would be totally unable to make myself out to be an idiot as you are doing."

Hilyard winked at me and continued his play acting by walking ponderously and awkwardly towards the door. I stifled a laugh. The wind rattled the draughty windows and added to the sounds of banging doors and shouts in the rooms above. I picked up a book and candle and settled myself on the stool beneath the priest hole. It was too cold to sit anywhere else in the room and from there I reasoned I could whisper to Thomas if the need arose.

They combed the house and the surrounding area for more than half an hour and at one point—hearing excited shouts in the direction of the stable—I feared they might have discovered something. I ran to the back window and saw one of them leading Hilyard's and Lee's horses. Another was leading my own. I ran back to my seat and prepared my answer to their questions.

Brown burst back into the room and pointed to the window. "Ha, mistress. And to whom might these three fine specimens belong?" I stood up and walked sedately to the window overlooking the kitchen garden. I peered into the darkness. "It is very difficult to see in the dark, but if you are talking about the three horses that appear to be eating and trampling my vegetables and herbs, they could be mine, my Aunt Dorothy Lady Crewe's and My Lord Bishop Crewe's. My Lord will be very displeased indeed should you have disturbed his animals, if indeed they are his."

I turned round and stared defiantly at Brown. He shifted from one foot to another and looked deeply uncomfortable. "Crewe's? Yes well, it is our duty to do everything to uncover those damned traitors, but I wish no disrespect to anything that belongs to the Bishop. We'll return them to the stables."

He turned and left the room as Hilyard entered it. I found I was shivering and he saw it and removed his coat. He buttoned it round me. "I know it's not just the cold, mistress, but you're doing well. Stay calm. I think they will leave now. I heard one of them saying they'd been sent on a wild goose chase."

We heard the front door slam shut and after a few seconds, horses' hooves clattered across the cobbles and echoed through the arch. Hilyard let out a long sigh and sat down heavily on a seat. I went to the fireplace and called up the chimney. "They're gone. It's safe to come down."

There was no reply and I became aware of gentle snoring up above. "Oh, heavens, Hilyard, climb up and wake him. If he turns over in his sleep, he'll come crashing down into the embers."

Hilyard smiled. "Well, mistress, that would wake him for sure."

◆   ◆   ◆

At five the next morning they were packed, saddled and ready to leave. Joseph and Cissy had been up since four preparing food and checking they had all they needed for their journey and whatever else they might encounter. Peter Cumin had brought Tom's horse at a quarter before five. Having been delayed in his task by a visit from a friend from Hexham, he had come to deliver Thomas's horse the previous evening just as the Bailiff and the messengers arrived. Recognising Brown, he had walked Midnight past them and taken the long route back to the smithy.

None of us had slept for long and I stood sleepily at the door, peering into the darkness. The three shadowy figures mounted their restless horses. Thomas's voice quavered a little as he spoke. "Take care, Dolly. We'll let you know what's happening when we are able. The Swinburne girls have offered their services to keep the Countess and others informed, so do not be anxious."

I pulled myself up to my full height. "Do not worry on my account. Rather look to your own safety and do nothing in haste. Lee, I am looking to you to see to your master's needs."

"That I will, mistress."

"Hilyard, thank you for your help. God speed."

"My thanks to you; I enjoyed our little excitement."

I nodded and turned to Thomas. "Goodbye, dear brother. God go with you."

"Goodbye, dearest Dolly. Raise a glass to our King over the water in the hope that he will be with us 'ere long." Thomas pulled on the reins and spurred his horse, and they disappeared into the gloom.

Joseph was laying the fire when I re-entered the parlour. He looked up and tutted, "thou art looking perished and famished. Cissy could get y'summat to eat. Mary's not yet here."

"Thank you, Joseph, but I feel too sick at heart to eat. Could you light the fire in my room? I shall retire there for a while. Perhaps I will sleep."

I sat at the table, surveying the crumbs of bread and cheese that were all that remained of the hastily eaten meal Thomas and his companions had consumed. There was a little ale in Thomas's tankard and I sipped it, pondering on the likelihood of their being captured before they had time to reach their respective safe houses. I wondered how long it would be before I heard that all was well.

◆   ◆   ◆

Not until more than a week later on the morning of the fourth of October, which dawned cold, crisp and bright, did I receive any news. I was reading in my room when I heard a rider come to the door. I dropped my book and ran down the stairs.

I reached the hall as Joseph ushered in one of the Swinburne sisters who threw back her hood and obviously had no time for pleasantries. "Mistress Dorothy," she began at once, "tomorrow you are to go to the horse racing in the meadow at Widehaugh, near Dilston. Be there by mid-morning." She glanced at Joseph who was hovering in the hall. "I can tell you no more and must be on my way." She turned away and reached for the door.

"Wait!" I cried, "You must tell me if my brother is safe. You need not fear to speak in front of Joseph." The girl looked uncertain and stared at Joseph. She breathed in, her lips pursed and turned to me. "God willing, you will see your brother tomorrow. It may be your last chance for some time. Wrap up well. I think winter has come early."

With that she swung open the door, mounted her horse with great agility and was gone before I had time to recover myself and thank her for her news.

I spent much of the rest of the day gathering together warm garments and hose for Thomas and seeing to the welfare of my horse, Chestnut. I retired to bed early leaving instructions that I would break my fast at six.

In the cold dawn the following day, Joseph adjusted the saddle bags on Chestnut and helped me into the saddle. "It's a bit of a load you be carrying. If they shift you'll come a cropper." Joseph's breath hung white in the air. I smiled down at him. "I will keep at a gentle trot. I have plenty of time to get there before they gather . . . for the races." Joseph, an expression of doubt on his face, nodded and stood silently as I clicked my heels against Chestnut's belly and moved slowly down the road.

Despite my slow progress, I reached the huge flat meadow beside the River Tyne at Widehaugh to find that as yet only a small number of Dilston villagers and stall-holders gathered at one end of the field, rubbing their hands together and stamping their feet. A few horses and riders were walking to and fro near the start of the course.

Another group of horses on the other side of the field were tethered to a fence, their riders huddled round a small fire. I recognised most of the faces but neither Thomas nor the Earl were among them. As I dismounted, the noise of riders made me turn to the east. I saw Charles Radcliffe at the head of the group and as they came closer I could see James just behind him, looking noticeably strained, though whether from the cold or from bad news I did not want to speculate.

They greeted me briefly and inquired if I knew when Thomas would arrive. I shook my head. "I have not seen him since he left for Bywell, but I would suppose that he will come from the same direction as you."

Charles dismounted and began to stride about impatiently. "We have ridden hard from our distant and uncomfortable hiding place on the moors at Shafto Crag and your lazy brother cannot get here on time from Bywell!"

"Charles," James intervened, "You cannot berate Dorothy nor imply criticism of her brother because we have suffered hardship." I held my tongue and breathed slowly, wondering why I had ever felt in the least interested in Charles.

James came closer and smiled at me. "We have found it necessary to move about a great deal due to the tenacity of the usurper's spies and lackeys. We stayed at your sister Margaret's house in Low Staward after we left Sir Marmaduke's hunting lodge."

"My sister? How is she?"

"Well enough. She and her husband were most hospitable but we had to move on to the cottage of a tenant of mine in Newbrough when we got wind of a bailiff heading in our direction."

"Did you hear of Thomas's close shave with the messengers?"

"I did. It seems we all have stories to tell."

"And why did you move to Shafto Crag?"

"Well, we heard that the messengers were close by, so the Swinburnes suggested we should hide well away from this area but close enough to Capheaton that they could supply us with food and keep us abreast of developments. We have not slept as well as we would wish out on the moors, so you must bear with our temper."

I refrained from commenting that it appeared that only Charles's temper had suffered.

A slowly increasing invasion of noise made me turn to watch as a good many more race horses and riders invaded the meadow and the races began in earnest.

A few minutes after the first race was completed a sudden commotion, again from the east, heralded the arrival of a group of riders whose speed was far greater than any before. At the head of this group I gradually recognised Thomas on Midnight, his fine charger, whose black coat glistened and steamed in the chill of the air. I watched with relief as they drew near. Thomas dismounted beside me and I lifted my arms to embrace him. "Now then, Dolly," he muttered quietly, kissing my cheek and taking my arms from around him, "We have much to discuss, so you must stand quietly by. I sent word so that I could see you before we leave, but there is no time for pleasantries."

I saw a change in his demeanour: there was a sense of purpose about him, a feeling of authority. I looked round at the expectant faces and could see that they—including James and Charles—hung on his word and were eager to hear what he had to say. My heart swelled with pride and I fervently hoped his news would lift the hearts of all those surrounding him, including myself. But when I turned back to him, I could see in his eyes that all was not well.

CHAPTER 24

WIDEHAUGH MEADOW

Thomas turned to James. "Have you heard the damnable news from the south?" James shook his head silently and the others gathered round. Charles stepped forward. "It must be particularly important considering you cannot keep to the agreed time for the meet."

Thomas did not react to Charles's sarcasm. Instead he straightened his back and took a breath. "I make no apology for m'lateness. It was necessary to wait for Oxburgh and Lee to return with the latest news from Newcastle, to add to that which we already knew. First of all, one of Widdrington's servants reported a few days ago that all his horses and guns were removed from Stella Hall by government forces before there was time to hide them. What is a good deal worse, it is most regrettable to have to report that in the midlands, the leaders of three uprisings have either been taken or gone into hiding, and it would seem that both invasions in the south and south-west have been repulsed or discouraged. Whatever the reasons—and I suspect treachery from Bolingbroke—they have not fulfilled their part of the plan."

A general groan, followed by mutterings, echoed round those gathered. Thomas continued. "That's not all. It's rumoured that the Lord Lieutenant Scarborough last week gave two weeks notice for the militias and trainbands to muster for the government."

Charles cursed loudly but James pushed past him and looked up into Thomas's face.

"In view of all this, have we received further orders?"

"None. Neither from Mar nor from France."

The consternation on James's face made me feel doubly afraid. Thomas bit his lip and continued. "It would seem to me that Mar's original plan for the main landing to take place in the north-east might be back into their thinking. It could be that the whole invasion force, perhaps with the King on board, might be heading for the Northumberland coast this very moment."

James stroked his chin, paced up and down and nodded to himself. "That is possible. And one thing is most clear to me: if we dither now and are taken like those in the south, the rallying point for the English part in the Cause will be lost. All our support in the west will be left leaderless, and without us the Scots will have no support from England to fight for our King."

Thomas nodded slowly at James. "Aye, we were to have risen when the force landed on our shores, but we have no choice now. It is some five or six days earlier than was intended, but we must appear in arms and rally our followers to the Cause forthwith."

Charles raised his brows and glanced at James. He put his hand on Thomas's shoulder. "I have underestimated you, Thomas. It seems you may have the qualities to be in command after all."

The expression on Thomas' face was one of doubt and surprise; precisely what I felt myself.

"Me? In command? Why not one of you or someone used to soldiering? Or Blackett?"

Charles grimaced. "From your question, I assume you have not heard the latest on Blackett. He went back to his grand house at Wallington and we think he has been contained there by Cotesworth. He may escape—if he has a mind to—but we cannot rely on his doing so."

Thomas remained silent, a frown on his face.

"So," James continued where Charles had left off, "as the only loyal Tory member of parliament present and representative of the chief Protestant family in this region, you—conditional to the agreement of our full party and official recognition from the Earl of Mar—are to be our General and lead us in battle."

"No!" My voice rang out in the clear, cold air before I had time to control my feelings and I felt my heart leap as they all turned towards me.

It was said and I could not take it back, nor did I want to. I took a breath and exhaled. "My brother will be a most loyal and brave supporter of the Cause and will no doubt fight as well as any, but he does not have the experience to be a general. He knows nothing of battles and strategies. Why, I know more from my history books than he does!"

I felt the embarrassment in the silence that followed. Oxburgh stepped forward. "Mistress Dorothy. A good number of us here are soldiers; to be sure we have fought and campaigned many times before. Himself has the good sense to know that he must listen to our advice, and what is more, he has the Earl of Mar's confidence and ear."

James walked across to me. He rested his hands on my shoulders and looked into my eyes. "And, you must understand that if we are to attract the greatest number of followers possible, our force cannot be led by a Roman Catholic. People will fear that our King might force his religion on his subjects if he is restored. We know he will not do that, but they will be much more assured of the truth if a Protestant general leads us."

I turned slowly to Thomas. "And you, Thomas, what is your opinion of their decision?" Thomas sighed and a smile slowly illuminated his features. "Well, Dolly, I see you doubt my abilities in that direction and I must confess it came as a bit of a shock; Mar had not decided when we last spoke. But the reasoning is right." He looked round at the assembled company. "I will do it, subject to the others accepting your proposal." He looked back at me. "Give me y'blessing, Dorothy, we have no more time to dally. We must be away before those blasted spies catch up with us again."

I knew, the moment he used my given name, that his mind was made up and further argument would be useless. Reluctantly, I nodded and hugged him. "God bless you and God speed," I whispered and turned away.

James mounted his horse and turned him round towards me. "My valet Wesby or some other courier will bring news to Dilston, Dorothy, so our good news will reach you."

If there be any, I thought.

Thomas cleared his throat and surveyed the assembled company. "Send messages to all our friends that we will meet tomorrow morning at Greenriggs."

James reined in his frisky horse. "The place near the top of Waterfalls Hill?"

"Yes, between Reedsmouth and Sweethope Lough. In a good Stuart stronghold."

He turned to me. "G'bye Dolly. God be with you." He smiled, leant closer and whispered. "And I forgive your outburst. I know it was because you are fearful for me. Worry not."

I forced a cheerful smile in return. "Goodbye, dearest brother. Take the greatest of care." He nodded and rode on.

"God speed you all!" I shouted and raised my hand in farewell as they began to move off. James and Charles nodded to me and waved.

I felt my smile fade as they cantered off towards the east and watched until they were well in the distance. I saw four of them peel off towards Dilston while the rest went in the direction of Corbridge. It was obvious that James and Charles must be going to see Anna Maria. With a jolt, I suddenly remembered I still had Thomas's warm clothes in my saddle bags. I too would have to go to Dilston so that one of the Earl's servants could convey them to Thomas.

I mounted Chestnut and cantered away without thought for the load he was carrying. Within fifteen minutes I was entering the kitchens at Dilston Hall.

I spied Betty bustling towards the door into the entrance hall. "Betty!" I called hastily, "I would speak to you. It is most urgent."

Betty halted in her step and looked me up and down. "Why, Mistress Forster! Whatever are you doing in the servants' quarters?" The kitchen maids and cook looked on curiously. I smiled at them in a manner I hoped would quell their suspicions, and went over to Betty. "I do not want to disturb the Countess. It is a small but important favour I would ask you. In private."

Betty ushered me out of the kitchen and along the corridor to a small room at the end, where Betty and her husband Charles Busby slept. The horse-hair mattress on the wooden slats looked none too comfortable. "Betty, do you know what is happening tomorrow?"

"I know that my master and his brother are staying this night and leaving in the morning. I know that my mistress has been sick with lack of news of him since he escaped from the bailiff and King Geordie's messengers. I know that we are all in danger if we are caught harbouring Geordie's enemies and I know that no-one who works here would dream of betraying the kindest, most generous of all masters in the whole of Northumberland."

I smiled. "Then there was no need for my caution. My favour is simply this. Please could you ask one of the servants accompanying the Earl tomorrow to take with him some warm clothes to give to my brother? I think their mission could take some time and winter seems to be coming early this year." Betty nodded and followed me back through the kitchen and out to where I had tied up Chestnut. I placed the bundled garments into Betty's hands. "When they have left, please tell your mistress I would be happy to return at any time if she would like me to visit, but I will not come unless bidden."

Betty nodded. "Like as not, she'd be glad of y'company, mistress. She's a lost young bairn when he's not here. I'll see she gets your message."

◆   ◆   ◆

When I reached Blanchland I was drained of all energy and my spirits so low that I retired to bed with some broth and one of my favourite books. I harboured the faint hope that reading could banish the fears that invaded my mind. It was not that I felt what the band of hopefuls were doing was wrong, but too much had already not gone to plan. Success depended on support from the Scots and French contingent. I knew that the highland clans were not noted for their liking of the English; nor for that matter, did they like the lowland Scots. They even spent much of their time fighting each other, often with great savagery. But, I reassured myself, they were unfailingly loyal to their King over the water. More than a hundred years before, the Stuart clan's James VI of Scotland had come to rule over the English as James I. That was reason enough for much pride despite their deep misgivings at their King ruling from London. Their fury at the forced exile of his descendant James II, and the usurping of his throne by the Dutchman William of Orange—even with his Stuart Queen Mary—knew no bounds. They had long been ready to fight for the Stuart cause; they were a fierce, proud and loyal people well versed in the skills needed for victory in battle.

My eyelids drooped and I removed the bolster from behind my back and lay down. My thoughts were still in turmoil. What about those in France? The court at St Germain and their supporters had encouraged the uprising and raised thousands of pounds for the Cause, but attempts to rise had been made before and failed. This time Ormonde and Bolingbroke had returned to France without, it seemed, much of a fight. Surely the King would not leave his loyal subjects to the mercy of the government's army? I imagined them landing on the Northumbrian coast, to the north of Bamburgh, sheltered from the North Sea by Holy Island.

I pictured myself in summer walking along the sands, sometimes chatting happily with John Armstrong, both touched by a soft breeze from the Farnes and looking to the sky as we heard the whistle of a red-shank piercing the air.

A great sense of longing overcame me and I began to weep into my pillow. Not only must I remain in Blanchland until some sort of outcome was achieved, but I could do nothing whatever to help or hinder that outcome.

CHAPTER 25

COMMUNICATION

2005

Monday evening's phone call was a text. "Things a bit hectic. In the middle of an endless list of patients, so don't ring. How did it go today? Is everything ok? xxx".

Disappointment surged through Cathy, but she didn't want to add to his obvious stress. "Job's fine. I'm fine and have lots to tell you about Dorothy when you have time. Don't work too hard. Talk to you later xxx".

She picked up her book and found the page she'd left earlier, but her eyes stared unseeingly at the turgid historical content. Jack was still on her mind and she found it hard to concentrate. She went to her computer and searched for an email full of new information that she'd forgotten to print out.

Just after midnight as she watched television in bed, Jack rang. "Hi. I was hoping you'd still be awake. I just wanted to speak to you . . . and now I don't know what it was I wanted to say."

"I can't believe that; you've usually got lots to say."

"Yeah, well I guess I'm tired."

"Sorry, I didn't mean to be flippant. Of course you must be tired. Are you in bed?"

"Yes."

"Me too."

"In that silky night slip thing?"

"Different colour, but yes."

"I wish I hadn't asked. It's my birthday on Friday."

"What! You didn't tell me."

"No, I was so mad that I had to work Friday and Saturday that I decided to postpone it to the following weekend. We can celebrate when I come up."

"How old will you be?"

"Thirty."

"Thirty? I didn't think you were that old!"

"You think thirty's old?"

"I mean you don't look that old."

"Being a mere child of . . . ?"

"Twenty-four. A few days before . . . the accident."

"Pretend I've got my arms round you right now."

Cathy closed her eyes. "I wish," she said quietly.

He was silent.

"Jack?"

"Yeah, I'm still here. You said you had things to tell me about Dorothy."

"Yes."

"So tell me."

"Yes, right. Let me get my brain into gear. Oh, yes. I got an email from my contacts in Australia. They'd been over here tracing their ancestors. They sent an attachment with some pages from a booklet by a Northumbrian historian called John Bird which, they said, told the story of Dorothy and how she rescued her brother."

"John Bird! That's the one I had that I couldn't remember. I'll have another look for it."

"Right. Well, I downloaded the attachment after I texted you but unfortunately it all came out as gobbledygook—different software maybe— but they said in their email they'd sent the booklet by post. Very frustrating. I did find a story on the internet about a Scottish aristocrat called Lady Nithsdale who dressed up her husband as her maid and the stupid guards didn't notice the difference and he escaped, so perhaps her story got used to explain how Dorothy got Thomas out of gaol. The one you read about in Bamburgh Castle, I mean."

"Yeah, it did say she and her maid got him out that way."

"Yes, well, at the moment I've got a very confused picture about what she might or might not have done. Anyway, the new book about the Jacobites should arrive tomorrow and I hope it'll tell me more. Bit of a sad person, aren't I? Sitting alone in my little flat, reading history."

"Of course you're not. You're doing great. You really are into it, aren't you?"

"Yes. I am. I feel a real empathy with Dorothy now I know so much more about her, Thomas and the various rebels, even though a lot that I've found out is difficult to untangle. It keeps me occupied and stops me from thinking about things I don't want to think about."

"Yes, a bit of therapeutic detective work. I hoped that was how it would work." Cathy decided to let him think his explanation was right. The truth was, she often used it to take her mind off him.

"So, you still haven't found the definitive version of exactly how Dorothy might have saved her brother and what you've found conflicts with what I found out in Bamburgh Castle. It looks pretty hopeless."

"Perhaps, but I'm going to keep looking."

"Great stuff."

"And now, I think it's time for sleep."

"You're right. I can sleep in, but you've got work in the morning."

"This morning, actually."

"Yeah. Sorry for keeping you awake. Take it easy and don't overdo things. I wish I was there to see how you are."

"I'm fine. Really I am; you don't need worry about me."

"Good. I think about you a lot. And worry. Do you ever think about me?"

"Yes . . ."

"Often?"

"How often would you like?"

He was silent.

"Jack?"

"Sleep well, Cathy."

CHAPTER 26

THERAPY

On Tuesday evening, Jack rang again. "Have you had a good day, despite my late phone call?"

"Fine, but there's something that's a bit worrying that I didn't tell you."

"Oh, Cathy, what?"

"The last two nights I've dreamt about Tom."

"Go on."

"Well, I don't usually remember dreams, but this was so startling that I could replay it in my mind when I woke. Tom was showing me he wasn't dead at all and saying he was glad I wasn't hurt. I woke up, and for a split second I felt so happy, until I realised it'd been a dream. Am I going crazy?"

"Of course not. It's not unusual. I don't know why it sometimes happens but I think it might be your way of saying good bye to him. You didn't say good bye, did you?"

"No," she whispered.

"Oh Cathy, I know this sounds strange, but I really think this is one of our ways of coming to terms with losing people we love, particularly after a sudden loss and when we haven't said good bye. It happened to me when my grandfather died suddenly. I kept dreaming we were chatting and fishing together. It'll probably happen to you again until you've fully accepted it all."

She swallowed. "I . . . I thought I had accepted it."

"That was a bad way of putting it; what I mean is I think it's when your subconscious lets go; when you can finally accept that someone has gone and there's no need to feel any guilt."

"I don't think I'll ever feel that."

"You will. You certainly have no logical reason to feel guilty."

"It may not be logical, but the guilt is still there."

"It's a cliché, but I've got to say it. Give it time."

"Yes, I hope you're right."

"Cathy?"

"Yes?"

"Are you really ok?"

"Yes. I feel a lot better now I've told you and you've explained it a little; there's no one else I could have told."

He expelled a breath. "You've no idea how good it is to hear you say that."

"But why didn't you suggest pills or some sort of psychotherapy? Professional, I mean."

He laughed. "Are you suggesting I'm not professional?"

"No, of course not!"

"I'm kidding, Cathy."

"Oh . . . well, anyway, you sort of took it on, unpaid, didn't you?"

"You haven't had my bill yet."

"Perhaps I'll have to find a way to repay you when you come north."

"Perhaps? I'm going to demand full payment!"

"Oh yes? What would that be?"

"I'll let you know."

Cathy paused and blew some air. "Um, can we get back to the therapy bit? Do you believe in anti-depressants when someone is in the kind of state I was?"

"Actually, in many cases, I don't; as long as you have family or friends you feel you can talk to. But it's not an easy thing to do. Grief's a particularly hard one to deal with, but it seems as if everyone wants quick fixes whatever their problems are. I happen to believe that having to deal with unhappiness, problems, challenges and whatever else may come along—hopefully with help from someone—is what life is all about."

"Yes, I think you're right. I don't like the idea of taking pills either, but I don't think I could talk about my feelings and thoughts to someone I didn't know and trust."

"You unburdened yourself to me and I was a stranger."

"Yes, but that was different. I was in a bit of a state and, I think, vulnerable to your persuasion. I'm not like that normally, but I felt I could trust you. I don't know why."

"No regrets, though?"

"No! You were what I needed. You saved me from myself and I'm really grateful, but what happens to all the people who haven't got someone who'll listen or who don't want to talk anyway?"

"That's where my argument collapses. We have to do something, but handing out pills is like putting plasters over an infection. We're not taking away the cause."

"You're absolutely right. I'm so lucky you were there."

"I'm glad I was. I get panicky at the thought I might have been a few minutes earlier and missed you."

"Oh, Jack, that's a horrible thought. But you're right, you were a stranger, but you made me feel I could talk to you."

"I'm not so sure I would be as effective with someone I didn't care about."

Cathy paused. "As in, how a doctor would care about someone?"

"More than that."

"But you acted so detached when we started researching in Hexham!"

"Well I had to give you time to be a little more together."

"So now I'm a little more together . . ."

"Let's see how things go when I get there."

"Right."

"Cathy, I'm going to have to go, coffee time's over."

"Oh Jack, I've got lots to tell you about Thomas from the new book I was telling you about. It really wasn't fair how he was blamed for the failure of the Preston battle."

"Can we do that tomorrow?"

"Sorry, I just don't want to stop talking to you."

"Me neither. I'll ring you tomorrow. Probably quite late. I'm on a different shift and then I'm going straight out in the evening. I'll ring when I get back."

"What exactly is your job at the moment?"

"I'm working in A & E."

"Oh, why didn't you tell me?"

"You didn't ask."

"Sorry."

"What for?"

"Being so preoccupied with myself that I didn't ask."

"That's ok."

"Not really, but thanks for being so understanding. You really are a lovely man. Talk to you tomorrow. Take care."

"You too."

◆   ◆   ◆

Next evening, after four hours submerging herself in writing Dorothy's journal, she was still waiting for his call at midnight. She felt a little disturbed, but decided not to ring in case he'd fallen asleep. They'd exchanged brief texts early that morning but she'd heard nothing since. She lay awake, still hoping he'd call, got to sleep around two, slept in late the next morning and was hastily grabbing her coat when her mobile rang. She clutched at it and saw it was him. She pressed the key.

"Morning Jack."

"Cathy, I'm so sorry."

"Jack, I'm late for work. I really don't have time to talk."

"Josie went into labour nearly four weeks early. Did I tell you she was pregnant?" Cathy sat down heavily on the sofa. "No," she squeaked.

"She was in shock when her labour began, so I had to stay with her. We were at her farewell party at a restaurant, the only time we could get everyone together before she left which was supposedly in two week's time. It was after midnight. She said later she'd had a few twinges but ignored them as she had a month to go. We'd all been drinking and the ambulance took ages to arrive. She more or less gave birth in the lift in the maternity wing! It was quite nerve-wracking, especially when I was slightly, no, quite definitely under the influence. I was on automatic pilot for the delivery. I was beyond relieved when we got to the delivery room so the staff could take over!"

Cathy tried to wipe out the pictures that came into her head. "Where was her husband . . . partner?"

"It's a long story. To cut it short—she doesn't have anyone."

"Except you, apparently."

"I didn't have much choice, did I?"

"I don't know; did you?"

"What? No I didn't!"

Cathy closed her eyes. "Sorry. Was everything ok?"

"Yeah, fine. There is a downside, though."

"That was the upside?"

"Well Josie's fine and the baby's fine. I would say that's an upside!"

Cathy bit her lip, "Right. The downside?"

"The weekend after next."

"What about it?"

"She had almost two weeks to work out and now we've had to shuffle everything around. I've lost the weekend I was coming up. No-one else could do it."

"What!"

"I know. I'm as annoyed, frustrated, exasperated—et cetera—as you sound. I came in early this morning and I've just finished sorting it out. They're giving me Thursday and Friday at the end of the week after the lost weekend, and I don't have to be back 'till the following Monday evening. I can be up there by lunchtime on the Thursday. Any good?"

She closed her eyes. "Fine, but I planned to be in Bamburgh by then, probably the Lord Crewe."

"Ah, that'll probably take me till late afternoon, then. I'll drive as fast as I can."

"Don't even think about speeding!"

"No, ma'am!"

She laughed. "That bad, eh?"

"No, I don't mind at all. I'm glad you care enough to worry about me . . . I'll make sure I get to you in one piece. Just one thing before you go. You haven't talked about the flashbacks for a while. Have they gone?"

"Not completely, but I'm thinking about the good times Tom and I had together and concentrating on his good points. Dorothy was so protective and positive about her brother, even though he seemed to play hard and drink hard. My Tom—not exactly an angel of course—was affectionate, generous, easy-going and fun to be with. I've been horribly self-centred thinking only about my part in his death when I should have been thinking more about him. I think it was because my final words were an accusation. I realise now that I meant it as a reluctant giving in to what he wanted. I wish I knew if he took it like that."

"I'm sure he did. He'd know from everything you'd done for him over the years, that you loved him."

"I hope so." She stood up. "Jack, I'm horribly late now. I've got to go."

"Yes; sorry about the change in our plans . . . please take care."

"You too. Bye."

Cathy took a deep breath, picked up her new lap top and silently vowed to spend every spare moment at work getting up to date with her writing. If what she had in mind panned out, Friday would be filled with more than research and writing.

CHAPTER 27

SHOCKING REVELATIONS

In free moments between clients, Cathy plotted what she would do about Jack's birthday. At lunchtime, she went out and bought him a card, an expensive watch which she left to be engraved and some wrapping paper. After work, she went to speak to her manager.

"Maggie, I've a big favour to ask you."

"Oh? Well I'll see what I can do. Explain."

Cathy looked at Maggie's sunny smile and raised eyebrows. "It's Jack's birthday on Friday and I would love to go to London to surprise him. It would mean the whole of Friday off and I'll come back and work Saturday afternoon and come in on Sunday and stay until I've finished all the paperwork."

"Special, is he?"

"Very."

"I thought so, looking at your face every time you talk about him. Well, it'll be six days a week for you after your holiday, and the paperwork you're so good at will have mounted up and all be yours."

"I'll take it home if necessary."

"I'm a pushover for a bit of romance, aren't I?"

"You're just a good boss, Maggie. That's why our staff are so loyal." Maggie tossed her brown curls off her face and fluttered her eyelashes. "Just call me St Maggie. And see if your Jack has a single, rich, handsome and desperate cousin."

◆　　◆　　◆

Cathy glanced at the small packed suitcase as she rang Jack late on Thursday evening after almost four hours writing Dorothy's journal.

"Cathy! I was just going to ring you."

"Hi, Jack. How does it feel to be almost thirty?"

"I told you, I've postponed my birthday. It was going to be the weekend after next until Josie messed up my plans, but now it's got to be the weekend after that. I'll need twice as many presents by then."

"What had you in mind?"

"A glass of wine . . . and you."

"Oh . . . right." Cathy tried not to overreact as she got off the bed and walked into the bathroom. "Hang on a minute while I get into the bath before the bubbles disappear."

"Catherine Adams, what are trying to do to me?"

"Nothing. I just don't want the bath to get cold!"

"Did I tell you I had a vivid imagination?"

"Not that I remember."

"Well I do. Ring me when you're out of the bath next time." He expelled a breath. "Right. I finally found the John Bird booklet about Dorothy and Thomas. It said that it's thought that Dorothy *may* have made the journey to try and free her brother with a local blacksmith called John Armstrong, 'riding pillion'; but I don't know if it's true or just a guess."

"John Armstrong? That's amazing. Brilliant. He's the potential romantic hero in my story, although another blacksmith called Purdy is also mentioned so it's just a feeling. No proof so far."

"Woah! You can't be thinking she'd marry a blacksmith. That's a step too far for those days."

"I know and I could have got it entirely wrong, but I'm going to check it out when I go to Newcastle. I'm banking on finding her marriage at the records office in Morpeth in Northumberland. I've read more about Charles Radcliffe and he's definitely out of the picture as far as any romantic attachment with Dorothy is concerned. So, you've found that Dorothy was possibly clinging to John Armstrong's back as they rode to save her brother. How romantic."

"Romantic? Not riding for three hundred and forty miles in the freezing cold on icy roads, with rough inns, tolls and highwaymen."

"How do you know that?"

"I looked it up on the internet."

"Right. Well, I'm almost at that point again in the new book about the Rebellion. It was well after midnight last night when I finally tore myself away from it. It makes the story of the rebellion and its consequences so fascinating that I've found it difficult to put down. Hard to believe, eh? Me hooked on history! It's confirmed what I suspected about the historically accepted belief about the rebels that they became involved through desperation and with no choice but to fight when the government decided to arrest them."

"Yeah I remember."

"Well, this book totally demolishes those ideas. It shows how extensive and how well planned the whole uprising was and how wealthy and influential almost all of those involved were. I've reached this book's version of Thomas's actions during the campaign and although some of his decisions were a little questionable—partly because of lack of information, poor communication, other people's incompetence or resistance and partly because of so-called supporters letting him down—most of what he did was well thought out and sensible, considering his lack of experience."

Jack laughed. "Wow, I'd like you on my side if I ever need defending!"

"Don't laugh, I'm serious. I think Thomas has been unfairly maligned. Many of those captured *pretended* they hadn't planned the campaign and said they'd been forced into it by stronger wills. Not our Thomas. Now I'm dying to know what the book says about his escape and where it is that he goes."

"I bet it's not back to Bamburgh to hide in the castle for two years!"

"I'll let you know."

"Cathy, I need to sleep now."

"I feel a little drowsy myself."

"Just don't go to sleep in the bath."

Cathy stood up and reached for a towel. "Ok, I'm getting out."

"I wish you hadn't said that."

"Night, Jack, sleep well."

"Oh, Cathy, I just know I'm going to dream."

◆　　◆　　◆

Cathy was on the road by eight the next morning, the route programmed into the GPS stuck onto the shelf beside her. The car was larger than she was used to, but once on the motorway she revelled at its speed and handling. She sat back to enjoy the ride and imagine how surprised Jack would be when she arrived.

Driving in London was not quite as intimidating as she'd expected, but a few scary skirmishes resulting from the wrong choice of lane made her long for a narrow road with no choices to make.

When the sign for the hospital came into view she heaved a sigh of relief. After a few abortive attempts to find the correct car park and work out the ticket machine, she surveyed the buildings and smiled. Inside this forbidding façade was a man whose arms she wanted to be holding her.

She found the Accident and Emergency block, avoided the main doors where ambulances were pulling up and pushed through a smaller door into a long, wide corridor. It was largely empty apart from a smart trouser-suited woman with long, lustrous black hair walking away from her at the far end. Suddenly Jack emerged and ran to the woman with open arms, swung her round and kissed her as he dumped her back on the ground.

The shock of his sudden appearance and what she'd seen made Cathy hesitate. She bit her lip, reluctant to doubt him, but uneasy. She began to walk towards them, straining to hear what was being said and trying to rationalise what she was seeing. *An ex-girlfriend? But why would he be so ecstatic to see her? A family member? His two older sisters were in America and India. Maybe a cousin?*

She came almost to within hearing distance, but they were both wrapped up in talking to each other and Jack's eyes were so focussed on the woman that she began to think she should leave. She shook her head and told herself not to be stupid. She took another few steps and composed herself. "Hello, Jack."

Jack swung round and she saw shock take hold of his features, dissolve into surprise and finally an overpowering joy in a smile that took away her irrational fears.

He ran to her and swept her up in his arms. "My God, what are you doing here?" Before she could answer, he tightened his arms and kissed her deeply until, after what seemed like minutes of light-headed pleasure, he released her mouth and she gasped for breath. "To wish you happy birthday," she said faintly.

"I guess this must be Cathy," the woman said in an accent that had a suggestion of New York in it. Cathy smiled. "Ah. And I guess this must be your sister Sara."

"On the button!" laughed Sara.

Cathy felt a sudden vibration between her and Jack's body. He pulled away as it became a loud buzz, removed a small object and pressed a button. "Oh, sh . . ."

"Shoot?" offered Sara.

"Yeah, something like that. Got to go. Sara, would you take Cathy to my flat?"

"Sure."

"Thanks, sis." He turned to Cathy. "Oh, Cathy, I don't want to go, but I have to. I still can't believe you're here." He got out a bunch of keys, pressed them into her hand and hugged her to him. He kissed her again, briefly, pulled away and ran down the corridor.

Sara smiled. "Well, isn't this nice? You haven't been to his flat yet?"

"No."

"We'll have to take a taxi."

"I've rented a car."

"You have? Oh, great. I'll go get my bags. They're behind the counter in the entrance."

Sara glided along the corridor and round a corner and immediately launched into a request for her bags as the receptionist was trying to placate an irate man. Sara leaned forward. "'Scuse me? I need my bags, now!" The receptionist frowned and lifted open a flap. "Help yourself."

Sara stepped forward and picked up two large suitcases with surprising ease. She clicked out the handles and smiled at Cathy. "Which way to the parking lot?"

Cathy walked through the nearest door and pointed. "Over there."

Sara strode out ahead of her and glanced up at the sky. "Geez, this weather. We shouldn't have to go out in it to find the car. Wouldn't you think they'd have an underground lot?"

"Well, I suppose it would be better, but this hospital has been here a long time, I think. They mightn't have had more than a handful of cars to find spaces for when they built it."

"I guess. It certainly looks pretty ancient from the outside."

"Yes, I suppose it does. How long have you been in America?"

"Oh, must be twelve, thirteen years now. Why?"

"You seem thoroughly Americanised."

"Not to them, I'm not. They still seem to think I'm a Brit, even though I've got U.S. citizenship."

"You're married to an American, Jack said."

"Was. Don't tell my mother. She's still waiting to hear I'm pregnant."

She threw her cases into the boot and slammed it shut, making Cathy wince, and climbed into the passenger seat.

Sara glanced round as they pulled out on to the road. "Stop, stop. Let me think. Right, take a left." Cathy accelerated round the corner. "No! Stop." Cathy glanced in the mirror and screeched to a halt. Sara frowned and looked round. "Ah, this is where we are. I get it. Take a right."

"You're sure?"

"Absolutely."

Cathy kept as cool as she could as Sara continued to issue directions which sometimes meant a sudden change of direction or that they had to reverse to avoid going down one-way streets. "They've changed the damned route I know," Sara complained.

Cathy continued to follow Sara's directions until they turned into a road lined with elegant Edwardian houses. "This is it. I'm just ready for a party, aren't you? I wonder who'll be there. I came back a couple of days early for it. I hope there's plenty of food. I'm famished now, so I can't wait seven hours. Tell you what, we'll get lunch somewhere."

Cathy's stomach lurched. A party? She hadn't been invited to a party.

Surely Jack wouldn't arrange a party and not invite her? Of course he wouldn't. But someone had, and she wasn't invited.

Sara pointed. "He's up on the second floor. I guess you could call it the penthouse, but it's small with only two bedrooms. Let's go up."

"Actually, I'm not sure I should stay."

"What?"

"I don't know anything about a party. Jack didn't . . ."

Sara's mouth dropped open. "But Jack doesn't know anything about it either. My mother's organised the party—with help from Charles. There must be some mistake. Perhaps the invitation has gotten lost in the post. I told her email was a better idea."

Cathy frowned. "Sara, if your Mum didn't invite me, I can't just turn up."

"Most certainly you can! Jack would go ballistic if you're not here when he gets back. Now let's get our things upstairs, then we'll go to the little Bistro just down the road."

Sara got her cases out of the boot, turned on her elegant heels and clicked up the steps.

CHAPTER 28

AN UNINVITED GUEST

Cathy wondered if she was doing the right thing as she followed Sara. It hadn't taken much to persuade her; the last thing she wanted to do was drive back and not see Jack, but a nagging doubt remained. His mother didn't want her there.

"The keys?" Sara was standing with her hand outstretched.

"Oh, yes, sorry." Cathy delved into the pocket in her jeans and smiled as she handed them over.

Sara flung open the door. "Welcome to Jack's. Ok! I guess you'll be in Jack's room so I'll put my cases in the second bedroom."

"Oh, Sara, I don't know if Jack . . ."

"Course he will! I saw that kiss and the look in his eyes."

"No, really, we haven't reached that point."

"Could've fooled me. Especially when he's expecting that he's got you mostly to his self."

"And your Mother?"

"Ah, now, he might have a bit of a problem with her, but nothing he can't fix if he wants to."

◆　　◆　　◆

Cathy hung up the black, low cut top that was meant only for Jack and wished she hadn't been so easily persuaded by Liz to borrow it. She unrolled the black, lacy, almost see-through skirt and laid it on the bed with the black stockings. She went to find Sara.

"Sara, I've got a problem."

"Oh, yeah?"

"Yes. The clothes I've brought are not for a birthday party, especially when your mum and, I suppose, Jack's friends and colleagues are going to be there."

"Oh, right, let's go review the outfit."

Sara smiled as she looked at Cathy's top and skirt. "Oh, I think we can do something with it that will knock them out, but be modest enough for my Mother. I brought you a roll of deep blue cloth near enough the colour of your eyes. It's got gold threads and they'll reflect the lights in Jack's living room beautifully. We'll try it out when we get back from lunch."

"You brought me it, from America?"

"Yeah. Jack told me about you a couple of weeks ago. Actually, I thought he'd had a few too many when he described you, but he got you scarily right. He's nuts about you, isn't he?"

"What?"

Sara put her head on one side. "Well he didn't actually say that, but he hasn't talked about anything else but you for the last few calls."

"Well he hasn't said that to me."

Sara paused. "Well, of course, he had a bad experience a while back, so maybe he's being a bit cautious this time."

◆   ◆   ◆

Sara finished folding and winding the blue material round Cathy and tossed the rest over Cathy's shoulder before securing it at her waist. She stepped back. "What do ya think?"

"Amazing. It doesn't entirely cover my cleavage, but . . ."

"Hey, you don't want to cover up your best assets, although come to think of it, you got more than your fair share of assets."

Cathy laughed. "You're really good for my confidence." She looked at herself again in the mirror. "Am I supposed to have a bare midriff?"

"Sure. It does look different with white skin, but it wouldn't look as good if I hadn't tucked your top into your bra. Bet Jack'll let you know how he feels tonight."

A loud chime sounded and Sara grabbed Cathy's hand and dragged her out of the bedroom to the front door. She swung the door open and beamed. "Mother, how wonderful to see you!" She kissed her on both cheeks.

"Who's this?" The disapproving look on Jack's mother's imperious face sent a cold shiver down Cathy's spine.

"This, Mother dear, is Jack's girlfriend."

"Well . . ." Cathy began.

Jack's mother turned her back on Cathy and confronted Sara. "Girlfriend? The northern girl he met on his trip to Newcastle? Hardly his girlfriend. I didn't know Charles had invited her after I . . ."

"I'm standing right here, Mrs Wood. If you're not happy about it, just say so and I can leave."

"*Doctor* Wood, please."

"Sorry; *Doctor* Wood!"

Jack's mother frowned at Cathy. Sara grabbed her mother's arm and led her to the sofa. "Hold it! Cathy's right to be a little cross. You were talking about her as if she wasn't here. *I* persuaded her to stay after I saw Jack's total delight when she arrived at the hospital after driving all the way down to wish him happy birthday. Apparently, Mother dear, her invitation got lost in the post."

"Oh." Jack's mother turned to Cathy and breathed deeply, her lips pursed. "Well, I suppose you'd better come and sit down. We need to have a talk."

Cathy walked slowly to the sofa and sat down. "What would you like to talk about?"

"First, your family. What does your father do?"

"He's been retired for almost two years."

"I see, and your mother?"

"She too."

"They are old?"

"My mother, fifty-two; my father, sixty-two."

"I'm fifty-five and hope to work for at least another ten years."

"Well, they'd both had enough of working abroad in the diplomatic service. My grandmother died two years ago and my mother wanted to come home and spend time with . . . my brother and me."

"Diplomatic service . . . ah. And what is your degree?"

"I don't have one. I work in a travel bureau."

Sara flopped down on the chair opposite them. "Mother; enough of the inquisition. And Jack told me Cathy is brilliant and gave up doing her degree to look after her fifteen year old brother."

Cathy blinked. "He told you that?"

"Sure he did. That and a lot more. Right, shouldn't we be doing the food, Mother?"

Dr Wood nodded thoughtfully. "Yes, we certainly should. My cases and food boxes are down in the entrance hall. You and she can bring them up, can't you?"

◆   ◆   ◆

Just after six, the flat began to fill with Jack's colleagues and friends. The women were curious about Cathy and the men more familiar than she wanted.

"Jack can pick 'em, eh?"

One of them slipped his arm round her waist. "No point in wasting time when he isn't here, though; I'm Chris."

Cathy took hold of his wandering hand and twisted it behind his back. "I agree. No point in wasting my time." She pulled away and sat down. The space beside her was immediately filled by another of Jack's colleagues. She grimaced as his hand wandered along the back of the sofa and he began to tell her about his day.

"Just before we began an operation, a student nurse rushed in and confessed she'd misunderstood the instructions about operating the autoclave. Stupid cow! We had to postpone the op. and now it'll cost more to keep the patient in an extra night and tomorrow's schedules will be chaos. And she wasn't supposed to be disinfecting the instruments anyway! Probably something to do with the cuts or admin got it wrong. That's the kind of thing we have to put up with! Dance?"

"Actually, I need to speak to Sara."

Sara was deep in conversation with one of Jack's colleagues, so Cathy slipped away, tired of medical chit-chat and unwanted attention, and went into the bedroom and lay on the bed with a book. Not until she heard the front door bell did she emerge into the noisy party.

She watched Jack's mother swing open the door and smother a bewildered-looking Jack in her arms as loud happy birthday wishes rang out. His mother pulled a beautiful, bejewelled woman in a glittering sari in front of him and was obviously introducing them. He nodded and said something, his eyes searching from left to right round the room and finally settling on Cathy. He beamed and strode towards her, wrapped her in his arms and kissed her, accompanied by whoops and whistles from his friends.

He took her face in his hands. "Wow! You look stunning, gorgeous." He stepped back and looked her up and down. "Where did you get this from?"

"Your lovely sister."

Sara appeared beside them. "You like?"

Jack laughed. "What do *you* think? Thanks, sis." He kissed her cheek and looked back at Cathy and pulled her back into his arms. "I should be cross with you. You kept all this from me, didn't you?"

She blinked, "but I didn't . . . I mean . . ." She avoided his eyes.

"Cathy; you didn't what?"

"Um, in your words: it'll keep."

"Cathy, tell me."

"Later, maybe. Let's dance."

He released her, took hold of her hand and pulled her through the door into the corridor. Charles came out of the bathroom at the far end and winked and Jack grimaced, opened the door to his bedroom and pulled her inside.

Cathy gasped at the brusque way he'd handled her. "Please, Jack. People have come for your birthday and you've hardly spoken to anyone."

Jack held her shoulders and looked into her eyes. "Tough. This is more important. Holding things back from me and being evasive is not the way to make a relationship work. And I want it to work."

"What? You've been evasive with me and refused to explain things when we've talked on the phone."

"We're face to face now. It's different. I can see in your eyes something's wrong. I want to know what it is."

"You're making this more serious than it is."

"If it's not serious, what's the problem with telling me?"

Cathy pulled away and sat down on the bed. "Ok, but you won't like it. I didn't know about the party."

"What! Charles organised a party and didn't ask you? I'll kill him!"

"No, it wasn't . . ." She bit her bottom lip.

Jack stared at her for a moment and sat down beside her, breathing heavily. "My mother!" he hissed, "Of course. She had an agenda. Sunita."

"Sunita? Is she that beautiful woman your mother shoved in front of you?"

He nodded. "She's the younger sister of a woman my mother tried to marry me off to, five or six years ago. Then there was another when I was already seeing, um . . . someone else."

"Someone else? Does she have a name?" Cathy tried to look into his eyes, but he looked away and stood up. "You don't need to know. It doesn't matter. Let's go back in." He strode to the door and opened it. Cathy walked through the door, turned back and put her hand on his chest. "Stop. Are you sure you're not keeping something back from me now?"

He looked down at her. "Just remember I want this relationship to work."

"So you said." She turned and walked quickly into the sitting room and pushed through the crowd of swaying dancers to the kitchen at the other end.

Jack caught up with her as she reached for some champagne. "I thought we were dancing."

"I want a drink."

"Let me do it for you."

"It's already open. I can manage." She poured her drink and sipped it before it bubbled over the top of her glass. She walked out as Jack poured his own.

Cathy sat down on the empty sofa, staring ahead. The door bell rang again. She watched Jack go to the door, glass in hand, and open it as the music stopped. A startlingly attractive, golden-blonde haired woman with ruby red lips swept through the door. "Jack, darling, happy birthday!" She flung her arms round his neck and kissed him full on the lips.

He pulled back. "Josie! I didn't know you were . . ."

She linked her arm through his. "I heard about it, so of course I had to come. I wouldn't miss your birthday party, would I?" Suddenly she pulled away, went back through the door and picked up a baby carrier. She handed it to Jack. "Put William Jack in your bedroom, will you? Oh, and you must remind me to get my winter coat from your wardrobe before I leave. It's getting colder!"

There was a collective holding of breaths as eyes looked in Cathy's direction and she felt as if she'd been punched in the ribs. Jack looked grim as he picked up the baby carrier and walked towards the bedroom. Cathy stood up, downed her drink and made for the corridor. She passed the door to the bedroom, where Jack was putting the carrier on her bed, and walked into the bathroom.

She decided she had to leave. She waited until she heard Jack close the two doors and slipped out. In the room, she got out her case and took her clothes out of the wardrobe. She unclipped the clasp at her waist and quickly unwound the material until she was left in her own clothes. She took off her black top as the door opened and Jack walked in.

"Please leave," she said, coolly. She pulled on her woollen sweater as he reached her and put his arms round her. She tried to pull away but he held her tightly. "Cathy, please listen to me."

"Why on earth should I? All that rubbish about not being evasive and keeping things from each other. You and Josie. That's where you got 'darling' from. How could you!"

"Cathy, I'm sorry, but it's complicated. I was going to explain later when we were alone. And I never called her darling!"

"But she called you 'darling'. Let go of me. I need to finish packing."

"Please, Cathy. Please don't go."

Cathy struggled out of his arms and resumed packing.

CHAPTER 29

PAIN

Cathy looked up as Jack sat down on the bed and put his head in his hands. His shoulders sagged and she felt a pain in her stomach. She packed her black top and slowly zipped up the case. He looked up. There were tears in his eyes. Knowing very well she shouldn't, she couldn't stop herself going to him and pulling his head against her. "Oh, Jack, please don't cry."

He wrapped his arms round her for a few moments. Suddenly he looked up, pulled her on to his knee and buried his face against her neck. She stroked his hair, feeling his pain. He looked up. "Have I blown it?"

She couldn't think how to answer him. The sensible thing to do was to walk away, but she wanted his arms round her and his lips on hers. "I don't know. You were my rock. I thought you were perfect. And a few minutes ago you made me feel bad for not explaining about your mother and all the time you were hiding your relationship with Josie. How do I deal with that?"

"My relationship with Josie is over; was over more than a year ago."

"She doesn't seem to think so, and you still seem very involved."

"Look, I can tell you everything if you want me to, but I'd rather not. I'd rather concentrate on us."

"I'm not sure there is any 'us.'" The words came out before she had time to think what she was saying. She felt him flinch. He moved her off his knee and stood up. He held her shoulders and looked into her eyes. "Do you really mean that, or are you just trying to punish me?"

She blinked hard as tears began to ooze from her eyes and he sighed and wrapped his arms round her and pulled her against him, her head against his chest. They remained unmoving, until William Jack stirred and began to whimper.

They both looked anxiously at the snuffling baby. A knock on the door startled them, but the baby settled back to sleep.

Jack went to the door. "Who is it?"

"Sara."

"Come in."

Sara came in and stared at both their faces and the blue material on the bed. "Oh, Cathy, ignore drama queen Josie. She knew what she was doing with that kiss and that coat line." She looked at Jack. "And you should stop playing the pathetic fall guy. It's time she found someone else to lean on."

Jack rolled his eyes. "Geez, Sara, you make me feel about two years old. It's not that simple."

"It's perfectly simple. Tell her it's time she moved on because you have— you can still be a friend, but that's all you'll ever be. Slip a shiny ring on Cathy's finger. Josie'll soon notice."

"Anything else, sister dear?"

Sara smiled. "That's all!" She turned away.

"Sara, wait!"

"Yep!"

A smile crossed Jack's face. "Tell Josie that William Jack's crying, will you?"

"But he isn't."

"Just pass on the message, Sara."

Sara shrugged her shoulders and nodded.

Jack led Cathy back to her case. She looked at him. "William Jack's asleep."

"Yes." He unzipped her case and pulled out the black top. "Put your arms up."

"What?"

Jack lifted up Cathy's arms and pulled her sweater off before she could react with more than a quick gasp. His ran his eyes over her, dropped her top and pulled her to him. He kissed her deeply, entwining his tongue with hers.

Suddenly the door flew open and someone walked in. Cathy opened her eyes and saw Josie standing there, her mouth opening and closing. Jack released Cathy's mouth and the iron grip he had on her body and turned.

"Ah, sorry Josie. He seems to have gone to sleep again." He turned back to Cathy and picked up her top. "I think you should put this on before we go back in."

When Cathy looked again, Josie had gone. She pushed Jack away angrily. "That was brutal! And you used me to hurt her!" She slipped the top on, walked to the window and rested her hands on the windowsill to stop herself from trembling.

He turned her round to face him. "Cathy, I'm sorry but I've tried again and again, as kindly as I could, to tell her we're never going to get back together. Maybe this time, she'll believe me."

Cathy turned back to the window, still shocked and seething. "You used me!"

He stood close against her back, wrapped his arms round her and kissed the back of her neck. "Please forgive me. It was a stupid thing to do. I didn't think it through. She hurt you and I wanted to hurt her."

Cathy turned her head. "It was you who hurt me, by not telling me the truth about her. All she did was fight for what she wanted . . . you!"

Jack tried to kiss her cheek, but she turned away. "Don't!"

He pulled his arms away and she heard him expel a breath. She closed her eyes in an agony of indecision and realised she could have stopped him kissing her after Sara left, but didn't; she'd instantly forgotten Josie might appear, so perhaps he had. She turned round slowly and saw the misery in his eyes.

"Oh Cathy, I've really messed up this time, haven't I?"

"Yes you have. What you did was wrong."

"Yes." He turned away, his head down and leant his hands against the wall.

Cathy suddenly realised she didn't want to hurt him. "I hope you realise you've got a lot of making up to do, to both of us."

He turned round and a smile flickered across his face as he locked his eyes on hers. "Does this mean you haven't given up on me?"

She raised her eyebrows, shrugged her shoulders and gave a quick smile. "Let's just say I'm putting it on the backburner, for now!"

There was a knock on the door. "Jack!"

"Come in Sara."

Sara popped her head round the door. "You absence has been noted and Mum wants you to come and cut the cake."

"Right. Just have to get this sari back on and we'll be in."

"Oh no, Mum's a stickler for getting the folds right. I'll do it and we'll be out in a moment and, Jack, I'm afraid she has plans to make a bed for you on the sofa, so if you had any ideas about getting together, you'll have to wait until she and I go to Bedford tomorrow."

Cathy caught Jack's surprised glance and smiled. "Jack has work early tomorrow and I'm going back to Harrogate. I have to be at work at 2 p.m. . . . so we'll have to put that idea on the back burner."

◆   ◆   ◆

Charlie came across as Cathy and Sara entered the room. "Sorry about the invitation, Cathy. I did try, but well . . . you understand, don't you, Sara; it's not easy to go against what your mother wants."

Cathy smiled, "And after my mum bribed you with a roast lunch and apple pie! How could you?"

"Yeah, well, Jack's mad at me as well for not telling him about it. He cornered me this afternoon and made me promise to take Sara out to dinner—Ade's on duty—so you could be alone and I still didn't tell him."

"So he wanted rid of me, did he?" Sara stood with her arms folded.

Charlie's eyes widened. "Oh, God, Sara, only after he'd had a couple of hours with you! Don't be mad at him."

Sara laughed. "Chill out, Charlie. I'd already had my welcome home."

◆   ◆   ◆

Jack followed Cathy into the bedroom after the last party-goer left. "I need my clothes for the morning," he said, loud enough for his mother to hear. He shut the door and took Cathy in his arms. "Do I take it from what Sara said that you were expecting to sleep with me tonight."

"I didn't expect anything until you kissed me at the hospital. And then

I found out about the party and nearly went home."

"What?"

"I didn't think I was wanted! By your mother, anyway."

"I'd have been devastated if you'd gone."

"Well I was upset. I thought it would only be the two of us, then there were three and then a roomful, including your mother!"

"I know. I thought of nothing else all afternoon. I even called at the chemist on the way home. I kind of assumed you wouldn't be on the pill."

"No, I'm not. I did the same yesterday."

"Oh, Cathy, I do want you, but not like this. I'd feel like a naughty child, creeping around and keeping quiet and imagining my mother giving us both looks of disapproval—at the very least—in the morning. And it's already after one and I have to be up at six . . . and I want it to be a relaxed, beautiful experience."

"As I said to Sara: another thing we'll have to put on the 'back burner.'"

He smiled. "You have no idea how much I wish I'd never said that."

She laughed. "You will wake me before you go, won't you?"

"Oh, yes; I need a glimpse of that slip you wear to get me through the day."

CHAPTER 30

DISAPPOINTING NEWS

1715

For ten days, I heard nothing of the band of hopefuls. On the evening of the fifteenth of October, Lee arrived. I led him to a seat by the fire and threw a blanket over his shoulders. I made him sip a hot drink of bramble juice until he regained some feeling in his hands. He looked up at me. "My master wanted you to be acquainted with what has taken place. We have assembled at Hexham."

"Hexham! But why? I thought the first object was to take Newcastle."

"Aye, it was, but we've been beset with disappointments." He sighed. "At first all went well." He took another sip and looked up at me. "From Greenriggs our party of sixty horses met west of Rothbury, with those of like mind from Coquetdale. Many others would have joined us as infantrymen, but they had no weapons so it was decided not to take them with us until Newcastle had fallen. We needed the arms we would capture, you see, and anyway the agreed plan was not to begin until we were joined by the forces from the Earl of Mar."

I nodded. "Yes, that had some logic."

"Aye, well my master sent messages by sea to Mar reporting we had only one hundred and sixty horses and that he had sent messages to those in Lancashire and the Scottish border that they should join us. My master also told him that Newcastle had promised to open its gates to him but he would need reinforcements of at least two thousand foot and five hundred horse."

I rested my hand on his arm to halt his account. "You mentioned they had only one hundred and sixty horses. Where were those from all the families across Northumberland and Durham who promised help?"

Lee bowed his head and looked at the floor. "Many did not come."

"Go on."

"We stayed the night in Rothbury, mostly in the public houses. We later discovered that a man whose house was used to billet a dozen or more men, rode to Newcastle to tell them we had risen. Anyhow, James III was proclaimed in Rothbury and Warkworth. We camped on Lesbury Common. My master saw it as a good place to wait for reinforcements, it being easy for the Scottish troops to reach us from the border and yet only thirty miles march south to Newcastle. My master expected forces from France to land nearby in Alnmouth as that had been Mar's original plan. But we waited almost a week and no-one came from Mar or from the sea."

Lee paused in his narrative and stared into the fire. Suddenly he seemed to rally and smiled up at me. "The Widdringtons brought nigh on thirty horses from Widdrington castle, but even with all of these, we were still not more than three hundred horses. The Earl and my master had thought that by now our strength would be a thousand horses. It was a great disappointment . . . but worse was to come." He paused again to sip some of the soothing drink. I sat down, my heart heavy, willing him to continue.

He sighed and began again. "On the Saturday—the eighth of October I think—our agent Lisle was sent to Newcastle to see how things were, and did not return, so it was thought he was captured."

He looked at me, seeming to try to put a brave face on it. "We had some good news on the tenth. Lancelot and Mark Errington led the capture of the castle on Holy Island. We needed the island as a base to send signals to the ships expected to arrive there from abroad. But our attention was taken from that exploit when it was learned that the advance guard from the government's Regiment of Foot had passed through Newcastle and were advancing upon us with great speed."

I gasped. "Were any taken?"

"They did not reach us. At first my master did not believe this intelligence. He said he would have known about it from his spies scattered about the region. But at last he was persuaded by Lord Widdrington to send a troop to contain the government guard at Felton Bridge. This they did, but they knew there must be more foot and probably many dragoons on their way."

"When was this?"

"Two or three days ago. We should have gone into action on the eleventh, but by the thirteenth, with no others joining us, no signs of reinforcements by sea, nothing from Scotland and then the news that Holy Island had been retaken by government troops from Berwick, we had no choice but to leave. We proclaimed James III in Alnwick and Morpeth."

Lee turned to me, an anxious look on his face. "My master was still confident that if we went to Newcastle our friends and allies would open the gates to us. Blackett had assured us he would rally the keelmen and many others loyal to the Cause, y'see. But we had intelligence that no such thing had happened and even that some of the keelmen had helped take the cannon from Tynemouth to Newcastle for the government, so they deemed it safer to retire to Hexham for the present. It is an easy journey east to Newcastle, is it not?"

I nodded, stood up and began to pace the room. "What is their intention now?"

"No plans have been made as yet, but the troops are glad to be back where many of them are on home ground and they can rest and regroup. My Lord Derwentwater has gone to Dilston; my master sent Charles Widdrington back to Manchester to persuade the Lancastrians to rise immediately and again he sent dispatches to Scotland to encourage the Scots to join us. We cannot understand why Macintosh is so delayed. Mar promised his advance some time ago."

I looked at Lee and saw the weariness in his eyes. "Will you stay the night in a comfortable bed?" He shook his tousled head. "No, mistress, I must return now. We do not know what the morrow will bring."

Before Lee left, I made sure he took with him bread, cheese, boiled beef and some pickles. I waved him off into the cold darkness with a note for Thomas full of love and good wishes. I made no reference to their situation for fear Lee would be taken and the government learn of their plight. I walked slowly into the parlour and sat beside the fire, staring into the flickering flames until Joseph persuaded me to retire to my room.

I lay in bed fretting about their seemingly hopeless situation and fervently hoping the government troops would stay in Newcastle and not proceed to Hexham before Thomas's force moved on. I thought about James who must now be with Anna Maria. I wondered if the countess still felt as much enthusiasm for their undertaking.

I grasped the quilt and felt the need to be positive. Tomorrow I would go to church before the service and pray for their deliverance and—God willing—their victory. I would visit the Countess the following Monday, despite having received no invitation, because the Earl would have returned to his pitiful army and Anna Maria would surely be feeling low.

I lay for a while unable to sleep, my mind going through what Lee had said and though I tried to resist it, my attempt to raise my spirits began to fail. I was forced to admit that victory seemed to have become a faint hope.

I rode to Dilston in bright sunshine on Monday October 17th. The cold weather had not relented but the sun lifted my spirits, and as I had heard nothing to the contrary, I assumed that nothing untoward had happened.

I was ushered into the nursery by Betty and found the countess playing on the floor with her son John. She sprang up when she saw me and ran to embrace me. Her familiarity surprised me. She clutched at my hands. "Dear Dorothy, I am so glad to see you. I got your message from Betty and James also said to send for you, but I feared that your reluctance for their venture and then what has happened since, might have angered you."

I looked into Anna's pretty face. Her eyes were filled with anxiety and she looked even younger than her twenty-two years. I smiled as brightly as I was able. "I am not angry and I am not against what they are doing. In fact I am all for it. I merely questioned the timing of the venture. I did not come before because I thought it was not my place to come unbidden."

Anna's face relaxed. She called the nurse to take charge of her son, grasped my arm and led me to the drawing room. She beamed at me. "James came to be with me last Saturday. We talked late into the night and hardly slept. I knew most of what had transpired; James has kept me well informed. But I must confess that I was surprised that they had retreated to Hexham. He seems not to be fully in agreement with some of the decisions Thomas has made, but believes that the Scots will join them ere long and they will soon march on Newcastle and take it."

She flopped onto the sofa. "Did I tell you that I am with child again? No, I can see by your expression that I did not. It hardly shows. James is delighted. He and I were reminiscing about our youth in St Germain-en-Laye and the walks we used to take in the gardens and woods of the Chateau. Yesterday we vowed that one day we will take both our children there. I was schooled in my later years at a convent in the town but spent my weekends at the Chateau. It was so beautiful. We would walk along the low walls on the west side of the estate and look down to the River Seine and Paris in the distance beyond. The city used to shimmer in the heat of the day and even at a distance we could see how fine its buildings were. At the time I was one of many young ladies who attended the Prince and his cousins, but I only had eyes for my James even then. He told me on Saturday that he had always felt the same, even before our betrothal."

A look of anxiety suddenly clouded her face and she stood up. Her hands grasped the front of her bodice and then covered her mouth. "Oh Dorothy, I hope this business will soon be over. Surely those that have held back will see their mistake and rally to the Cause?"

I struggled to find words to comfort her. "I hear Charles Widdrington has gone to alert the Lancastrians and I know that Thomas has again sent messages to ask the Scots to join them immediately. As the numbers grow, perhaps it will attract the ditherers."

Anna Maria's face broke into a smile. "Yes, yes; that will surely happen."

The door opened and Betty entered with a tray of food and drink. She put it down on a side table and stood with her hands on her sturdy hips, a look of stern concern on her face. "P'raps, Mistress Forster, you can persuade m'lady to take some sustenance. She hasn't eaten enough to keep a sparrow alive this last week or so, when she should be eating enough for two."

I nodded. "We will both eat your delicious offerings. Is that not so, m'lady?" Anna nodded and smiled.

◆   ◆   ◆

I left Anna Maria with a promise that I would visit regularly and did so twice within a week. On the Friday—the first of my two visits—I learned that Thomas and the others had left Hexham somewhat hurriedly on the Tuesday evening. Thomas had received news that the government's army had come together under Carpenter and had reached Newcastle; the city was fully defended and more troops were on their way. What was more, Cotesworth had been given permission to gather together his own forces to seek the so-called rebels and attempt either to take them or to scatter them widely so that they had no chance to become a threatening force.

Thomas, Widdrington, James and Charles concluded they could not now succeed at the objectives they had been given. As they ate their supper, news arrived that Lord Kenmure had reached Rothbury from Scotland. Thomas at once struck camp and gave orders to move there. He also sent messages that they should all later meet up with the other Scottish forces under Macintosh at Coldstream on the border between England and Scotland.

Anna Maria tried to make the best of the news as she related it to me. "It would have been so much more dangerous to attack the city with so many defences in place. On the borders we can fight them on territory familiar to our army but which will seem confusing, bleak and dangerous to the government forces."

I nodded and tried not to show the concern I felt. "When they are a larger force," I began, "they may draw Carpenter away from Newcastle and be able to sneak another way and catch the city unawares."

Anna Maria clapped her hands. "Yes, yes. I think that is how it may be."

The nurse brought young John to eat with us, and later we wrapped up well and took a turn round the elevated gardens that were bathed in wintry sun. The Countess began to talk of how good life would be when it was all over. "No doubt we shall be called to court in London and will partake of all the pomp and ceremony that is so lacking at the present time. We will have no-one there who cannot speak English. Even our French cousins will be prevailed upon to learn it, although we will keep a good facility in the French tongue—James and I speak it to each other quite often—for it will help in keeping good relations with France."

I smiled and kept my counsel. I felt they were a long way from making such plans, but if it pleased the countess to talk of such things I was happy to let her continue.

My second visit in pouring rain on Sunday 23rd October brought news of a personal nature so shocking that the snippets of news on the progress of the loyal band later seemed of little consequence.

The countess' news—which she had learnt just that morning—had done little to alleviate her fears for her husband. Observers on the coast had reported that earlier in the previous week, King James and the allies in the ships from France, receiving no welcoming signals from Holy island, had moved on, and this filled her with anxiety. It was hoped that the ships had continued north to Scotland but nothing was known for certain.

There being little else to talk about and the countess in rather low spirits, I was considering taking my leave when Betty came in unbidden saying that a gentleman from Adderstone had arrived to see me.

The tall, burly figure of my dear friend John Armstrong, followed by a younger and slighter youth, entered the room. John bowed to the countess and turned to me. I looked at the troubled expression on his handsome face and my pleasure at seeing my friend and my curiosity to know why he'd come, turned to apprehension. I sprang up. "John, is it my father? Is he ill?"

"No, Dor . . . Mistress Forster. Please sit down. This young lad has ridden with great haste from your uncle's house at Stene. He went to Adderstone to find you. When he came to have his horse shod, I offered to take him by the quickest route to Blanchland, but we met with her ladyship's butler, Thompson, as we crossed the bridge from Corbridge. He told me you were here."

I sat down, my face feeling numb, and looked first at the youth and then back to John's unwavering gaze. "You have found me. What is your news?"

"It is your aunt, the Lady Crewe."

I sprang up again. "She is ill?"

John moved closer, a look of sadness on his face. "Oh, Dorothy, you must prepare yourself for a shock. I'm so sorry to have to tell you . . . that your aunt passed away a week ago to this day."

As John's face swam before my eyes, my head buzzed and I felt strong arms take hold of me as I passed into darkness.

CHAPTER 31

GRIEF

I felt myself being lowered onto a seat and sniffed the overpowering aroma of smelling salts. A rough hand gently lifted a lock of hair from my forehead and I opened my eyes and looked up into John Armstrong's concerned grey eyes. I remembered at once what he had said: my aunt was dead. It seemed impossible. I had realised she was not as strong as she used to be, but not that she was near death. I raised myself up.

"How, John?"

He waved the youth forward. "Will, give Mistress Forster the letter." Will moved forward hesitantly, and thrust an envelope into my hand. I turned it over and saw the seal of Lord Crewe. My hands shook as I pulled it open. The letter was dated October 17th and had no personal greeting.

'It is with the deepest sadness that I must inform you of the death of your Aunt, my beloved wife Dorothea, on the sixteenth day of October. The deep concern and agitation caused by the knowledge that the King's messengers were seeking to arrest your brother sent her into convulsions from which she did not recover.

You may continue to use the residences at Bamburgh and Blanchland for the present. My page William has some money to alleviate your present situation. Think not to receive more, excepting—for the sake of your Aunt's love for you—a portion of the revenues you collect for me which will be yours until I am with her once again.'

I turned the letter over but there was no more. No signature and no mention of my name. Tears sprung to my eyes and the letter dropped from my fingers. Will knelt down to pick it up.

"If you please, Mistress Forster, I'm to see it burnt before I leave and to give this purse to you."

I looked at the purse and turned away. Anna Maria came forward and offered her kerchief. I took it gratefully and dabbed my eyes. I turned back to Will. "Burn it, if you must."

He came forward and placed the purse in my lap and went to the fireplace where he stood for a moment. He turned back to me. "Would you read it again before I burn it, mistress?"

I shook my head. "No. The words are imprinted on my heart."

I sat in a daze. The Countess summoned Betty and asked her to give Will food and a bed for the night and to prepare a room for me. I stood up. "No, I cannot stay, I must go back to Blanchland, or perhaps, Adderstone, or . . . Bamburgh . . ." I turned to John. "Does my sister Margaret know?"

"No, only the family at Adderstone. I can take the news to her if you wish, perhaps tomorrow, after I take you to Blanchland. You can collect your thoughts there and take time to decide where you would go next. But this night, you must stay here."

His tone was gentle, but firm, and I knew he was right and was grateful he was making the decision for me. I nodded, unable to say more. Betty stood, her hand on the door. "I'll have the fire in your room blazing before y'can climb the stairs!" She turned to the Countess. "Will I find a place for John Armstrong to bed down, m'lady?"

Anna Maria looked uncertain. It was obvious she found it hard to place him in his correct station in life. I stepped forward, unable to stop my voice wavering as I spoke. "He is a man of property and should be treated as such, if you will."

John smiled gently at me and we both failed to acknowledge that his property was the smithy he worked in and the small room behind it.

◆   ◆   ◆

The following few days were an unhappy blur of grief and fatigue. The only constant comfort was the presence of John Armstrong.

He was gone only three hours on the day after we returned to Blanchland. He instructed Cissy to take over his job of sitting with me and persuading me to take some sustenance to regain my strength while he went to sister Margaret's home in Low Staward.

I found it hard to understand why the short journey from Dilston had taken such a surprising toll on me. All my strength seemed to have gone and I found it difficult to take more than the occasional drink of herbal tea or chicken broth. I wondered if I should try to send word to Thomas. I did not see it would do any good, but felt it wrong for the news to be kept from him. There was no reason to tell him the cause of our aunt's death. He was not as fond of her as I had been, so it would not be so great a blow.

At the end of the week James's valet, Wesby, arrived with news he had recently brought to the Countess. He said Anna Maria had asked him to inform me of it before he returned to his master.

I was relieved to hear that on the previous Saturday, October 22nd, Thomas's party and Kenmure's troop had at last met up with the main body of Scottish reinforcements under Macintosh's command in Kelso on the Scottish side of the border. Wesby confided that James had been extremely annoyed to learn that Macintosh's frustratingly late arrival to join them had been caused by his failed and unplanned for attempt to threaten Edinburgh. Now that they were in Scotland, Kenmure had assumed overall command which would only be relinquished to Thomas if they crossed back over the border.

I wondered how Thomas would take his sudden demotion. It seemed unnecessary to me and quite possibly disturbing to the troops. Wesby smiled at me. "My mistress felt that such good news would help lift your mood. She said that if you felt well enough to come tomorrow, she would be pleased to see you."

I rose from my chair and walked slowly to the window. I suddenly realised I had a great need to return home. "Thank her Ladyship for her kind thoughts. Please inform her that I am to begin my journey to Bamburgh tomorrow and will call on my way."

◆   ◆   ◆

As John and I came within sight of Dilston the following morning, I steadied my horse and brought him to a halt. "Oh, John, I cannot separate that place from the news of my aunt's death. This is the first unhappy death connected with the campaign. I cannot help wondering how much more pain and grief this whole undertaking may cause." I turned to him. "Should we have left well alone? Should we have left the foreign usurper to his uncomfortable throne until such time as a new king was needed?"

John looked steadily at me. His eyes were full of compassion and his look gave me a strange feeling of comfort. "I cannot answer your question. I lack the knowledge to understand the fervour which seems to grip those who would rebel. I am a simple man who wants nothing more than to earn his daily bread and lead a quiet, untroubled life. I have no wish to fight, unless in defence of my home and family."

I pondered his words. "You live alone, John."

He looked away. "Aye, I do. But, God willing, I hope that will not always be the case."

I kicked Chestnut into action and we moved on down the track. I found John's simple philosophy comforting. We'd been friends for many years, yet rarely talked about personal matters. I enjoyed helping him learn to read, but we talked mainly about books or discussed any difficulties I might be having as mistress of Thomas's domains. He'd come to Bamburgh at the age of sixteen at the same time that Thomas and I took up residence at the manor, and he remained with Purdy until he became smith at Adderstone five or six years previously. I glanced at his handsome profile and yet again was somewhat surprised that he should have reached the age of twenty-six without being caught by one of the unmarried women in the area.

Adderstone was only a hamlet but there were a good many villages and towns in the area that held fairs and fetes where girls and women were on the look-out for striking young men like John. Gypsies often appeared at such gatherings and cast spells to bring the women luck in finding husbands. I often mused how it would be to live such a life. I sometimes felt trapped in my social circle and the demands that I be limited to those deemed to be of my own class. How much simpler to be free to join in those festivities and the rituals of the games that my servants took part in to find their partners!

We entered Dilston Hall just after midday and found to my dismay that a party was in progress. I felt it inappropriate that I should be part of such festivities so soon after my aunt's death. We were ushered into the dining hall where the table groaned with meats, poultry and piles of sweetmeats.

Anna Maria spied me and rushed over to greet me. "Good news, good news, Dorothy. We heard yesterday that the government's troops under Carpenter are exhausted after searching for our army in alien and difficult countryside, and are so inferior in numbers that we can now defeat them and go on to take Newcastle. We held a party last night and are having a celebration luncheon before the remaining guests leave." She clapped her tiny hands together and beamed at me. "Are you not pleased, Dorothy? Newcastle will be ours, London will soon after admit defeat and the whole country will come over to us. Do sit down and eat. You look as if you have been starving yourself."

I looked round at the noisy revellers and shook my head. "I cannot stay, I have some distance to ride today, but I wished to bid you farewell for the present. I am returning to Bamburgh."

The look of disappointment on the Countess's face almost made me waver. "Oh, but I thought I might persuade you otherwise. Who will I have to share my thoughts with and celebrate the successes?"

I waved my arm towards the happy company quaffing their drink and laughing with such abandon. I forced a smile. "You will not be alone. And it is not so far. Your carriage would reach our home in a day or two if you wish to sample our hospitality. I may return shortly, but I have been away from Bamburgh too long. There will be much to do."

Anna Maria shrugged her shoulders and gave a weak smile. "If you have made your decision I should not try to change it. We will throw another party when all is won. I shall expect you to attend. God speed you on your journey."

We embraced and I left the room, thankful to be away from the noise of revelry. I found John in the entrance hall, gnawing on a chicken leg. "You may stay if you wish, John, but I cannot."

He looked taken aback, threw the bone into a soup bowl and followed me out. "Do you think I would stay for the sake of a meal when you have such a journey before you?"

I was startled by the hurt and anger in his voice. I watched him stride across the courtyard to the stables and bring out our horses. He helped me mount and I took the whip from his hand. "I did not mean to upset or insult you, John."

He bowed his head. "I know. Forgive me; I should not have spoken to you in that manner." He paused and looked up. "I think we should stop at the King's Head in Corbridge. You should eat before we continue further."

I nodded and he swung onto his saddle and kicked his horse into a gentle trot. I followed, grateful he did not canter, for a trot was all I could manage.

Later, in the gloom of dusk at Capheaton, we found shelter for the night and were given assurances that any news would be brought to Callaly and on to the smithy at Adderstone. John Armstrong promised he would then convey it to me in Bamburgh.

Late on Sunday evening we rode into Bamburgh and as our horses climbed the hill to the village I bit my chapped lips and felt tears coursing down my cheeks.

John saw to it that I was fed and warmed by a blazing fire and stayed long enough to drink some hot spiced punch, but insisted he must return to Adderstone. He had been away from his work long enough. His customers would be impatient if he stayed longer.

I stood up and thanked him for all he had done and squeezed his large strong hand between my small white ones. He hesitated, clasped his free hand against mine, bowed his farewell and was gone without a word. Only then did I realise how much I would miss him.

CHAPTER 32

AFTER THE PARTY

2005

"Morning gorgeous!"

Cathy surfaced, feeling Jack's lips on hers. "Mm. Morning." She forced her eyes open and blinked. "What time is it?"

"Nearly seven. Got to go in a couple of minutes."

Cathy sat up and flung her arms round his neck. "You can't. You should have woken me up and I'd have had breakfast with you."

"Looking like that? I don't think so. I wouldn't have made it into work. Anyway, my mother was up making breakfast—and checking I slept on the sofa—when I woke."

Cathy giggled, "Mothers can make you feel like a child again, can't they?"

"Well, it's easier to take the line of least resistance and keep her happy." He kissed her again and hugged her close. "So, have you forgiven me for last night's horrible mistakes?"

"Wait a minute." She kissed him. "Yes, I seem to have."

He smiled. "Text me before you set off and when you get there. I'll be a nervous wreck till you do."

"I'm a good driver!"

"Maybe, but others aren't. Take great care."

◆　　◆　　◆

After a leisurely breakfast, Sara saw Cathy to her car. "I do hope you and Jack work out. Josie was so devious. I don't know how any self-respecting woman could try to trap a man into marrying her by pretending she was on the pill. I mean, I'm sorry she miscarried and all that and I'm sure Jack was wonderful about it all but . . . Oh my God, your face! He didn't tell you."

Cathy shook her head as her body went into shock.

Sara looked panic stricken. "Oh, but I'm sure he would have if you'd had more time alone. Oh, shoot! I'm such a loose mouth. I'm sorry."

"It's ok. Not your fault. Thanks for everything."

"Cathy, I think we should go for a coffee before you set off; give you time to get over this before you brave the traffic."

"No, really, I'm fine. I'll take it easy. Bye Sara. Enjoy your holiday."

◆   ◆   ◆

Cathy sat in the car and texted Jack. "Setting off."

He texted a reply almost immediately. "Thanks, I was beginning to think something had happened. Is everything ok? xxx".

"Fine".

Her phone rang before she had time to switch it off. She frowned. "What?"

"What on earth's wrong?"

"Jack, I'm running late. I don't have time to talk now."

"Don't do this to me. Tell me what's wrong."

"Just something you forgot to tell me."

"About what?"

"Can we talk when I get to work? I should be on my way by now."

She heard him sigh. "Promise to tell me later, then."

"I will."

"Right. Take care."

"Yes. Talk to you later." She switched off her mobile and set off. It took a supreme effort to make herself concentrate on her driving and forget she'd broken her own rule. The engraving on the watch she'd left for Jack haunted her. She'd committed herself; revealed the depth of her feelings before she was certain she'd fallen for someone she could spend her life with and, more importantly, someone who loved her enough to be completely honest with her. She felt sick at the thought.

◆   ◆   ◆

Cathy went into her office and switched her mobile on. She texted Jack. 'Back. In office. Very busy.'

He rang immediately. "Oh, Cathy, thank God you're back safely. We need to talk."

"I've got a lot to do."

"Well, I'm in the office now doing case notes, but I'm making time to talk. And so are you."

"But . . ."

"No buts. Sara rang."

"Oh."

"Yes, it is quite an 'oh' and I'm sorry you had to find out like that. I was hoping to explain everything when we were alone together in Bamburgh, but instead you got half of it last night and the worst bit this morning. Cathy, we didn't actually live together, just sometimes at her place and sometimes mine and then not very often."

"I don't think I want to know."

"Well, as my relationship with her didn't mean that much to me, I didn't really want to tell you, but I have to now. Please listen."

Cathy closed her eyes. "Go on."

"Well, Josie was in a hell of a state after she lost the baby. I was mad at her for deliberately trying to get pregnant to make me feel I had to commit, but I couldn't end our relationship when she was so vulnerable. We stayed in a casual, platonic relationship for almost six months until I hoped she could take it. I told her it was over and she went a little crazy and had a few flings. She ended up with a married doctor and after a couple of months got pregnant again. When he found out, he said she'd better get rid of it or they were finished. She refused and he dumped her. I felt responsible, Cathy. So I said I'd be there for her if she needed help. Big mistake. She actually wanted to move in last June, so I explained again that all we'd ever be was friends. Obviously, she didn't accept it. Until maybe last night, seeing us kiss."

"Oh."

"Just 'oh'?"

"I'm not sure what else to say. I'm sorry if you've been worried about my drive back, but I needed time to think things through."

"Oh, Cathy, I'm sorry it upset you and that you had to find out about it from Sara. It's the last thing I wanted to happen. Am I forgiven?"

"I've got a lot to think about; all that stuff about not holding things back or being evasive. But I guess . . . what you did for Josie was just you being you."

He was silent for a few moments. "So I'm not forgiven?"

"I'll probably forgive you in the end; I need to think some more. Your world is so different to mine in so many ways."

"My world? Are you talking about my mother?"

"No; London and the entangled world the medical profession seem to live and work in. I heard some of their macho conversations before you arrived. But not your Josie bit."

"So do you mean the fact that I'll be seeing Josie when she returns to work?"

"That doesn't help."

"Cathy. This is about us. Forget about everything else."

"I'm not sure I can. Look, Jack, I need to get on now."

"Right."

"Bye, Jack."

He rang off without saying goodbye.

◆   ◆   ◆

As soon as she got home from work, Cathy rang her parents to say she'd come for lunch the next day, unplugged the house phone and plunged into her writing. She didn't stop until hunger reminded her she hadn't eaten.

As she went into the kitchen, she switched on her mobile and searched her fridge for salad and cheese. She sat down and saw there was a message from Jack asking her to call.

"Cathy . . ."

"Hi. I've been writing. I just saw I hadn't switched my mobile back on, oh and I haven't plugged the house phone back in either."

"So I found out."

"So why did you want me to call?"

"To talk."

"Oh, I've plenty to talk about. I've got loads done in the last two hours. Did I tell you about the book I found which described Daniel Defoe's travels and his description of Newcastle in the eighteenth century?"

"No."

"It's been very useful. You wouldn't believe how much information I've found out about England and the north-east in particular at that time."

"Oh . . . good."

"Something wrong, Jack?"

"You tell me. I'm still feeling pretty stressed about the Josie thing and what you said after I explained and you seem to have moved on and . . ."

"What do you mean, 'moved on'?"

"Well, you're bubbling with what seems to me to be a slightly forced enthusiasm about bloody history; not me, not us."

"You should be pleased. You got me into this whole thing."

"Yes, but that was partly to stop you running away from me and partly to distract you from your depression and grief. Right now you seem to be using it so you can relegate me and us to an afterthought!"

"This isn't like you, Jack. You're usually so calm and rational . . ."

"Stop it, Cathy! This is me you're talking to and I don't feel at all calm or rational! Have you forgotten what it was like to kiss and be in each other's arms? I'm unhappy and frustrated and wishing last night and this morning could have been different and that my past couple of years could have been different. But it's happened and I need to know what you've decided, how you feel. If you think there's no future for us . . . tell me now!"

The shock of Jack's words shook Cathy out of the impersonal mode she'd tried to use. "Oh, Jack; it's not just what you were keeping from me or what you did last night during the party, though I found it all very hard to take. And there's nothing I'd rather be doing on a Saturday or any other evening, than being with you, but I had to keep writing or I'd have gone crazy thinking about how impossible it is for this relationship to work. If we lived closer it might be different, but we don't."

"You think it's impossible?"

"Well, your career's in London and mine's here and at the moment my parents need me . . ."

"Right, so one minute you're saying there's nothing you'd rather be doing than being with me and the next you're saying it's impossible. I don't think I can take any more of this conversation. Call me tomorrow if you have anything more positive to say."

CHAPTER 33

DECISIONS AND SURPRISES

Cathy lay awake in the gloom of early Sunday morning feeling panicky and pathetic. She glanced at her bedside clock. Two in the morning was the wrong time to be thinking of calling Jack. She plumped up her pillow, hugged another and lay down again.

She was slowly losing consciousness when her phone sprang into action. She snatched at it and it skidded onto the floor. She almost fell out of bed in an effort to reach it.

"Hello."

"Cathy, I'm an idiot. It's my fault you're feeling negative about us. Just tell me if you still want me to come to Bamburgh."

"Oh, Jack, yes. I think it's the only way we can work out whether we should continue this relationship, and if so, how."

"So you really do have doubts about it."

"Not when your arms are round me, but when I'm alone and thinking about everything till my head hurts: yes."

"Right. Well, at least I know how to keep you positive in future. I found your present under my pillow a few moments ago when I was tossing and turning. I put it straight on. Thanks, Cathy. It's a beautiful watch. I hope you don't regret spending so much on me."

"I hope so, too."

"You know, I was never so incapable of looking at things coolly before I met you. I hate to think what would happen if I panicked at work and spoke before I thought. I'd have dead bodies on my hands."

"I get panicky too. I was indifferent to the men I knew before."

"But you're not indifferent to me, are you?"

"No."

"Good."

"Night, Jack."

"I'm going to hug the pillow and pretend it's you."

"I already was."

◆　　◆　　◆

Late afternoon, the following Tuesday, Maggie came into Cathy's office. "You've got a visitor. The delightful David."

"Please tell him to get lost."

"Can't do that. He's got a business trip to China and Japan and apparently you're the only one who knows how he likes things done."

Cathy looked through the glass partition and saw his eyes were on her. She turned away, looked at Maggie and grimaced.

"Sorry, Cathy, but he has brought us a lot of business."

Cathy rolled her eyes. "Ok. Send him in." She studiously avoided looking at David as he read out his schedule of meetings in various cities and she made notes on her computer. "Is that it?"

"Yes, as far as the business side of it is concerned."

"Fine. I'll get back to you as soon as I've made some tentative bookings. Would you like to do any tourist trips while you're there?"

David moved his chair closer and touched her arm. "If you came with me, we could do any trip you wanted."

She glanced at him. "David, I thought I'd made myself perfectly clear about how I felt."

"That was when that arrogant Asian was hovering around."

"Enough! You can take you disgusting prejudice out of here and forget about getting any help from me!"

"Ok, ok. Chill out! That was a joke."

"It didn't sound like a joke."

David put his hand on hers and she pulled it away and stared at the screen.

He began again. "Cathy, what I meant to say was that you were in a bit of a state then and he obviously took advantage of the situation. If we'd been alone . . ."

"If we'd been alone I would have said exactly what I said then."

"Are you sure about that?"

"Yes!"

Maggie burst through the door. "Cathy, I need to speak to you. Urgently. Privately."

Cathy glanced at David and walked out of the office.

Maggie grabbed Cathy's arm and led her to the door. "It's Jack."

"What's Jack?"

"He came to see you . . ."

"Jack's here?"

"Yes and I asked him to wait until you'd finished with David and he was watching you both and . . . oh, Cathy, his face . . . he walked out when David put his hand on yours!"

Cathy ran out into the murky dusk and looked wildly down the street. She couldn't see him. She looked up the hill and saw him at the top and about to cross the road.

She shouted his name as loud as she could, but he didn't hear above the noise of the traffic. She ran up the hill and shouted again. She prayed he wouldn't try to get away when he saw her. As she drew closer, she shouted, "Stop, Jack!" He swung round and saw her. She crashed into him and flung her arms around him. "Jack, please don't go! I had to see David; Maggie's been so good and he was going to take his business away, and it doesn't mean a thing . . ."

"Whoa! Stop and take a breath." He tipped up her chin. "Cathy, I wasn't going anywhere, well, not back or away from you. I just couldn't stand watching him touching you and taking advantage of the situation. If I hadn't left, I'd have come in and punched him!"

She expelled a breath and looked up into his eyes and he took her face in his hands and kissed her softly.

There was a dismissive growl behind Cathy. "Argh! Why am I not surprised?" David's face was twisted into a snarl. "Guess what! You can forget the bookings. I'll do it on the internet. It's not rocket science. As you know, Cathy dearest, you don't have to have a degree to book a few flights."

He turned to Jack. "Did you know she's frigid? You're welcome to her."

Jack stepped forward, his eyes flashing angrily, but Cathy pushed between them. "No, Jack; he's just lashing out because I've hurt him. Just leave it."

"Hurt, am I? Don't you believe it. I don't need you, Cathy. Not at all!"

She turned to face him. "Look, I'm sorry this happened, David. I know how I'd feel if it was me. I really thought you'd accepted it was over."

David's shoulders slumped and his head went down for a moment. He looked up and the fight had gone out of his eyes. "You're not the only fish in the sea, y'know."

Cathy shook her head. "Absolutely not."

David turned away and strode off down the street. She watched him go and felt Jack's arms close round her from behind in a possessive hug. He kissed her neck and cheek. "Does he always talk in clichés?"

"I'm afraid so. Especially when he's upset. Now I have to go and explain everything to Maggie and beg her forgiveness for losing a client."

"I have a feeling she probably already knows."

◆　　◆　　◆

Maggie turned to Cathy, a resigned look on her face. "I think I might have made a mistake telling you Jack walked out. Hey ho! Can't win 'em all. I don't think you're going to get much done now, so you might as well go home. Perhaps you could come in half an hour earlier tomorrow."

Cathy nodded, "Sorry, Maggie," and walked into her office.

As she picked up her bag and coat, she saw Jack duck below Maggie's desk, retrieve some red roses and give them to her. He appeared to be whispering urgently to Maggie and stopped and looked guilty as Cathy emerged from the office. He turned to her as Maggie smiled briefly and gathered up her files.

◆　　◆　　◆

Cathy said very little apart from giving Jack directions as he drove to her flat. He parked the car and put his arm round her shoulders as she walked to her door. "What's wrong? Upset about Maggie?"

She looked up at him. "Yes; I suppose those roses were an attempt to make it up to her . . ."

"Yes. Sorry about that. I'll get you some more."

"And the whisperings?"

He looked away. "Ah, well, just flirting a bit. She *is* very attractive."

"Look at me and say that."

Jack smiled at her and kissed her nose. "You'll find out, eventually, but you're not going to get it out of me today. So, was that all you were so thoughtful about?"

"Well, that and wondering about you turning up on a work day and also me having made David so unhappy. You've only seen the bad side of him. He can be obnoxious, but he can also be quite sweet and thoughtful."

"And good for business. Bad timing on my part, eh?"

"Well, it would have been better if you'd let me know you were coming."

"*You* didn't."

She shook her head. "Maybe what happened both times is a lesson to us both."

"No surprises in future, then?"

Cathy smiled. "Oh, no, some surprises I like—birthdays, anniversaries."

"I'll try and remember."

Cathy keyed in the code to the main door and they ran up the stairs to her front door. She giggled and fumbled with the keys as Jack started unbuttoning her coat. They almost fell through the door as it opened and he kicked the door shut and pulled off her coat. He shrugged out of his coat and sweater and peeled her top off. He shook his head. "Don't know how I kept my hands off you last time I did that."

She laughed and put her hands on his chest. "You said you were hungry on the drive over."

"I'm ravenous, but it can wait." He picked her up in his arms. "Which door?"

She nodded to the door on the left. "I don't think I made my bed this morning."

"Perfect." He carried her along the corridor and into her bedroom.

"Jack, we need to talk about this."

"What is there to talk about?"

"Me and my . . . oh, Jack, you heard what David said. I'm not very good at it."

He laid her down on the bed and appeared to be trying to suppress a laugh.

"It's not funny! I'm not terribly experienced and the experiences I've had, I found sort of . . . underwhelming. Rubbish, actually."

Jack lay on his side and pulled her close. He covered her face in kisses and slowly began to undress her, kissing her bare skin as he revealed it. He continued to kiss and caress her until she moaned with pleasure and wanted more. He lifted his head. "Shall I stop now?"

She threaded her arms round his neck and brought her lips close to his. "Don't you dare!"

◆　◆　◆

Cathy roused from dozing as she felt Jack kiss her brow. "Wake up sleepy head."

She snuggled against his skin. "I want to stay here forever."

"Mm. Not underwhelming, then?"

She smiled. "I can't think of words to describe it. Nobody told me how totally overwhelming it could be. You're an incredible lover."

"If I am, it's because it's you. Frigid? David's an idiot. You're sensational."

She looked up at him. "Do you mean that?"

He smiled. "Of course I do . . . overwhelming for me too . . ." He took a breath. "Right. Now I'm really famished. Haven't had anything since eleven this morning."

She sat up. "Ok, we'll eat." She yawned. "I wonder who was ringing the house phone. Not many people know my number and it's ex-directory."

"David?"

"No, and I don't think I'm going to hear from him again."

"Right, come on, we need a quick shower and then we'll eat. Carry-out or go out?"

"You decide. I'm still floating."

◆   ◆   ◆

The doorbell rang as she stepped into the shower. She frowned. "Ignore it. It's probably kids. Halloween or Guy Fawkes or something." It rang again.

"Shall I chase them away?"

"Well, I suppose it might be a good idea to give them some money so they don't come back. The other flats are empty, so no-one else is going to answer."

Jack went to get dressed, glanced fleetingly at her a minute later as the doorbell rang again, blew a kiss and disappeared. She washed her hair and stood under the shower, her face wreathed in a continuous smile.

Tired of waiting for him to come back, she got out, towelled her hair and wrapped herself in another. She thought she heard Jack's voice and wondered if he was ordering food. She heard more voices and wondered if he'd turned on the television. She padded out of the bathroom, along the corridor and into the living room.

Her eyes widened as she saw her parents' shocked expressions. "Oh, it's you . . . I thought it was . . . I mean, hi, how are you both?"

Her mother's eyes blazed as she walked towards Jack. "How dare you take advantage of my daughter when you know she's still vulnerable? You're a doctor, you're supposed to understand these things!"

Cathy ran to Jack's side. "Mum! Don't say another thing. And there's no 'suppose' about it. He's a wonderful, understanding and deeply caring doctor. If it wasn't for Jack, I'd still be a pathetic, depressed heap!" She slid her arm under his arm and along his back. He said nothing as he cupped her bare shoulder and pulled her close. She looked up into his smiling face and looked back at her mother. "And he hasn't taken advantage of me at all. If I'd had my way, this would have happened last week!"

Cathy's mother shook her head and pursed her lips. "And what if you get pregnant?"

"We're not fools, mother."

Her mother walked to the window and looked out. "She's all we've got now," she whispered. Suddenly she spun round and faced Jack with anger in her eyes. "How dare you take her away from us!"

"Alice, dear . . ." Cathy's father put his arms round her.

"Mum, no one will take me away from you! Whatever happens, I'm not leaving here as long as you want me to stay."

Jack turned to Cathy, his expression quizzical.

Cathy's mother put her head on one side. "You're saying that now, but I know how one's priorities can change when . . ." She pulled away from Henry's arms and walked towards the door. "Time to leave, Henry." She walked out. Cathy's father began to follow her, but he looked back when he reached the door. "She has a short memory. I could tell you how we got together; but maybe not. She'll come round. We came, Cathy, because your mobile was off and there was no reply to your house phone. We were worried. You weren't yourself last Sunday after your trip to London on Friday."

"Sorry, Dad."

"At least I understand now why you didn't answer."

"Henry!" Cathy's mother's voice was sharp.

"Coming dear!"

Cathy shut the door and walked into Jack's open arms. "Well," she grinned, "that went well!"

CHAPTER 34

FRUSTRATING NEWS

1715

For almost a week, I heard nothing. Early on Saturday morning, the fifth of November, John arrived as I sat at breakfast.

"Pardon me for disturbing you so early but I have much to do today; Thomas Smith, the Holy Island blacksmith, has gone with your brother and I'm sharing some of his jobs with Purdy as well as my own. But I received two pieces of information late yesterday and I felt you should know them before I began work."

I left my meal and waved him to sit beside me near the fire. "Go on. I have heard snippets of rumours this week that bothered me a great deal."

He sat down. "I will try to relate it as accurately as my memory will allow. First, one of Clavering's servants came from Callaly with news of last weekend. It seems there was no engagement with Carpenter as hoped for by the Earl."

"Why not? I thought it was the reason for Anna Maria's celebration."

"That is what I understood but the servant said that the Scots disagreed with the English on such a course of action when they held their Council of War, so instead they headed towards Jedburgh."

"Jedburgh! But that's still in Scotland. What was the reasoning for that?"

"I don't know. A roundabout way to Newcastle?"

"And what of Carpenter?"

"His government troops struck west to head them off. The English urged the Scots to march back into England and engage him before he crossed the border but the Scots disagreed. It is thought the Scots did not wish to enter England, but I do not know if that is the case."

"That is possible."

"Aye. Well I cannot remember all the details of what happened next except that some time later the English tried again to persuade the Scots to make an attempt on Newcastle. They argued that with their local knowledge of the area they could move with speed across the western hills and fells into Tynedale. Captain Hunter was even sent ahead to prepare quarters for the army, but it seems that the Highlanders refused to cross the border and the plan had to be abandoned."

I sprang up and paced the room. "What frustration my brother and the Earl must have felt. What fools they all be! One group wants this and another that. Cannot they see they must make compromises and look to what is best for the Cause?" I turned back to John. "Go on."

"Well, it seems that Carpenter and the government troops got to Jedburgh and found that your brother's army had moved on. Meanwhile your brother received intelligence about Carpenter and the poor condition of his men. This time—the government's army now being in Scotland—the Highlanders were all for engaging them."

"And?"

John shook his head. "Still they did not. Your brother thought they needed more cavalry to be certain of victory and the lowland Scots were adamant they should move on and take Dumfries."

I continued to pace up and down. I felt my frustration might turn to anger if I stopped. John's eyes followed me round the room. "Shall I go on?"

I nodded.

"Well, at that point Charles Widdrington rode in with letters which changed the whole course of action."

I sat down, my attention on John's face and my hands bunched tightly together.

He continued. "The letters said that if Lord Kenmure would advance into Lancashire, the High Church Tories and Catholics of Manchester would rise forthwith and provide twenty thousand men. A thousand were already in arms and the gentlemen of the north-west eager for action."

I shook my head and breathed deeply. "But Carpenter was not defeated.

Did they not see that he would remain a danger if they did not engage him?"

John shrugged his shoulders. "I know not, but the Council agreed to march into England with your brother in command again. Unfortunately, some men from Teviotdale in Scotland and many of the Highlanders deserted them. The rest of the army turned south, and Charles Widdrington was sent back to inform the Lancastrians they were coming."

I turned to stare into the fire. After a moment I turned back to John. "Is that all?"

"Not quite. Last night one of the Swinburne sisters arrived. She had already been to your father's and been given short shrift from Madam Forster."

My anxiety instantly turned to anger. "That woman! She would turn St Peter from her door if she thought he wanted something that might endanger her cosy existence."

John frowned. "You have seen little of your stepmother these last years. She is well thought of in Adderstone."

I felt admonished, but could not let his rebuke pass. "I lived with her for many years when I was young. She did much to sour my father's opinion of Thomas."

John held my eyes. "People can change."

I lowered my lids. "Go on with your story, please."

He was silent for a moment. "Well, the Swinburne woman's horse needed attention. She was going to ride here and I explained my connection to you and said I would convey the message. She was thankful to tell me her news and stay the night before returning home."

I looked questioningly at John. "Oh?"

He smiled. "I gave her my bed and slept in the smithy."

"I did not mean to question your sleeping arrangements, John."

He raised his brows. "I just wished to make it clear."

His face became serious again. "She told me your brother and his army had entered Brampton on the first of November. There he received a number of dispatches from Mar which showed that news sent by your brother to Mar had not got through to him and he had little knowledge of what had been happening."

"No doubt the government did their best to stop the messages getting through."

"Aye, that may be the reason. She also said that Carpenter and the government army are now in Corbridge, waiting for your brother to march back towards Newcastle. He will have a long wait, for your brother is pressing on towards Penrith in the Lake District. That is all she knew."

"Penrith! Oh John, I fervently hope their decision is the right one. Taking the north-west is not the same as cutting off the government's supplies of fuel from Newcastle."

"No. I mulled over all you said about their plan for doing that. With the numbers they had then, it seemed to me a foolish enterprise. The Swinburne woman said that after all this time they still have less than two thousand."

I gasped and looked up, alarmed at his words. I saw him pale. He leant forward and took my hands. "But they have the promise of twenty thousand. That will be more than enough."

I closed my eyes and nodded silently.

I released my hands and stood up. "Thank you John. You said you have much work to do today. I too."

I held out my hand and he stood up slowly and took my hand, gently rubbed his thumb across my fingers and bowed his head briefly. "I will return if there is more."

◆   ◆   ◆

When I had received no further news by Wednesday 9th November, I rode to Adderstone before dawn and in pouring rain to inform John Armstrong that I would ride to Callaly to see if the Claverings had any further news.

I found him hard at work. I removed my gloves, untied my wet cloak and stood warming myself in front of his blazing fire. I told him of my plan. He wiped his hands on his apron. "Is that wise in this weather?"

"I must know what is happening."

He stood silently, his eyes on me.

I continued, "I will return tomorrow. I just wanted you to know I am gone from Bamburgh."

He folded his arms. "If you wait till the morra, I can come with you."

"There is no need. I have regained all my strength and know the road well. It is not yet seven o'clock. I can be there mid-afternoon if I ride hard."

He looked uncertain. He reached into his pocket and retrieved a linen kerchief. He held it out to me. "Your face is wet."

I shrugged my shoulders. "There is no point; it will get wet again. At least it is less cold than it was. I will call in on my way back tomorrow." I moved towards the door, retying my cloak. He came over to me and put a hand on my arm. "If you are determined to go today, make sure you stop for no-one on the road. I am not happy you're travelling on your own."

"John, I have been riding these parts on my own or with my maid since I was twelve."

"Not on your own as far as Callaly, and why is your maid not with you?"

"Thomas does not trust her and her family with our business."

"Then wait till I can go with you."

"I will be back before you notice I am gone."

His mouth tightened. "You are a headstrong woman, Dorothy Forster!"

I felt myself blushing and a little angered. "Good-bye John. I *may* see you tomorrow, *if* I have a mind to." I turned away with a flourish, opened the door and ran to where Chestnut was tied to the mounting block. I untied him, climbed the stone steps and sprang onto his back.

As I broke into a canter I heard John wishing me God speed; I did not look back, but as I turned at the end of the road, I realised I had left my gloves.

CHAPTER 35

CALLALY CASTLE

The journey to Callaly Castle took longer than I anticipated. The road had become a quagmire and I reached the castle as dusk was overtaken by an inky blackness. Chestnut was in a sorry state having slipped and tottered his way for many a mile. I had to dismount and walk with him for some distance more than once.

I entered the grounds of the castle knowing I looked bedraggled and mud spattered. I was received with some surprise which turned to amazement when it was realised I had come alone. I was ushered in and given food and dry clothes. Only then did I realise I had not eaten since early breakfast.

As I climbed stiffly up the fine staircase to my room later that night, I turned over in my mind what I had learnt from my hostess. They had received news that very day of a fine victory the previous Thursday. The Bishop of Carlisle and High Sheriff of Cumberland and Westmorland had assembled the County Militia on Penrith Fell to engage with Thomas's army on their route south. There were more than fourteen thousand government troops and yet when they heard of the approach of Thomas and his army, they had all fled leaving their arms behind them.

Greatly cheered by their bloodless victory and gift of more arms, Thomas's troops had marched into Penrith unhindered and gleefully proceeded to enjoy the dinner prepared for the Bishop and his men. It had been a welcome turn of fortune for they had been dispirited by the non-appearance of Cumbrian Jacobites who had promised to join them. The Bishop had imprisoned a number of them in Carlisle Castle, but what had happened to the others was not known.

The army advanced and on the road to Lancaster, Charles Widdrington arrived and said they were eagerly awaited by the Lancastrians and that James III had been proclaimed in Manchester where a troop of fifty men were armed and waiting to join.

I climbed into the cold bed and pulled the covers up to my chin. A troop of fifty! Where were the twenty thousand promised?

◆   ◆   ◆

As I prepared to leave Callaly on the morning of Thursday 10th November, two riders arrived. One was John Armstrong, the other a servant I recognised as belonging to the Swinburnes of Capheaton.

I watched them both being ushered to the back of the house. This had not happened to John when we arrived together. I felt angry that he was being treated that way, but in truth it was obvious to the household servants from the clothes he wore that he was not a gentleman. I knew they might have lost their positions had they erred in their judgement of his status, but I wondered why they did not recognise him from before. I concluded that their attention had been on me and he had simply been accepted as my protector.

I was curious to know whether the servant might be bringing further news but went first to speak to John. I saw the relief on John's face when he saw me.

I smiled at him. "I see you are checking up on me. Did you think I was incapable of reaching my destination?"

He did not return my smile. "My worry was not with you, but with those that ride these parts with evil intent."

"I had nothing of worth for them to steal."

He glanced round at the interested onlookers, came closer and lowered his voice. "There are many bands of horse thieves and in some cases when they spy a woman, they are not always looking for jewels."

I blinked and decided not to ask what he meant. I hoped I had misunderstood. I stepped back and surveyed the room for the newly arrived servant. I saw him in the corner pulling off his boots. "Henry, do you bring news for Madame Clavering and myself?"

He shuffled forward, cap in hand. "Yes, mistress." I waved him and John in through the kitchen and into the hall, and asked a passing servant to find Madam.

◆   ◆   ◆

Henry glanced at Madam Clavering and myself and puffed out his chest, cleared his throat and began. "At midday last Monday, they entered Lancaster in a fine show, their swords drawn, drums beating and colours flying. The English led the column wearing their red and white cockades, and the Scots blue and white." He paused for effect and looked at us.

"Go on, go on!" Madam Clavering snapped, her eyes full of anxiety. Henry looked taken aback. "Yes, Madam. Well, the inhabitants of Lancaster and their leaders had not expected to be on General Forster's itinerary so were not prepared, and when the Colonel of the militia got together only six hundred men, but no reinforcements from the government, he retreated. General Forster's army marched in and took the town, seized six cannon from a ship in the river—and a good deal of brandy beside—and about a hundred men joined the Cause. They also freed Thomas Siddal from detention in Lancaster Castle—y'know, the feller 'as led the riots in Manchester last June?"

I did not know of the man, but made no comment. "Continue, Henry."

He turned to me. "Well, mistress, there's not much more 'cept they heard that the leader of the Regiment of Dragoons in Preston had also retreated and they mean to go there next."

"Preston?" I stood for a moment in thought. "That's quite far south, is it not?" Madam Clavering shrugged her shoulders and dismissed Henry with a wave of her hand. I looked anxiously at John as Henry disappeared back through the kitchen door. "Could you thank . . . ?" John nodded, handed over my gloves and disappeared after Henry.

A servant brought me a cloak. It was not my own, nor was I wearing the breeches I had arrived in. Madam Clavering had ordered they be thrown out and had insisted I accept a brown velvet dress and a woollen shawl to cover my shoulders. She had also given me what she dismissed as an old, but warm velvet cloak with a fur trimmed hood. I had not possessed such a fine set of travelling garments for some years, and was pleased I hadn't worn my best breeches for the journey there.

◆   ◆   ◆

As soon as John and I were out of sight of Callaly Castle, I hitched up my skirts and swung my leg over Chestnut's shoulders to sit astride him. John looked across at my revealed, stockinged legs and raised his eyebrows in my direction. I returned his gaze with a look of defiance.

"It would take forever to ride side-saddle!"

"I made no comment."

"Your expression was comment enough!"

He smiled, clicked his heels, and set off at some speed.

◆   ◆   ◆

More than a week passed before I received news I had hoped would never come.

The Countess's butler, Thompson, was ushered into my drawing room just before nine on the morning of Friday 18th November. He looked tired and drawn and would not be seated. He walked about the room wringing his hands and licking his lips. I had to catch his arm to restrain him. "For heaven's sake, Thompson, say what you have to say. My pulse is racing from your heavy looks and sighs."

He looked at me with such pity that my heart went cold. "Thompson!" I cried, "Tell me. Is my brother hurt or . . . dead?"

"Dead? No, he is not dead, but they are all as good as. All is lost. They are captured and being taken to London. My Lady has great need of you at Dilston. You must come or she will go mad with fear for His Lordship's safety."

I gasped and sank into my chair. "But Thompson . . . I don't understand. Everything was going so well. How? When?"

"I do not know the answers to your questions, mistress. The news came late yesterday afternoon and my Lady sent me to you straight away. I have ridden through the night, but very early this morning went first to Callaly for directions."

I stood up, sent Thompson to the kitchen to find refreshment, and went out into the hall to call for Jenny. I focussed my thoughts on nothing but getting ready for the journey. I gave orders for two horses to be made ready and asked to see Alan Reed who did all the heavy work in the manor, and whom I knew could ride well. I made Thompson promise he would rest and not leave until the following morning and asked him to call in on John Armstrong on his way back and tell him the news and where I had gone.

After a hurried meal, the three of us set off, Jenny riding pillion with Alan, and reached the Great North Road not long after twelve o'clock. Despite Jenny's complaints we continued without stopping, sometimes cantering, sometimes galloping, until we reached the outskirts of Alnwick.

The latter part of the week had been bitterly cold and the roads were covered with hard-packed snow, yet although we had to take great care to avoid deep drifts in some places, we made good time.

We took the road to Rothbury as Thomas and I had done at the beginning of the whole affair. We reached Rothbury and were able to look for rooms before it was fully dark. The small tavern provided us with hot food and for myself an adequate bed, though Jenny and Alan had to share a palette with a thinly stuffed horse hair mattress in a poky back room. I was asleep before eight and we were all up and on the road by seven the next morning. It was icily cold and a wintry shower began as we started our journey.

Our reception by Anna Maria at Dilston in the late afternoon was tearful and punctuated by repeated declarations of her gratitude that I had come so swiftly. It was many minutes before she could compose herself and feel able to explain how such a catastrophe had taken place. Her voice was agitated and at times her words gabbled in such a way that I found her hard to understand.

She began, "they reached Preston on Wednesday the ninth of November or Thursday the tenth—I forget which—and were joined by a great many gentlemen with their tenants, servants and attendants so that their strength was by then between three and four thousand men. So great was their confidence at such a response that they took time to rest and enjoy their success." She broke off and looked at me. "A quite reasonable thing to do, don't you think?" I refrained from commenting, anxious not to slow her account, but nodded.

Anna Maria closed her eyes and began again. "They were informed that Carpenter was hurrying down from the north and that the government commander at Chester, General Wills, was making various preparations against them . . . but the promises of support for them in and around Manchester made them brush off such threats. But on the Friday evening, James got word that Wills was preparing to march on them. The Council of War decided to post guards around the town and they put the army under orders to prepare for action."

Anna Maria began to pace up and down the room. "The next day your brother—briefed by Oxburgh—countermanded those orders and gave new orders to continue their march to Manchester. But it was too late. Our guards reported that Wills was approaching the bridge over the river outside the town. Your brother went to review all positions and found that Macintosh had, without orders from him, withdrawn the detachment led by Charles to protect the bridge over the River Ribble on the road from Wigan. Your brother ordered that Macintosh and Charles should take the forces forthwith and fight the army led by Wills on the town outskirts."

The Countess paused and took a sip of wine, her voice growing fainter as she continued. "Macintosh refused. Later your brother went to him again, urging him to advance before it was too late but again he refused. Instead Macintosh suggested that they should barricade the streets of Preston so that the cavalry would have to dismount and face them at close range. Your brother threatened Macintosh with a court martial for rejecting his advice and for cowardice. It made no odds. Then it seems your brother retired to his quarters, some thought in a fit of pique, as had Widdrington some time before."

She looked at me. "I cannot understand why your brother did not insist that Macintosh follow orders. James would have done so, had he been in charge." She continued. "At two, the fighting began and continued until dusk. Francis Simpson, one of James's servants, said that James and Charles fought bravely throughout. Their forces repulsed every attack and were still in possession of the town at sunset, but by eleven the next morning they realised that the town was surrounded. There were whispers that Wills had been joined by Carpenter and by the Earl of Carlisle and Lord Lumley's forces."

Anna Maria paused and dabbed her eyes. "What happened next seems somewhat confused. It is believed that Oxburgh and that grump Widdrington—who by all accounts had taken no part at all in the fighting—advised your brother to negotiate with the enemy because their numbers were too great to overcome. This he did. James did not want this and Charles was furious it should even be considered. Many others accused your brother of all manner of things. The Scots refused to abide by his decision and sent their own emissary to Wills."

I covered my face with my hands, my mind numb. Anna Maria's wavering, hysterical voice continued but I found it hard to concentrate.

"They were given until the Monday morning to come to a joint decision. A hostage was required from both the Scots and the English . . . Macintosh and my James offered themselves up!"

The silence that followed that awful statement penetrated my anxious imaginings as I tried to stop myself thinking about the consequences of it having gone so wrong. I looked up at Anna Maria. Tears were pouring down her face. I went across and put my arms around her.

After a few moments of quiet weeping, Anna Maria insisted on finishing her account. "Charles and some of the Scots had earlier proposed to the Council that they should attempt a break-out and fight on, but Macintosh said that all had been agreed and it was too late. Francis Simpson managed to escape and brought this news to me. He thinks others escaped, certainly a good number of the Highlanders. But, for the rest, they are all now in the hands of the government. We can assume they are being taken to London."

The implication of her final sentence was frighteningly clear. It meant prison, and for the Lords, the Tower. The penalty for treason was transportation. Or death.

Anna Maria began to pace the room. Between sighs, she said she had already given instructions to prepare for her journey to London within the week.

I was appalled. I protested against such action and used all my powers of persuasion to stop her from contemplating such a journey in the appalling weather that had now taken hold. I cited her unborn child as well as her son. Anna Maria rebuffed all advice. She insisted she must speak to the King and plead for his mercy in the name of her son and unborn child. She would say that James was an unwilling participant, persuaded into action by stronger parties who had called on his support, and knew nothing of the plans and had taken no part in their preparation; others had plotted and drawn him into their treacherous intentions.

Anna Maria sank down on the nearest seat, wracked by sobs. I stared at her in disbelief and suddenly knew that if it were in James' interest, Anna Maria would see to it that Thomas and the others became the scapegoats for all the planning and failures of the rebellion. Such was the force of a love so strong that any wrong was permissible, should it result in her husband's reprieve.

I left the next morning without speaking my mind. It would achieve nothing and would have meant we would have parted enemies. I swallowed my hurt and wished Anna Maria every success in ensuring James's freedom and in truth did dearly wish that it would be so. I had a great fondness for the Earl and did not blame him in any way for what had befallen. He was an honourable and admirable man, but he also adored his wife and might be persuaded for love of her to say things that were not in his own mind to say.

I rode through the snow behind Jenny and Alan, barely noticing my discomfort. I searched my mind for words to explain to the authorities what Thomas had done in a way that would clear his name and achieve his release. I knew it was futile. Whatever else I might do, the truth could not be denied. He, like all the others, had gone into it knowing the price of failure. He would not pretend innocence and I would not try to persuade him to do so. I could not see what I, or anyone else, could do to save him.

CHAPTER 36

THE SPLIT

2005

Liz chewed thoughtfully on her lunchtime pizza. "So you're saying the not-so-saintly Jack expects you to just quit here and go and live with him in London."

"Yes. After my parents left and we were sharing a carry-out, he asked if I'd meant it when I said I wasn't going to leave them, because he'd assumed I'd go and maybe work in London at our main branch and live with him. I was astounded."

◆　　◆　　◆

"Jack, we haven't known each other for long and we've only just admitted we love each other."

He released her from his arms and sat up on the sofa. "Does the length of time matter? Anyway, I pretty much fell in love with you from the moment you stumbled through the heather into my life."

"Really?"

"Yep. Even with your pale, tear-stained face you took my breath away. Your eyes knock me out every time. And the rest of you, well . . . I suppose at first it was just an unbelievable attraction, but it developed into a full blown, passionate love by the time you fell asleep in my arms that first night. I had an overwhelming urge to protect you. I was terrified you were going to walk away from me the next morning. At first I kept quiet about how I felt because I didn't want you to feel you had to respond out of gratitude. When I began to think you had some feelings for me, I didn't dare tell you how much I love you or ask whether you loved me, in case it didn't come close to how I feel. Obviously, it doesn't."

"How can you say that? Didn't you believe what I put on your watch?"

"Ah yes, the inscription. 'All my love always, Cathy' I didn't notice it was engraved until my bedside light shone on it early this morning. So I leapt in my car at 2 p.m. as soon as my shift was finished and drove here like a madman because I believed it."

"It's true, I do love you, very much."

"Just not enough." He began to pace the room.

"Jack, surely you wouldn't expect me to leave them so soon after . . ."

He came back and took hold of her shoulders. "Cathy, you didn't give a time limit, like a couple of months. You said no one would take you away from her and that you wouldn't leave here as long as she wanted you to stay."

"I felt so sad for her and I wanted to stop her hurting."

"So you hurt me instead."

"I didn't mean forever."

"I thought you might have learned not to say what you don't mean!" His words hit her like a physical shock and she pulled back and bit her lip. He expelled a breath and pulled her close. "I'm sorry; that was a crass thing to say. Forgive me." She looked up at him and nodded. He held her for a moment, released her and ran his hands through his hair. "You could have such a good career in London and maybe take a degree. We could get married if you want."

"And if we decided to start a family?"

"We could think about that later, much later."

"I'd want that sooner rather than later."

"Ok, fine, if that's what you want."

"And then we'd have both sets of grandparents hours away. I don't want that. If you really want to be with me, why don't you come and work here?"

"I probably wouldn't get anything until next summer and there's no guarantee that it would be anything like the salary I have in London and if we wanted to start a family, a nanny would be expensive . . ."

"A nanny! What are you talking about? I would take care of my children myself!"

"What about your career? Isn't that important to you?"

"Bringing up children is the most important thing you can do! I want to be there for them."

Jack frowned and shook his head. "You'd want to be tied to the house with no adult conversation while I was on eight hour shifts? Often longer! You'd go bananas!"

"Believe it or not, babies can be taken out in the fresh air! They don't melt! And I do have friends!"

"Your friends would probably be at work!" He came back and stood next to her, breathing heavily. "You know what my father said to me after he and Mum split up?"

Cathy shook her head, hardly daring to breathe.

"He said that you can't help who you fall in love with, but it's not enough. You have to agree about the important things."

"And we don't?"

"We don't seem to." He sat down and put his head in his hands. "Oh God, Cathy, I didn't think you'd feel like this. You've thrived on the research you've been doing. Surely you couldn't be happy changing nappies and watching daytime television."

"Give me some credit."

He looked up. "I do. That's why I don't understand."

Cathy folded her arms round herself. "It's a good job we found out how diametrically opposed we are in our ideas of marriage before we committed to each other," she whispered.

Jack moved across, took her in his arms and held her tight. "Oh, Cathy. I love you so much." He kissed her forehead, her cheek and her lips until she was unable to stop herself responding passionately and allowing herself to be led into the bedroom.

◆　　◆　　◆

"Oh, Liz, we didn't talk about it again. Just more mind-blowing love-making and complete contentment in his arms."

"Mind-blowing? Right. Sounds like Jack is pretty experienced."

"I think by the time you're thirty you'll have had a lot more men than he's had women!"

Liz looked startled "Ok. Stay cool. You're a lost cause, aren't you?"

"What do you mean?"

"You're crazy about him. Despite the Josie thing and the disagreements about bringing up kids and not agreeing about where you'd live, you couldn't really give him up, could you?"

"I don't think so. But he might give me up . . ." Cathy frowned and looked away.

"Mightn't be a bad thing."

"What? Do you have to be so negative? Has Matt found someone else or something?"

Liz glowered. "Oh, him. He wasn't that good anyway; all sweetness and light at first until I refused to be browbeaten into going to a rugby match and then yesterday he had me shopping for him! I mean, all that pretentious cooking nonsense; shopping for food is just not my thing. He actually shouted at me for getting the wrong kind of rice! I walked out. Anyway, you're changing the subject, I think it's strange Jack didn't try to sort it out before he left this morning."

"He didn't say a thing, but he was so loving and passionate even after everything we'd said to each other."

"Oh, Cathy, you're so naïve. Most of them are passionate. After all, they know they're guaranteed to get satisfaction every time."

"But he made sure I did too, more than once . . . each time."

"Oh, wow! When you said mind-blowing, I didn't realise you meant that good. We've got some thinking to do. We have to make sure you hang on to him if you can. Leave it with me. I'll get back to you."

◆   ◆   ◆

Later that day Cathy tried to eat supper, but was distracted by mounting anxiety and pushed it away. Jack had texted as soon as he got back to his flat just before her lunch with Liz and she'd replied. She'd texted him from work in the late afternoon when he was supposed to be having a break and as soon as she got home, but there was no response either time.

She sat at her computer, glancing every few minutes at her mobile that reminded her how much time had passed since she'd tried to contact him. She sent another text. Eventually, she put Jack out of her mind and began to type furiously.

Just after ten, he rang. "I've just come to my locker and seen your texts."

"In the hospital?"

"I don't have a locker in my flat, do I?" he snapped. She felt as if he'd punched her in the stomach. Her mouth opened but she couldn't speak.

"Oh, Cathy, I'm sorry. I'm totally knackered, but that's no excuse for taking it out on you."

She swallowed. "I must have misunderstood your shift hours."

"No, I was called in early just after I texted you I was back. I've been here ever since. A huge pile up on the M25 just before lunch on top of the normal morning influx. Two of them died on me. One was just nine years old . . ." The emotion in his voice made her ache for him.

"Oh, Jack, I wish I was there to hug you."

"Don't. I spent the whole of the journey back thinking about yesterday, last night and waking up with you in my arms this morning. And then I have the lousiest day imaginable and you're not here."

"I don't know what to say to make it better."

"You could tell me you're getting on the next train, but that's not going to happen, is it?"

"You know I can't."

"So this isn't going to work, is it? You were right; the whole situation's impossible. You don't want to move here and . . ."

"That's not fair!"

"I'm not saying you don't have a reason for staying there, just stating a fact. For me it would be maybe three or four hours, perhaps more depending on the traffic—twice a day—too much for a daily commute . . . so we live apart; see each other for a night, maybe two, now and then. Not much of a future, is it?"

Cathy felt a pain beneath her ribs and couldn't speak.

"Cathy?"

"What?"

"Am I right?"

"I . . . I don't know what to say."

"And no solution?"

"If you don't want to come here, I can't think of one."

"I can't just quit and move; it doesn't work like that!"

They sat in silence for a few moments.

"So, the situation looks pretty hopeless, doesn't it? Cathy?"

"Yes, but as it happens, you have a great get-out clause."

"What the hell are you talking about?"

"I had a phone call this afternoon. One of our London staff's been taken ill. She was going to do a tour with a group of Americans and I'm the only one free who's done the tour before. I've had to cancel my trip to Newcastle and instead be at Heathrow to meet them early on Saturday. So, I'll be taking the train tomorrow and brushing up on my history and geography monologues . . ."

"How long will you be away?"

"Ten days; so you have a great excuse to get on with your life without me and cancel your holiday. Unless you want to go to Bamburgh alone next Thursday." He was silent. Cathy felt waves of pain tightening round her waist.

She heard him swallow. "I won't be doing that now." He sounded as if he was going to choke.

She wrapped an arm round herself, holding her phone so tightly with the other hand that her fingers tingled. "Right . . ." She felt numb and her eyes filled with tears. Unable to say goodbye, she switched off. He didn't ring back.

◆   ◆   ◆

Jack rang at seven the next morning.

"Why are you ringing, Jack?"

"Cathy, I'm here if you want to talk some more. It came out all wrong last night; maybe we can find a way to be together. The last thing I wanted to do was to . . ."

"Give me more grief? Too late! Because that's what you've done and I think we agreed there wasn't a way to be together and . . . I won't be needing your 'support' any more. I'll deal with any problems I have and I won't answer your calls or texts, so don't bother sending them!"

"Cathy, for God's sake, don't do this! We don't have to lose touch."

"What! Jack, do you remember saying our situation looked hopeless, impossible and living apart wasn't much of a future?"

"Yes, but . . ."

"What's changed, Jack?"

They were both silent for a few moments.

Cathy took a breath. "What we did last night . . . was break up. Let's leave it at that."

She rang off and switched off.

◆　　◆　　◆

Liz looked startled as she drove Cathy to York station and heard about their split. "Ok. Wow! That was pretty final. Not what I had in mind to hook him at all and looking at your face, I'd say you're not entirely happy you said that."

"I'm totally devastated. I now know what being heartbroken means. But what was there left to say? I remember pleading with my parents not to send me away to school in England when they told me about it. It made it hurt more when they rejected me and what I wanted. I decided I would be the one to make this decision, before Jack did."

"Mm, get your point. Pity."

CHAPTER 37

SHOCKING NEWS

1716

Early in March, four months after Thomas's incarceration in Newgate prison, horrifying news carried on a ship from London to Newcastle spread like wildfire across Northumberland and Durham.

I was shocked beyond belief and most deeply saddened to hear that our dear cousin James, Earl of Derwentwater, had been beheaded on Tower Hill in London on the twenty-fourth of February.

Despite every effort made to plead for clemency for him from the House of Lords, members of the Commons and many others—including a personal plea from poor, heavily pregnant Anna Maria not long before his execution—the King had not been moved.

All the Lords had been impeached for high treason on the ninth of January. The countess lodged in the Tower with James from December until mid-January when there was an outbreak of smallpox. Before she left, James made his case to the authorities. He pleaded that he had not been privy to or involved in a plot to remove the King, was not prepared for such action, had not committed any cruel, severe or harsh action during the fighting and had given himself up at the first opportunity.

When I read the news sheet account of the content of his plea, I could hear the pleadings of Anna Maria. Widdrington made a similar but more lengthy appeal, as had Lords Nithsdale and Nairn. Two others had offered no mitigation. The Earl of Wintoun pleaded not guilty and said he did not recognise this George, Elector of Hanover, as his king.

It said that when James was asked if he had anything more to say before the sentence was passed, he again repeated how unprepared he had been, it having been a sudden and unplanned action. He protested his future loyalty to King George and asked that they consider the effect on his wife and children. Widdrington, Kenmure and Nairn made similar pleas.

In the end, James died a brave and noble death. On Tower Hill, after spending a good deal of time in prayer, he apologised to his friends for pleading guilty to treason and said that he had never held any other but King James as his rightful and lawful sovereign. He explained his reasons for what he had done for his king and country. He said he had rejected the offer of a reprieve if he renounce his religion. This was against his honour and conscience and he would die a Roman Catholic. He went to the block without a word of reproach to either his executioner or those who had condemned him.

I was not alone in my grief. The consternation throughout the north-east was heartfelt. People remembered what a good and generous master he had been and how cruelly let down by many of the families upon whom he had counted.

Some, such as the Reverend Patten who had turned King's evidence in prison, were openly despised. Those Jacobites who held Sir William Blackett to have had some hand in the failure of the uprising got their own back on him. They spread word in Newcastle about his involvement in the plot and his disloyalty to King George, with the result that he was slighted and ridiculed by the inhabitants who were largely loyal Geordies.

The tragic news made me angry at all those who had assured me that the government would not dare to execute Thomas and might even release him in time. I now felt certain that being Anglican and a Member of Parliament would be no barrier to them using his death as a warning to others. I decided to go to Adderstone to make a final plea for help before I committed myself to the only course of action left open to me.

As I rode carefully along the icy roads, I thought with bitterness of my father's journey to London earlier in the year. Not only had he not tried to help Thomas in any way, but he had gone instead to make a claim to avoid forfeiture of the family estates.

Most of the other families involved in the rebellion, particularly the Roman Catholic families who had suffered deprivation before, had put their estates in trust or made other arrangements long before the rising, so that they would not lose their inheritances if the uprising was unsuccessful. Two months before the uprising, even James entrusted his deeds and family papers to Martin Swinburne, a tailor who lived in Upper Dilston and whose sisters were the couriers, until they could be transferred to Capheaton Hall where Sir William and Lady Mary Swinburne could secrete them and so foil the Commissioners.

Thomas had taken no such measures. He was his father's heir and certain to lose not only the mines he already held but also all that he would inherit, so my father went to London to claim he had settled two thirds of the estate on his wife.

The Commissioners hearing the case were told that she had been, and possibly still was, his housekeeper and rejected the claim. He had therefore rewritten his will. Thomas was bypassed and the Adderstone and Carham estates were settled on my younger brother John and my half brother Ralph, respectively. I listened with disgust to my father's assurances that I would not be left destitute. I left Adderstone Hall in a fury that he had done nothing to plead Thomas's case and I had not returned until now.

I reached the small wood of firs, pines, wych-elms and rowan ash that sheltered Adderstone Hall from the cold northern winds. I followed the winding track to the Hall my father built when the Pele Tower was deemed too insignificant for my ambitious stepmother.

She received me with a look of distrust, but reluctantly allowed me in to see my father. The parlour was filled with the fumes of the coal-burning stove and my father's pipe. He looked warily at me as he sat on his great oaken settle, book in hand.

"Now then, Dorothy, I hope you are not come to stir up further aggravation between your step-mother and myself."

"No father, I simply ask if you mean to leave Thomas to his fate or will help me succeed in my quest to contrive his escape."

My step-mother sprang out of her high-backed chair, a look of outrage on her face. "Would you have your brothers and sister reduced to the mercy of the poorhouse?"

I looked at John, just two years younger than myself, sitting meekly in the corner with his eyes cast down and at thirteen year old Ralph and young Mary who sat at their mother's feet. "I do not wish harm on any of my family. I mean to go to London to do what I can to help Thomas. If father, or John could have accompanied me, we might together have pleaded his case without resorting to other means. From your reaction, it is quite clear I can expect no such help from either of them, so I ask merely for a strong horse and a little money to add to that I already have. Do not worry that I will burden you with my plans; for as yet, I have none."

My father stood up and came towards me. "Dorothy, Dorothy, you cannot ride to London. Even in my carriage it was a long and arduous journey through deep snow and ice. It is one of the worst winters we have ever had. They were roasting ox on the frozen River Thames when I was there! The weather is not much better now. The roads are rough and once you are past Wetherby, there are highwaymen. The inns are mostly, at best, rough and dirty. You must not go. We must trust to the mercy of the court."

I stared incredulously at my father. "As poor, dear James did? I think not. I will go whether you help me or no." My step-mother tutted impatiently. Father shook his head and sighed. After a moment he beckoned me to follow him. He took me into his small office, retrieved a key from his waistcoat pocket and unlocked a small drawer in his walnut desk.

"I cannot spare more than sixty guineas, but you can have my fittest and strongest horse. I will tell Jim to saddle him for you."

"Thank you father."

"You were always a strong-willed child."

"That is why it was best that I left as soon as possible when Madame became your wife. It was not you I wanted to be parted from."

"I know, I know, but I needed someone to look after the household and she was a good housekeeper. She is not so harsh as you think. She only wants to protect Ralph and Mary's future. And John's, of course."

"Of course. Perhaps John should be encouraged to find a wife. He is twenty-six, almost twenty-seven and still clings to your shirt tails."

"Adderstone will be his, so he has no other place to go."

"And Ralph will inherit Carham," I said, resignedly.

"He will. Though, God willing, not just yet."

"Please God, not for a long time yet." I looked into my father's care-worn face. "I do not mean to make you anxious. You must not worry that what I do will cause you to lose your estates. I know they mean much to you."

"They do, but then so do you and Thomas. It may seem that I have abandoned him but he was old enough to know the consequences if he failed. Indeed you are old enough to know the retribution that could fall on you should you be discovered aiding a traitor."

"Father! How can you call him that?"

"I can, because it is the law of the land. His was a brave but foolish enterprise. Many of us could see the appeal, but understood the folly of it. I pray you will both be spared and will not rue your actions."

He went out into the hall and called for Jim. He gave instructions for Ebony to be saddled. I kissed my father's cheek and he held me to him for a moment. He stepped back. "Ebony will need to be shod."

"I am going to see John Armstrong anyway to tell him what I intend. I will have to leave Chestnut here. Please take care of him. Give my regards to the others."

I left the Hall and walked to the stables. I was overawed by the size of my father's horse, but with the aid of Jim mounted him at last and headed for the smithy.

John was not at work but I found him in his room sitting reading close to the fire. He stood up, a look of surprise on his face. "Dorothy! Come and warm yourself. I did not expect anyone to be out on such a foul day."

I sat down beside him on a bench by the fire, a little disconcerted that he should use my Christian name so casually. I composed myself. "You have heard what they did to the Earl?"

"I have. It's a terrible thing. I'm sorry; you must be deeply distressed. I would have visited you but . . ." He turned away.

I sat for a moment collecting my thoughts. "John, I have my father's horse Ebony outside and he needs to be shod. Will you do it for me now, please? I'm going to London to try and help my brother."

John sprang to his feet. "To London! What foolishness is this? You cannot make such a journey on your own."

I stood up, my hands on my hips. "Do not tell me what I can or cannot do. No-one else is prepared to go and help Thomas, so I must. They have executed poor James and Kenmure and since Nithsdale escaped from the Tower I am sure they have others in mind to make up for his loss. Those in Newgate Prison like Charles Radcliffe and Thomas will be next. I am going and if you will not help me with Ebony then I will take him to Purdy!"

John looked at me for a moment and I was surprised to see a mixture of anger and exasperation on his face. "Of course I will take care of Ebony, but who will take care of you?"

"I will take care of myself."

"No! I will not let you go alone."

"*You* will not let me?"

"No!" He took a breath. "I will come with you and I will *not* take no for an answer."

I saw grim determination on his face, his eyes defying me to argue. I felt I should be annoyed that he was taking command of the situation and telling me what would happen, but I also felt great relief that I might not be alone and I could not stifle a quick smile in his direction. He turned away and breathed deeply.

I moved closer. "John, I am truly grateful to you for making such an offer, but you must consider that you would be putting your life at risk, as well as your livelihood."

He swung back to face me. "I am quite aware of the consequences both of my actions and of what you intend. When do you wish to leave?"

"Tomorrow."

He nodded. "We will use only Ebony. It will cost less to keep one horse on the road and it will not be so dangerous if you ride pillion behind me."

"I am as good a rider as yourself."

He raised an eyebrow. "But easier to keep in check if I hold the whip."

I saw a faint smile on his face. I felt I should say something to put him in his place, but could think of nothing.

He continued. "You will also then be able to ride side-saddle, in skirts, without it slowing our speed. I do not think they will look favourably on a young woman in breeches in London. And for safety, as we have similar colouring, you can act as if my sister."

Before I could think of a reply he threw on his coat and went outside.

I followed him out and watched him feel the saddle and lift up Ebony's hooves one-by-one. He looked back at me. "I have a longer saddle which is thicker. It is for two riders and will be quite comfortable enough for you. Go back into my room and keep warm. It will take time to light the furnace and replace his shoes."

I was becoming increasingly impatient at being told what to do. "I hope, John, that you will not take advantage of this arrangement. This is my enterprise and I will make the decisions as to what we will do and how we will do it!"

He stood, his eyes fixed on mine and didn't move.

"So," I continued, feeling uncomfortable at his steady stare, "I will go and keep warm while you prepare him for our journey."

He continued to look at me, his expression unreadable and with a slight nod of the head and the merest raising of an eyebrow, he spoke in a firm voice. "Yes, Mistress Forster."

I knew he hadn't deserved my rebuke but was unable to think what I could say to put it right.

◆   ◆   ◆

We reached Bamburgh as the moon rose brightly and the stars began to sparkle in the clear sky. It was bitterly cold and I was glad of John's broad, warm back to cling to as Ebony trotted slowly up the road to the manor house. We supped early and I retired to bed before nine, leaving John in the kitchen finishing his October ale.

I laid out my clothes ready for the morning and filled my leather saddle bags with extra woollen clothes, stockings and mufflers. I had resolved to wear the velvet cloak Madam Clavering had given me. Besides being warm, I felt it would command a certain respect from people I might have need of impressing.

I climbed into bed and thought about John in the room below me, a great relief flowing over me that he had seen fit to join me in my quest. Despite feeling a mixture of excitement and apprehension, I slept better than I had done for some time.

CHAPTER 38

THE GREAT NORTH ROAD

We were delayed by a blizzard on the first day of our journey and had a slippery and slow day's ride and a night in the Grey Nag's Head in Morpeth. We approached Newcastle in late afternoon on the second day.

The horizon was filled with plumes of smoke and steam which mingled and hung unmoving above the Castle Keep and the walls and buildings of the city. I wished we did not need to spend the night there, but the difficult conditions had slowed our ride and Durham was out of reach for that day.

Newcastle is considered a fine town and indeed has many fine buildings and shops, but the acrid fumes and smoke that often blow up from the ironworks and the ships carrying coal and lead from the nearby mines add to the city's normal secretions. The pall sometimes settles over the city, lending it a grey and suffocating atmosphere that takes away the pleasure of its architecture.

Our night in the George Inn near the parish church of St Nicholas was noisy, but warm and friendly, despite their misguided loyalty to the Hanoverian King.

After a late breakfast the next day, we crossed the stone bridge to the south side of the River Tyne and up the busy, steep streets of Gateshead. It was almost an hour before we left the dirt and grime behind. The snow of the previous days had turned to unpleasant sleet that stung our eyes and the slippery slush beneath poor Ebony's hooves made him snort with effort as he struggled on.

The sun was beginning to set in a clearer sky when we finally saw Durham Cathedral in the distance, its tower standing proudly above the trees to the south-west of the road. I leaned to my right and pointed, "See,

my Uncle Crewe is bishop of that great and splendid cathedral. Are you
not impressed by its size?"

"Aye, it's a fine sight. Have you thought where we will stay this night?"

"I have only stayed at the castle on my previous visits, but I have heard
that there are one or two comfortable rooms at the Big Jug Inn in Claypath,
if they are not taken, and I heard it said they serve wholesome food."

"That sounds promising. 'Tis just as well you know the town for it is
all new to me."

"Further south we will have to leave to chance finding us lodging, for
I have never travelled beyond Durham. And John, I've been thinking, if
I'm to be your sister, you must call me Dorothy."

We rode on a little further and John turned his head towards me. "In
that case I must also be allowed to speak as if to a sister."

I leant forward to his right side and looked up at his face. "An elder
sister, whom you must respect, John."

He glanced back and I saw a smile hovering around his mouth..
"Yes . . . dear sister Dorothy."

As we got closer to Durham I saw that dusk was rapidly approaching.
My bones ached despite the more comfortable saddle. For a second day I
was sitting astride Ebony, having found that riding side-saddle on the first
day had proved too difficult and uncomfortable on a journey which had
to be taken with care and a tight grip on the saddle. Despite trouble with
my skirts I found that the voluminous cloak had been useful in covering
most of my legs and I rode more easily that way.

The Great North Road eventually swung down into Durham and I was
thankful when at last Ebony's hooves clattered down the cobbles of Claypath
and we reached the Big Jug with its smoky warmth and hot spiced ale. I
had barely finished my stew when my lids began to droop and I took my
leave of John and fell on my bed fully clothed.

The early morning was icily cold and not helped by a north-easterly
whipping down the road as we set off. As the road curved round between
the closer rows of buildings and into the market square, I was grateful
for the warmth that John's body gave me as he guided Ebony across the
slippery cobbles along Saddler street and down towards Elvet Bridge.

We passed the prison on the west end of the bridge and rode across to Elvet. I glanced up and down the street.

"That disagreeable woman, Lady Mary Radcliffe, lives in this street. She is no doubt moving heaven and earth this very minute to be sure of keeping her wealth, regardless of James's death and Charles suffering in Newgate Prison."

John turned to face me and frowned. "I think she will not be the only one doing that hereabouts. I don't like to hear bitterness in your words, Dorothy."

I was taken aback to receive such a rebuke and surprised to feel chastened. I resolved to watch my tongue in future.

Although the roads became less rough as we journeyed south, the inns were often less comfortable than our first three stops. When the weather was fine I found myself exhilarated by the speed we rode and the vista of the frosted countryside we went through, but what I was totally unprepared for was finding that there were times when the two of us had to share a room and once—together with strangers—not only a room but also what was offered as a place to lie.

I was thankful that John made certain that nobody lay near by placing himself between them and me. None removed clothing and all used their outer garments as extra covers in the freezing rooms, but it gave me added comfort to know that his presence made it certain that none would search me for money while I slept.

Hidden beneath my clothes I had a little more than two hundred guineas left from the three my uncle sent after my aunt's death and the sixty from my father. Over the past three months I had already sent near a hundred guineas to Thomas when I received word of his need to pay five pounds a week for his food and lodging in the prison, and a further five pounds for a room to himself. Thomas also had to pay twenty-five guineas to be released from his leg shackles, and more recently another ten per week to have a room in the governor's house rather than a chamber on the common side of the prison where he had first been interred. He had used up his own money within a few weeks of arriving in Newgate prison.

Lee, who was allowed to leave the prison to seek money and buy food and drink for his master, had managed to beg substantial amounts from known sympathisers in London, but these handouts were not reliable. I knew I would probably need a good deal of what I had left if I was to get him out and safely away.

Time and again I wondered what conditions he was living in and with what kind of people he shared those conditions. If they were as rough and lacking in good manners as some of the travellers John and I met, I knew he would not be happy. I found myself shocked by the behaviour and language of some of them, whether they were travelling the roads by public or private coach or, indeed, horseback.

On entering one freezing ante-room ahead of John, a man dressed in some finery restrained me by the arm. "Well, my pretty one, I can keep you warm through the night!"

John swung round and grabbed the man's collar. "Stay far away from her and keep your leering eyes and randy comments for those that are as low as you!"

I had never heard such strong words from John and was surprised. I knew then that I could not have made the journey without him and was grateful.

There were more than two weeks of travel in freezing weather after we left Durham, and we experienced frequent demands for road tolls of a penny per horse, and skirmishes with coach drivers making it necessary for us to take action to avoid being mown down. We stayed two nights in Boroughbridge to give Ebony time to recover from his burdensome load and at the end of twenty days of exhausting, bone-aching journeying, he at last brought us to the outskirts of London.

As we rode on through the city, I found the increasing noise and smells overwhelming. The din of the cries of peddlers, clocks chiming, animals snorting, street musicians and the shouts of passers-by as they tried to make their opinions heard by their companions, added to the rattling iron wheels and horses' hooves clattering over the stone cobbles.

I had often thought myself lucky to live away from the noise that city dwellers had to bear in Newcastle, but this was a great deal more deafening, the volume of traffic being so much greater. I could not believe that people would choose to live in such mayhem. I found myself longing to find lodging where I could be the sole occupant of a quiet room and a bed to myself. I tried to convey my thoughts to John but even though I shouted, he did not catch all I was saying.

After a short while he brought Ebony to a stop outside an inn, swung his leg over the horse's shoulders and jumped off onto the stony ground. He held his arms aloft to help me down. I winced as I slid from the saddle, supported by his strong arms. He looked concerned. "Are you hurting?"

"I ache all over. Thank goodness we've reached our destination at last. I need to rest."

"I don't know if this will be where we stay, but Ebony can rest while we have a meal and find out where we are." I wanted to protest that I could go no further but did not have the strength.

After our meal of cheese, bread and pickles, I sat back in my seat and sipped the ale which had been the only drink on offer. The room was smoky and noisy but warm, and I felt a little better. John leaned forward and raised his voice so I could hear him over the din.

"I have the address of the house of John Purdy's kinsman who used to live near him in Lucker before he came to London. He'll be able to help us find rooms. I think our purpose would be better served if we were not in inns where . . ." He looked round furtively.

I nodded. "Yes, John. I understand your thinking. I did not know you had spoken to Purdy."

"I went to see him from the manor house after you had gone to bed the night before we left. I knew his relation lived in London and Purdy was happy to be of help. I think we should go there now if we can find the way."

I sat for a moment, reluctant to leave the warmth but knowing he was right. I stood up. "Then go we must, before I fall asleep on this uncomfortable seat." I threw on my cloak and pulled up the hood while John showed the landlord the address and asked for directions.

As darkness fell and people scurried fearfully along the streets, we finally found the house in a road near Drury Lane. Purdy's cousin, an aged though still strongly built man with sharp eyes, made us welcome and it was good to hear a familiar accent among the strange sounding speech we heard on the streets.

He and his wife asked no questions as to our purpose and insisted we stay with them that night and find other lodgings in the morning in the light of day. Purdy was still a smith like his cousin and had a small stable nearby. He assured me that Ebony would be well cared for and his wife showed us a small room upstairs at the back of their house which contained a bed and a chair. I glanced at the bed and at John. He turned to Mrs Purdy.

"Dorothy will be comfortable in this room. I would ask that I might sleep in the parlour. A chair would suffice."

"You are not married?"

"No."

Mrs Purdy nodded. "I will fetch you a blanket. You must choose for yourself which will be the least uncomfortable chair to sleep on. You are a big man. Perhaps the mat in front of the fire would be best."

The following morning I descended to the parlour to find that John—with the help of Purdy—had already found rooms in a lodging house nearer to Newgate. It was in Holburn and not far from the top of Snow Hill where the road led down to the prison.

Purdy warned us that the streets off Snow Hill and in the Old Bailey where the prison was, were full of footpads, street scourers and pickpockets and we would do well to carry pistols. John stood in thought for a moment. "I think I will find some kind of bludgeon. I have no knowledge of guns and no wish to acquire it."

I nodded. "That will suffice. I think most thieves and vagabonds will look at John and turn away to find easier prey. And I do not intend leaving his side other than to enter the prison."

Purdy looked disconcerted, shook his head and tutted. "Well, you must do as you will, but be wary at all times. You know we are here if you need further help. I will see that your horse is ready for you whenever you need him."

I touched John's arm and he nodded and felt in his pocket. "Here are five guineas for your care of Ebony." Purdy protested and shook his head but I insisted. I saw his wife Lizzie was happy to see him take it.

Our lodgings consisted of one room with a fireplace, a large bed, a small table, two wooden chairs and a leather armchair. There was another tiny room next to it with a marble-topped wash stand with bowl and jug and a wooden clothes-horse. We had agreed that we should spend as little as possible on our lodgings, but I could not help but wonder about our sleeping arrangements now we were fully alone. I sat down and looked at the bed. John saw where I looked and came to me with raised brows.

"Another small room will be free within the week. I can return to Purdy's until then if you wish, but as we have slept together for a number of nights, I thought it would not bother you. You did not complain and I would be happier if I was close by."

"John, I was grateful for your protection and comforted by your nearness and I would be fearful without you now. It is just that I find the lack of privacy taxing. It is not something I am used to."

He stood looking at me for a moment. "If you will allow me to take the leather chair, I will bring the furniture out of the wash room into here and I can sleep in there."

"I would not think of having you sleep in that freezing room! We will find material to make a screen round my bed. I will be happy with that, though I do not think you will sleep well on that chair even near the fire."

He smiled. "I have no trouble sleeping. Now, are you visiting your brother today?"

"Most certainly. I am eager to see Thomas and I must find out what possibilities there are to help him escape. We will buy some food and drink for him on the way. That will put him in even better spirits."

The sickening smells and raucous sounds that greeted us as we neared Newgate prison made me hold my kerchief to my face and grab hold of John's arm for comfort. The clamour increased as we reached the gate. We knocked at a door in the gate and a small flap opened and the head of a turnkey appeared and asked our business.

"I am come to visit someone who lodges in the Governor's house."

He peered out and looked us both up and down. "Well, well; and which of those traitors do you wish to see?"

I fought to keep my face expressionless. "General Forster."

"Ah. That one. It's my thinking his life is made too easy for one who would've had us all back to popery, inquisitions, tortures and burnings of so-called heretics."

I stiffened and yearned to argue the case with him but a sidelong glance and a warning squeeze of my hand from John checked my impulse.

I swallowed. "Please would you let us in?"

The turnkey sneered at us and pointed to a heavy iron door to our right. "That's the way into Mr Pitts's house." His head disappeared and the flap came down.

I looked at John. "I suppose Mr Pitts is the governor."

After a few minutes of knocking, a heavy-set man opened the door, pistol in hand and asked my name and business. Before I could finish my explanation, Lee pushed past the man and grabbed my hand. "Oh, Mistress Forster. I thought I was dreaming when I heard your voice. I cannot believe it. Your brother refused to ask you to come." He turned to the man holding the door. "Jonas, this is my master's sister. I can vouch for her."

The man nodded and stood aside but barred the way to John. "Not you. One visitor at a time. Relatives only."

I opened my mouth to protest but John stopped me with a hand on my arm and a frown. "I'll wait outside. Give my regards to your brother."

CHAPTER 39

AN UNEASY TRUCE

2005

"Honey, it was terrific! The beautiful lake District in the late Fall, snow on the mountains round Loch Lomond; that stupendous castle in Edinburgh, the cathedral and castle in Durham to die for and romantic inglenook fires in old inns. Couldn't have asked for more. You made our holiday and we had a whip round and this is for you."

"Oh no, Joe, that's very kind but . . ."

"Hey! Do you want upset me when I'm leaving and not looking forward to the flight?"

"No, but . . ."

"I don't want to argue! Take it."

Cathy took the envelope and kissed Joe on the cheek.

"Gee, honey, you made my day."

One by one they hugged and kissed her and waved as they filed through the gate, showing their passports and boarding passes. Cathy smiled and waved until the last one disappeared from sight. She slipped the envelope into her bag and turned round.

Jack was standing a few feet away. Cathy gasped and looked for something to lean on. "What are you doing here? How did you know where I'd be?"

"I phoned Maggie."

"Why?"

"To find out where and when you'd be here. She said you're going to Newcastle on Friday, to continue your research."

"What's that got to do with you?"

"I want to come too. I've worked almost every day since you left, so I have seven days free and I want to know the end of Dorothy's story. You owe me that."

"No!"

He came closer. "No strings, Cathy. Just two friends trying to find the end of Dorothy's story."

"No. I couldn't . . ."

"Just searching for information and visiting places. Please, Cathy; I need to do this."

Cathy looked into Jack's eyes and saw pain. Her instincts told her it would be unbearably hard to do and merely prolong the hurt she'd hoped would slowly heal, but she yearned to be with him again, even if for only a short time.

She forced herself to look into his eyes. "*If* I say yes, you have to promise not to touch me, not to say anything about feelings or what happened between us."

He stood for a moment and looked down. "I promise." He looked at his watch. "Cathy, I have to catch a train in ten minutes. I need an answer."

"It really does have to be strictly research and nothing else."

He nodded.

Cathy knew she should say no, but she didn't. "Ok. I'll text you the details of the hotel in Gateshead. 8 a.m. breakfast, Saturday."

He looked steadily at her. "I'll have a pot of coffee waiting."

◆   ◆   ◆

Cathy frowned as her phone rang late on Friday evenng. It was Jack.

"What?"

"Just thought I'd let you know I've arrived."

"We said 8 a.m. breakfast. Don't make me regret giving in to you."

"Right. Night, Cathy."

"Night." Cathy switched off her phone, grabbed a pillow to hug and closed her eyes.

◆　◆　◆

Cathy stood outside the dining room and prepared herself to face Jack again. If they were just acquaintances now, why should it be so difficult? She took a deep breath and walked through the door. A figure silhouetted against the window on the other side of the room stood up and waved. She moved forward hypnotically until she reached the table and sat down as he pushed the seat under her. "You didn't need to do that."

He sat down and looked into her eyes. "Morning Cathy. Coffee?"

She nodded irritably and unfolded her napkin. He poured coffee into her cup. "Seen the view?"

She turned. "Oh, yes. Incredible. It said the view was good on our details. Lots of bridges across the river, and that glass building across the road is the Sage Music Centre, isn't it?"

"Yes. We should take a look."

"It's not on my agenda."

"Ok. What are we doing today?"

"Well, I don't know what you're going to do, but I'm going to spend the day in the Central Library in Newcastle."

"Me too, then."

She took a sip of coffee and looked up as a waiter came to the table. "Good morning Sir, Madam; would you like to order now?"

◆　◆　◆

Jack stood up. "Great breakfast, eh?"

"Yes. Delicious. A bit more than I'm used to, though. I think I'll walk to the library."

"It's quite a walk. We should take my car."

"You can if you want. I want to walk."

"You know where you're going?"

"I've got a map."

Jack looked at her for a moment, his eyes narrowed and he shrugged his shoulders. "Good luck! See you there."

Cathy went back to her room and picked up her backpack and the internet map showing the route to the library. It didn't look far and she wondered why Jack had looked so doubtfully at her. If he thought she couldn't follow a map, he was wrong.

She strode down the steep hill as the rain started. Getting across the Swing Bridge was simple, but when she took out the map at the other end, it was hard to shield it from the deluge. Some of the names smudged, but she knew the general direction she had to take and refused to worry she might get lost. Wet hair dripped down her face and onto the map and she put it back in her backpack and strode on.

She avoided a motor bike as she crossed a road and suddenly thought about Tom. His name still caused her heart to take an occasional plunge, but no longer automatically set off the chain reaction of unhappy thoughts and images that triggered pictures of her flight after the crash. Sometime she woke from her dreams about Tom and almost felt it was his attempt from beyond to make her feel better. Almost, but not quite; she knew it was just her subconscious playing tricks. Jack had more or less said so.

She wove up through streets, took a wrong turn which meant that after fifteen minutes she had to double back, and walked on until she came to the Eldon Square monument. Suddenly, her confidence failed her and she stopped a man and asked the way to the Central Library.

He smiled "I'm going there myself. This way. Come under the umbrella."

She hesitated for a moment. "Oh, thanks. I was about to go in the other direction."

"Well, if you wanted to go to the footy, that would be great, but for the library, it's this way."

Her phone rang. It was Jack. "Where the hell are you? It's nearly an hour since you left."

"I'm almost there."

"Couple of minutes," the man said smiling at her.

"A couple . . ."

"I heard." He rang off.

"Oh, dear, is he cross?"

Cathy smiled at the man. "It's not a problem."

◆   ◆   ◆

Cathy found the room where the local history books were kept and searched the room for Jack. He shook his head when he saw her. She took her backpack and coat off and wiped a rivulet of water from her face with the arm of her sweater.

"Didn't you have an umbrella with you?" Jack whispered, an incredulous look on his face.

"I left it in my car and I didn't know it was going to rain!"

Heads turned and Jack put his finger to his lips, dived below the table and pulled out a towel. He got up, walked round to her and began to towel her hair. She snatched it from him. "So you knew it was going to rain and just didn't bother to tell me," she whispered angrily.

"I assumed you'd watch the weather report, until I saw you striding off without an umbrella in your hand. It could have been in your backpack, but I brought the towel just in case it wasn't." His face was too close to hers for comfort and she sat down and finished towelling her hair.

He went back to his chair and sat down. He leaned forward and began to whisper. "That book in front of you has some info about the Forster family and their wills. Mine has some family trees and what they call the family pedigree, but there's a lot of it and we can't discuss it here. There are some more books I want to look at. I'm going to do some photo-copying in a minute and I think you'll have to copy some of the info in your book too, so we can take it all to a café. It's going to be a very late lunch by the time we get through them all."

"Right. I'll get started."

◆   ◆   ◆

Cathy took a sip of coffee. "I don't think I told you what happened to the captured Jacobites after the battle in Preston."

Jack shook his head. "No."

"It was awful. Some were herded into freezing prisons or churches; some were squeezed into terrible conditions in ships to the American colonies, but the professional soldiers, the leaders and the aristocracy were marched down to London in freezing weather to be tried for treason. They must have been absolutely exhausted by the time they got there and then were jeered at and had unmentionable things thrown at them. All the Lords were imprisoned in the Tower, but Thomas, Charles Radcliffe and many others were in Newgate Prison, which sounds a really bad place to be, although not as bad as the worst."

"Add the terrible weather that winter. And I don't suppose there was any heating."

"They would have some mangy blankets, maybe, but Thomas was quite lucky or maybe just clever. He was in a room with a fire in the governor's house attached to the prison."

"How did he manage that?"

"Money."

They sat looking at each other for a minute until Cathy dragged her eyes away from Jack's. She looked down at the pile of papers on the table. "A parcel arrived from my contacts in Australia, just before I left yesterday. I haven't opened it yet, but it should contain John Bird's leaflet."

"Ah, I forgot mine."

They read silently for a while and Cathy highlighted the parts she wanted to make notes about. She glanced at Jack and he was drawing a line round a passage on the copied page. He looked up and she felt as if she'd been caught stealing the silver. He took a breath. "Did I tell you Josie had a party last Saturday?"

"You know you didn't."

"Yes. A 'wet the baby's head' party."

Cathy grimaced. "How nice! Still William 'Jack'?"

"Well she couldn't really change it when everyone heard her call him that, could she?"

"So, if she invited you, you must have told her we'd broken up."

"No. I haven't told anyone. Not even Sara." He looked down. "None of their business," he said quietly.

He picked up his papers and stood up. "I'm going to finish these back at the hotel. Do you want a lift or do you want to look like a drowned rat again?"

She glared at him. "I don't want anything from you! I'll make my own way back!"

"Fine!" He hesitated for moment as if he was going to say more, turned away and stomped out of the café.

CHAPTER 40

REVELATIONS AND FRICTION

Cathy took a taxi to the hotel, went straight to her room, tore open the parcel from Australia and began to read the letter and booklet inside. She was relieved that it confirmed what she'd read in other books. It said it was thought that John Armstrong had accompanied Dorothy to London, but if what she found had happened to Thomas was true, in the end, they'd both lost their brothers.

◆　　◆　　◆

She lay in bed unable to sleep and wondered how Dorothy would have felt losing her brother—if what she'd read had really happened—and knew it had to have been a terrible blow after all she'd done. Yet, somehow, she'd carried on. But not alone. She wrapped her arms around herself. *I didn't save my brother and I'm not going to have a happy ending.*

It was the first time Cathy had cried herself to sleep since meeting Jack and she woke with an anxious feeling and remembered strange, mixed up dreams she wanted to forget. She rolled over and the glowing green numbers on the radio alarm clock showed it was five o'clock.

She got up and made a cup of tea. Her face in the mirror was a mess and she was glad Jack wasn't there to see it; why she felt like that, she refused to think about.

She forced herself to go back to bed and watch the rolling news for an hour and almost fell asleep. At seven, her phone rang.

"Cathy, I think maybe I'm asking too much; if me being here is too hard for you to cope with, I can go back to London."

A shock ran through her body. "Is that what you want to do?"

"No."

"Oh."

"But I'm finding it hard."

"Yes."

"Shall we see how today goes and make a decision this evening?"

"Oh, Jack, I don't know . . . yes . . . perhaps."

"Right. I'm going to breakfast in about ten minutes. Coming?"

"I need a shower. My hair needs washing; as you said, it's a mess."

"Oh, Cathy, I'm sorry about the rat's tails comment. I don't know why I said that; I've never seen it or you look anything but beautiful."

"Stop."

"Yes, ok. Well, I'm famished. I only had a beef burger and chips last night—room service."

"Me too—well, a sandwich."

"We need a good, breakfast, don't we?"

"I don't feel like eating."

"What? Look, I'm putting my doctor's hat on now. You need a decent breakfast. Go and have your shower. I'll give you fifteen minutes and if you're not down by then, I'll come up and hammer on your door."

◆   ◆   ◆

Cathy opened her napkin and put it on her lap. "I was thinking about what Dorothy had to go through just to get to London and then stay there and visit that disgusting prison . . . she had to have a lot of courage to contemplate a journey she'd never done before and attempt to spring him from prison. And here I am in this luxurious hotel and I'm struggling to handle a failed relationship and just keep going with the research. I'm pathetic."

Jack had flinched when she mentioned "a failed relationship" and now he was staring into his coffee. He looked up. "Not pathetic; just hurting. You're not the only one."

"So why are we doing this? I'm not sure I can keep doing this with you."

"We'll make a decision this evening, like I said. It's Sunday, so we can't do much research. Let's do some sightseeing."

Cathy looked up as the waiter put a plate in front of her. "I didn't order."

The waiter looked confused and glanced at Jack. Jack nodded. "That's fine."

The waiter put a second plate in front of him. "Thank you madam, sir. Enjoy!"

Cathy waited until the waiter had disappeared. "You ordered for me?"

"Yes. I just thought you'd be hungry and would like scrambled egg and smoked salmon. Was I wrong?"

"That's not the point!"

The waiter returned with a bottle of champagne in a bucket. Cathy looked at Jack, mouthing, 'what?'

Jack smiled and Cathy had to bite her tongue. He leant forward. "Well you chose the hotel, so I thought . . ."

A sudden anger surged through her. "What are you trying to do, Jack? You're not going to make everything right with a smile, smoked salmon and champagne!"

She threw down her napkin and walked out.

◆   ◆   ◆

Cathy pulled out her papers, her mind and body feeling out of her control. She tried to force herself to take in the information she'd found in the library but couldn't concentrate. She told herself it was just writer's block; nothing to do with Jack.

She lay on the bed feeling bewildered and hungry and knowing she'd been irrational. Jack had been trying to do something nice and she'd been ungrateful and impetuous . . . and probably embarrassed him in front of the waiter. She picked up her phone and punched in his number.

"Yes?"

"I'm sorry."

"Right. So am I. I find it hard not to want to . . ."

"I'd like to see the Sage and the Baltic Art Gallery," she said hurriedly.

"With me?"

"Yes . . . if you want to."

"I'm having breakfast. Two plates of scramble and smoked salmon. You'll have to wait until I'm finished."

"Call me when you're ready, please."

"Right. I'll put the Champagne in my room fridge, shall I?"

"It would be a shame for it to get warm."

"I'll be ready in ten minutes."

◆　　◆　　◆

They looked up at the sweeping curves of the Sage before they went through the automatic doors. After a few steps inside, they stopped and gazed around. Jack smiled. "Quite a place, eh?"

Cathy looked up and began to turn, trying to take it all in. The vast glass roof swept over the two auditoriums and the huge entrance hall of the Sage and curved down to the north revealing a living picture of the river, its bridges and Newcastle. "Stunning. I heard it was unique, but it's more than that. The space is amazing."

"And it's even better when it's dark. Shall we see if they have any returns for either of the Halls this evening? We could eat in the restaurant here first."

She hesitated, feeling a little distrustful of his motives. "If you want."

"Is that a half-hearted 'yes' or a 'not really'?"

"Jack, I'm feeling a little half-hearted about everything but this place at the moment, but it's fine by me if it's what you want to do."

Jack looked at her and turned away. "Right; I'll go and see if there are any tickets."

◆　　◆　　◆

They ran down the steps from the Sage, crossed the road and continued on down to the riverside. They rode the lift of the Baltic art gallery, walked round the exhibits for half an hour and came back down to the river.

Jack turned to Cathy. "Come on to the middle of the Millennium Bridge. You get a better view of both buildings from there."

Cathy walked up the slope of the bridge, stood in the middle and looked southwards as the glass lift moved up the converted flour mill. The artworks had made her think, but she left feeling confused and a little cheated. She felt she should have understood what the artists were trying to say, but hadn't. She turned to her right and gazed again at the huge, curved, strangely shaped Sage building, its glass panels reflecting light across the river. "It looks like a glittering, enormous flat slug with its head and tail cut off."

Jack laughed. "Don't let the locals hear you saying anything derogatory about their buildings."

"I wasn't being derogatory; or I didn't mean to be. I think it's spectacular; totally different . . ." She looked at Jack. "Just a bit slug-like."

He smiled again and took her hand. "Come on. I'm dying for a good cup of coffee. And maybe some tapas?"

Cathy frowned, shook her hand from his and walked towards the Newcastle side. Jack walked beside her and pointed. "See that tall building that says 'Newcastle Cooperative Society' at the top?"

"Yes."

"Well, to the right of that, behind the riverside pub, is the Spanish restaurant where we can get the coffee and tapas. What do think?"

"Fine."

Jack turned to her. "You're sure?"

"Yes."

"You've gone all monosyllabic on me, Cathy. Was it grabbing your hand that did it?"

"Yes."

"Right."

◆   ◆   ◆

The two places left free were on an upholstered bench against a wall and they were squashed together on their corner of the long table. Jack smiled at Cathy. "I didn't realise it would be so popular. Perhaps we should share a mixed plate of tapas."

Cathy glanced at Jack. "Whatever."

They ate and drank in silence until Cathy saw Jack jab a piece of battered fish. "Hey! You've already had three of those and I want that one."

Jack looked at her, his eyebrows raised. "Didn't know you were counting." He lifted the fork to her mouth. She hesitated. "Please put it down. I want to use my own fork."

Jack leant forward and put his lips to her ear. "We've shared forks of food and a lot more, Cathy! Eat the bloody fish!" He brought the fish to her lips and she opened her mouth and began to chew as she felt tears spring into her eyes.

He put the fork down, slid his arm round her and pulled her against him. "Please don't; I didn't mean to make you cry, " he whispered.

She gulped as his cheek touched hers. Her lips were against his ear. "Take your arm off me or it's going to be really embarrassing when I pull away and slap your face."

Jack released her and sat back. Cathy swallowed the remnants of the fish, picked up her wine and downed it in one. She turned to Jack. "Please let me out."

He stood up. "Where are you going?"

"The hotel."

"We haven't finished."

"I have."

◆   ◆   ◆

She walked briskly along the quayside towards the Swing Bridge until she reached the colourful stalls set out on the wide pavement. She began to browse a music stall and bought a DVD for her parents and another which reminded her of Tom.

She was crossing the bridge when Jack caught up with her. Her heart leapt and she turned away and looked straight ahead. He strode ahead and turned to face her.

"Stop. It's not working, is it? You can't bear me touching you and I can't stop wanting to." He pulled out two tickets, grabbed her hand and closed her fingers round them. "You need to find someone else to go to the concert with."

He strode off and Cathy leaned against the rail feeling a pain that took her breath away. She peered down at the swiftly moving river which had turned a gloomy grey, reflecting the rain clouds that were darkening the sky.

She hated herself for wanting Jack's arms round her again and hated herself for walking out on him, but he'd broken his promise. It had made her want what she couldn't have and now she'd driven him away and he probably wouldn't try again. And even if he did, what was the point? They'd split up and neither could compromise on where they could be together or what they thought was important in a marriage.

She tried to quieten her fast beating heart by taking long breaths. She fisted her hands, knowing for certain that Dorothy would have found a way to make things right.

She ran across the bridge and up the hill and reached the hotel just as Jack was driving up the ramp out of the underground garage.

CHAPTER 41

NEWGATE PRISON, LONDON

1716

I felt deeply unhappy that John was being excluded from the governor's house, but nodded to him and turned to Lee. He took my arm. "Come, I'll show you to my master's room."

We found Thomas seated by a fire talking to another man. As we entered, Thomas sprang up, a look of astonishment on his face, and paled as if he had seen a ghost. I ran over and threw my arms around him. I felt his arms close round me and listened to his muffled voice saying my name over and over again. He released me and I saw tears in his eyes. "Dolly, whatever are you doing here?"

I glanced at the man still seated by the fire. The man stood up and offered his hand. "Sir Francis Anderton, who would wish to be at your service but who finds himself at present unable to be so. If you would excuse me, I must return to my room."

I smiled at him and shook his hand. "Dorothy Forster; thank you for keeping my brother company. I am sure it gives him great comfort."

Sir Francis bowed and left. I sat down in his seat. Thomas leant forward. "Why have you come, Dolly?"

"To help you escape."

"On your own?"

"No. John Armstrong insisted on accompanying me and I'm very grateful he did."

He sat silently for a moment. "I've been here for more than four months. Why now?"

"The situation changed when we heard about James. Before that awful deed there was much talk that the government would be lenient rather than make martyrs of you all. We heard that many had been sent to the colonies in Virginia, Carolina and Jamaica and would return in time. And some of those imprisoned in the west seemed to escape easily. Did you know that Lord Widdrington's brother, Henry, and the Charlton brothers escaped from Wigan prison?"

Thomas shook his head. He sighed. "That may be, but it seems they've kept some of the truth from you, Dolly. Haven't you not heard of those that were shot later and those that died of cold or the fever, crowded together like dogs in filthy, freezing prisons? The Governor, Pitts, is full of stories of our men in prisons in Chester, Lancaster and Liverpool and how much worse I would have suffered had I not been so fortunate as to be brought here. There are others festering in the prisons in Fleet and Marshalsea. I wake from nightmares and think of the suffering our brave soldiers have endured. We only lost two or three in battle, but we have lost many more since. And . . . the government having dealt with the Lords, it's our turn next."

I took his hand. "Thomas, why did you not tell me all this? Your letters spoke only of a need for money and were cheerful about your situation."

Thomas shrugged his shoulders. "When neither John nor Father came, I could not expect help to come from any other. You should not have come."

I felt his pain but could say nothing that would comfort his feeling of neglect. I squeezed his hand. "When I heard about poor James, I realised that your life was in danger and I could no longer rely on the King having mercy on you. We have to get you out of here. Tell me, do you know how Lord Nithsdale escaped from the Tower?"

Thomas looked at me with new hope in his eyes. "Pitts told me that it is said it was Lady Nithsdale's doing. She generally visited him with her maid, but on that day slipped in almost unnoticed by a relief guard without her maid but with the maid's clothes beneath her garments. At the end of the day, Nithsdale dressed in the clothes, and the regular guards, expecting two ladies to leave as usual, let them out and they got clean away." Thomas laughed. "The droll thing is, he was pardoned the next day and so all the effort was not needed. But they could not have known that, for all other pleading had come to nought."

I sighed. "Well, we cannot repeat that, especially as I don't have Jenny with me, but there must be a way." I sat in thought. "You seem to have a great deal of freedom here. The door of this room was not locked."

"It is locked at ten in the evening when Pitts and his manservant, Jonas, retire for the night, and is not opened till eight the next morning."

"And who holds the key to the front door and this?"

"Jonas. And he is a strong, armed man and faithful to his master for he gets a portion of the fee we pay, so do not look to help from that quarter."

"Do you know how long it will be before they bring you to trial?"

"Mr. Pitts says that bills of indictment for high treason are being prepared on eleven of us. Charles Radcliffe was not among the names, though he is here, lying low and trying to keep out of their notice. The bills could be found at any time and our trial is likely to be held seven days from then, certainly before mid-April."

I gasped and my heart beat fast. "We could have less than a month!"

Thomas smiled weakly and shrugged his shoulders. "I have resigned myself to it. As yet, I do not know how I will plead. If I refuse to acknowledge Geordie as King and plead not guilty, I will hang. If I plead guilty and throw myself on the mercy of the court, it is said I might be sent to the colonies. So I can either be a traitor to my King across the water and be exiled . . . or die."

I stood up and felt a new determination take hold of me. "You will do neither. We will find a way to get you out of here. Out of the country, I think, for they will not turn a blind eye to you as they have done to some."

Thomas smiled fondly at me. "It would please me beyond measure if it were possible, Dolly. I am frit of dying, but I don't want to be remembered as a turncoat and coward."

◆ ◆ ◆

Over supper by the fire in our room, I explained to John the time constraints we were under. I asked John for his ideas on how we could help Thomas escape.

He frowned and his eyes were anxious. "My thoughts as I waited for you 'midst the smell and clamour of that awful place, were that whatever we do must not include you having to enter that den more than necessary. Purdy told me the place is full of unimaginable behaviour and drunkenness and there is much sickness: gaol fever, they call it."

I saw I had to reassure him. "The governor's house is set apart and quite respectable. Thomas's room is not unlike this room, other than having a small barred window which looks out onto the prison yard, and a strong iron door. There is no other person in the house but a gentleman called Sir Francis Anderton and, of course, Lee. My visits do not put me in any danger."

I saw John was somewhat relieved and smiled at him. He gave a quick smile and his eyes held mine. I felt a strange sensation, but tried not to let it disturb my concentration and began again. "Now then, it's urgent that we make a plan and carry it out as soon as possible. My feeling is that I must make Jonas trust me and somehow use that trust to steal the key to the door and . . ."

John clenched his fists. "You are not thinking straight! That would be too dangerous. He would notice! What we must do is make a copy of the key so he does not have time to be suspicious. For that, we need an impression. I do not like the idea of you putting yourself in such a situation but it is all I can think of."

"I would need wax for that, would I not?"

"We could use wax, but I think the less we have contact with shopkeepers who might remember us or become suspicious of our intentions, the better. We can use moist clay wrapped in a wet rag. You should be able to hide it beneath your cloak."

I felt a smile creep across my face. "Yes, I could get the impression when Jonas was not looking. I must find out where he hangs the keys."

"He probably keeps them about his person."

"Perhaps I could take him ale or wine and get him drunk so that he sleeps, and take the impression that way."

John stood up and paced the room. "It is all too dangerous. If he caught you, you could be thrown in prison too!"

"John, I would not risk all unless I felt sure it was possible to succeed."

He sat down and looked into my eyes. "Promise me you will do nothing until we have thought of all the pitfalls and are ready with our plan."

I smiled at him. "I promise. I know you think me impetuous, but I can be cautious and patient when the need arises. Now, we will need to have horses ready for Lee and Thomas and we must somehow book a passage on a ship to France. They cannot stay here."

After much discussion, we finally agreed that when the horses were bought and the passage booked, I would take the clay on every visit to Thomas until such time as an opportunity arose to use it.

Purdy gave us directions to Leigh in Essex where we could find ships for France. John persuaded me it was best if he made the journey alone. The journey would be tiring and the inns unlikely to be anything but rough and dangerous. He would be there for perhaps two or three days and he made me promise to stay in our rooms unless to go out in daylight to buy food at the shops in Holborn.

"I mean to frequent inns in Leigh where I can ask questions and listen to the drunken gossip of the sailors. Not until I find a Captain I think I can trust will I book the passage. I need to take twenty guineas as a holding fee, with the promise of more when the Captain's passengers are about to board."

I listened to him with mounting pride. He might not possess the same level of education or social class as myself, but he had an innate common sense and inspired in me a feeling of admiration and total trust.

I felt strangely bereft after John left but quelled my impatience to visit Thomas and tell him of our plans. I had promised to wait until John returned and wait I would. I passed my time by buying material, needles and thread and sewing a pocket inside my cloak big enough to hold the ball of clay and a key. I also bought broad sheets that printed the latest news so I could keep informed should there be any moves to bring the trial forward.

Late in the afternoon of the third day, John returned. When the door opened, I was so relieved and pleased to see him that I ran unthinkingly to him and hugged him. I was surprised to see he was embarrassed and gently pushed me away. I wondered if he had left someone at home who was awaiting his return. I stepped back and composed myself. "I was worried you might have run into difficulties. I am pleased to see you back safely."

He breathed deeply and nodded. "And I am glad to find you safe. I thought my decision to leave you here alone might have been wrong." He removed his coat and sat down. "I've booked the passage on the early morning tide on the 11th of April. Next, we must buy the horses. I think it is better if you are not seen purchasing them. People might remember you when the deed is done and the news spread abroad."

"They might remember you! You are a very striking figure of a man."

"A pretty face is the more likely to be remembered. I can pass for a servant buying horses for his mistress. And no-one knows my name."

♦   ♦   ♦

On subsequent visits to Newgate, I took note of the governor's and Jonas's routines and their interaction with Thomas and Sir Francis. I decided not to tell Thomas the details of our plans. It was obvious that much ale and whisky were consumed and I was wary of him telling all when he was in his cups. I reassured him that the plans were well in hand and would be revealed when it was time.

I arrived one morning to find him pleased to have made contact with two of the others imprisoned in the rooms round the Press yard of the prison. Since Thomas's indictment, Lee was no longer allowed out to perform errands of any kind. Thomas managed to persuade Jonas—with five guineas in his pocket—to take open letters to Peregrine Widdrington and Colonel Oxburgh, inquiring as to their health and situation.

He received a reply from Oxburgh saying that many Jacobite sympathisers brought in money which kept them well fed and able to drown their sorrows with liquor and that he hoped Thomas kept cheerful. He also asked if Thomas knew that the Countess Derwentwater had been delivered of a daughter at the end of March. I had heard nothing from Anna Maria since she left Dilston and hoped she was being well taken care of.

Thomas was a little perturbed that Peregrine had been sick with the fever and unable to write, but had read the note and asked Jonas to convey his good wishes. I remembered Peregrine's fresh-faced good looks ten years previously and how ardently he had pursued me until persuaded by his family that our religions did not mix and my fortune was too meagre. I fervently hoped he would recover.

I continued to observe Jonas as often as I could but was frustrated to see that the keys never left the belt round his middle. I noted which key he used for the front door and saw how it hung on the key ring. I showed a friendly interest in him whenever I felt it right and encouraged him to confide in me. Occasionally, I took him small gifts of mince pies or caraway cakes and saw he appreciated them without becoming suspicious of my intentions. One evening visit revealed him merry, but not drunk enough to be in a stupor or fall asleep.

I was becoming discouraged and agitated as the deadline came nearer and still I had been unable to find an opportunity to take an impression and could not see a way of doing it. I prayed for a miracle, but in the event, what transpired was even more unexpected.

◆　　◆　　◆

On the sixth of April I entered the governor's house late in the afternoon when I knew the governor would be on his rounds. I immediately noticed a change in Jonas's demeanour. He looked drowsy and I thought at first he'd been drinking, but it seemed more than just the effects of drink for his skin was shiny and damp and he had a strange odour about him. I expressed my concern and asked if I could do anything for him. He complained of a headache and pulled at his collar. I noticed a purplish rash on his neck and sores on his hand. A plan formed in my mind.

"Let me make you a hot toddy to comfort you. Tomorrow I will bring some herbs to ease your headache."

He shivered and sighed heavily. "'Tis only the fever. I have had it before, but I'm strong and well fed and will throw it off again."

I moved back warily and turned to walk across the stone floor towards the steps that led to the door to the stairs above.

"But," he called after me, "the toddy would be welcome."

I nodded and ran up the stairs, my pulse racing. I reached Thomas's room and quickly explained my plan to him. He helped me prepare the drink with a great deal more whisky than water which we heated on the fire. He dropped in some cloves from the cupboard where he kept his spirits and ales. He chuckled. "I'm well versed in this and though I'm loath to part with m'whisky, it's in a good cause."

I returned to Jonas to find him seated by the door. I offered him the tankard full to the brim with the mixture, and he took it gratefully. I left him and returned to Thomas.

Some time later, Lee tiptoed down to the anteroom and spied on Jonas. He returned with a smile on his face. "He is well asleep and snoring. Let me take the impression for you."

I shook my head. "No, if he wakes and finds me there he will think only that I am looking to his health. He might distrust your intentions. Stay here and make sure I'm alerted if the governor should return. If I get it done, I'll wake him and ask to be allowed out."

I put on my cloak, took out the parcel of clay, unwrapped it and lay it on the table. I replaced the wet rag in my pocket. My heart was pounding. I smiled uncertainly at Thomas, quickly doubled my thumb in my right hand to ward off danger, picked up the ball of clay and left the room.

CHAPTER 42

THE KEY TO FREEDOM

When I reached the anteroom, Jonas was still snoring loudly. His keys were hanging loosely by his side. I knelt down on the floor and took the weight of the largest key in the palm of my hand. I waited to see if he would stir, but his snoring lessened and his breathing became quiet and regular and I knew he was in a deep sleep.

I pressed the key into the clay as John had shown me and slowly removed it, my hands shaking. I put the clay on the floor and wiped the key on the lining of my cloak. Gently, I let it hang as before, carefully wrapped up the clay in the wet rag and put it into my pocket.

I tiptoed across the stone floor and back up the steps, went quietly through the door and stood there for a moment composing myself. I burst back through the door, letting it bang, and ran noisily down the steps and across the floor. Jonas did not stir. I shook him and called his name. It was a full five minutes before he was awake enough to register his situation.

"What! Have I been asleep, Mistress Forster? Hell fire and damnation! Is Mr Pitts about?" He fingered his keys and levered himself up out of the chair.

"No, Jonas, he has not returned. I think you had a nap but he did not see it. I would be grateful if you could let me out."

John emerged from the shadows across the road as I came through the door. I ran over, leaned against him and whispered. "I have done it."

He put his hands on my shoulders and brought his face close to mine. "You're shaking."

"I was so afraid Jonas would wake."

He took my hand. "We'll return to our rooms and you can explain all there."

Although a chime somewhere struck seven of the clock when we got back, John decided he must use the mould to make the key immediately. He had found a smith on the edge of the city on his way back from booking the passage in Leigh. He'd made friends with the man and they'd drunk together. It was possible the man might be a little suspicious at the sudden need for a key to be made this late in the day, but John judged that so long as the right price was paid, he would quell his curiosity. I disliked the idea of him going off at that hour.

"Why not use Purdy?"

He looked at me and shook his head. "The noise that firing up the furnace and hammering the key will cause could raise his neighbours' suspicions. If there are enquiries later, it might prove difficult for Purdy."

I nodded and was grateful he was thinking clearly, for my mind was still in turmoil.

It was almost midnight when he returned and I had imagined all manner of ills which might have befallen him. I restrained myself from embarrassing him again and merely welcomed him back and asked to see the iron key.

"Was the impression adequate for your needs?"

"I think so, but before we use it, I will have to try it in the door."

"How?"

"If I wait till early morning, I can try it then without them stirring. I will do that tomorrow night. There will be no moon and I will have to trust that no-one is about to see me. If it works and needs no work on it, we will be able to carry out our plan on the evening of the tenth."

"Then I will tell them tomorrow what we have in mind so they can think about the parts they have to play. I will warn Thomas against over indulging for the next few nights."

John nodded. I looked into his eyes for reassurance and comfort, and found them in the smile he returned.

The next afternoon I was shocked to see the governor's door opened by the turnkey we had spoken to at the gate next to the governor's house. He looked suspiciously at me as he let me in and refused to say what had happened to Jonas.

Thomas explained that the turnkey was standing in for Jonas whose fever had felled him. Lee had tended to him through the night and reported that he was now a little better and would probably be back on duty in a day or so.

I sat, head in hands for a moment, then sat up and straightened my shoulders. "I hope our plans will not have to be put back. We cannot proceed until Jonas is well. His trust in your good behaviour is crucial to our plan." I saw I had their attention. "We have a key to the front door, horses ready and a passage to Calais booked early on the eleventh."

Thomas gasped and leant forward. "Tell me more."

I smiled at them both. "The evening of the tenth, Thomas, you must wear your nightshirt over your travelling clothes and somehow lure Sir Francis and Mr Pitts into your room and keep them drinking there. Get the governor merry if you can."

I turned to Lee. "Lee, I have seen Jonas go to the cellar for ale. Your task is to go down and talk to Jonas, persuade him to get you an ale and find a way to trap him in the cellar. Now, dear brother, you must find an excuse to leave your room and come down to the hall where Lee will be waiting with the key. When you get out, you must lock the door from the outside and leave the key in the door. That will give us some time to get you away."

I looked at their astonished faces. Thomas sat there for a moment nodding and smiling at me. He suddenly looked at Lee. "I hope you are right that Jonas will recover. We do not want to have to change our passage." He turned back to me. "We heard today that the Bills of Indictment have been posted. The trial is within the week, on the 14th. The time is short."

◆   ◆   ◆

On the morning of the 10th of April, Jonas opened the door to me and I was able to show genuine pleasure at his recovery. I had not slept the night before, knowing that if he did not return, our plan would come to nought or at the very least the passage to France would have to be changed. John had proved to his satisfaction that the key worked the lock and I was carrying it with me, but it would have been in vain if the obnoxious turnkey had still been in charge.

I went to Thomas's room, gave the key to Lee and reminded Thomas of the part he had to play.

When I rejoined John I saw the relief on his face when I told him we were able to carry out the plan that evening. We spent the rest of the day packing our saddle bags and clearing our rooms. At seven we went to sup with the Purdys and insisted they take five more guineas for their kindness to us and their care of the horses. We made our farewells to Mrs Purdy and went with Purdy to his stables to collect the horses.

Together we walked the horses to Holburn and continued until we turned the corner to go down Snow Hill. We tied the horses to the rings next to the mounting blocks of an inn a little further down the hill from the governor's house. We waited in the shadows of the building across the road from the prison, where we could also keep an eye on the horses.

Just before nine of the clock, the door opened and my heart lurched as Thomas and Lee emerged. Lee put the key into the lock and turned it. They came quickly across to the shadows and I pointed to the horses. We walked briskly to our mounts and were up and off into the night within five minutes of their escape.

I experienced a mixture of elation, exhaustion and deep sadness during more than six hours journeying to Leigh. I was deeply thankful that our plan had succeeded but I had no way of knowing when I would see Thomas again.

As we rode along, I listened to their gleeful conversation about how Lee had jammed the door to the cellar while Jonas was finding more beer and how Thomas had plied the governor with wine and excused himself from the room pleading the need to use the necessary in the room above. They laughed and seemed exhilarated at their freedom and talked of life in France with their King.

I felt excluded and my head ached and swam through lack of sleep. I listened to John as he occasionally gave them directions and told them the name of the ship and its captain. He explained that their horses had to be left at the captain's rooms as part payment for their passage and that a balance of one hundred guineas was due.

Thomas cleared his throat. "We have a little money, but will need more to buy horses in Calais and to live on until we reach the court at St Germain-en-Laye."

I could not bring myself to reply. John looked back at me but I closed my eyes and leant my aching forehead against his back. He answered for me. "We have kept back fifty pounds for your use. What is left is needed for our journey back to Bamburgh."

Thomas nodded, looked across at me and was silent for a while. I knew he was thinking of his home and wondering when he would be able to return. In my heart I could not feel any optimism that it would be soon—if ever.

◆   ◆   ◆

Their departure went according to plan. As John and I watched them being rowed out to the ship, the promise of dawn was heralded by a faint glow of light in the sky to the east. I felt a sudden giddiness and was not sure if it was the emotion of the moment, tiredness or something more. After all the feverish activity of the last few weeks, it seemed impossible it should suddenly be all over and Thomas gone. He had thanked us both profusely, hugged and kissed me briefly with tears in his eyes and climbed into the boat before I had time to say more than a quick farewell.

I strained my eyes and watched until the small boat merged into the darkness of the swelling waters. I could see the lights of the ship beyond them and suddenly felt an overwhelming conviction that I would not see him again in my lifetime. I turned to John with tears running down my face. I swayed towards his dark figure and he caught me and held me steady. I felt him put his cold hand on my forehead.

"You are burning. Are you ill?"

"I do not feel well . . . my head aches . . ."

He picked me up and I laid my heavy, throbbing head against his chest as he walked to where Ebony was tethered. He lifted me up onto the horse's shoulders and leapt on behind me. "Lean against me. We cannot begin our journey home. We will have to find lodgings until you are well."

I felt his strong arm hold me as Ebony walked on. I lifted my head. "Can it be the fever, John?"

His arm tightened. "I do not know, but we must find a place to stay. If anyone will have us."

I drowsed until the movement came to a stop. I opened my eyes and saw the outline of a cottage by the roadside. John lifted me down and sat me on one of the saddle bags against a low wall in front of the building. I heard him knock on the door until it opened and a woman's voice remonstrated at the intrusion.

"I'm sorry to wake you, ma'am, but my . . . sister is ill and cannot go further. It may be that she has a fever so if you have a dry outhouse you could spare us, I will tend to her."

The woman came over to me and shone a candle in my face. She peered closely at me, pulled my hair away from my face and neck and felt my head. She went back to John.

"Bring her in. We have more rooms than we need."

"But, we have reason to believe it might be a very catching fever—the typhus I think they call it—and you might become ill yourself."

I waited, hoping the woman would not send us away.

"Son, my brother and I survived the Great Plague in London in '65 when all our family and friends were taken and ourselves only ten and twelve years old. We have lived a good and useful life on this farm since then and were blessed to inherit it from our uncle when he passed over. If the Good Lord sees fit to take us now, then so be it. You have your lives ahead of you. Bring her in."

CHAPTER 43

INDECISION

2005

Cathy waved and ran round to the driver's side of Jack's car. He let the window down and looked at her with hurt in his eyes. "What?"

"Where are you going?"

"Do you care?"

"Yes."

A car pulled up behind and sounded a horn. Jack pursed his lips. "Get in!"

Cathy ran round and climbed in. "I'm sorry. It was a childish thing to do, to walk out on you, but you . . ."

Jack raised his hand. "I know." The man in the car behind leaned on his horn. Jack looked at her. "Put your seat belt on!"

Cathy clicked the seat belt in place and sat back. Jack stepped on the accelerator and the car shot out on to the road and turned south. Cathy glanced at Jack. "So, where are we going?"

"I don't know."

"Have you checked out?"

"I thought about it, but I didn't."

"I know I angered you because what I did was embarrassing, but you broke your promise."

"I've just said: I know! Oh, Cathy, I'm not angry just because of what you did. More about the situation we're in because of the decision you . . . we made. It's very hard to go from intimate to platonic."

Cathy nodded and heaved a sigh. "Please let's go back and get ready for dinner and the concert."

He drove on for a few minutes without speaking and eventually swung round a roundabout and headed north again.

◆ ◆ ◆

They walked back to the hotel from the concert and spoke platitudes to each other about how good the music had been. Cathy remembered the same unnatural feeling of forcing herself to make impersonal comments after going to see a film with David. After a while she and Jack lapsed into silence and she realised he must be feeling the same.

◆ ◆ ◆

Cathy slid the card into the lock on her room door. "Would you like a coffee?"

"In your room?"

She nodded. Jack looked at her for a moment and shook his head. "No, thanks."

"Oh, ok. Well, thank you for this evening. It was great; the food, the music . . . and the company." She reached up and kissed his cheek.

He pulled away. "What the hell was that?"

"Just a thank you."

"So you can do that, but not me?"

"Well, I was thinking during the concert that if we're just friends now, it would be ok."

"Were you really?" The sarcasm in his voice stung her. "Well it wouldn't. Unless you want to sleep with me?"

Cathy stepped back and Jack grimaced. "I didn't think so. Night, Cathy."

◆ ◆ ◆

On Monday morning, the drive north to the records office in Morpeth was as silent as breakfast had been. They arrived late and found the room full and all the machines occupied. They found a leaflet that described how they could do a search and Cathy looked for the drawer that would contain details about Bamburgh parish. She sat waiting for a machine and watched Jack looking at rows of books. He pulled one out, looked across at her and went round the corner, out of sight.

Twenty minutes later a monitor became available. The details on the fiche were hard to decipher, but Cathy eventually found the records that showed Dorothy's birth in 1686. She began to look for any details of Dorothy's marriage from 1716 onwards, got to 1740 and gave up. Jack appeared. "How are you doing?"

Cathy looked up at him. "Not very well. I can't find her marriage, so I'm going to look for her death in the name of Forster." Jack stood behind and leaned his hands on her shoulders as he looked at the screen. "I thought you assumed she might have married the blacksmith."

"I did and I've put that in my notes for the 'journal', but I can't find it on any of the parish records."

Jack brought a seat and leaned close to her. "What about the copied sheets I gave you? The family tree said she died in 1767 and had married John Armstrong."

"Really? That's what it said may have happened in the John Bird booklet, but no-one else did. Why didn't you tell me you'd found it too?"

He put his head on one side. "We weren't exactly on good terms and I assumed you'd go through what I gave you with a fine tooth comb."

"I just flipped through and didn't notice that. So, if I find her death in 1767, we can assume the rest is correct."

"I suppose."

Cathy leant forward and scrolled through the ancient handwriting until she reached the 1760s. She searched for Dorothy, Forster or Armstrong, until she got to 1770. She sat back. "Nothing."

"So the bit about John Armstrong could be wrong too."

"Oh, Jack, I hope not."

Jack lifted up the book he'd been reading. "I'm afraid this book confirms what you've just found. Someone has gone through all the Armstrong family births, marriages and deaths and put them together in this book. There's nothing about a Dorothy Forster marrying John Armstrong."

◆　　　◆　　　◆

A pensive silence was broken by the intermittent pouring of wine or request to pass the vegetables as they ate dinner. Jack took a sip of wine and looked at Cathy. "So is there any point in going back there tomorrow?"

"I want to, but you don't need to come."

"I mightn't. I promised to buy some things for Charlie that he didn't have time to do because I took him to Bamburgh. And as we're driving on to Bamburgh on Wednesday, it's the only time I've got."

"Fine."

On Tuesday afternoon Cathy travelled back to Newcastle from Morpeth in driving rain, pleased she'd found something Jack had missed but frustrated that it wasn't Dorothy and John's marriage. She spent the rest of the afternoon going round the Newcastle shops trying on shoes and buying a glitzy scarf for Liz.

◆　　　◆　　　◆

She kicked the door to her room shut and dropped the bags on the bed. She was unzipping her coat when someone hammered on the door.

She opened the door. "Oh, hi . . ."

"Where the hell have you been?" Jack took hold of her shoulders, his face close to hers and full of fury.

"Jack, you know where I've been!"

"I've been trying to get through to you all day and your phone's been switched off!"

"You know I turn it off when I'm driving and in the records office. I just forgot to switch it back on when I got to Newcastle. It's not a crime!"

"For God's sake, Cathy! You said you were coming back at lunch time. It was gloomy and pouring with rain like on the night of the accident. I was terrified you'd had one of your flashbacks and something terrible had happened. I even called the police to see if there'd been any accidents!"

Cathy pulled away and sat on the bed. "I didn't think . . ."

"No you didn't!"

"I'm sorry."

Jack sat down on the bed beside her and pulled her to him. She didn't resist. She needed his forgiveness.

◆　　◆　　◆

Cathy sipped her soup and looked at Jack. "I looked at a couple of other parishes."

"There must be many more than that."

"There are; loads. I also found that some of the records have been transcribed into easy-to-read print in large books. I'd like to finish having a look at those tomorrow on our way to Bamburgh. So far, no luck with the marriage and there are only a limited number of parishes covered by them."

"You can't give up now."

"No, I know, but I'm beginning to have doubts about the whole thing."

"Dorothy and John Armstrong?"

"Yes, and I'm even doubting that she went down to try and rescue her brother. When I think of the number of history books or pamphlets you or I've read which say things like, 'it is said that' or 'she is believed to have'. It's only in novels that it's said with conviction."

They were both silent for a few moments.

"Cathy, remember I told you about the stories like the one about the Scottish raiders in the mist in Blanchland not being in history text books and yet locals knew of them because they were folk tales passed down through the centuries ?"

"Yes."

"Well, all the details may not be entirely accurate but I like to believe that the general gist of those stories is true, so Dorothy's has to have some basis of truth."

"You're a romantic."

"And you're not?"

"I think I'm also a realist. A doubter. I need proof."

"In that case, I hope you'll get it. You could be disappointed."

"Yes, but I hope not. You know what, even though I haven't found a record of their marriage in the Parish records, I'm going to search again for a Dorothy Armstrong in the deaths."

"*We* are going to search."

"Ok. *We*."

SOUTH TO NORTH

1716

On the morning I awoke, my mind at last clear and my body almost free of aches, I lay a while with my eyes closed and tried to recall what I could remember of the past few days. Visions of John's troubled face and his hands applying wet cloths to my face and feeding me broth were confused with memories of the woman bathing me and applying lotions to my face and body. I remembered a feeling of helplessness and trying to tell them something, but could not remember what is was.

I could hear the sound of regular breathing. I opened my eyes and lifted my head. John's head was resting on the pillow next to me but his large frame was wedged into a chair beside the bed. He looked pale. I went cold at the thought that he might be ill and have caught the fever from me.

I leant across and touched his forehead. It was warm but not hot. I heaved a sigh of relief and he opened his eyes. He sat up, blinked and stretched. He smiled. "You're awake. How are you feeling?"

I smiled at him. "Well, I think." I sat up and looked at my bare arms and saw a number of healing sores. I looked at him.

He nodded. "You also had spots and rashes on your neck and . . . other places. Mistress Ward knew what to do. I don't know how I would have managed without her help. You were fevered and restless much of the time."

"How long have I been ill?"

"Almost a week."

"A week! How can that be?"

"You were barely conscious, so the memory of it must be lost. Do you really feel well? You slept soundly most of yesterday and through the night. I cannot believe the illness is gone. You were so poorly."

"I feel a little weak and am not yet ready to dance a jig, but I think I am recovered." I looked down at the shift that was not mine. I looked up to see my clothes draped across a chair on the far side of the room. I turned to John. "This is not mine. How did I come to be dressed so?"

He bit his lip and looked away for a moment. "Forgive me. When we got you inside you were burning and bathed in sweat; your clothes clung damply to you and though hot, you were shivering as if your body would fall apart. She said she had to cool you down with sponges of cold water and had a shift you could wear while your clothes were washed and dried. She found she could not do it on her own. I . . . I could not refuse to help . . . I had said I was your brother."

A shock ran through my body and I lowered my eyes and turned away. He touched my arm. "Please don't be angry. I had no choice."

"I'm not angry, John. Just a little . . . shaken. It had to be done." I turned to him and smiled. "Dear John, thank you for all you've done for me in my quest and these past few days. I think I owe you my life."

He smiled and smoothed away a lock of hair from my eyes. I lay back, shocked at the intimacy of his gesture. "I think I will rest a while. You should go and get some proper sleep yourself." I closed my eyes and heard him stand up and walk to the door. The door opened and closed quietly and I lay for a long while, unable to sleep.

John rode to London early the next day to do some errands for the Wards on condition they would allow him to pay for what was needed. He confided to me that he also wanted to find out the latest news.

He returned late in the evening and thrust a large sheet of paper into my hands. It was a proclamation offering a reward for Thomas's capture. It described him so well, that I was deeply grateful he was safely in France.

' . . . Middle stature, inclining to be fat, well shape'd except that he stoops in the shoulders, fair complexioned, his mouth wide, his nose pretty large, his eyes grey, speaks the Northern Dialect . . . a reward of £1,000 to any who should apprehend him.'

I looked at John and saw there was more. He looked steadily at me.

"Dorothy, Peregrine Widdrington died of the fever and I'm afraid the authorities were mightily discomforted by your brother's escape. Those that remain in prison have been arraigned, including Colonel Oxburgh and the man they are now certain is Charles Radcliffe, and are to appear before the courts in May. It is thought many will not escape execution."

◆   ◆   ◆

Another week passed before John would consider starting our journey home. As he secured our saddle bags outside the cottage, Mistress Ward restrained me by the door, leant close to me and whispered. "I wish you both all the happiness you deserve. He's a fine man; you could do no better."

I was startled and stood with my mouth open. Mistress Ward smiled. "He didn't fool me with that sister story. I have lived with my brother all my life and never has he dealt with me with such tenderness and love as John did with you. God speed you on your journey, my dear."

I took a deep breath and hugged her. "I owe you so much. I can never thank you enough for what you've done. I pray to God you will not suffer for it."

Mistress Ward shook her head. "Don't fret. You've given me the satisfaction of bringing you through the illness and also a story to tell. That's thanks enough."

◆   ◆   ◆

John insisted I ride in front of him in case I felt weak and lost grip with my knees or my hold on his waist. Now that time was not pressing on us, we stopped more frequently than on the journey down. Sometimes we stayed for two nights if John thought I looked tired. He insisted on finding comfortable rooms even if they were a little off our route. More often than not I had a room to myself. I was surprised to feel lonely on those occasions and even more surprised to feel glad when we had to share a room.

It was into May when we finally rode along the coast road beside the sandhills between Seahouses and Bamburgh and I saw my castle to the north standing proudly on the horizon. I was unable to stop myself bursting into tears. This day I had ridden behind him. John slowed down and looked back at me. "Do you want to stop?"

"No, I want to get home; as fast as we can." I dried my tears, stood up on my stirrup and held on to John's shoulders. I had ridden side-saddle on this final day so I could ride sedately into Bamburgh, but now I pulled up my skirts and swung my leg over Ebony's back. John laughed and I clung to his back as our faithful horse broke into a canter.

As we rode up the road into the village, we saw crowds of people lining the street, shouting greetings and cheering us. I was bewildered. "What is all this?"

John shrugged his shoulders. "All I can think is that I talked to one of the Swinburnes in the inn in Morpeth last night and he has spread the news of what you did. He said the fact of Thomas's escape was already known and much talked about, but no-one knew how, although they suspected your absence had something to do with it."

We reached the manor and John jumped off and helped me down. We were surrounded by a crowd of well-wishers and staff curtsying and fussing round me. I was happy to hear their praise for what I had done and pleased to see their obvious delight at my safe return, but felt uncomfortable that they seemed to regard me alone as being the heroine. I protested that I could not have done it without John's help and they nodded, glanced in his direction and continued to shake my hand and say how brave I had been.

It was some time before we could reach the door. I was relieved when we finally entered and closed it behind us. I smiled at John and grabbed his hand.

"Come!"

I turned towards the door to the kitchen, meaning to take him through it and out into the back garden. He stood firm, breathing deeply and loosened his hand from mine. "If you would permit me, Mistress Forster, I must return to Adderstone. I've been away long enough."

I spun round, shocked at his words and the change in the tone of his voice. I felt tears spring to my eyes. "I thought . . . we were friends, John. I have so much to thank you for and I wanted you to share my delight at being home and feeling the salt wind in my face again."

I saw him glance uncomfortably at Jenny Lee who was picking up the saddle bag of clothes. I frowned. "Please take my clothes to be washed, Jenny, and ask cook to begin supper." Jenny curtsied and left.

I turned back, uncertain how to speak to him. "Please John. Just a few minutes more." He stood for a moment looking at me and seemed undecided what he should do.

I grabbed his hand. "Please."

He nodded reluctantly and we walked through the kitchen, out into the garden and took the path down to the bottom of the grassy slope.

I leaned against the wall, breathed in deeply and looked across the sea towards Holy Island to the north. I turned my gaze to the Farne Islands and then to the castle high on its cliff. I listened as the grasses whispered in the breeze and the gulls cried eerily above us. "Are we not the luckiest people to live in such a county and a place as beautiful as this?"

"We are."

I felt his presence close to me and he put his hands gently on my shoulders. I reached up with both hands and pulled his arms around me. I was shocked to feel him shake himself free and pull away.

"No, for pity's sake, Dorothy. Do not do this to me!"

I stood for a second, unable to comprehend his words or actions. I spun round, a feeling of deep hurt flooding my body. I saw he'd backed away and was breathing deeply.

I gulped for air. "I'm sorry John. I have misunderstood. I thought . . . I thought you had a fondness for me."

He threw his head back and exhaled in exasperation. "And what use would it be if I did? Coming back here . . . it is so obvious. We are so far apart."

I relaxed and raised my eyebrows. "You mean that you are a man of property and I shall be homeless and without income when my uncle dies; perhaps even sooner if he finds out what I did?"

I scrutinised his face and saw that my attempt at light-hearted comment had not changed his mood. He shook his head. "You know what my meaning is."

I took a step closer. "Oh John, you are the finest man I know."

"And you the finest woman! But generations of privilege cannot be bridged. It's too big a gulf." The emotion in his voice touched me deeply.

I swallowed, knowing it was in my power to win or lose what I wanted most. "Then I will leap that gulf if you will catch me. I love you, John."

I watched him shake his head in disbelief. A questioning smile crept across his face. I smiled back at him. He hesitated for a moment and I lifted up my arms to him.

He sprang towards me and gathered me up into his arms and buried his face in my hair. "Oh Dorothy, I have loved you so long. I never dared to hope . . ." He kissed my hair and set me back on the ground. "You are sure? Really sure?"

"More sure than I have ever been about anything before."

He leaned over, cupped my face in his hands and kissed me gently on the lips. I felt such an overwhelming surge of love that I threw my arms round his neck and kissed him so strongly that he staggered slightly as he wrapped his arms around me.

We stayed locked in each others arms and talked until the sun went down. We knew that there would be prejudice and constraints, perhaps even strong opposition to our union and I was anxious as to the outcome. But I was certain about one thing: our social differences were unimportant. I was prepared to fight to be together. Our success in saving Thomas had given me the hope that I could sweep aside any obstacles. John cautioned patience. "I have waited and hoped so long; I would wait another ten years now I know you love me."

I smiled at him. "John Armstrong, if you think I'm going to wait that long, you are sadly mistaken. Whether my family disowns me or not, I mean to spend my life with you and I'm not one to be dissuaded from something once my mind is made up."

He nodded, smiled and rested his forehead on mine. "So be it, my love."

TRAGEDY

2005

On Wednesday morning Cathy and Jack left the hotel in tandem and were in slow moving traffic within minutes. She looked at the back of Jack's head in the car ahead and thought how easy it was for them to hurt each other without meaning to. It was chilling to remember what happened to Tom after her rash words and actions.

She shook her head, trying to clear images of the accident, changed up into third gear as the speed of the traffic increased and told herself to concentrate.

I wasn't to blame for what happened to Tom! I reacted to his wishes at a moment when he at last took control and didn't leave it to me to make the decisions. He was looking after me. I spent years doing my best to care for him and we had good times and I don't need to feel guilty about those years. Dorothy and I have a lot in common: years of trying to keep our brothers in check and looking after them. And losing them.

There were tears in Cathy's eyes, but this time they weren't only for Tom.

◆   ◆   ◆

Cathy followed Jack—leaving a safe distance between them—until they came within a few miles of the turn off to Morpeth. In her rear mirror she noticed a car, similar to her own, racing up the outside lane followed by another close behind. She couldn't believe it when they both slipped into the space between her and Jack. She slowed down and noticed a sign that said the road narrowed ahead and the overtaking lane was blocked. She hoped they wouldn't try to overtake Jack before the road narrowed.

A minute later another fast moving car appeared in her mirror and grew large at a frightening rate. The barriers were in sight.

Inwardly, she screamed to Jack to watch out. The car passed her and she watched in horror as it suddenly pulled to the left. She stepped on the brake and changed down a gear as she watched the car narrowly miss Jack and slam into the car behind him, which in turn caused a glancing blow to the following car which spun into her path.

Her instant decision was to hit the flimsy-looking barriers rather than the car. The wheels screeched as she turned the steering wheel, pressed the brakes and slammed into the barriers; they gave way easily but pieces of flying wood turned her windscreen into a spider's web. She slowed down as she scattered cones around the road. She strained to see through the cracks in the windscreen and saw Jack's car ahead parked on the hard shoulder. She pulled up in front of it and sat gasping.

Before she could release her belt, Jack had opened the door and wrapped his arms round her. "Oh God, Cathy! I thought it was you. Oh, Cathy . . . thank God . . . do you hurt anywhere?"

She swallowed, shaking. "I don't think so. Oh, Jack, it missed you by inches!"

He held her, his cheek against hers. After a moment, he helped her out and wrapped his arms round her again. He was shaking too. "Are you sure nothing hurts?"

"The belt cut into me a bit when I hit the barriers, but I wasn't going fast by then and the head rest softened the blow to my head."

"Does your neck hurt?"

"No. I'm just a bit sore here." She pointed to her ribs.

"Show me."

She unzipped her coat and lifted up her sweater. He looked at it and prodded her skin gently. "Doesn't look too bad. Tell me if it begins to hurt." She nodded. He put his arms round her again, his lips against her ear. "I have to go and see if I can help."

She pulled back. "Yes. What can I do?"

"Ring 999 and sit in my car."

"Jack, please, I want to help."

"Cathy, you've just had a crash; a nasty shock."

"Jack . . . I've got to help . . ."

He looked at her and his eyes closed briefly. "Ok, but it won't be a pretty sight. Get the first aid box out of my car and bring it to me after you've rung."

He ran off and she phoned for an ambulance and was told someone had already rung and help would soon be on its way. She reached into her car and got out her own box and collected Jack's. She had to brace herself as she walked towards the damaged vehicles and began to hear cries for help, moans and sobbing. A few of the motorists held up by the accident were standing gazing at the scene and looking dazed.

The next fifteen minutes were an adrenalin fuelled blur as Cathy followed Jack's instructions as he assessed each victim. They both put on gloves before she began to do what he asked and her last task before the medics took over was to hold a large pad on a man's chest to stem the blood oozing from his wound. The relief she felt as she heard the ambulances was written on Jack's face too. A third ambulance arrived just after the police.

Jack briefed the emergency care workers and within twenty minutes all but one of the victims were being ferried to local hospitals. Cathy grabbed Jack and pointed. "What about him?" Jack shook his head and turned her away. "He was the first one I looked at. Nothing could be done. Another ambulance is on its way to collect him."

◆　　◆　　◆

Cathy watched her rented car being towed away as she sat in Jack's car. A dreamlike feeling swept over her. Jack's voice penetrated her thoughts as he got into the car. "Are you really ok?"

She nodded. "I don't know how you cope with dealing with such horrific sights and such terrible injuries every day."

"It's not always like that."

She turned to him. "Oh, Jack, I hope I did everything right."

He put his arm round her. "You were brilliant. You did your best, and that's all any of us can do."

◆   ◆   ◆

"Eat, Cathy."

She looked up. "Yes." She picked up the soup spoon and began to sip the creamy liquid in the café they'd found in the High Street. "We've missed the morning session. We have to get there for when the afternoon one begins."

"I think we should give it a miss and go straight to Bamburgh so you can rest."

"No! I want to finish looking at that book I told you about that's easier to read. I have to. The record office isn't open tomorrow or Friday."

She could tell he wasn't happy with her decision but knew he wouldn't fight it.

◆   ◆   ◆

Cathy flipped through the printed Bamburgh parish record of burials in the 1760s and turned the page into the '70s.

"Look at this!"

Jack looked up from the book he was reading again about births, marriages and deaths of the Armstrong families. "What?"

"If she did marry John Armstrong, this could be her. It says: May the seventh 1771, 'Dorothy, wife of Mr. John Armstrong of Crookham, in Ford Parish."

"How old would that have made her when she died?"

"Um . . . about eighty-five, if it was her."

"That's very old for those times.

"Lord Crewe was a similar age when he died."

"Really? So why do you doubt it was her?"

"Well, it just says Dorothy. I mean, how do I know which Dorothy it was? There were lots of Dorothys scattered all over the records in many different parts of the county."

"But you couldn't find a Dorothy *Forster* under burials in Bamburgh?"

"No."

"Or Blanchland?"

"No, nor anywhere else I've looked."

"So, take a leap of faith and believe it."

"I'm sorry, I need more proof that it really was her because I haven't found a record of their marriage. I suppose they might have just lived together and she took his name."

Jack shrugged his shoulders and put his book in front of her. "Have a look at this. I remembered something I read on Monday, but dismissed." He pointed. "This entry in the Warkworth Parish Records: it's an epitaph to the death in October 1728 of Elizabeth, daughter of Dorothy Armstrong, Hauxley. I looked up Hauxley on their map and it's on the coast—remember the reference in that novel you were reading about her husband being a fisherman?"

"Oh, yes, but a novel can be wrong."

He flipped the pages. "Ok, but there was also another reference from Corbridge Parish. Look; under baptisms it records that on the thirteenth of August 1721, Elizabeth, daughter of John Armstrong was baptised."

"You think it might be the same one?"

"Well it's quite near Blanchland if they were living there at the time, but we have no proof it's the same Elizabeth or the same John."

Cathy suddenly felt excited. "I've just remembered! Dorothy had an elder sister, Elizabeth, who died young, so she could have named a daughter after her couldn't she?"

"I suppose."

"Right, I'm going to go back to the fiche to see if the death is recorded in the original handwritten records."

She went back to the monitor. Five minutes later Jack returned with a book in his hand. "Come and read this."

"But . . . oh, look Jack, there it is: May, 1771!"

Jack looked over her shoulder. "Great." He took her hand and led her to the seats round a low table. "How about this?"

Cathy looked at the book and giggled. "Great title! *Historical Register of Remarkable Events*."

Jack smiled. "Yeah. It has a list of things that happened during the eighteenth century. I looked for 1715 to see about the rebellion and it says pretty much what we already know, but it has a footnote. 'See May 5th 1771, page 281.'"

Jack flipped the page and held it for Cathy to read.

Died, at Crookham, in Northumberland, in a very advanced age, Mrs. Armstrong, sister to General Forster, who served in that capacity under the Pretender in 1715, a lady of great knowledge and amazing activity and fortitude in her youth. When her brother was imprisoned at London she was permitted to see him, and, having a piece of clay in her pocket, took thereon the figure of the prison door key . . .

"I read about the clay impression somewhere and included it in my story!"

Jack nodded. "Yes, well, the only thing that makes me wonder if it's all true is that it says she came back to Newcastle to have the key made and then went back to the prison. I think that's unlikely."

Cathy frowned. "Absolutely! It was a difficult journey and could take two or three weeks to go just one way in those days, especially through ice and snow."

"And Newcastle would have been the worst place to come to have the key made. They were staunch supporters of King George, weren't they?"

"Yes; that's how they got the name of 'Geordies.'" Cathy sighed. "So I need to find something to corroborate what that says. It could have just been some imposter trying to cash in on the story of her courage."

She stood up and suddenly felt faint. She blinked as a black shadow crossed her eyes and there was a buzzing noise in her ears. She felt Jack take hold of her. He sat her down. "You've gone ashen. Put your head down." He stroked her back until she sat up and smiled wanly. "I'm fine now."

Jack stopped her attempt to stand up. "Sit there until I get you a drink." She watched him rush to the drinks machine and feed it with coins.

She took the cup, gulped down the hot sweet tea and made a face. "Ugh! I'm fine now, honestly." She stood up and smiled at Jack. "See!"

"You're not going to do any more research. We're leaving now. I'll get your coat."

Cathy looked at the expression on Jack's face and decided not to argue.

◆   ◆   ◆

Jack unlocked the door to her room and carried her case inside. "Go and lie down."

"I need to unpack and hang up my clothes."

"You need to lie down and sleep, if possible. I'll do your unpacking."

"But . . ."

"Do I have to pick you up and throw you on the bed?"

"You wouldn't . . ."

"Try me!"

She kicked off her shoes, lay down and watched as Jack quickly emptied her case, put her lap top on the desk and stowed away her clothes in the wardrobe and drawers.

She sat up. "From what I saw, it's a fantastic village, isn't it?"

"Yes, and tomorrow we'll take a proper look, but right now you have to sleep."

He closed the curtains. "I'm taking your door key so I can come back and check on you. I'll wake you up when it's time for dinner. Do you mind if I read about Dorothy on your computer when I come back?"

"Um, all right. Let me open it up." She got up, logged on and found the document. She looked up at him and he raised his brows and pointed to the bed.

"Ok! You're being very . . . pushy!" She lay down.

Jack smiled, leaned over and kissed her forehead. "Sleep well!"

◆   ◆   ◆

Cathy woke to the sound of her ring tone. She opened her eyes as she heard Jack's voice.

"No, she's fine . . . yes, it was; very similar." He looked at her as she sat up. "I'll pass the phone to her, shall I?" He mouthed "your Dad".

"Hi, Dad."

"Cathy, we've just come back from dinner with friends and switched on the news channel and there was a car just like your rented one smashed up in this horrific accident on the A1 . . ."

"Yes, it wasn't mine, just similar. I'm fine. Jack was just ahead of the accident and I had to swerve out of the way and my windscreen was shattered but . . ."

"What! Are you sure you're ok?"

"Absolutely. Jack was wonderful. He looked after the victims and made me sleep when we got to the hotel in Bamburgh and I feel great now. Oh, Dad, you must bring Mum here; she'd love it."

"We have been, just after we got engaged, but it's probably changed a lot. Well, now we know you're ok, we can sleep easy. Please pass the phone back to Jack."

"Oh . . . ok. Love you both." She handed her phone to Jack.

"Hi . . . yes, of course I will . . . a bit of a mark from the seat belt and she was shocked, but that's all . . . we did, but . . . um . . . yes, I do, very much. Right; night." Jack switched off and turned away.

Cathy stood up. "What time is it? I'm so hungry."

He turned back. "After nine. Why don't we have room service?"

"Fine. Is there a menu on the desk?"

◆   ◆   ◆

Cathy wiped her mouth. "That was delicious. You've been very silent. Didn't you enjoy it?"

"Yeah; it was good. I've never seen you eat so much or so quickly."

"I didn't have much breakfast or lunch."

"No."

"What's wrong, Jack?"

He shook his head. "Nothing really . ."

"But?"

"I was just thinking how lucky you are to have a father who . . ." Jack's thoughts suddenly seemed to drift away.

"You've never talked about your father and come to think of it, neither did your mother or Sara."

Jack looked up. "He's dead. Three years ago."

"Oh, Jack, I'm so sorry."

Jack stood up, walked to the window and opened the curtains to the pale moonlight. "My parents split up just over five years ago after a massive row about my mother trying to manoeuvre me into a relationship with Sunita's sister. He was against what she did with both Serena and Sara. Especially when Serena went to live in India. They weren't arranged marriages, just gentle pushes; parties, dances, dinners. It was all about meeting the right kind of people. Dad could see what she was doing and didn't like it. He wondered if she regretted marrying him. I heard him ask her that. She said she didn't, but I'm not sure he believed her." Jack sat down on the bed. "They started arguing about everything and sniping at each other even when I was there and eventually my mother ordered him out. He went."

"What did he die from?"

Jack stood up again and turned away. "I visited him a week before he died. He said he still missed my mother every day. I said I thought she missed him too and told him to go and see her or ring her. He said he'd think about it . . . but he didn't. He killed himself seven days later."

A shockwave spread through Cathy's body and she jumped up and ran to Jack. She flung her arms round his neck and put her cheek against his. "Oh, Jack, please tell me you wouldn't ever . . ."

Jack closed his arms round her. "Of course I wouldn't! No matter how miserable I was. I'm still so angry with my father. It left us all feeling shocked, devastated, helpless, sad and guilty; wondering if we could have said or done something or—in my mother's case—if what she'd said and done had made him do what he did. It changed her a lot; though she still can't stop herself from trying to find women for me. Perhaps if I'd given in five years ago, none of their fighting would have happened and he'd still be alive."

"It wasn't your fault! It was between them. And you said the right things to him. You couldn't have said anything more positive. He alone made the decision to do what he did. Oh, Jack . . ." She held him tightly.

Jack pulled back and held her face in his hands. "You still love me, don't you . . . don't you, Cathy?"

She looked into his eyes. "It's impossible to stop loving someone just because you think you ought to. And you make it more impossible when you keep looking at me the way you do and saying things and touching me and holding me, even though you promised not to!"

He smiled. "I lied. You didn't really think I'd give up on you that easily, did you? I love you so much." He kissed her lips softly. "Love seems too small a word to describe how I feel about you." He shook his head. "This is crazy! We love each other; we've got to be together. One of us has to give in about where we live!"

Cathy pulled away. " Well, it can't be me. You don't see how my father looks at me when I leave; even just to my flat! And my mother has changed. She was even tearful when I went on the tour. How do you think they'd be if I said I was going to live in London!"

Jack stood for a moment, his expression grim. He turned away and slipped out of the door.

◆　　◆　　◆

After a restless night, Cathy was up and dressed before eight the next morning. She'd gone to Jack's room after he left and lifted her fist to knock on his door. But there was nothing to add; she'd meant what she said. She went back to her room and lay for a long time wondering if she'd finally made him give up on her.

She looked at her watch. 7.55 a.m. She rang Jack.

"Uh, huh, oh, hi."

"Hi. Did I wake you?"

"Yes. I didn't get to bed for another two hours after I left you."

"Why not?"

"Tell you later. You better go on down and eat. I need to have a shower and find some clothes."

"Right."

◆　　◆　　◆

Cathy was finishing her poached eggs when Jack strode into the room, carrying a sheaf of papers. Her heart turned over as he came close and sat down.

He ran his eyes over her but didn't smile. "Nice top you're almost wearing."

"It's the only clean top I have. Liz persuaded me to buy it. Don't you like it?"

"Low cut and bare shoulders . . . what's not to like? Can't wait to see what else you're wearing." There was an edge to his voice that made her feel uncomfortable.

"A mini skirt and tights."

"Right. I rang the hospital and everyone's out of danger, though one of them is still in intensive care, but stable."

"That's great! What a relief. You were amazing."

"Not really; just did what any doctor would do. You were the amazing one. Not many people would be as calm as you were. So, what are we doing today?"

"Well, if you don't mind, I'd like to take a look at Adderstone Hall and see if we can find Crookham or Berryhill. I want to know where Dorothy ended up."

"Right. But first, listen to this. I gave you these papers a couple of days ago, but they were at the bottom of your case and it didn't look as if you'd looked at them, so I did, before I read your 'Dorothy Forster Journal' while you were sleeping. Totally fascinating, by the way. I don't know how you've done it, but I was absorbed from beginning to end and it's not normally the kind of thing I read."

"Oh, good. I've got a bit of tweaking to do here and there and also the end of the story and an epilogue to write, but I'm glad you think it's ok."

"It was, more than just ok. Right. On some of these sheets that I photocopied from a book in the Central library, there's a section called 'Evidences of the Pedigree of Forster of Adderstone.'"

"Oh, I did read some of them, but I forgot to tell you I found that Dorothy's father left her £1,000 in 1725."

"Yeah, probably enough to buy a row of houses in those days. Did you read anything else?"

"I don't think so."

"Ok. In the will of Dorothy's nephew- son of her brother John—John Armstrong was left a yearly allowance in the 1760s."

"Oh! Her brother John hadn't even married by 1716 so her nephew must have been more than thirty years younger than Dorothy when he died. So, you think it was 'our' John Armstrong?"

"Who else? And the ninth 'evidence' on the list, is a letter to a distant relative from a Miss Isabella Forster, this time the *daughter* of Dorothy's brother John. First of all she mentions her 'Aunt Armstrong', then later, 'Mrs Armstrong.'"

"She doesn't say Aunt Dorothy Armstrong?"

"No. Now you're being picky. Who else could it have been?"

Cathy sat for a moment. "Yes; Dorothy only had two sisters, Margaret who married John Bacon and Elizabeth who died young. So Isabella only had two aunts who lived into adulthood and we know that Aunt Dorothy on her mother's side was dead and called Crewe, so Aunt Armstrong *has* to be our Dorothy."

"Exactly."

"Wow! Thanks, Jack. That's brilliant."

"Yeah. Well, I think I'd better get something to eat."

He went to the cereal table and Cathy realised he hadn't smiled or touched her since he'd walked out of her room the previous night.

CHAPTER 46

DESTINATION

Cathy and Jack sat on a bench further up the hill from the hotel. She looked southwards down the road that skirted the foot of the huge cliff, on top of which was Bamburgh Castle. She turned her head and looked through the triangle of trees to the large stone house where Dorothy and Thomas had lived. They'd been to photograph it and the church of St Aidan where Dorothy and Thomas had worshipped.

"It's a lovely village and a fabulous castle. I don't care if a lot of it *is* mostly nineteenth-century, it's probably similar to what it was before Dorothy's ancestors let it fall apart. And I can see why she was happy to come and live here."

Jack sat back. "Mm. So, you want to find Berryhill? I thought it was only Crookham we'd be looking for."

"Yes, but one of the family trees I found says Dorothy married 'John Armstrong of Berryhill, Parish of Ford'. I don't know where Crookham or Ford Parish is; do you?"

"I've heard of Ford. It's a model village somewhere in north Northumberland near the Scottish border."

"Near here?"

"Well, about the same distance north, but well inland. I've got a map."

"I'd definitely like to go there."

"Ok."

"Oh, and there's another thing I forgot to tell you. Last week I found a book which has excerpts from Rev Patten's book and also from King George I's 'Annals of 1716' that you mentioned. It says something similar about Tom getting the Governor of Newgate prison drunk and pretending he was going upstairs to the 'necessary'—euphemism for the loo, I assumed—and instead going to where his valet had locked the gaoler in the cellar, taking off the nightshirt covering his clothes, leaving it on some steps and escaping using a key someone had provided. I checked in my author's book and he says that the key was 'obtained apparently by his sister Dorothy'. Isn't that brilliant?"

"Mm. So did that convince you you'd got it right?"

"It helped. I thought at first it was possible he could just have been upholding a generally accepted and well-loved traditional tale. But what you found in the pedigrees convinced me."

Jack looked steadily at her. "You know, Cathy, the research and writing you've done in such a short time is phenomenal."

"Thank you, I think. Next thing, a degree with the Open University!"

"Yeah, why not? After this, it'd be a piece of cake."

"Actually, I've been thinking about it."

"Go for it."

"Researching this made me realise how much I missed the challenge. Thanks."

"For what?"

"It was you who got me into it."

"That was just a ploy to stop you running away from me."

"You can be quite devious, can't you?"

"Well, I was worried I'd lose touch with you and you'd drive off and do something awful to yourself."

"I'd have been on your conscience . . ."

"Something like that. And the fact that I was instantly besotted. But I thought you needed something else to concentrate on and I was mildly interested to find out more about Dorothy and her brother. But I probably wouldn't have had the determination or patience to do what you've done."

"Oh, Jack, you're being ridiculously modest. You're the most patient, caring and understanding man I know; well, mostly. Except when you think I'm being unreasonable."

"Hm, I should be recording this so I can play it back next time you get me in a twist."

"So . . . there could be a next time?"

"Maybe."

◆   ◆   ◆

The drive to Adderstone village took only ten minutes and the tree-lined lane they presumed was the way into Adderstone Hall was off the main road not far from the village.

Jack slowed down beside a stone-built building and pulled over so he wasn't blocking the way. Cathy stepped out to take a closer look. She'd expected a much larger building and was puzzled. A man came out of one of the doors, through a gate and onto the road and she walked towards him. "Excuse me."

He smiled and looked her up and down. "Yes, pet."

"I just wanted to know if this is Adderstone Hall."

He laughed. "Why no! It's much grander than this. These are holiday cottages. There's another lot up at the farmstead and others dotted around. The wife knows more, but I think these might have been the stables at one time. The rest have got all kinds of names to do with history or sometimes jobs."

"Really? Do you know any of the names?"

"Just a minute, I'll get the wife."

"Oh no, I don't want to bother her . . ."

"It's nay bother, she loves a gossip."

◆   ◆   ◆

The woman came out of the cottage as Jack brought Cathy's coat and helped her get into it. He zipped it up.

Cathy was surprised. "You didn't need to do that."

"Yes I did, before another man undresses you with his eyes," he whispered.

The woman reached them. "Now then, Jack says you want to know about the cottages."

"Jack?"

The woman looked uncertainly at Cathy. "Yes, Jack, m'husband. Was it not you he was talking to?"

"Oh, yes. Yes it was, sorry. It's just that my . . ."

Jack offered his hand. "I'm Jack too. Nice to meet you."

The woman shook his hand. "Well then, what a coincidence! What do you want to know about the cottages? Are you wanting to stay here?"

"Not at the moment, we just wanted to know their names and maybe have a look at the Hall."

"Oh, you can wander round the grounds—sixty acres of it, it said in the blurb—if you're staying here but I don't think you can actually go in the hall unless you hire it for a wedding or something like that, but I can show you where to get a glimpse. Come on."

"Oh, I don't want to take up your time; you're on holiday."

"It's not a bother. We were thinking of going for a coffee in Bamburgh with the grandchildren but it's much too early yet. Jack was just seeing how the weather was when he saw you."

She trotted off down the road and Cathy and Jack had to walk fast to keep up with her. "Jack said you wanted to know the names."

"Yes."

"Well, before we left the area two or three years ago I knew the names, but things have changed a bit. Up at the farmstead they had some named after saints from the area like Bede, Oswald and Aidan. D'you know the church in Bamburgh? That's St Aidan's."

"Yes. We've seen it, just up the road from where we're staying at the Lord Crewe."

"That's right. Now then, what else did they have up there? Ah yes, Stewards, Shepherds and Blacksmiths."

"Blacksmiths? Did it used to be a blacksmith's?"

"Ee, pet, I've no idea. Mebbie. And here in the grounds of Adderstone Hall these four are just called stables one, two, three and four. Oh, and two more; Gardeners and Toms."

"Toms?"

"Aye, it is a bit of a funny one, that."

"Actually, a man called Tom Forster lived here in the eighteenth century, didn't he?"

"The general? Him that led the Jacobites? Yes, I know about him and about him living here, but d'you know, I never made the connection. I just used to think it a bit of a funny name. M'brain must've taken a holiday! Anyhow, I think they sold some of the cottages, or they're for sale. The only ones I've heard people talk of now is Stewards, Shepherds and Oswalds. Well . . . Oh, look, there it is."

Cathy looked to where she was pointing. The Hall was a square, solid-looking building on two floors with a huge Grecian-looking portico in the middle, supported on substantial columns. The chimneys, on what appeared from a distance to be a flattish roof, were large and squat.

Cathy turned to the woman. "Do you know if it's the same building the general lived in with his sister and the rest of the Forster family?"

"Ee, I'm not sure, but I don't think so, pet; I think there've been a few different buildings there. I did hear that the General's father built a new house to take the place of the old Pele Tower but I think both of them are long gone."

"Right, well, thank you very much, erm . . ."

"Mary." Mary turned and started walking back.

"I'm Cathy. Thanks for your help. It does seem like a lovely place for a restful holiday."

"And they've got a riding school, tennis, croquet and a mini golf course, so there's more to do than just relax. So d'you think you might come for a holiday here sometime?"

"It's possible, but at the moment we're just interested in finding out where the general's sister Dorothy lived."

"She lived in the castle. She saved him from the Tower, you know. Dressed him up in her maid's clothes and got him out. They were going to execute him."

"Yes, I know she saved him, but I think he was actually in Newgate prison, where the Old Bailey is now, and . . ."

"Really? That's not what I heard."

"Well, history can be a bit like that, can't it? It's sometimes difficult to know which version is right. I could be wrong."

"Well, I know the bonny lad Derwentwater was in the Tower. Have you heard about the Derwentwater lights?"

"I remember them being mentioned, something to do with when he was executed?"

"Yes, it was the Aurora Borealis, of course. It was a bit weird that the lights shone so violently. But it was when they got his body back home, not when he got his head chopped off. Anyhow, they called them 'Derwentwater's lights' for quite a long time. People used to be very superstitious round here, some still are."

"Do you come from here?"

"I was born in Alnwick, Jack too, but we live down south at the moment. Near Durham; to be near our daughter."

Cathy suppressed a smile. "I'm from Harrogate."

"Oh, I wouldn't go that far south, even if they moved again. I think we'll probably come back here soon. It's not the same down there, really."

They'd reached the car. Cathy smiled at Mary. "Thanks again for your help. It was very kind of you. Please give Jack my thanks too."

◆   ◆   ◆

Crookham turned out to be in the emptiest and wildest piece of countryside Cathy had seen since leaving Blanchland. The road wound through rolling countryside from Adderstone to Wooler where the brooding Cheviot Hills dominated the western horizon. Jack drove north towards the Scottish border and Cathy was increasingly aware they were driving in comfort through the kind of terrain Thomas and Derwentwater's army had tramped and ridden in one of the worst winters many had known.

Four or five miles from the Scottish border and the town of Coldstream, they almost missed the turning off to Crookham village. The village was tiny and off the main road on the east side. They drove through the small cluster of houses before they realised that was all there was. The nearest farm down the hill from the village was not called Berryhill or Crookham Farm. They continued along the road and Jack took the first road off to the left. He parked at the side of the road and they spread out the map he'd brought. They discovered they'd turned off the road to Ford and were on a road that would take them through a place called Heatherslaw and join a road to Etal village.

They poured over the area around Ford but couldn't see Berryhill or Crookham Farm. Cathy was about to fold up the map in frustration when her eyes wandered to the north of Etal and settled on the word 'Berryhill'. It was obviously a farm and the contours showed it was on a hillside on the east side of a road. She pointed. "Look, Jack!"

"Oh, yes, and I suppose Crookham isn't very far from Berryhill, but why did the records call him 'John Armstrong of Crookham' in later life?"

Cathy ran her eyes over the area around the village. Suddenly the name 'Crookham' caught her attention to the north-west of the village, just off the curving main road. It was a farm called 'Crookham Eastfield'. Jack followed her finger. "Wow!" They looked further along the road on the map and saw 'Crookham Westfield'.

Cathy sat back in the seat, totally bewildered. "So there are three possible farms and a village! We should drive round and take a look at all of them, but without looking at ancient farm deeds which we have no right to do, there's no way of knowing the truth. Perhaps he was born at the farm in Berryhill but tenanted one or both of the Crookham farms, or perhaps he owned Berryhill and both Crookham farms. Or maybe they just lived in a house in Crookham."

She looked at Jack and shrugged her shoulders. After a few moments, a strange feeling of satisfaction crept over her and she couldn't suppress a smile.

"You know what, whatever the truth is, Dorothy lived with John Armstrong in this beautiful, wild countryside and that's enough. She must have missed the sea at Bamburgh and the gentle beauty of Blanchland, but she was content to live out her long life here with John Armstrong and he loved her enough to make sure that when she died, she was buried with her family in Bamburgh . . . oh, Jack!"

Cathy turned away, opened the car door and climbed out onto the muddy edge of the road, her hands against her mouth. Jack joined her and tipped up her chin. "What's wrong?"

"She loved Bamburgh, but she came here."

"Yeah."

"To be with the man she loved."

Jack smiled. "Ah."

Cathy put her hands on his shoulders. "Perhaps I could persuade Maggie to let me go part-time and I could stay with my parents for part of the week and be with you for the rest of the week."

He raised his eyebrows. "Well, I might be able to take that for a short time, but not on a permanent basis. While you were doing your tour and I couldn't see you, talk to you or even text you, I was totally lost; empty. I need you 24/7."

"You know I can't do that!"

"So that's why I spent a couple of hours last night searching for jobs in York, Leeds and Harrogate."

"What?"

"Mm. Some of them I'm a bit over qualified for; one I'd love to get but would be quite a step up, and there are a couple of sideways moves. I've registered my interest in all of them, but it'll probably be near June next year before I can actually move—unless one of them is desperate."

His eyes were fixed on hers and glowing with love.

She put her arms round his neck. "Did I mention I adored you?"

"I don't remember 'adored'."

"Or that I love you desperately?"

He held her tightly. "No, but keep saying it. I need to hear it. I thought I'd wrecked everything. I was stressed and needy that day when I said those things about us not working out. I wanted you so much and it felt as if you were rejecting me. Oh, Cathy, you've no idea how much angst and panic I've lived through in the last two or three weeks. Before I met you, no-one affected me so completely."

She laughed and kissed him. He held her in a possessive grip, kissing her deeply until her head swam and she pulled away, breathless.

"What about our mothers? My mother is so prejudiced. Can you handle that?"

"I can handle anything as long as you love me."

"And your mother? She's going to be so angry."

"Oh, she was when I told her to give up trying to find me a wife because I wouldn't be with anyone but you; but she'll come round when I tell her you're pregnant."

"But I'm not."

Jack smiled. "We'd better get back to the hotel and start practising, then."

"And you don't mind me being a stay-at-home mother?"

"No; you were right. I had ten days and nights to think about it. I remembered there was always someone there for us; usually my father or my grandmother. My mother was working full time, but Dad organised his business life round us. Now, please, no more questions. I want you so much and we're miles from Bamburgh . . ."

"I noticed a B & B as we came through Crookham."

"What? Wow! How am I going to keep up with such a brilliant wife?"

"I don't remember you asking me to marry you."

"Ok. Marry me."

"That's not very romantic."

"Well, when we're not standing in mud, I'll go down on one knee and beg you to marry me. Good enough?"

She brought her lips close to his. "Perfect."

BAMBURGH, NORTHUMBERLAND

1740

So here I stand, in this much-loved place once more; my dearest Thomas buried in the family crypt in the church of St Aidan behind me.

In 1722 they asked him to take command of another attempt to bring James Stuart to his rightful throne, so they understood that the failure of 1715 was not his. He refused that mission, but "King James" made him Steward of the Royal Household in France and then in Italy; a post he held for many years.

Thomas died of an asthma in Boulogne in '38. I believe he was on his way home. They brought his body across the sea and buried him in Dover, but my nephew John Bacon, son of our sister Margaret, brought his body back to be buried here. May he find peace.

◆ ◆ ◆

I hear a footfall and need not look to see who is there. The hands that come to rest on my shoulders are strong and give me comfort. I turn my face to him.

"John, my love, when I die, promise to bring me here to rest next the sea."

His face clouds and he frowns and holds me close. "My dear heart, only if you promise not to leave me for at least another twenty-four years."

I take his hand, kiss it and look into his eyes. "I will do my best; and you know, once my mind is made up . . ."

Lightning Source UK Ltd.
Milton Keynes UK
UKOW05f1600190215

246539UK00001B/3/P